THE SCAPEGOAT
David Stanley

PAPER★STREET

Paper Street Publishing

Paper Street Publishing

ISBN (ebook) 9781916176386

ISBN (paperback) 9781916176393

www.davidjstanley.com

www.paperstreetpublishing.net

This book is for

Lindsey and Connor,
all the backup I'll ever need

1

THE HOUSE WAS HIDDEN from the road by a high wall and thick stands of trees on both sides of a curving driveway. As he swept around the last bend the building seemed to appear, huge and threatening, like a horror movie castle. A line of cars and SUVs were already parked out front and he added his personal vehicle to the end. He glanced up as he stepped out his car. A single light burned in one of the windows and Coombes knew it would be in the room where the body lay.

His partner, Grace Sato, was talking to his lieutenant, who appeared to be on the point of leaving. He'd skipped breakfast and coffee; he'd shaved in his car as he drove, but still he was the last to arrive. At least he was wearing his best suit.

"Glad I caught you, John. I wanted to impress upon you the need for sensitivity in this case. The guy might seem like old news, but he's connected everywhere. If you stand on his toes, I doubt I can save you."

"Got it."

Coombes gave his name and badge number to a uniform with a clipboard, then stooped down to pull on a pair of Tyvek shoe covers. When he straightened back up, he saw Gantz still standing there. He pulled on nitrile gloves, his eyes fixed on her face.

"Promise me," she said.

"You know me, Ellen. I'll treat him with the respect he deserves."

"That's what I'm worried about."

He wondered why he was there at all since he wasn't even on rotation, but not for long. Becker was officially on call, but he was about to retire and had one foot out the door.

"Do we know how the killer got in? I assume there's an alarm."

"Alarm, security cameras, private security patrols, the whole bit. Looks like the killer bypassed the alarm then wiped any footage recorded by cameras once he was inside. TID are going to see what they can recover, but don't hold your breath."

It was unusual for his lieutenant to visit a crime scene and he figured she wasn't just here to ask him to play nice. There was certain to be a political element to the case and a good result would help to shore up her position downtown.

"I never do, L-T."

Coombes turned and walked inside the building.

He saw a lot of expensive properties in Homicide Special, but this was the first one he'd seen where pictures hanging on the walls were all of its owner. It looked like he'd had oil paintings produced from photographs of himself. They were in the style of old masters and were loaded into appropriately vintage gold wooden frames.

"Wow, check out the selfies," Sato said.

He nodded morosely as they started up the stairs. The portraits continued next to them at shoulder-height in a diagonal line. They were beyond ridiculous, yet strangely not that much of a surprise based on what he thought he knew about the subject of the paintings.

As he came to the top of the stairs he was looking straight into a room.

Elizabeth Walton lay face-up on the pale oak floorboards with the top of her head toward him and her feet facing the window. She was wearing a thin nightdress, a gold watch with a small face, and some kind of necklace.

Coombes squatted down next to the body.

2

Dark purple marks wrapped around either side of Walton's neck, and across the front where the killer's thumbs had pressed down. Her face was unnaturally pale, almost blue, and her eyes were open and glassy. Near the hairline on her left temple, was another bruise where a fist had struck her.

The way he liked to think of things, this wasn't Elizabeth Walton. Her body was just that, a body. The spirit, the soul, whatever you wanted to call it, was gone. That was the part that was Elizabeth. Whatever was left, was just evidence of a crime, of a life cut short.

Walton's hair was fanned out behind her head, wild and tangled. Coombes put a gloved hand down on the floor and leaned down to look at where her head was resting on the bare wood. There was blood there, like thick molasses.

Coombes straightened up, anger flaring in his chest.

He hadn't known Elizabeth Walton, but it changed nothing. He wanted to find the man that did this and extract some form of revenge. And it *was* a man, there was no doubt about that. Almost all the cases he worked the perpetrator was a man. It was barely worth the effort to pretend otherwise.

"What are you thinking, Johnny?"

He let out a slow breath and spoke in a neutral tone.

"Our guy hit her, here, knocking her to the floor. He crouched over her and began to strangle her. Pinning her to the floor and preventing her from calling out. Judging by her injuries, her assailant was probably twice her size. There's an impact injury at the back of her head, but it doesn't look like it's from being knocked to the floor. I think he lifted her by the neck then slammed her down, hitting her head repeatedly off the floor until she passed out. Then he finished it, crushing her windpipe with a downward pressure from both thumbs."

"It seems excessive, doesn't it?"

He glanced up at Sato. "Go on."

"Well, like he could have killed her quicker but was drawing it out."

"Like he was enjoying it."

"That it was *personal*," she said.

He nodded. When you got right down to it, strangulation was the most personal way to kill someone. Looking into their eyes and choking them to death with your bare hands. No gun, no knife. It didn't get more intimate or brutal than that.

Two crime scene techs appeared behind Grace in the doorway wearing coveralls and carrying aluminum cases. He recognized one from a previous crime scene. Carrie Dupont.

"Detective Coombes. Are you messing up my crime scene?"

"Not my style, Carrie."

"*Hmm*," she said, unconvinced.

He looked back down at Walton before leaving.

Even after what had happened to her, he could tell that she'd been a beautiful woman. Her skin was smooth and flawless, her bone structure perfect. She'd taken care of herself, and had enjoyed a good life right up to the point it had been taken from her.

"Okay," he said to Sato, "let's speak to him."

2

HARLAN TREMAINE STOOD ON an oak deck overlooking the covered swimming pool that sat to the side of his Brentwood property. He was wearing a bespoke gray suit, dirty white sports socks and no shoes. A comet-trail of dried blood ran down the side of his right hand.

Tremaine half-turned and looked back at Coombes.

"What did you say, Detective?"

"I said, what time did you find the body?"

The former Governor of California appeared to zone out for a moment before coming back.

"About half six. I was about to go for my morning run and found the window at the back door broken. Glass was spread across the floor. There was dirt on the marble heading toward the stairs. They were boot prints; I could see the tread pattern. I got a bad feeling. They were headed up toward Lizzie's apartment."

"Then what happened?"

"I got the Benelli from the safe and went upstairs. I found Lizzie on the floor of her office like a slaughtered animal. I searched everywhere looking for that bastard, praying I'd find him so I could send him straight to hell. He was gone."

It was no surprise to him that Tremaine owned a shotgun, his position on guns was a matter of public record. Coombes wrote *he was gone* in his notebook, then flipped back to the previous page where he'd written brief details from the initial police report.

"You say you found her around six thirty?"

"Yes."

"We don't have you reporting her death until seven twenty-six." Coombes looked up from his page, watching the other man closely. "You couldn't have spent all that time searching your property. What were you doing during those fifty-six minutes?"

"I don't know. It was like I disappeared."

Coombes hadn't voted for Tremaine but he hadn't voted *against* him either so he supposed he needed to take more responsibility. He wondered what a former governor needed with an attractive full-time member of staff that lived in his home.

An idea came quickly to mind.

"What was it that Elizabeth Walton did here?"

"Lizzie helped run my charitable foundation."

"Anything else?"

If he took his meaning, Tremaine didn't show it.

"The truth is, she *was* the foundation. I was just a figurehead."

The time lag in reporting the death bothered Coombes, as did the fact that he'd answered the door to first responders wearing the suit he wore now, not the running gear he'd been wearing when he found the body. Changing clothes was in the same ballpark as hiding evidence. He made a note to get hold of his original clothing for testing.

"Do you know anyone who'd want to hurt Miss Walton?"

Tremaine shook his head.

"What about you? Do you have enemies?"

"About five million people. Do I think one of *them* broke in here and killed Lizzie to hurt me? No, and screw you for saying it."

Anger made the other man's eyes bright and focused. For the first time in the interview, it felt like Harlan Tremaine had actually seen him. He remembered the warning Gantz had given him when he arrived and decided for once not to lean into the anger.

"My condolences on the loss of your friend, Mr. Tremaine. I speak plainly, without malice. A trait I believe we may have in common. My only aim here is to put the person that did this in a box or in the ground. Are we good?"

"Put this guy in the ground, Detective, and I'll buy you a new car."

Coombes pretended not to hear this. Attempting to bribe a police officer was a felony but so was threatening one and if he arrested everyone that did that then prisons would be full inside a month. To be a cop, you had to first be a realist.

Besides, it wasn't like he didn't need a new car.

"I notice your hand has blood on it. Is it hers?"

Tremaine looked at his hand, surprised.

"I don't know."

"We'll need to photograph it and take a sample. Don't wash it."

Tremaine said nothing. He looked like he'd shut down, that he was broken inside. It felt like there was something else going on, something big and he was holding it back.

The only thing he could think to explain it, was that Tremaine and Walton had been in a relationship. Perhaps she'd wanted to end it and, in a rage, he'd killed her. It explained the blood on his hand, the change of clothes, and the delay in calling the police.

In any case, Coombes didn't like it when people close to a victim were covered in blood they couldn't explain. Perhaps there was a more innocent explanation.

"Did you touch anything at the scene before you called it in?"

"Her nightdress. The hem was gathered at her waist and she was exposed. I pulled it down so that she was covered. I knew she'd be photographed by your people. She didn't deserve to be immortalized like that, like she was some kind of stripper or porn star."

Coombes understood, but tampering with evidence was a no-no.

"You say she was exposed, should I assume she's not wearing underwear?"

"Correct."

"Was the hem up by her abdomen, or lower?"

Tremaine's face screwed up in disgust.

"You think she was...assaulted as well?"

"It's something we have to consider, unfortunately."

"Far as I recall, it was across the top of her legs. Higher at the sides than the middle."

Coombes pictured the scene. A man had pinned Walton to the floor, his hands around her throat. Her legs would've been pumping, trying to escape, trying to get him off her. The light material of her nightdress would slide down her thighs and gather at her waist.

"Probably nothing," he said. "Let's get your hand processed."

Tremaine looked across at Sato with disdain.

"Do you not get to speak, Detective?"

"It's my job to witness everything you say to my partner. If you make a move to threaten him while he's holding his notebook, it's also my job to shoot you in the face."

"I guess you voted for the other guy, huh?"

"If I could've voted twice, I would have."

They returned to the room where Elizabeth Walton had been murdered. The forensic technicians were gone and they once more had the room to themselves, supposing you didn't include Walton who still lay on the floor. Plastic bags were now attached to both of her hands to protect any evidence that might be under her fingernails.

When you were close enough to strangle someone, their hands were close to you.

He took in the room properly for the first time.

It was a home office with a desk and a computer. The walls were oak paneled up to a dado rail, with deep blue and black flocked wallpaper above. A wingback leather chair sat next to the door facing the desk. The leather was held in place by a line of black metal studs. It was a masculine piece of furniture and for this reason, Coombes could only imagine the former governor sitting on it while Walton worked.

Watching, puffing a big cigar.

Tremaine was strong and muscular beneath his suit. His bicep was big enough to cause his sleeve to become tight when he lifted his arm. Then there was the bruise on Walton's face; it was on the left, making her assailant right-handed. Like Tremaine.

Coombes put the idea aside for now.

A laptop computer lay open on Walton's desk next to a lamp with a horizontal green shade. He saw the back of a picture frame and when he moved around the desk, saw that it was a picture of Elizabeth Walton standing next to a goofy teenage girl.

A daughter perhaps.

He pressed the space bar on the laptop and the screen lit up, prompting him for a password. Coombes didn't bother guessing. A spiral-bound notepad sat next to the laptop filled with names, telephone numbers, and dollar amounts. Around them were curly doodles and little faces. Some of them happy, some of them sad.

Coombes imagined Walton on the phone, her pen always moving. He flipped back through the pages and they were almost all the same. Names, numbers, dollar amounts. It had to be related to her charity work for Tremaine. The dollar amounts were substantial, the lowest figure he saw was for $15,000, which had a very sad face drawn next to it.

She hadn't been balancing her checkbook, that was for sure.

He took a photograph of the ten most recent pages using his cell phone, then of the other items on the desk, finishing with a closely-cropped picture of the photo frame. Walton looked younger in the picture, maybe by as much as a decade. The teen would be in her mid-twenties by now. Heartbreak was in store for her, and he might be the one to deliver the news.

Coombes opened each of the three drawers to the right side of her desk. Inside were the usual office stationery, a pair of reading glasses, boxes of hard candy, and some out-of-date nicotine gum that looked long forgotten.

No Post-It Note with the laptop password conveniently scrawled on it.

Coombes didn't think it mattered. Assuming Tremaine wasn't the killer, the man who was hadn't done it for anything on the laptop or he would have taken it with him. He had broken into the former governor's mansion, either to commit a burglary, or with the intention of harming Tremaine. It appeared that the killer had entered the wrong side of the building and Walton had caught him before he could leave.

Her bedroom was right through the wall.

The logical takeaway from her nightdress was that the man had made a noise loud enough to wake her and she'd come to investigate. Probably because of the alarm system, she'd imagined it was Tremaine himself making the noise and had no cause to worry about her safety. Sometimes, he reflected, those who lived a good life lacked the critical imagination required to imagine things taking a turn for the worse.

"Are you mad at me?"

He glanced up at Sato. "For what?"

"For what I said to Tremaine. About shooting him in the face."

"No. Look, you have nothing to worry about with a guy like Tremaine. He's not going to report you. If you apologized to him, he'd be disappointed. You showed him what you're made of and that you're not afraid of him. He respects that, and so do I."

"Still. I shouldn't have said it."

Coombes said nothing for a moment.

"Aside from his politics, what do you think of him?"

Sato chewed her lip.

"Maybe his foundation does good things, but it's *him*, you know?"

"Grace, I'm asking you if you think he's good for this."

Her mouth fell open in shock.

"Are you kidding? No. I don't think that at all."

If someone who was ready to shoot a potential suspect in the face thought he was innocent, maybe he should listen to them.

An undoubted problem with working in Homicide, was that you saw the worst side of people all the time. After a while, it was easy to believe that it was a fair representation of the wider population.

He felt himself slump. Without caffeine in his system, he was flagging and his mental focus lacked clarity. It was a situation he resolved to fix as soon as possible.

"Let's take a look at her bedroom."

They walked into the hallway and into the next room along.

A double bed lay to the right, with a nightstand on either side. The floor was carpeted and he could tell from the wear pattern which side of the bed Walton had used to get in and out. There was a large closet on the wall next to the door, a dressing table and mirror on the left and a window opposite.

He opened the closet and saw a line of fussy, conservative clothing.

Serious clothes, for a serious job. While her nightdress had highlighted every curve of her body, these clothes spoke of nothing but professionalism and confidence in her abilities. Of having no need to leverage her appearance to get what she wanted.

He felt the case against Tremaine begin to dissolve.

If the two were mixing business with pleasure, something Coombes knew a little about, he'd doubtless want her dressed a certain way. Tremaine was a testosterone guy, a guns and ammo guy. He'd want the full cliché.

Behind him, Sato whistled.

He turned and saw she was at the dressing table, with the contents of a clutch purse pulled out in front of her. Her cheeks were flushed and her eyes were alive. Coombes moved closer and she held up Elizabeth Walton's wallet. There was a clear window inside, showing a California driver's license. Grace lightly tapped her gloved index finger next to the date of birth. He glanced up at her, surprised.

"Is that right?"

"If it isn't, it's the best damn fake I've ever seen. Who would even fake being older past the age of 21? Nobody, that's who."

"I thought she was in her forties."

"You and me both," Sato said.

Elizabeth Walton was 61 years old.

"I hope I look that good when *I'm* in my sixties," he said.

"You don't look that good now, Johnny."

"*Right.*"

He saw an iPhone sitting on a charge mat on Walton's nightstand. He picked it up and the screen lit up and buzzed. Face ID. He walked through to her office where Walton still lay on the floor awaiting collection. Her tongue was partially sticking out and there were strong petechial hemorrhages in both eyes. Coombes had experienced mixed result trying this before, but he had nothing to lose. He pointed her iPhone at her face and when he turned it back, it was unlocked.

He swiped up, and at the same moment, heard doors slamming outside.

Coombes went to the window and glanced out. Two black Suburbans were now parked in front of his personal vehicle and six suited men were gathered around them. He stepped back from the window and called out to Sato.

"Grace, we've got company."

"Who?"

"FBI."

"You're kidding."

"I wish. Whatever you're doing, nail it down fast."

He returned to Elizabeth Walton's cell phone and brought it back to life before it shut off again.

The feds would take the phone, he had to get everything he needed off it now. He saw nothing in Messages or WhatsApp that could lead to Walton being murdered and moved on. Next, he brought up the recent call record and using his own iPhone, photographed several screens' worth of names or numbers.

Going back to the beginning of the year, there were only calls from three named contacts; Harlan Tremaine, Amy Tremaine, and Cora Roche. He brought up the details for each and took a photograph of their contact information.

The unnamed numbers would all have to be checked, and there were a lot of them. Coombes heard the feds moving through the hallway downstairs, they'd be with him in seconds.

They were looking at the selfie gallery.

He was in the office, which he figured was the first port of call for the agents who would want to see the crime scene, whatever their interest in it might be. He stepped quietly out into the hall and into Walton's bedroom where Sato was flicking through a leather-bound journal.

Coombes changed apps on Walton's cell, bringing up her email.

He didn't need to unlock her laptop to see her email, it was all mirrored onto her cell. There were no threatening subject lines and it appeared that all were work-related. The names of charities were in a lot of them, along with words like *fundraiser, gala, evening,* or *lunch.* He photographed the inbox anyway, then put his cell away.

He heard the fast rumble of a man's voice in the room next door. Something about the energy in it was wrong, but he couldn't put his finger on it.

One thing was for sure. his job would be a lot easier if he could take the cell phone with him and give it to the feds if and when they needed it. He muted her iPhone, started a maps navigation to the federal building, and slipped the cell into his pocket. The maps app would keep the screen alive without needing Walton's face to unlock it again.

"You ready for this?"

Sato nodded. "As much as I'll ever be."

3

FOUR MEN STOOD IN the home office staring at Walton on the floor. None of them were wearing gloves or shoe protectors, and the vibe was that of four businessmen at an expensive restaurant waiting impatiently for a maître d' to seat them. One was fat with thinning hair, one had a beard and bushy eyebrows, one looked like he'd just got out of college, and the last had a face as gray as poured concrete.

Coombes figured the fat man was in charge and turned to face him.

"Fellas. I'm Detective-"

The man lifted his palm to cut him off.

"We know who you are. Detective Coombes with an e, formerly of the US Army; Detective Sato, formerly a security officer with the Japanese Consulate. I'm Special Agent in Charge Tobias Henderson and this is my team."

Henderson didn't introduce them, there was clearly no point.

Coombes noticed that Eyebrows was almost standing on Walton's outstretched hand. The lack of respect made him angry.

"This is awkward, Henderson. I never heard of you before."

The SAC clenched his jaw so hard that a muscle the size of a walnut popped out around his molars.

"All that matters, Coombes, is that we're taking it from here. You just got started, so I assume that you've got nothing. The best possible time for a change."

He decided to leave that alone for now.

"What's the Bureau's interest in this?"

"Amy Tremaine was kidnapped off the street on her way to work."

Coombes was still for a moment, processing the new information. The two crimes had to be linked, but he couldn't make the pieces fit. Had the killer come here first looking for Amy?

"I'm going to save you some time, Henderson. We've processed this room, the one next door, and the point of entry downstairs. None of it is going to help you with a kidnapping investigation, so how about you get the hell out of my crime scene and tell your friend with the eyebrows not to stand on the corpse on his way out."

"I don't take orders from the LAPD, you little punk."

"And I don't take orders from Justice. Brentwood isn't federal land, or a Native American reservation. If you tell me this is *national security issue* I will laugh in your face and so will the chief. Our turf, our rules."

Henderson came forward to square-off but he was four inches shorter than Coombes and had to crane his neck to maintain eye contact. Behind him, College Boy looked like he was about to start laughing.

"Your chief will be my next call, Coombes, make no mistake."

"I hope so. Because in exchange for giving you a piece of this, he'll insist we get a piece of the kidnapping. Joint Task Force. He's big on the optics of inter-agency cooperation. The two of us shoulder-to-shoulder in front of the TV cameras. Are you ready for that?"

Henderson considered it for a moment. Too long. Any pause was the same as conceding, anybody in the room could've told him that but by the time it occurred to the SAC it was too late. A sour flavor seemed to form in Henderson's mouth before he spoke again.

"All right. You take the homicide; we'll take the kidnapping."

"You say that like you're giving me something. I already *had* the homicide. I want a background to the kidnapping to eliminate possible avenues from my investigation."

"Are you high, Coombes? That's never going to happen."

"Broad brush strokes, that's it. Or I take it to the chief myself. Jackson and I are on good terms, by the way. Ever since I closed the Ferryman case. I've played golf with him more than once. The man has a dark sense of humor, we get on like a house on fire."

"I pity your lieutenant, Coombes, putting up with this all day."

"Then we have a deal."

Henderson nodded once and turned away, walking out the room. The other three agents walked out after him. College Boy flashed him a wide grin as he left.

He followed them down the stairs and out into Tremaine's driveway. For the first time he registered that there was now only one Suburban parked out front and it dawned on him the significance of the missing SUV.

"You took Tremaine."

Henderson turned to face hm. "That's right."

"What if I have more questions for him?"

The SAC said nothing and instead looked amused.

"You told Tremaine not to tell me about the kidnapping before I interviewed him."

"Look at you figuring things out, Coombes. It's like watching a child taking its first steps. One last thing and it's non-negotiable. I'm going to need the phone."

Coombes took out Walton's cell and threw it fast at Henderson's head. The agent caught it one-handed, fumbled it, then caught it again.

"*Eat it.*"

Henderson glanced at the screen, which was still lit up with a map.

"The federal building. What a *great* idea. Guess I'll see you there."

The G-men got into the big SUV and Coombes watched it take off down the driveway. Sato came over, the back of her hand casually brushing against his leg.

"You really play golf with the chief?"

"Of course not, but he didn't know that."

"I don't know how you do it, Johnny. You tore that guy a new one like you were peeling a banana and he's a head cheese at the Bureau."

"He got Tremaine *and* Walton's cell phone, so I figure he came out ahead. All we got to keep what was ours by rights anyway."

Sato said nothing and they walked over to where their personal vehicles were parked as an unmarked van made the turn through the gates and headed toward them.

"Can you handle things for a couple of hours? I've got my...thing." She shrugged, embarrassed. "It's Tuesday, you know?"

They'd been given mandated time with a psychiatrist after an officer-in-volved shooting at the end of the previous year. Specifically, when he'd shot a suspect who pulled a gun on them. An investigation had ruled in his favor, but gave them both compulsory time with a psychiatrist. It was a meaningless protocol, designed to cover the department's ass in case they went rogue at a later date. Like they were wild animals that were going to become rabid killers after their first taste of meat.

"You're still doing that? We've been cleared for active duty."

"I find it helpful to talk to someone, thought I'd keep going for a while."

"Talk to me, I'm your partner. It's practically in the job description."

Sato turned away from him and watched while the Coroner's people sat on the loading area of their open van and pulled on their coveralls.

"You're not *just* my partner though, are you?"

4

He watched Elizabeth Walton being loaded onto a gurney and get strapped in before she was transported down the stairs to the van outside. Also watching, were the line of selfie photographs that seemed to act like an honor guard composed entirely of Tremaine.

After she was gone, he stood in her now-empty office and stared at the floor where she'd been. All that was left of her life was a blood stain on the floor.

He recalled Tremaine saying he'd searched the property for the killer, shotgun in hand, and decided to follow in his footsteps.

The mansion had twenty-eight rooms including the two he had already been in and he quickly photographed each one using his cell phone in case he needed to remind himself of the layout or check for something later.

Technicians were still working around the presumed point of entry and around a closet containing the security system. He then walked around the grounds, which were substantial, and examined the entry gate.

It wasn't known where the killer had breached the outer perimeter, but it probably wasn't at the gate as there was a concentration of security sensors and cameras there. Far simpler to climb the wall to the north, where thick trees provided plenty of cover.

That only left Walton's car, a silver Lexus.

She hadn't been killed in her vehicle but it was a fact that most victims knew their killers beforehand. If there was a chance to find the killer's identity inside the car, he'd take it. Using keys from her bedroom, he unlocked the

Lexus and opened the passenger door, the side her killer might have used if she'd given him a ride.

Coombes bent down so that he was sitting on his heels outside the vehicle. He examined the floor. There were no impressions on the mat, no dirt, or visible hair or fiber evidence. He checked under the seat, his gloved hands reaching under for a forgotten object loaded with fingerprints.

Nothing. The car looked brand-new.

The only thing of interest was a black box clipped to the driver's side sun visor. He didn't know what it was so he took a photograph of it in case he needed to find out later.

Twenty minutes had passed and he was getting nowhere, so he returned to his car and drove to the federal building. To save time with the lobby metal detector, he left his weapon in his glovebox and took the elevator to the fourteenth floor.

The reception area was behind a thick glass wall that to Coombes had always been the perfect metaphor for their relationship. Only light traveled both ways between the FBI and the LAPD.

He gave his name and five minutes later the lean-faced college boy he'd seen at the former governor's home came out to see him. The other man smiled and held out his hand toward him, something no FBI agent had ever done before.

"Special Agent Barnes."

"Detective John Coombes."

They shook hands. Maybe he'd found a fed he could trust. Barnes led him through a security door and escorted him inside.

"You know, I was special once. Didn't stick."

"Army CID, I saw that in your file."

He knew the only reason Henderson had allowed his visit was to show him that there was nothing for the LAPD to do here, that this was *Bureau business*. It made no difference to him what the other man's motivation was as long as he got what he needed.

An agent in a glass-fronted office saw him and quickly began closing the blinds, drawing his attention to a large-scale map on the wall before it was hidden. The map was covered with drawing pins, too many to count. They were working an angle, which meant they had something.

The SAC sat at a computer nearby with his sleeves rolled up. With his jacket off, Henderson looked fatter than ever and his white shirt was soaked through at the armpits. Coombes' mother had taught him not to judge a book by its cover, but he'd been in the Army since then, and had found doing just that often kept you alive.

Henderson was an asshole; he'd bet his last cent on it.

Barnes directed him to sit at a desk, then quickly leant in and typed a password into the computer. The login screen cleared and an image was frozen on screen.

A street scene.

The sidewalk where Amy Tremaine had been kidnapped, he supposed. It was taken by a camera that looked through a window at a little higher than eye-level. This was unusual, as most security cameras were mounted high aiming down with all that meant for distortion.

Barnes rolled the clip.

People walking past, mostly in the same direction.

After a moment, a white panel van pulled to a stop, the two nearer tires riding up onto the sidewalk. The side door rolled open and a man wearing track pants and a zip-up hooded top jumped out.

His right hand was unnaturally flat at his side, like he was about to slap someone.

He took two confident strides forward and put his hand across the mouth of a woman who had just passed him. She reacted with surprise and his hand dropped down to her waist as he turned her toward the open doorway of the van and boosted her effortlessly inside.

The man got back inside and closed the van door as it pulled away.

The whole incident took less than five seconds.

"Jesus," Coombes said.

"He had a strip of duct tape in his hand. Covers her mouth first to prevent her from screaming, leaving both hands free to maneuver her inside the van."

He glanced at the mouse, then up at Barnes.

"Do you mind?"

"No, go ahead."

Coombes dragged the playhead to line up the clip so that it was paused with the kidnapper a step behind Tremaine, his hand blurred as he reached forward to grab her across the mouth. He studied it for a moment in silence, soaking it up.

Based on the time recorded in the corner of the footage, Amy was abducted over an hour and a half after Elizabeth Walton's body was discovered by Harlan Tremaine. Easily possible for the same people to pull off both crimes.

"I assume there's not enough to identify him?"

"No. We can't get facial recognition from the side of his face; we need eyes, nose, and cheekbones. Honestly, it's a miracle we have this footage at all."

For the first time, Coombes wondered where the camera had been.

"Why? Where did you get this?"

"Small electronics store next to the abduction point. Has a drone in the window, it's on fishing line so it looks like it's hovering. It's fitted with a camera that records people on the sidewalk. I saw it for what it was straightaway. Owner says it's for security and I believe him. Didn't come across as a pervert to me."

The description of the drone was familiar. He stood and took out his notebook.

"Okay, run me through the victim's timeline."

"Amy Tremaine took the Metro from MacArthur Park to Pershing Square every morning, then walked to the Schiff & Cornell law practice via the Starbucks on 6th and Grand. We figure her kidnappers knew where she worked and moved backward from there."

Coombes made a note of this and looked up.

"What makes you say that?"

"MacArthur Park is a better abduction point."

"All right," he said. It came to him where he'd seen the drone before and decided it would be his next stop. "What about the license plate?"

"A dead end. We pulled it off another camera but it's a fake. Kidnappers cloned a pre-existing vehicle, which is pretty smart. A patrol car running the plate would get no red flags."

"Her cell phone?"

"Tossed out the window and destroyed by passing traffic."

Coombes thought for a moment, looking down at the screen. Barnes' workstation was immaculate. No notes, no coffee cup rings on the desk, no food wrappers. Just keyboard, mouse and two plastic business card containers, nearly full. Mason Barnes, special agent.

"Are you looking at any work connection?"

Barnes frowned. "In what way?"

"A problem with a client, or with someone she went up against?"

"That's not an active area of investigation."

"The former governor then?"

Barnes glanced at the SAC. Henderson was deep into something on his computer, mashing keys on the keyboard. It didn't have the rhythm of someone typing, it sounded like a kid hitting random keys just for the hell of it. Barnes nodded.

"So there's been a ransom demand already?"

"Came in about ten minutes before you arrived."

A quick demand was a bad sign. What you wanted to do was leave a longer gap, let the victim's family marinate until they were good and tender. Let their worries feed on themselves. Once they start to think that all is lost, *then* you come back with the ransom demand. At that point, relief will make them accept any figure a kidnapper chose. When a kidnapper asked for an amount quickly, they almost always got seller's remorse, believing they asked for too little. From there, things tended to take a turn for the worse.

"That was fast," Coombes said.

"I know," Barnes replied, like he was admitting Tremaine was dead.

He remembered the office blinds being closed.

"You've got something cooking already, don't you?"

"Look, I've already said too much."

"You've hardly said anything at all."

Henderson appeared next to him, faster than he would've expected.

"That's *enough*. The Bureau has the abduction, LAPD has the murder. That was our deal. You work your side of the street, Detective, we'll work ours."

"This is bullshit. There's *no* federal case to answer here. Not with the murder, not with the kidnapping. You're pushing me out of *my* case. I have jurisdiction, not you."

Henderson's face turned scarlet as two agents came up behind Coombes.

"Get this prick out of here. Use restraints if you have to."

Coombes glanced at the men and laughed.

"Please. I could snap these two *underwear models* like twigs."

"I'll show him out," Barnes said. "*Right*, Coombes?"

"Whatever, I'm done anyway."

He pushed past the men behind him and walked toward the exit. Barnes rushed to fall into step next to him. Coombes had nothing against the young agent, who'd tried his best to answer his questions. The guy had it bad if he had to work under Henderson all day.

"Were you a cop, Barnes?"

"Yeah. I still am."

He glanced at the FBI agent.

"All right. Then you have to realize our cases are the *same* case and splitting them down the middle increases the likelihood that another woman is going to die."

"I agree, but the Bureau has more experience with kidnappings."

The elevator arrived and they got on. They were all alone.

"How about this, Barnes. You and me work together. Back channel. Anything I get, I share with you; anything you get, you share with me. All that matters is the woman."

Barnes screwed up his face.

"I'm ten weeks out of the Academy, I can't do it. Henderson doesn't like me much better than you, he'd bounce me right out the Bureau."

The elevator doors opened and they walked in silence through the lobby and out into the area in front of the building. People in suits were coming and going. His own suit made him fit right in, nobody gave him a second look.

"Your lead, what is it? You don't have to give me names or anything."

"We believe our suspects are responsible for a series of dog kidnappings."

"*Dogs?*"

"Hear me out. We're talking about pets of the super rich here. Some of them don't have children so their pet is like family to them. You wouldn't believe the bubble they live in. Diamond-studded collars, two-thousand-dollar grooming bills; these people let their dogs lick inside their mouths, it's disgusting."

Coombes nodded, he was frequently disgusted.

"All right, I see it, but that can't be the whole thing."

"We think they have some kind of access to these homes. A security or catering company, something like that. They're on the inside, they know who to hit. Who's vulnerable, who can liquidate a lot of cash quickly. It would surprise you. Some of these people are holding on to properties by their fingernails, living off cat food. Those people don't get hit."

"What about Elizabeth Walton?" Coombes said. "You figure she gave up Amy's work address, then they killed her to keep her silent?"

"No. We can't explain that. You can find out where Amy Tremaine works using Google, her name's right on the firm's website. Walton's death doesn't fit the pattern or make any kind of tactical sense."

"You think this is the first time they've taken a person?"

Barnes shook his head.

"It's the first we've heard about, but you saw how that guy moved. They're pros. A real slick operation. My feeling is we only know about this one because somebody got killed."

"How do you square that with the quick ransom demand?"

"Maybe they realized they made a mistake taking the governor's kid. They're exposed and the longer it continues, the worse it gets. So they want to off-load her as quickly as possible. The pressure to catch them eases if she's returned."

"*Or?*"

"Or she's already dead and they need the money to relocate until things blow over. I know the situation, Coombes. Look, I've got to get back up there, I've been too long already."

"One more. Where does the FBI really fit into this?"

Barnes shrugged.

"Tremaine called the U.S. Attorney, that's it."

5

THE SPACE IN FRONT of the electronics store was a crime scene, but there was no police line protecting the area, no uniforms limiting access, no crime techs dusting for prints. It was like nothing had happened. A door had opened and a woman had vanished without trace.

Coombes turned and looked at the storefront.

It had a single large window and a door to the side. A box with a strobe advertised that the store was protected by an alarm, but there was no sign of an external camera covering the sidewalk.

Sidewalks belonged to the City, aiming private cameras at public land was illegal, although that didn't stop many from doing it. When challenged about an illegal camera, it was common to hear that it was only a dummy, or that it had stopped working years ago. The camera would remain and nothing would be done to remove it.

Everyone had something better to do.

The store owner had hidden his camera in plain sight on a drone that appeared to hover at the top of the window. It was both a security measure and an advertisement for a product they sold. Barnes had come here and seen it for what it was, but Coombes wasn't sure that he would have.

The agent was good.

He walked into the store and saw a man standing behind the counter with a friendly smile. It looked like he'd been watching Coombes stare at the drone in the window and had taken his interest and expensive suit as a sign of a big purchase to follow.

"Help you?"

He pulled his jacket to the side to reveal his badge.

"Detective Coombes, LAPD. I want to see the drone footage."

The man's expression soured.

"You got a warrant?"

The store owner had rolled over for the FBI and given them what they wanted, but it was clear he couldn't expect the same treatment. For him, he'd need a warrant. The man had watched his cop shows, he knew his rights.

Coombes glanced around the store and saw it was aimed at the security and surveillance market. Alarms, cameras, drones, motion-activated lights. Everything a paranoid person could ever need. But there was something else. Cameras built into photo frames, clothing buttons, jewelry. Suitable for private investigators, or perhaps, federal agencies.

"I have friends who left the department, set out their own tent, you know? Mostly cheating spouses, wandering daughter cases, that type of thing. They always have good things to say about your store, your equipment."

The store owner's stance changed and he saw a flicker of pride on his face. They were going to be able to work something out. He sensed an anti-government vibe and decided to lean into that a little.

"Feds are freezing me out," Coombes continued. "By the time a warrant comes through, chances are, the girl's dead. You know who I'm talking about, who her father is. That's a lot of heat coming down the pipe for everybody. I just want to see the footage for myself, check the feds didn't miss something important. If there's nothing there, then I don't waste time on a dead end that could be better spent elsewhere. What do you say?"

"All right, it's through back. Just don't get excited by anything else you might see there."

The man lifted part of the counter to let him through, then took him down a corridor piled high on one side with boxes containing crossbows and samurai swords, up a flight of stairs and into an office with no windows.

Next to the door was a sink, coffee machine, and a refrigerator. A desk was pressed against the end wall under a framed print of a president Coombes hadn't voted for and who he didn't want to continue breathing.

A laptop sat open on the desk next to an all-black Smith and Wesson 1911.

Coombes sat in front of the computer as the old man explained his system.

Unlike the state-of-the-art cameras inside the store, the jury-rigged drone had no interface of its own and simply produced a list of files which could be viewed with a media player. He saw that there were two clips for that morning and one for each of the proceeding days. It was easy to guess why, the footage had been interrupted by the FBI after the abduction and a new clip had started.

The biggest surprise was that the FBI had left the store owner with not only the original footage of the abduction, but the laptop computer that stored it.

He'd worked four previous cases that overlapped with the Bureau, and in each case they had taken possession of all evidence and any equipment connected to that evidence. It seemed to Coombes like this was an oversight by Barnes who was under a lot of pressure to save a woman's life, but a mistake that would soon be corrected.

He started the earlier clip from that morning.

The time was encoded at the top right of the screen and he fast-forwarded to near the time of the kidnapping and resumed playback. It was the same footage he'd seen at the federal building. On rewatching, it was clear to him that the kidnappers knew exactly what they were doing.

Smooth, efficient, professional.

Only two bystanders seemed to realize what had happened, everyone else had their head buried in a cell phone, or were focused on the task of maintaining distance with other people on the busy sidewalk.

He could see why the location had been chosen as a grab point, it was perfect. Aside from the hidden security camera, of course. He rewound the clip and restarted playback. Once again, the man threw Tremaine inside the van, jumped in after her, and closed the door as it pulled into traffic. There was no one else in the rear compartment, just the driver up front.

A two-man operation.

The expression caught on something as he thought it. Because of the angle of the camera, the driver was obscured. It was therefore possible that the driver was a woman. He made a note in his notepad.

Driver, female?

There was no reason to think this based on the footage alone. But if Barnes was right, and this was a team that had started out kidnapping dogs, then there was a chance they were dealing with a *Bonnie and Clyde* type couple on an escalating crime spree.

He watched the clip through again, but found nothing more.

Amy Tremaine passed the same spot every day on her way to work and then on the way back home. The kidnappers knew she was going to be there, because they knew her routine. Knowing where she worked wouldn't have told them her route, they had to have followed her at least once beforehand, perhaps each way to determine the best time.

He glanced at the store owner, standing over him.

"This is going to take a while. You can go out front if you like."

The man's face twisted.

"Look, I don't know. I should stay I think."

Coombes shrugged like he didn't care. Doubtless this meant the man had things on his computer that he didn't want to share with the LAPD or the FBI. He saw the store owner was now holding a mug of coffee.

"Any chance I could get one of those?"

"Black okay?"

"*Perfect.*"

When the old man turned away, Coombes took a thumb drive out his pocket and plugged it into the side of the laptop. He dumped the weekday files going back three weeks onto it. The files were large and the transfer would take several minutes.

Coombes glanced back and saw that the store owner was already on his way back. At times like this, he would normally rely on Sato to run interference for him. It could be hard to see past her face, her smile, the hint of something in her eyes.

He minimized the copy window and put his iPhone on top of his thumb drive. The drive made his cell phone tilt up at an odd angle, so he used the corner of his notebook to make his cell lie flat and began making notes about the kidnapper to justify its position.

Hair color, build, approximate age.

He didn't worry about the approaching store owner reading his writing, he could barely read it himself.

"You think she's dead, son?"

Coombes stood and took the mug that was being held out to him, his whole body in front of the laptop and his cell phone. He took a long drink and nodded his head with exaggerated thanks at the man's mediocre coffee.

"Unfortunately, yes."

"Such a waste. They always take the pretty ones."

Coombes had heard this sentiment before in one form or another and he knew it wasn't true. People just remembered some more than others, cared about some more than others. Based on their looks, their race, their religion. He said nothing and instead took another mouthful of coffee.

The world could be a terrible place and humans had developed belief structures that enabled them to cope.

People that mattered, people that didn't.

A buzzer sounded in the store below; the first customer since he'd arrived. The old man reluctantly went to deal with it and Coombes took the opportunity to check on his file transfer. He was in time to see it hit 100%. He ejected the drive and checked the copy window had also closed.

31

Now that he had his own copy of the footage, he felt little desire to remain where he was with either the old man or the framed buffoon looking down at him as he worked.

Coombes left and dipped his head in thanks to the store owner who had a drone sitting out on the counter for two young Latinos. He decided to visit the Starbucks Amy used every morning while he was in the area.

It was a brief walk, but he felt breathless by the time he arrived.

He was used to dealing with murder victims, people that were *definitely* dead. Though he suspected Amy Tremaine was dead, he had to work on the premise that she wasn't, that she could be saved if he could find her in time. Like Schrödinger's cat, she was both dead and alive at the same time and the pressure this caused was exhausting.

He ordered his coffee to go in case he had to leave early and got a table facing the door. It occurred to him that the server hadn't asked his name yet the barista had put the coffee down in front of him regardless. He turned the paper cup around and saw that it had *COP* written on it. He would've laughed, except that some ugly backstory probably lay behind it.

At least it isn't PIG, he thought.

He plugged his thumb drive into his tablet and brought up footage for the day before the kidnapping. Looking first for Amy, then for the figure that had leapt out the Ford Transit. Her timing was almost identical to the day of her abduction, less than a minute difference. She walked through shot, calm and assured, oblivious to the coming danger. He saw no one that matched the kidnapper, or anyone else that was acting suspiciously.

Coombes jumped the footage on eight hours then left it playing back at four times normal speed while he drank his Americano. He wasn't sure when she finished work, so he had to sit and wait. Eventually, she entered shot at ten past seven. Amy looked tired, but showed no concern about her safety. If one of her clients had threatened her that day, he would have expected to see something on her face.

Grabbing her on her way home was never going to be ideal for the exact reason he had already found. Amy had no fixed finished time. She was a conscientious worker and finished whatever she was working on before heading home, even if that meant working late. He supposed there might also be days when she finished early, depending on workload.

Short of tracking her movements with a GPS tag, it would be impossible for anyone to guess when she would enter the abduction zone.

The mornings were a different story.

Her timing then was consistent, controlled by the D Line timetable. She used the same Metro service every morning got off at virtually the same time and walked to work via Starbucks for a last-minute pick-me-up. Her routine was highly predictable and made the task of abducting her painfully easy.

Based on this realization, he decided to focus on morning footage, going backward one day at a time. He was able to quickly locate her each day. Confident, happy. Believing that her work helping others was making a difference.

He found what he needed on the second-to-last file.

Seventeen days before he bundled her into the van, her kidnapper walked along the street directly behind her. Close enough, that he could've reached out and put his hand on her shoulder. As they were about to exit the frame, the man stopped to look around, seeing the potential of the area as a kidnapping point.

The trees planted on the sidewalk before and after limited visibility and caused pedestrians to move in a uniform manner. After the abduction there was a direct feed onto West 5th Street, then a straight shot onto the 110. It appeared to be a professional risk assessment and it came to Coombes that the man was likely from a military or law enforcement background.

This was the moment it was decided, he thought.

Coombes paused the video to analyze the man's appearance. On this day, he was wearing a dark-blue suit jacket over navy jeans, with a white shirt with no tie. Smart, but casual. He wore a pair of wrap-around sunglasses with legs that that sat straight and didn't hook around the ear. On his wrist was a watch on a green fabric bracelet known as a NATO strap.

A military field watch.

The watch had 12 and 24-hour times on the hour markers and was simple but durable. A Hamilton, he thought, perhaps a Seiko or a Timex. A design classic, but something of a relic.

Modern soldiers wore digital watches encased in chunky black plastic. Field watches were from a bygone era and as a result, were either worn by officers who wanted to distance themselves from the lower ranks, or sons who had inherited a war watch from their father.

Coombes added the information to his notebook and circled *military background*.

He considered the man's change of dress. It was a complete overhaul from the man in track pants, sneakers and warm-up jacket that had sprung out of the van to abduct her. This smart-casual look would not have alarmed anyone, Amy Tremaine included.

It was the perfect camouflage.

Grabbing Amy off the street in broad daylight in the heart of downtown was dangerous. The location was less than a mile from LAPD headquarters, and both marked and unmarked vehicles were in the area all the time. Once she got off the Metro, it would've been a five-minute walk to Starbucks and another five minutes back to her office. Most of that route was too exposed or had too much traffic to make for a viable kidnap point.

It meant that instead of a ten-minute window to capture her, it was more like 15 seconds as she passed in front of the electronics store.

This was their one shot, all or nothing.

So why take her here, not as she left her home?

Her apartment in MacArthur Park was far from the safety of her father's home in Brentwood. She'd rejected his lifestyle and his values, but that hadn't taken the target off her back.

Barnes thought the area around her apartment offered many more potential abduction points and he had to agree. The agent had concluded that the reason they hadn't taken her there was because they didn't know where she lived.

In the light of the earlier footage, that made no sense.

A kidnapper that ran recon on a target three weeks prior to an abduction wouldn't just recon one end of the route, they'd do the whole thing. They'd track her all the way home, traveling with her on the Metro, right up to the door of her building.

Coombes shook his head.

The kidnappers didn't need Elizabeth Walton for anything.

Now that he knew which day to look at and how his perpetrator was dressed, he could re-trace their route using Metro security cameras. Somewhere there'd be footage that could identify him. He added this to his notes and finished his coffee. When he put his cup down, he glanced at the image frozen on his tablet just as the power saver turned the screen black.

He caught a glimpse of something at the last second.

Coombes woke the screen again.

Amy Tremaine and her abductor right of center frame, moving to the left as before. Behind them, however, another man was looking straight at them. Coombes dragged the playhead and saw the second man's head turn as they walked past.

He scrubbed the playhead backward and forward, faster and faster, amplifying the small movement. The second man's head followed Amy perfectly. Watching her every moment. Coombes paused on a frame when he was facing straight toward the camera.

The second man was tall and muscular, with a shaved angular head.

He looked like bad news.

The worst news you could imagine.

Like a killer who would think nothing of murdering innocent young women once they were no more use to him. If it was indeed a two-man operation, he had to be looking at the driver. Coombes zoomed in tight on the paused video with his fingers. There was almost no degradation in image quality. The man's face was sharp and unobstructed. They'd be able to run it through facial recognition for an ID.

Coombes smiled.

Maybe the morning hadn't been a wash after all.

6

COOMBES RETURNED TO THE Police Administration Building, the head-quarters of the LAPD, and the home of Robbery-Homicide. He needed to start assembling the pieces he had so far to see if a picture was forming, and to help him decide where to go next. He decided first to get Gantz up to speed with the kidnapping of Amy Tremaine and the arrival of the FBI. When he finished, she sat back in her seat and looked him in the eye.

"All right, I'll bite. What do you want?"

"What's that supposed to mean?"

"John, the entire time you've worked here, you've never once updated me on a case unless I asked you to. So, you want something. Spit it out."

"I could ask you the same question, couldn't I? You've never come to a crime scene before and told me how to conduct business. What's that about?"

"Tremaine has enough money to burn down the department. My presence was to reassure him that he was in good hands and that I had my best man on the case."

Coombes shifted from foot to foot and she smiled at his discomfort.

"So. What was it you wanted?"

"I passed Becker's desk on the way in. He's sitting there like he's waiting to have a tooth pulled. I get why you didn't want him to lead the investigation, but if he's doing nothing, I'd like to bring him into this. I have a lot of numbers to run down and any one of them could lead to Amy Tremaine. I figure all hands on deck, no?"

Gantz nodded.

"That's a good idea, but office duty only, okay?"

"Lieutenant?"

"He is not to go outside the building, are we clear? I promised his wife."

A void opened up inside him. He knew what she was going to say, but he asked it anyway.

"What happened?"

Gantz sighed, her eyes dipping down to her hands for a moment.

"He said he was cleaning his gun and it went off. Missed his head by a quarter inch."

"But you don't believe that."

"Of course not, and neither does his wife. His service weapon is now in my drawer. Not everyone is ready for retirement and he's been a cop for a long time. My concern is that he could put himself in danger intentionally, or otherwise. So, he stays in the building until he's end of watch, no exceptions. Aside from that, use him how you wish."

Coombes nodded and walked to the door. Becker needed to keep his mind busy, he thought. To feel useful. Benching him like this was the wrong move.

"John? You look like you spent the night on a sofa."

He turned back, surprised by her insight.

"There are worse places to be."

Gantz made a knowing face.

"Keep trying, Coombes, it's all you can do."

He nodded and left the room.

If he knew one thing about himself, it was that he *wasn't* going to keep trying. Not with Julie, not anymore. He was done.

A tall paper to-go cup sat on his desk. A Starbucks Grande, his second of the morning. There was another on Sato's desk, although she was currently absent. It made him feel bad about the way he'd handled the psychiatrist issue.

She'd caught him by surprise, that was all. Now, because of his reaction, she thought she needed to apologize by getting him a coffee.

The coffee was the same temperature as the sun, Sato wasn't long back. It would be an easy ten minutes before he could drink it so he set the cup to one side and transferred the pictures he'd taken at the crime scene from his cell phone onto his computer. After he'd done this, he spent a couple of minutes reviewing them on the big screen. It was easy to miss details in the heat of the moment, or on his cell phone.

No new details were popping out for him, so he moved the photographs to a new folder on his network drive. He remembered the drone footage of Amy Tremaine's abduction and transferred that over as well.

While Coombes waited for the large files to transfer, he wrote a brief message on a Post-It Note and stuck it on top of Sato's coffee cup.

Sorry for being a dick. J x

He walked across the detective bureau to where Becker's desk was located and saw from the other man's face that he'd gone from a simple tooth extraction to a double root canal.

"Mark, I need a huge favor."

Becker's pained expression cleared and he smiled.

"John. Didn't see you there. What can I do for you?"

"I need help running down some details. It's not sexy, but I need someone sharp and I immediately thought of you. Do you have a minute?"

"In fact, I've got four days to fill. What do you need?"

Coombes laid out the basics of the case so far, the screenshots he'd taken of Walton's cell phone and the long list of unidentified phone numbers that he needed to convert into names and addresses. It was grunt-work of the worst kind, suitable for a newly-qualified rookie, but it was enough for a light to return to Becker's eyes.

"I'm on it."

"Don't slow-walk this one, Mark, I need it ASAP. There's plenty more where this came from if you want it."

Becker took no offense and appeared grateful at the prospect. Coombes had been in the same position himself more than once. When faced with long hours with nothing to do, the smallest job would be stretched to fill the time available.

Sato was back at her desk when he returned, her head in a book.

A Post-It was sitting on the lid of his own coffee with three Kanji characters carefully printed on it. Coombes pointed his cell phone at it to translate it.

Forgiven.

He peeled off the note and stuck it to his cubicle wall. There was a small collection of notes up there already. Kanji was an art form to him; he could look at it all day.

His coffee had finally reached drinking temperature and he drank the top third in a rush. Coombes stood and looked over the divider at Sato and noticed for the first time that she was wearing nitrile gloves.

"What are you reading?"

"Walton's journal. She wrote everything down on paper. Stream of consciousness stuff. What it means, I can't say. I should've left it with Dr. Kenner, see what she made of it."

"Read something."

"All right." Sato cleared her throat. "*January 6. Saw a teenage girl in Walgreens today. Her ass was hanging out and she had a busted lip. Fourteen years old, if she was a day. A middle-age man was hauling her down the aisle by her arm. It was impossible to tell if he was a date, or her father. I suppose I'm in no position to judge. Out of curiosity, I followed them. She picked up a pregnancy test. I said nothing, it was already too late.*"

"All the entries are like that?"

"Pretty much."

"What's that 'no position to judge' mean?"

"I assume she saw something of herself in the girl."

"Anything to move the case on?"

"No, but she's a riot. She could've run a podcast with this stuff."

He drank some coffee while he thought things over.

"All right, give me five minutes to make some notes and I'll catch you up on the rest of my morning. In the meantime, I want you to look at recent social media posts made by Elizabeth Walton, Amy Tremaine, Harlan Tremaine," he paused to check his notebook, "and someone called Cora Roche."

He spelled the last name as Sato wrote it down. Her head came back up.

"Looking for what?"

"Links between them, changes in circumstance or behavior. Find out if Walton was dating someone. You wouldn't believe how often a victim posts a happy picture with their killer before it all goes to shit."

Sato nodded, like she could imagine it all too easily.

Coombes turned back to his computer and opened a new spreadsheet. Using an existing template, he quickly mapped out a timeline for the day, separating the Walton events into one column and the Tremaine events into another. He included when the LAPD became involved, when they arrived on scene, and the same for the FBI.

When he finished, he stared at the row representing the fifty-six-minute window where Harlan Tremaine said he had 'disappeared'. It wasn't unusual for people to lose time. Hell, he probably lost five minutes himself every time he went into the shower stall.

Fifty-six minutes.

That was a *lot* of time to lose.

Coombes supposed that part of his problem with Tremaine's statement was that he had a pre-existing idea about who the man was from his time in office: his appetite for keep-fit and bodybuilding; his stance on guns; and his love of gas-consuming cars and SUVs.

The man's posturing was pure testosterone, virility, and adrenalin. This was at odds with someone who spaced out for almost an hour at the sight of a dead body. His eyes continued to move over the data.

On the face of it, the two crimes split easily in two.

The only chronological overlap between the two columns was the time period where he'd extrapolated when Amy Tremaine had to have left her apartment, and the time she spent riding the Metro to Pershing Square. Since she was a victim, this was no overlap at all. There was plenty of time for Walton's killer to get across town and abduct Amy.

He realized that Sato hadn't seen the footage yet.

"Grace, leave that just now I've got something to show you."

Sato rolled her chair along the floor until she was sitting next to him.

Coombes played the clip of the abduction first, then the earlier clip of the reconnaissance run. She sat in stony silence as the events unfolded, her eyes moving around the screen. He could tell that she was imagining herself in Amy's position, which was not the reaction he'd had. He moved clear so that she could replay each one herself.

After she'd watched each clip three times, he cut in.

"What do you think?"

"That's definitely our guy," she said. "Do the FBI have this?"

"They have the abduction; I don't know if they found the other one."

She studied him for a moment.

"You don't want them to have it, do you?"

"If we give it to them they'll shut us down, if they don't know, they can't."

"It's easier to ask forgiveness than get permission?"

Coombes smiled. "One of my favorite quotes."

"No kidding. Ok, so this is our guy. What can we do with it? Is this going to be enough to identify him? You can only see this side of his face and his ear. It could be anyone."

He nodded. She wasn't wrong.

"I let you see it three times for a reason. It was kind of a test. I figure that if you didn't notice, neither would they, assuming they got this far."

Sato's eyes flicked back to the screen and he began to replay the scene then paused it with the background figure looking straight at the camera. She still hadn't seen the man, her eyes focused instead on the foreground.

Coombes pointed at him.

"This guy at the back watches Amy like he's locked on target. I'm sure he's not the first guy to turn his head as she's walked past, but he looks like a stone-cold psycho, so I'm thinking he's involved. We have his whole face, more than enough to ID him. If we get *this* guy then maybe he gives us *that* guy and hopefully that leads us to Amy Tremaine. Not to mention one of these two assholes probably killed Elizabeth Walton."

"I like it," she said. "Just out of interest, how badly did you piss off Henderson when you were at the federal building?"

"He threw me out on my ass, why?"

Grace didn't look surprised.

"Facial recognition is an FBI system, right? So your new buddy probably set all their databases to notify him of whatever we submit. Facial, fingerprint, DNA, whatever. Bureau gets results a lot faster than we do, so they will beat us to the punch every time."

He ran his hand back and forth through his hair.

She was right.

It was even possible that Henderson had suckered him into working the case using reverse-psychology and that Barnes was in on it by providing enough information to get him started. If they got a juicy hit, the feds would swoop in and steal it out from under them and present it as their own.

Coombes smiled.

He'd been working on a solution without realizing it.

"We get Becker to submit everything, they won't be tracking him."

"Becker's on this too?"

"Gantz had him running down his clock sitting at his desk, so he's going to be helping out with computer stuff, phone calls, warrants, whatever we need."

"Perfect. They'll never see us coming."

Five minutes later, the video landed.

7

COOMBES HAD READ A science fiction book once where bad news travelled faster than the speed of light. It had been a satire, and he didn't read too many of those anymore. The real world was now all the satire he needed.

Amy Tremaine's ransom video was posted onto a Chinese video-sharing website at 13:31 L.A. Time, and it took Coombes only eight minutes and forty-seven seconds to hear about it. In that short period of time, the equivalent of one tenth the population of the United States had watched the clip.

He assumed many lived elsewhere and some had watched more than once.

The picture was fuzzy at first as the lens attempted to focus. Black, with something suspended like dust in front of it. A light snapped on and a greenish-blue line appeared at the top of the picture.

A water tank.

A flash of movement and suddenly Amy Tremaine appeared in the middle of the frame surrounded by bubbles. She was wearing a cobalt blue shirt and white briefs. She fought her way to the surface but a muscular arm at the top grabbed her head and pushed her back under the water. Amy's arms and legs pumped furiously in the water, then she reached up and fought the hand that held her in place.

Ten seconds. Twenty. Thirty-five.

The seconds ticked away at the corner of the video. Time seemed to slow down, but they were still only a third of the way through the footage.

Coombes was holding his breath along with her.

At seventy-two seconds in Amy twisted her head sharply to the side, freeing herself from the hand holding her, and swam to the surface. She managed to get a breath down before she was pushed under again. The hand now gripped her by a fistful of her hair.

There was no way to escape from a hair-hold.

Amy's eyes grew wild with panic. She looked straight at the camera, pleading for help. An understanding seemed to pass over her face and with it a level of focus.

No one was coming to save her.

She'd have to save herself.

Her hand shot out and hit the glass. Hard enough to make a dull thud. She did it again, then again. Water slowed her hand's movement, robbing it of momentum. On the fifth try, using her right foot braced against the glass behind her, and her left hand in front, she hit the glass hard enough to cause a star fracture on the surface of the glass. She was able to repeat this again, causing another star fracture next to the other one.

The effort drained her of all her strength.

Amy pointed at the person holding the cell phone, then her body went slack and her arms fell limp down at her sides. The kidnapper caught her and pulled her effortlessly out of the water. The clip ended the way it had started in darkness.

For a proof of life video, it looked a lot like she died at the end.

"Goddamn," Coombes said.

He turned to Sato and saw that her cheeks were scarlet and her jaws were clamped together. She was staring fixedly at the screen, at the black rectangle where the video had played.

After a moment, a tear ran down her cheek.

"I never thought I'd say this, Johnny, but I feel sorry for Harlan Tremaine. That poor woman, it's disgusting. Men are sick."

"We're going to have to watch this a bunch more times."

"Watch it if you want, I've seen enough."

He understood her position. Sato could be emotional at times, but in a lot of ways that was a good thing. The job had taken most of his emotion and he was the poorer for losing it.

"All right. Based on her height, see if you can work out likely tank sizes. I figure a tank this big didn't have someone's pet goldfish in it. We find the tank, maybe we find a lead."

She turned to him with the high beams on.

"I know the drill; you don't need to spell it out like I'm a child."

"She's still alive, Grace. Take a breath."

Sato said nothing and rolled her chair back around the divider to her desk. He was still looking at the top of the divider when he saw her put on a large pair of headphones she kept on her desk.

For the first time, it dawned on him that she used the headphones to control when he was able to talk to her.

They were for blocking him out.

Coombes sighed and turned back to his screen.

He opened his notebook to take notes and played the clip again. The first take away, was that the cell phone shooting the video *moved*. It wasn't attached to a tripod or anything else, someone was holding it. This wasn't a huge surprise, since they already knew there was more than one kidnapper, but he made a note of it anyway.

Based on what he could see of the kidnapper's arm, he figured he was looking at the same man he'd seen following her in the drone footage. Because of the gender split that he usually saw on cases, Sato associated herself with the victims, while he associated himself with the perpetrator.

The arm looked like his own arm.

If anything, the kidnapper's arm was stronger, more muscled.

Using his own build as a benchmark, he estimated that the kidnapper weighed in the region of 190 pounds.

On screen, Amy began hitting the glass again.

It impressed him the way she'd sufficiently overcome her panic to take action. A tank like that would be strong, designed to hold back the weight of a lot of water. She'd caused two cracks. If her kidnapper had pulled her to the surface to let her breathe, then shoved her back down, it was highly possible that next time she could've broken the glass.

She'd run out of air, pure and simple.

The clip ended and he'd learned nothing he didn't already know.

Coombes started it again with no real hope that situation would change. The brutality of what he saw didn't become easier to look at, instead it seemed to build with each viewing. Anger was suffocating him. He couldn't imagine what it would be like for Tremaine to see his daughter treated like this. The man had already agreed to pay her ransom.

This was what seller's remorse looked like with a kidnapping.

There was nothing to identify the man in the clip. A lot of guys in the service had tattoos. Not having them didn't mean much, except that he probably wasn't ex-special forces. He didn't think he'd ever encountered a special forces veteran without ink, it was like a tribal tradition. Coombes made a couple of notes then scrubbed forward to just before the end of the clip, when Amy appeared to point at the lens and paused the clip again.

The pointing made no sense to him, what did it mean? Was she pointing at the kidnapper, or was it aimed at her father?

He stopped playback and saw that the view count had increased by fifty-eight thousand. It had to be trending around the world.

Coombes minimized the browser so he didn't have to look at it anymore. The kidnappers weren't messing around, that was for sure. They'd kill Amy if they didn't get what they wanted, which was now 5 million dollars.

Hopefully, five million reasons to keep her alive.

8

Sato stood in front of a water tank, staring at fish on the other side. The glass rose up above her head by around six inches. Amy Tremaine was six inches taller than Sato. Even if the tank had been identically damaged, it was too small to have been the one in the video. Amy's feet had been suspended in the water above the base. None of the tanks they'd seen were damaged, coming here was a waste of time, just like the last four venues they'd checked.

The tanks were either too small or too big.

He had committed too much time to this quest to find the tank and now that he knew it, all he wanted to do was abandon the whole investigative string and begin again somewhere else.

"I'm sorry, but we just don't have a tank of the size shown in the video."

The aquarium manager, Manuel Garcia, wrung his hands in front of him, his face contorted into what Coombes could only assume was meant to be a smile.

"What about behind the scenes?"

"I don't take your meaning."

"The other aquariums we visited had tanks that the public don't see. Where they put new fish before they are put out for the public."

"Ah, yes. The nursery tanks. I can show you them if you like, but they are not like the one you're after either. Nursery tanks are long and low to the ground for easy access."

Behind Garcia, a man in his 20s was mopping the same section of floor over and over. Shooting glances at them, then turning away. The man was skinny and had wild red hair. Coombes had seen this behavior before. Sometimes it meant the person had something going on and was nervous about the arrival of the police. Other times, it was boredom.

"All right, never mind that. Can you at least identify the tank that was in the video. Give us a likely manufacturer, model number, something like that."

Garcia shook his head.

"No, I can't. That's just it. I never saw one that shape before and I've been in this business for 30 years. The dimensions...the glass. It's all wrong."

"The *glass* is wrong?"

"There is no way she should've been able to crack the glass like that. The bigger the tank, the stronger the glass. It should've been half an inch thick. A thousand-pound mako might get through that, but not a hundred twenty-pound woman. No offense to her."

"What does it mean that she cracked it?"

The manager shrugged.

"My guess? It's not a tank at all, it's a display case."

"Like in a museum?"

"Exactly. They're not rated to hold water, just display items to the public in a way they can't get at them. Stuffed animals, waxworks, whatever."

Coombes sighed.

They were going to have to start over and draw up a list of new locations to search. It hadn't occurred to either of them to check for display cases.

The man with the mop had disappeared.

Perhaps he realized that there was no threat, that his supervisor hadn't turned and pointed him out. *That's him there, the man you're after.* Coombes found he was disappointed. Chasing down the red-haired man and tackling him to the ground would've provided welcome stress relief.

"Thanks for your thoughts, Mr. Garcia, they've been helpful."

Coombes put his notebook away and they walked toward the exit. Sato had spoken to each aquarium beforehand and none had mentioned tank damage or a break-in. Coming here had always been the longest of long shots. Yet if they'd stopped there this new angle about display cases would never have come to light. People always gave him more in person, it was a mistake to think you could do the job from a desk.

"Amy Tremaine was kidnapped this morning, right?"

He glanced across at Garcia. "Right."

"It's just, the video is dark. It looks like it was shot at night. We open here at 9 a.m. and our staff are here from about 8. That's going to be the same wherever you go, aquarium or museum. The place where they shot this, it looks closed. Abandoned even."

"We figured it was in a storage area, somewhere not open to the public."

Garcia nodded in understanding. "*That's* why you were asking about our nursery tanks. Well, I wish you luck, Detectives. I hope you find that poor girl soon."

"So do I," Coombes said.

The manager split off from them and walked back toward his office.

There was always another reason not to rely on telephone interviews. People lied to the police all the time and it was a lot easier to lie when you weren't face-to-face with a seasoned cop. Coombes detected no subterfuge from Garcia, only a genuine wish to help. If he'd been hiding something it would've been right there on his face.

The doors rolled open and he saw the skinny man was leaning against the wall. Coombes turned toward him and put his hands on his hips. It was a power stance designed to amplify the size of his body while displaying both his badge and gun. The man was vaping from an e-cigarette and his hand shook as he held it to his mouth.

Coombes said nothing and let the silence build.

"You're here about that video of the girl in the tank?"

"That's right. You know something?"

Sato formed up on his right, her hand resting on the grip of her pistol. She was a lot smaller physically and was happy to let her sidearm do the talking.

"Whatever I tell you stays between us, right?"

"Depends what you tell me, doesn't it?"

The man's face twisted; it wasn't the answer he wanted.

"Look, I know where they shot that video. It's not an aquarium or a park, it's a...private club. If it got out that I was a member, I'd lose this job. We deal with children here; management take a hard line with family values."

The man cared more for his job with a mop than he did for Amy Tremaine. Coombes moved closer and dropped his voice into a low growl.

"The address. *Now.*"

The skinny man gave him the number of a building on La Brea Avenue in Mid-Wilshire. They were in Long Beach, opposite the Queen Mary. The whole of L.A. was between them and their destination.

He looked at his watch. Sixteen thirty. At this time of day, it would take them close to two hours to get there.

"Name?"

"*The Hard Limit.*"

"*Your* name."

"Joachim Nelson."

"What kind of club is it?"

Nelson's face colored. "It's a sex club. S & M. Anything goes."

"What's usually in the tank?"

"Performers. Couples. Strangers. Doing everything you can imagine."

"Have *you* been in the tank?"

Nelson nodded. "Everyone's been in at least once."

"How many members does the club have?"

"It could be 80, it could be 500."

Coombes could just imagine the DNA pool he was headed toward.

"You're not going to call and warn these people, are you Nelson?"

"If they knew I told you I'll be kicked out. I like it there."

"That much, I believe."

Coombes turned and headed back to the car.

People could be disgusting. Every day his job rubbed his face in it and he was no longer surprised by anything. Strangers screwing inside a water-filled tank for everyone to watch.

"How did I do?"

"You did great, kid."

"So you'll call and let me know?"

"Sure will."

Just another day in L.A.

He'd heard of clubs like *The Hard Limit*. Places that used private memberships to operate outside the law. Coombes got into the car and watched Grace's perfect face as she put on her seatbelt. She'd been against coming here and was quiet now it had paid off.

He started the engine and moved slowly out of the lot. They had a long way to go and every minute they spent not moving was a minute that evidence could be getting destroyed.

The obvious solution was to send Becker to babysit the scene until they got there but Gantz had been clear, Becker wasn't to leave the building.

That left him with hoping for the best; getting backup from Mid-Wilshire station; or bringing the FBI up to speed.

He mulled over the best option.

Calling in the FBI would show them he was a team player and might facilitate more movement of information on their shared case.

Coombes started laughing as he pulled out the parking lot.

"What's funny, Johnny?"

Sato's eyes seemed to sparkle when he laughed.

The FBI would never give him more information. If he told them about *The Hard Limit,* they'd pretend they knew about it already then go over there and black hole any evidence. He'd never see a clipped fingernail of it.

Telling the FBI about the club would be the same as arranging to have someone burn the place to the ground, everything would be lost.

He glanced at Grace.

"Just thinking about our friends at the Bureau."

"You think they'll come here looking for the tank?"

"Doubt it. They'll have computers that can work out dimensions from the video. They will look at manufacturers, then whoever they shipped them to. Right now, they will still be sitting on their asses waiting for a match. We got two leads coming here, coming to the *wrong place.* We got lucky, sure, but you have to put yourself out there to get the luck or it will never come. Feds don't think that way."

"You believe that *display case* angle then?"

"It's certainly believable."

Sato was silent as he lined them up on the 710, heading north.

"I take it you don't think so?"

"It just seemed like he was trying to diminish her, that he couldn't imagine a woman being strong. If a man had been in that tank, he would've said squat about the cracks."

"You're probably right, but that doesn't mean it's not valid."

"You don't get it, Johnny. There's a constant barrage of shit women have to put up with; running us down, robbing us of agency. That's when we're *not* being strangled, and drowned, and murdered. I'm sick of it."

Coombes nodded, then after what he hoped was a suitable interval, reached over and turned up the AC. There was a white noise aspect to the car's air conditioning that he had always found relaxing.

His mind returned to the unsecured crime scene at *The Hard Limit.* The rate the view counter had been jumping under the video of Amy Tremaine made it more and more likely that other members at the club would recognize the tank, even if the owners hadn't seen it yet.

It was only a matter of time.

Coombes discounted the idea of inviting uniforms from Mid-Wilshire to trample over all the evidence, he needed someone he could trust.

He knew just the guy.

9

BILLY LASS STOOD GUARDING the doorway to the club with a huge grin on his face. Three men were arranged around his feet in various states of having their ass handed to them. Bouncers, Coombes supposed. Big men, with shaved heads. Each seemed to have a freshly broken nose, presumably something they picked up trying to gain access to the club.

"Hey, Billy. How's the family?"

"Not bad. Looks like little John's getting a baby brother or sister."

Coombes smiled. "That's fantastic news."

"It's something all right. I got three hours sleep last night with the one we've got."

Lass had been his partner many years ago and had named his son after him.

"When do you guys leave for San Francisco?"

"Couple of weeks. I'm going to miss this place."

Coombes nodded and made a mental note to see his old friend before he left town.

"These guys give you any problems?"

"That big one there," Lass pointed at one of the men on the sidewalk. "He scratched my knuckle as he collapsed."

Billy laughed, amused with himself.

"Anybody get inside before you showed up?"

"Nah, you're good. The geek squad went in about forty minutes ago wearing moon suits. The club owner is sitting in that lime-green Honda over there, and the bar manager is in the black Firebird across the street next to your Charger."

Coombes turned his head to look at each car but he could see little inside. If they took off before he interviewed them it could take a while to run them down, but interviewing them before he saw the scene was likely a waste of time and he'd spent a long time looking for this tank.

The two men could wait.

"All right, we're going to go inside, see what we're dealing with here."

Billy nodded and stepped to the side.

"TID left gloves and shoe protectors inside the door."

Grace looked at Lass and did her best to smile.

"Billy."

"Grace."

Inside, the club had a smell he couldn't identify. He was pretty sure he didn't *want* to identify it and pulled on the shoe protectors quickly. A flight of stairs opened out into a large industrial space that was painted black. There was a high ceiling with a mezzanine level above and a doorway to what were probably private rooms.

The tank Amy Tremaine had been put into was in the middle of the floor, the cracks she'd made in the glass lit up by a portable light unit. The technicians had obviously finished processing the tank because they were both over at a bar packing up equipment.

Coombes approached the tank and studied the star fractures.

He held his gloved fist up for scale. About three inches across, four or five inches between them. A crack extended out from one toward the other, stopping just short. If the two had connected, it might've been enough to break the glass.

Coombes leaned in close and tilted his head up to see the top edge. It looked like a thin green line.

"Still think that's a display case, Johnny?"

There was a hard cynical edge to Grace's voice.

"No, but it's no aquarium tank either."

"What then?"

"A custom build maybe. Garcia was right, the glass is too thin."

"Don't you start with that sexist crap."

He turned to Sato. Her cheeks were flushed with anger, her eyes piercing.

"Look for yourself. It's quarter inch, Garcia said it should be half inch."

He waited until she looked up before continuing.

"This takes nothing away from her, okay? She's a fighter."

Coombes didn't like having to justify himself, but he was willing to cut Sato some slack. Too many of the victims they saw were women who had met their fate at the hands of a man. Things landed differently for her and they always would.

He headed over to the bar and noticed that his shoe protectors kept sticking to the floor. He had a fair idea why, and he did his best to shut it out.

The technicians had a line of metal cases ready to go.

"Detective Coombes," he said.

One of the technicians looked up.

"I'm Yeager, this is Ramirez."

"You guys get anything from the tank?"

"Not a damn thing, it's been wiped down," Yeager said.

"Which is more than you can say for the floor," Ramirez said.

The technicians laughed, but Coombes couldn't get there. He'd busted his ass trying to find the tank and it was all for nothing.

His cell phone vibrated. Billy Lass.

"Billy, what's happening?"

"The owner's back with the bar manager. Should I send them up?"

"May as well," Coombes said, before disconnecting.

He turned to Yeager.

"What about the other rooms?"

"It's set up like a karaoke place, except instead of singing, people get tied up and whipped. We saw no evidence that your victim was back there. My opinion? They came to use the tank, then left."

Two men and a woman appeared at the doorway. The woman was a knock-out, which he figured made her a bartender. That left a man in his thirties with longish feminine hair and a man that looked like an accountant.

"Which one of you is the owner?"

"That would be me," said the man with long hair. "Don Chase."

He held out a hand to shake, but Coombes ignored it.

"We're going to need a list of your members, Chase."

"Can't do it."

"You think I can't get a warrant?"

"I'm sure you could, I'm saying that it wouldn't do you any good. We don't *have* a list of members. If we don't keep a list we can't be compelled to hand it over. Our members like their privacy and we learned the hard way from our previous club."

"How do you control access if you don't know who they are?"

"Members are given a key fob. There's no ID on it, just an anonymous token."

"What's that?"

"The way the developer put it, it's like a gift card for Netflix. Those cards have no value until it's added by a cashier, the recipient scratches off a panel and there's a code to type in. The code gives you access to the gift value, but not the identity of who bought it, or their credit card number. Our key fob has RFID, you hold it up to the panel downstairs and it reads the token."

"All right. Then I'll need a list of your credit card transactions."

"Oh, that was just for the gift card example. We use a cash app."

"What about buying drinks at the bar?"

"Same answer. If you dig into that you'll find names but they'll all be John Doe, or Jane Doe, something like that. No one puts a real name into a cash app, it defeats the point."

The owner smiled; his eyes full of fuck-you.

Coombes absorbed it for a moment, then reached out and grabbed Chase by the hair, yanking his head backward as he frog-marched him over to the tank of water.

"Hey, hey, hey!"

"Did you see the video?"

"I saw it! I saw it! Let go of my hair!"

Coombes tightened his grip, twisting the man's hair in his fist. The TID men turned to watch the show, curious to see where it went next.

He was a little curious himself.

"One of your customers half-drowned a woman. I want names."

"I don't *have* names, I told you."

"How many members do you have?"

"I'd have to check my laptop."

"*Guess.*"

"Over seventy."

"How many of them are men?"

"Forty? Forty-five?"

"How many are muscular military-types in their early-forties?"

"What? I don't know!"

"Listen, Chase. We can come back when you're open and get IDs directly. Keep coming back until we get the person we want. Maybe you don't go out of business, maybe you do. I'm saying I can live with it either way."

"All right. There's maybe three men like that but I still don't know their names."

"Am I not being clear enough?"

"They busted up my tank! If I knew who did it I'd tell you, okay?"

"John, let him go."

Coombes turned to see Grace behind him.

"He can't tell you what he doesn't know, besides, we don't know if it *was* a member. The club is on social media, I just looked. Over a hundred thousand followers. The tank is in a lot of the pictures. It's more likely our guy saw it there than he was a member."

"And if he *didn't?*"

"If he didn't, putting this man in hospital is unlikely to change anything."

He released Chase and raised both of his hands in frustration.

"We found the tank and we get *nothing* from it?"

"Not true. We found out for sure Amy didn't die here. That's not nothing. Harlan Tremaine will be very glad to hear it. He might even get some sleep tonight."

Grace rested her hand on his arm.

It looked like nothing, but the gentle pressure of her fingers through his suit jacket cooled him down. He could feel the red mist dissipating and calmness returning.

As the rage left him, an idea took its place.

He turned back to the owner and the other man shrank away from him.

"You said that you had a club before this one, what was it called?"

Chase eyed him carefully, looking for the angle.

"*The Black Feather*, why?"

"Another club for perverts?"

The owner bristled. "BDSM enthusiasts."

"And the tank was at your previous club?"

Chase's face froze. He saw it now, the land mine under his foot.

"I've answered enough questions, Detective. You want any more, you're going to have to charge me with something. I'm sure my lawyer will tell me to say nothing, however."

Coombes smiled.

A refusal to answer was still an answer.

The tank *had* been at the previous club, and that club had been raided. It was likely to him that some, if not all, the names that were now protected by anonymous tokens were previously exposed when Chase had been forced to hand over his list of members' names.

All he had to do was reach out to vice and get a copy.

"I think we're done here, Mr. Chase."

10

CORA ROCHE WORKED AT Titan Two Reality, a special effects company based in Burbank, a block north of Warner Bros and Disney Studios. It looked like any other industrial unit, but the inside walls were lined with Plexiglas cases containing robots, monsters, dinosaurs, and aliens. Many were familiar to Coombes from movies he watched before he met his wife.

He approached the front desk and leaned into a young man's airspace.

"We're here to speak to Cora Roche."

"Can I ask who you are and what it's regarding?"

"No."

The man's eyebrows shot up at that and it looked like he was about to say something else when Coombes clenched his teeth and leaned forward some more. It bored him that mindless drones like this thought they had the right to his identity *and* his business simply because they were the first point of contact.

The man forced a smile and picked up his phone.

While he waited for Cora to come out front, Coombes stepped back from the desk and stood next to Sato who looked like she was holding a laugh inside.

"Jesus, Johnny. It's like you're not even housebroken."

"You know, Grace, you're easily in my top ten favorite partners."

Her mouth opened into a little O that pulled at something inside his chest.

After less than a minute, a woman with blue hair came out from the back. She wore dark eyeshadow and lipstick, had full sleeve tattoos, and was entirely clad in black. Her eyes swept nervously around the room before fixing on him. Somehow, he looked like what she expected. As she approached, he counted seven piercings in one ear, four in the other.

"Cora Roche?"

"Yes?"

"Detectives Coombes and Sato, LAPD."

Her shoulders sagged. "This is about Lizzie."

"That's right."

Roche rocked back on the heels of her biker boots and took a deep breath. Her face turned pale like she was about to pass out. They didn't have time for that, he needed to pull her back.

"What is it that you do here, Miss Roche?"

"I design prosthetics for movies and TV."

Coombes pointed at an alien in one of the cases.

"Like that?"

"No, that's creature effects. I do wounds. Cuts, bullet holes, exposed bone."

He nodded casually, like he often met someone who spent their day designing injuries, and glanced around the reception area. There were people standing about drinking coffee and laughing like they were in a Starbucks.

"Is there somewhere we can speak privately?"

"My manager's on vacation, we can use her office."

They followed her past the reception desk and through a door marked *staff only* to a long corridor. A chemical smell hung in the air and it seemed to draw closer as they moved deeper into the building. Roche moved through a door which opened automatically and they entered an airlock space with a second door that opened after the first closed behind them.

They were in what looked like a lab, with two long tables and amber-colored lighting overhead. Ten women wearing white coats sat working at the tables, none of them looked around at them. The chemical smell was now like a soup, he didn't know how any of them could stand it.

Empty, disembodied faces were suspended down the center of the tables. He recognized some of them, they were the faces of actors.

Sato looked at them in disbelief.

"These are silicone?" She asked.

"The skin is, the hair is real. Every strand is put in by hand, it's a labor of love. In a mid to long shot you can't tell the difference between a stunt man and an actor."

Coombes said nothing.

A mask of this quality would be extremely convincing on security footage, either to establish an alibi or to cast blame elsewhere.

They came to an office and went inside. Coombes took out his notebook, his eyes fixed on the woman with blue hair. The room was small and seemed to become smaller still with the door closed. Out of sight of her co-workers, Roche's demeanor crumbled and tears rolled down her cheeks.

"What happened to Lizzie is too much, I can't think about it."

"The two of you were close?"

"She was my best friend. My only friend."

"I'm sorry for your loss, Miss Roche. We'll try to get through this as quickly as possible. When was the last time you saw each other?"

"I last saw her the day after New Year's but we spoke almost every day. I guess you know that already. It's why you're here, isn't it?"

Coombes nodded.

"And how was she when you last spoke?"

Roche shrugged. "The usual. Excited, distracted. All that charity stuff really got her going. Helping other people, that's what she was all about."

"Was it normal for the two of you to go so long without meeting?"

Roche dug a tissue out her pocket and blew her nose.

65

"Some months were busier than others. January and February were usually pretty quiet but I was used to her losing herself to the cause. She was focused, mission-orientated."

He studied Roche for a moment.

The colored hair, the piercings, the dark makeup. She was a very different person to Elizabeth Walton, with her prim business suits and starched white shirts. They appeared to be at opposite ends of the spectrum, to say nothing of the age difference between them.

Despite this, a deep bond had formed.

"How did you and Miss Walton come to know each other?"

"We went to the same yoga class. I sucked big time and she took me under her wing. She had a way of making everything fun and I stopped being embarrassed about sticking my ass in the air. Later we took a self-defense class together, it just kind of built from there."

Cora Roche looked at the floor and seemed to go somewhere else, perhaps thinking about how the self-defense class hadn't helped her friend when she was being strangled.

"Was she having problems with anyone?"

"She never told me if she was and she told me everything."

"What about relationships? Was she dating?"

"Lizzie would sometimes cancel on me, say she was *seeing a friend*. It was the only thing she was private about. I got to thinking that the *friend* might not be the same as the time before, and that didn't matter to her."

Coombes wondered if Walton's discretion might not owe more to her date being married. It was a frustrating detail for her to have kept back from her best friend, but probably not relevant if her death was linked to the kidnapping.

"What about the former governor? Any tension between them?"

"Those two were like an old married couple. She'd worked for him so long she could finish his sentences. I asked her once if there was anything there and she just laughed."

"What did the laugh mean to you?"

"That he wasn't her type, obviously."

"Any idea what her type was?"

"I honestly don't know. I stayed with her dozens of times and often thought she was going to make a move on me, but she never did. It's too bad, I would've rung her bell."

Coombes tilted his head to the side.

"You stayed at the Tremaine mansion?"

"God, no. This was at her apartment downtown."

He frowned and glanced at Sato. She shook her head.

"We don't know anything about an apartment. Do you remember the address?"

"South Hill Street, I don't know the number. I posted pictures of it on Facebook once but she asked me to take them down. Said she didn't want other people seeing it. I assumed she meant Tremaine. I heard her take a call from him there once and she told him she was at her sister's. I don't blame her. She ate and slept most days in his home. I couldn't do that. The best thing about work for me is leaving at the end of every day."

It was a point of view Coombes could easily understand, having had the occasion to both eat and sleep at the PAB. Sato took over.

"Do you still have those photographs of the apartment?"

"Having them and finding them are two different things. They were probably on the cell I lost last year. None of that stuff was backed up."

Sato opened her iPad.

"Would you recognize the building if you saw it again?"

"Of course."

Sato pulled up South Hill Street on Street View and stood shoulder-to-shoulder with Roche, the screen between them. He watched upside-down as Grace moved the camera car down the street, turning the view from side to side to see the buildings, then on again.

"That one," Roche said, pointing.

Sato glanced around. "You sure?"

"It's a building, not a man in a dark alley."

A half-smile formed on Coombes' face.

He liked Roche, for what that was worth. Sato zoomed in on the building number and he wrote it down and closed his notebook. They were done here, and all they'd learned was that the victim didn't have an enemy in the world. The apartment, he knew, would be a dead end.

It probably *did* belong to her sister.

"Again," he said, "I'm sorry for your loss."

The prosthetics artist fixed him with a stare.

"I'm not stupid, I know what's happening. Everything's being put into finding the governor's daughter. News channels don't even mention Lizzie anymore, just Amy."

"You have my word that's not the case, Miss Roche."

He could see that she didn't believe him. Roche was right. The living always took priority over the dead. If he could save Amy Tremaine at the expense of finding the truth behind Walton's death, he'd take it.

He held out his card toward Roche and when she made no move to take it, he put it down on the table in front of her and tapped it twice with his index and middle fingers to get her to focus on it.

"If you think of something, give me a call."

Coombes left her to her thoughts and walked through the lab where they made actors' faces, to the doorway. Sato drew alongside and they continued on through the airlock, toward the company's lobby area. As they were passing the plastic cases with aliens and robots, his cell phone rang. Gantz.

"L-T, what's new?"

"Tremaine wants to see you again, sounded important. Tell Grace to sit this one out. I think he likes you."

"What's not to like?"

Gantz ignored that and read out an address near Fairfax.

"Is that an FBI safe house?"

"It's his gym."

11

HARLAN TREMAINE'S GYM WAS located only eight blocks from Coombes' home. As a result, he'd driven past it many times without realizing that such a famous establishment was right on his doorstep. It had a shabby-chic appearance with faded whitewashed brick and looked like it was on the point of going out of business. The run-down look disappeared as soon as he opened the door and he saw the high-gloss interior, straight out of a movie spaceship.

An attractive blonde eyed him suspiciously.

"Are you a member, sir?"

"I'm here to meet Mr. Tremaine."

"Ah, yes. Here we go."

The woman lifted a gym bag from under the counter and placed it in front of him.

"What's this?"

"Your clothes. You're going to be working out with Mr. Tremaine. He left this for you in case you didn't bring any. He's already inside."

"You're in luck, I already brought my own clothes."

Coombes held his suit jacket open so that she could see his badge and gun holster, then walked past her toward the changing rooms. The blonde said nothing. He moved through the men's changing room, past the entrance to a shower, and out into the gym.

It was packed.

He'd been in a few gymnasiums in his time, and they had almost always been near-empty. Not this one. Loud music thumped from every angle, full of energy. His wife's kind of music, not his.

He scanned the room, back and forth, looking for the former governor. It took a moment to find him as he was sitting at a machine, pulling down on a bar.

Coombes walked over, very aware of his suit and his street shoes. He was drawing attention. Maybe the change of clothes would've been a good idea. His clothing was going to limit how long he had with Tremaine whether he liked it or not.

Like a lot of gyms, there were mirrors all around. To help you look at yourself, to look at other people. If you saw that you were fat, shame propelled you to keep going; if you saw that you were looking good, it inspired you to keep going.

It was a win-win on the mirror front.

He saw that Tremaine was watching him as his arms slowly worked the bar down, then up again. Smooth and steady. There was no trace of anything on his face, no effort, no pleasure. It was as if pulling on the bar was like breathing in and out.

"You saw that video I suppose?"

"I saw. You have my sympathies."

Tremaine was silent for a long moment.

"I had already agreed to pay them, it wasn't necessary to do that to my Amy. Now of course, they want more money. The kind of money it takes a while to pull together."

Five million dollars.

Coombes nodded, impatient to be going. Whatever he was doing here, it didn't seem to be moving the investigation on, therefore it was a waste of his time. Tremaine's expression seemed to clear, the tension holding his eyebrows down in a hard line melting away.

"You're still wearing your suit, Detective."

"I'm still working. If I wasn't, I wouldn't be here."

"I took you for a man that looked after himself. You look capable."

Tremaine looked capable, that was for sure. Capable of pinning a woman to the floor and crushing her throat with his bare hands.

"I take care of myself."

"Oh yeah? How?"

The bar was still going up and down, rhythmically, like Tremaine had forgotten he was doing it. Coombes glanced at the stack of weights at the back. 180 pounds. It was almost his exact weight. The former governor was in incredible shape.

"Resistance mostly. Perps resist, I chase them down. It's great cardio."

"No doubt. What else?"

"I run trails in the hills, get some fresh air. Box a little too."

The bar stopped moving and Tremaine let his arms drop down into his lap. They were glistening with sweat and were flushed pink with blood though his tanned skin.

"Excellent. I used to box when I was younger. When you're in a fight, you think of nothing else. Surprisingly peaceful, considering you're trying to hit another man and avoid being hit at the same time."

More and more faces were turning their way.

Everyone in the gym had probably seen the video of Amy in the tank of water. But these were Tremaine's people, they would leave him alone. He was the outsider. The faces were looking at him, openly hostile.

"How about we take this somewhere else?"

"All right."

Harlan Tremaine stood and they walked toward the changing room. Before they got there, Tremaine stopped at a section with free weights. He lifted a huge dumbbell and began to do arm-curls. Coombes sighed.

"This wasn't what I had in mind, Mr. Tremaine."

"Relax, I'm nearly finished my routine."

Tremaine wasn't looking at him, or at himself in a mirror, he was looking at a woman less than ten feet away. She was wearing yoga pants and a top that barely covered her sports bra. The woman was about the same age as Tremaine's daughter, but it didn't appear that Harlan was thinking about Amy as he looked at her.

"What happened to your FBI friends?"

"I gave them the slip, they were driving me crazy. If someone was after me, they would have gone for me when they had the chance."

"I agree."

Tremaine glanced away from the young woman's flexing rear end to look at him. There was something in his gray eyes, something he couldn't read.

"I was curious about the origins of your name. About the spelling."

"It's pretty straightforward. My parents came to this country by plane, not on a boat."

"I like you, Coombes. You say whatever's on your mind, no filters. With that in mind, what I said before, I wasn't kidding. I want my girl back and I want the animals that took her dead. After that video, it's all they deserve."

"If that's what you wanted, you made a mistake involving the FBI."

Tremaine nodded.

"They would've gotten involved anyway. By bringing them into it, I gained a measure of control I would otherwise not have had."

Tremaine swapped arms with the dumbbell and resumed his scrutiny of the yoga pants. The young woman was now standing on one foot and stretching the other up over her head.

"I didn't become a cop to kill people, Mr. Tremaine. I'm in the justice business, not the revenge business."

"Yet sometimes, they can be the same. No? Let me tell you, when you're on this side of the fence it feels different. If this happened to you, you'd want the same."

"That's why I'm not judging you."

The dumbbell went back down on the rack with a heavy *clank*.

"I know that these things can go either way. Cornered suspects. Shoot-outs. All I'm saying, is that if that situation was to develop...well, I'd owe you."

This was why Tremaine hadn't wanted Sato here, Coombes thought. Repeating his offer in front of her would make it harder to pull off if the opportunity arose. Of course, if there *was* a shoot-out now through no fault of his own, it would appear to Tremaine that he'd done what he asked.

Even talking about it had compromised him.

"We didn't have this conversation."

Tremaine nodded again.

"I knew you'd understand."

When you are used to being surrounded by yes-men the truth often didn't get through. Tremaine expected to hear what he wanted and heard it anyway.

Coombes decided to drop it.

If he said he wasn't going to gun down a suspect in cold blood, what would likely happen is that the case would mysteriously be given to Wallfisch, another D-III detective at RHD. Wallfisch would doubtless be more agreeable to what Tremaine proposed but would be less certain to get his daughter back alive.

Amy had to take priority.

"Was there something you wanted to tell me about the investigation?"

"Yes, but not here. I'm going to hit the showers. I'll get you out front."

When Tremaine emerged from the changing room ten minutes later, he was wearing a blue suit, loafers, and a diver's watch on a chunky bracelet that looked like it weighed four pounds.

Coombes stood and prepared to walk toward the exit but the former governor shook his head and pointed up.

"I have an arrangement with the management here."

Coombes suspected the *arrangement* was that he owned the place.

They climbed up concrete stairs until they reached a door to the roof. A sign warned that it was alarmed, but no alarm rang when Harlan opened it. A brick lay on the other side and Tremaine used it to hold the door open.

"I want to show you something," Tremaine said.

They walked to the edge of the roof that overlooked the parking lot.

"The black Tahoe."

"Feds," Coombes said. "They followed you here?"

"No, they arrived about twenty minutes later which means they're up in my cell phone. I suppose switching from a Suburban to a Tahoe is considered undercover work in the FBI."

Coombes nodded and tilted his head to watch a black helicopter move through the deep blue sky. The former governor was taking his time getting to the point.

"You asked me if I had enemies, someone that might want to hurt me."

Here we go.

"That's right."

"Well, I did think of someone, but he's not an enemy. Not exactly."

Coombes frowned. "What then?"

"I guess you could say he's a super-fan. I post something on my socials and he's always the first to like it, no matter the hour. I'll post a video on my YouTube channel that's ten minutes long and he'll post a comment two minutes later. See what I'm saying? If he *watched* the video then his comment should be a minimum ten minutes after posting. He has to be first. He also set up a website about me and sells merchandise with my face on it."

Coombes felt a familiar rush and pulled out his notebook.

"This is good. What's his name?"

"James Anderson."

He wrote the name down.

"Have the two of you ever met?"

"Many times, though never by my design. I am asked to give keynote speeches all over California either related to my time in office, or to my foundation. So, I'll be giving a speech and I'll look down into the front row where the lights spill into the audience and I'll see him looking back at me, his cell phone recording me. Not once, Detective. Every single time. If I check into a hotel, he'll be in the lobby waiting for me, camera ready."

"How does he know where you're staying?"

"I guess he calls ahead and pretends to be a member of my staff. There are a limited number of hotels set up to cater to someone like me, so he'll only have a handful of calls to make. I'm not going to check into some sleazy motel because of some weirdo. Screw that."

Coombes thought for a moment.

"How long has this guy been doing this?"

"Since I announced my run for governor."

"Wow. That's a long time ago now."

"You're not wrong. At first it was flattering. I was trying to build my base and it made no sense to alienate anyone. He was dedicated, technically proficient, and was doing all this without being paid. For all I know, he helped push younger online audiences toward voting for me. I saw him as a bit of a clown. I'd laugh about him privately with friends. I figured it was the price of doing business; you're in the public eye, this is what is costs."

"I see that," Coombes said, nodding.

"I thought when I hit the term limit, he'd lose interest. Why would he continue, when I was no longer governor? I thought there was a light at the end of the tunnel, that the situation would resolve itself."

"But it didn't."

Tremaine shook his head.

"If anything, it got worse. Now that I'm a private citizen it feels like more of an intrusion. Back then I had a security guy, I was protected. Because of this joker, I now have a conceal carry license. I'm packing heat when I go to the Farmers Market in case this wacko decides to become famous at my expense."

Coombes sensed where this was going.

"How long ago did you file a restraining order?"

"Three weeks yesterday."

"Does he know where you live?"

"Are you kidding? *Google* knows where I live."

It was a solid lead, but Coombes couldn't help wishing he'd had it from the get-go rather than have this piece held back when he could've been hunting him down.

"Why didn't you tell me this yesterday?"

"You have to understand. It's a huge leap to go from invading my privacy to...what's happened. I thought he might come at me but I had nothing to base that on, just my gut. A worst-case scenario. Whatever he had going on, it was aimed at *me*. I didn't think he'd go after my girls, that he'd try and hurt me through them. Not for a second did I think that, or I would have taken steps to prevent it."

My girls.

The easiest approach would be to show Tremaine a screen grab of the man that followed his daughter, but since he was not long through telling him that he wanted the man dead, not to mention having a gun to hand, he decided to keep that to himself for the time being.

"Okay. How about you describe this Anderson character to me."

"White. Brown hair. Your type of build, but three or four inches shorter."

Coombes wrote this down.

"Anything else?"

"Sometimes he wears glasses. When I'm on stage the light bounces off them like two flashlights. When I've seen him outside, he always wears sunglasses, the type with straight legs that kind of rest on the top of the ear."

Coombes glanced sharply up from his notebook.

"Really?"

"Yes. I thought for a while his sunglasses had a correction built into them, but I have seen him wearing no glasses at all, so I assume he has contact lenses."

Tremaine hadn't picked up on his spike in interest and that was probably for the best.

"This is worth looking into so I'm going to get right on it. In the meantime, if you see this guy call me immediately. *Do not shoot him*. We need him to get to Amy and in that situation, he has all the high cards. The best bet is to locate him, track him back to where she is, then drop the net on him."

Tremaine said nothing, his eyes down by his feet.

"Look at me, Harlan. No cowboy shit, okay?"

Tremaine half-smiled.

"You really do have my number, Detective. We'll do it your way for now."

He put his notebook away and they turned away from the edge, back toward the roof exit. Coombes waited until they were almost there before he asked his final question. His tone light, conversational.

"Was there anything between you and Elizabeth?"

"I loved her, but not the way you mean. Lizzie was family. When my wife passed, she kept Amy and me going when we thought there was no reason to continue. Lizzie saved me many times over but when she needed me, I was fast asleep."

They were at the door now.

"Did James Anderson ever meet Elizabeth?"

"No, but he would know about her. He knows everything about me. It's all up on his goddam website."

12

A DARK-BLUE BMW SEDAN was parked in his usual spot in front of his home. He didn't know much about the brand; all their cars were kind of the same to him. Looked expensive. Fast. It looked, in fact, like it had just rolled out the factory door, it was spotless.

Coombes sat for a moment studying it.

Who did they know that owned a BMW? Julie's sister maybe. But she hadn't seen her sister in a long time, almost two years. They'd had some kind of bust-up that he'd never cared to find out about.

The Beamer had a vanity plate that hurt his brain to look at. CSECLSD. Case closed, he supposed. He frowned. That didn't sound like something his wife's sister would choose, she worked for Google.

He opened the car door and stepped out onto the street. A couple of vehicles passed before he could cross over.

Up close, the German sedan was larger than he thought, its streamlined shape seemed to hide its size. Chrome details, sparkling paint with an unbelievable high gloss. It looked good. Over a year's wages, that was for sure. Not that anyone bought cars anymore, they were all leased and this one would be no different.

He stepped right up to the glass to look inside, his hand shielding the sun. The windows were heavily tinted, but not illegal. He was able to see that it was unoccupied, and that a sea of black leather filled the interior.

Coombes continued up the path to his front door. The hair on the back of his neck was standing up, a primitive part of his brain was activating.

He'd experienced the same thing several times in the past, usually when he was about to be confronted by a dead body. He had learned to listen to his early warning system and not shrug it off.

Humans had survived for thousands of years not on luck, but by instinct. You didn't learn from mistakes if you were dead. Instinct was passed down, a genetic knowledge.

The lock didn't turn.

He pulled the key out and checked he'd used the correct one. It was. A simple flat key with the teeth on one side. He had two similar keys on his keyring, but he hadn't used them. He didn't think he'd ever mixed them up, the house key was on top of the stack, next to his car key fob.

He sighed.

There was a rocker switch on the inside that held the latch open or closed. Julie must've activated it by mistake. The surprise of seeing her sister again, maybe.

Coombes reached for the chime, then paused.

CSECLSD, that sounded like a lawyer's plate.

Things had been patchy between them recently. Was she seeing a lawyer about a divorce? Had she already changed the locks? The barrel of the lock looked the same, not fresh and shiny.

He lowered his hand from the chime.

None of this added up. No lawyer would come out here on business, they'd make you go downtown. Into their fancy office with their secretaries, their pot plants, and their corporate art.

He walked around the side of the building toward the yard. Halfway down was a window into the bathroom. As was normally the case, the window was open a half inch, then clicked shut on the inside. He took a steel ballpoint pen from his jacket and used it to turn the mechanism from the outside, then pulled it open.

There was some kind of commotion inside, he could hear it as soon as the window opened. He pulled himself up and through the opening then lowered his feet carefully so as not to make a sound. Whatever was going on, he didn't want to tip his hand.

He took off his jacket and set it over the edge of the bathtub. He was in good shape, but pulling himself in through the narrow window had caused sweat to break out on his face. He wiped his forehead with the back of his hand.

The hairs all down both arms were standing up now.

He drew his weapon then quietly opened the door.

Muffled voices. Anger. Back and forth, like an argument. Coombes swung his gun around, checking behind him where the kitchenette diner was, then back across, into the living room.

On the coffee table sat the laptop Julie used to run her web design company. The laptop was open, a screensaver moving around. Next to it, sat two empty glasses. Flutes, the kind people used for drinking Champagne. As far as he knew, they didn't own any such glasses.

He moved into the hallway and stared at a fat leather briefcase that sat on the tile. Next to it, was an equally fat dachshund that lay with its head resting on its front paws. The dog's brown eyes looked lazily up at him before closing again.

The wine glasses, the dog.

Julie's sister wasn't here.

It wasn't a home invasion.

He moved back toward the kitchenette. On the counter he now noticed a big black bottle. He was right, it was Champagne. The cork and its wire cage lay next to it. He sighed. It was obvious what this was, you didn't have to be a detective.

The bedroom door was shut.

The angry voices seemed to be coming from within. No, not anger. It was like a wild animal had been tricked into entering the room, then had the door shut on it. This animal was trapped inside, and it was tearing itself apart trying to get out.

Nothing good would come from opening the door, he knew that. Not with the Champagne glasses out there on the coffee table. The easiest thing would be to leave and return home at the regular time, pretend none of it had happened.

But he couldn't do that, it wasn't who he was.

He transferred his gun to his left hand then slowly turned the handle. The door opened a crack, so that the latch was outside the door frame. The sound coming from inside got louder. The sound on its own was more than enough but he couldn't stop himself. He had to go on. He had to see it with his own eyes. It was like removing a sticking plaster, you had to rip it off quickly in a single action. In the end, they said, it was better.

All the pain in one go, not drawn out.

With the gun back in his right hand, he kicked the door wide open.

Julie was on the bed on her hands and knees while, behind her, a heavily muscled man mounted her from the rear. They were both naked. Their heads turned to look at him. Julie wore some kind of gag and she started to laugh through it when she saw him. Saliva ran out her mouth, around the gag and onto the pillowcase in a thick, viscous stream. The man stared at him with a neutral expression, his bucking hips not stopping or slowing for a second.

The final piece of energy left his body.

He felt cold and disconnected. It was like a bad porn movie, except the woman was his wife. His brain couldn't accept what it was seeing. She was tied to the bed and gagged, yet her facial expression told him that she was enjoying every second. Perhaps more so, now he was watching.

This was the end for them, there was no way back.

The lawyer, if that's what he was, bared his teeth.

"Beat it, man."

Coombes felt his finger tighten involuntarily against the trigger of his weapon. He wanted to kill the stranger as sure as he wanted his next breath.

He forced himself to count to ten inside his head, the way his father had taught him. If you waited until ten, you generally made the right decision.

Julie was still laughing at him, she couldn't stop.

The cop part of him figured he could shoot the lawyer and later claim he thought the man was raping her. The gag and bindings, combined with the man's physicality, would sell it.

But he knew that if he pulled the trigger once, he'd continue firing. Julie's gagged laughter was destroying him. The laughter, and the smile that was pulling her eyes up at the corners. He'd kill both of them and, after that, he'd put the gun in his own mouth.

It was how these things went; he'd seen it before.

Inside his head, he reached ten.

He turned and walked into the hallway.

After a moment staring at the floor, he put his Glock back in its holster and retrieved his jacket from the bathroom. Mechanically, he pulled it on.

Coombes looked around.

He wouldn't be back here, there was nothing left for him. Already the house looked different, like he'd taken off a pair of sunglasses.

All around him he saw the same things, except now he saw how little of it was his. Julie had chosen everything, and he'd gone along with it because he'd loved her. If she wanted the floral drapes, who was he to say no? As long as she'd been happy, he'd been happy.

His eyes stopped on the television.

It was one of the few things he'd chosen. Julie hadn't cared too much about tech stuff, that was his field. He walked across to it and began to unplug the leads.

There were his suits as well of course, but they were in the wardrobe behind the man with the heaving buttocks. Most of them were old and needing to be replaced anyway.

He lifted the television off the hooks on the wall and carried it toward the front door.

It was a flat panel, but it was plasma, not LED. He'd bought early, and chosen the wrong technology. The picture was great but it was old now and not 4K. It wasn't even 1080p. None of that mattered now.

The *weight* was what mattered.

Coombes opened the front door and lugged the television down the path to the street, leaving the door of the bungalow open. He kept standing on the power cord. He paused to wrap it around the base, then lifted the television above his head. It was really heavy. The newer LEDs were light as a feather.

Reaching the sidewalk, he paused to get his breath back. Heads turned as people drove by.

He was in front of the BMW. *CSECLSD.*

"Close *this*," he said, and threw the television at the windshield. The showroom clean glass instantly turned opaque as it smashed. The car's alarm sounded; its lights flashed. The television slid slowly down off the hood onto the sidewalk leaving deep scratches in the paintwork.

Coombes walked across the street to his car.

It disappointed him that the television hadn't penetrated the glass into the cabin. The glass had been caught in some kind of safety film, designed to protect the driver.

He climbed into his car and slammed the door.

After a moment, the lawyer appeared outside his bungalow. He was still naked, still apparently, aroused. The man was a machine. He looked like a quarterback, not like any damn lawyer Coombes had seen before. The man ran down the path toward his ruined car and started randomly screaming with rage, his hands gripping his head.

He glanced at the rearview mirror and saw a bittersweet smile on his face. He hit the ignition and revved the engine, over and over, loud enough for the lawyer to hear. The man charged across the street toward him.

Coombes nailed the throttle and pulled the wheel hard over, aiming straight at the other man. He swung across the road, causing other vehicles to take evasive action. The lawyer's eyes popped open in surprise and he was forced to jump to the side to avoid the fender of the Dodge as it came toward him. It was hard to see over the hood, but it looked like he'd missed him by inches.

He hit the brake and lowered the window, looking down at the naked man that lay sprawled and bleeding at the side of the road.

"If I see you again, I *will* kill you. That's a promise."

The man said nothing.

He glanced up. His wife stood in the doorway, arms crossed. She looked the same as she always had, beautiful but slightly sour like she'd sucked on a lemon.

Probably the only thing she hadn't sucked today.

He was pleased to note that she'd taken the time to cover her body, there was only so much humiliation he could take. Next to him, the lawyer hadn't moved since he'd crashed down on the ground. Shock was kicking in. His hands were shaking by his side and his eyes remained wild from his near miss with the fender. The man's pumped-up quarterback body had finally gone slack and limp.

Satisfied, Coombes buried the throttle once more, leaving five feet of rubber behind him on the warm asphalt. He needed a drink. He needed to lose himself down a deep hole, where there was no light and no chance of being seen, even by himself.

His cell phone began to ring.

He considered not answering it, but the screen displayed his partner's face with a cheeky smile. Grace Sato, the one good thing in his life.

"Grace, what's the news?"

"We got a hit off facial recognition for our mystery man."

"*Fantastic.*"

"Don't get excited, we're probably looking at an eye witness."

"Okay."

"Anton Schofield, thirty-eight years old. Born in Munich, Germany to a Czech mother and a Russian father, moved to the US in '08. Looks like a real charmer, Johnny, but there's a problem. His name's flagged. He's a missing person."

"Give me the address."

13

SCHOFIELD'S HOME WAS LOCATED in the hills west of Laurel Canyon, half a mile above Sunset Strip. It wasn't exactly the kind of place that rolled out the welcome mat, and steel security barriers and impossibly high hedges were all around. Money lived here, and it didn't want you knowing about it. Were it not for his GPS unit, Coombes might not have found it at all, but there it was right in front of him.

The security gate was open and he turned in onto a short driveway that fed around the side of the building. Sato's car was already there, as was a Hollywood cruiser, and a Lexus SUV.

He got out and walked to the front door.

Nobody had gone in yet, he was just in time. Coombes nodded at the uniforms who stood back watching, hands on hips. A short Latina stood next to Sato with a huge bunch of keys. When the woman saw him she began to unlock the house.

The door had three separate locks, which either indicated a certain level of paranoia on the part of the owner, or an understanding that danger was close at hand.

The door opened and a beeping started.

Loud, insistent. For a moment he imagined coming home to this noise every day. You couldn't shut it out, it was deafening. He followed the woman inside, Sato next to him, her hand resting on her holstered weapon.

The Latina walked to a control panel and waved a dongle across the front.

Silence returned and he felt his heart begin to slow.

The woman came back over so that she was standing in front of them. She was wearing a business suit with a light-colored top underneath. The top appeared to struggle with the task assigned to it.

Or maybe it was exactly right, he couldn't tell.

She was nervous, she didn't want to be there, not if the owner lay inside somewhere dead.

"Sorry, we weren't introduced" he said. "Who are you?"

"Maria López. I look after some of the houses around here when their owners are away. They call, ask me to restock their fridge, or get a cleaner so it's ready when they come back. We get them whatever they want."

He nodded.

Rich people, they had so many homes that half the time they were someplace else. The other side of the country, the other side of the world. Being rich was hard, it was a full-time job living the life of Riley.

"When was the last time you heard from Mr. Schofield?"

"Not since October or November last year. I'd have to check my files."

"Is that normal?"

"No, he usually needs something twice a month, maybe more."

"What did you think of him?"

She avoided his eye.

"I don't know him, sir. I only met him once. Everything is by telephone."

"Well, did he seem like a nice guy?"

"He was different from my other clients."

"How so?"

The woman hesitated.

"He looked like one of those men that stand in nightclub doorways."

"Like security? Shaved head, muscles?"

"Yes."

He thought of *The Hard Limit* and the bouncers Lass had taken out.

"Anything else?"

"He had a tattoo on his neck." She pointed to her own neck, under her left ear. "An eagle with two heads, like it was looking both ways. It looked European. I thought he might be a Nazi. He looked at me like I was a cockroach."

"Did he frighten you?"

"I can't say that, sir."

"I won't tell him. He might be dead up there."

The woman flinched. Eventually, she nodded.

"All right, Maria. Leave the keys and a number where we can reach you."

She handed him the ring of keys and began to look through her purse. He looked at the keyring. At least ten metal keys, plus what he took to be a clicker for the security gate, and the dongle for the alarm console.

He looked up and saw that her cheeks were flushed.

She gave him a business card, which he exchanged for one of his own. Her card was superior to his in every way, as he knew it would be.

Maria López, residential property manager.

The ink of her name seemed to sit on the surface of the card, like it was three dimensional. It had a pleasant feel when you ran your finger over it. Super high gloss. Like it was written in blood, but in a good way.

He was in the wrong business.

Nobody got rich in the LAPD, though a few had when they'd left. Private security, high end. That's where the money was, not down in the gutter with the dead bodies where he was.

He looked her in the eyes and smiled.

"You think of anything else, give me a call, ok?"

"Okay."

She left quickly, wobbling a little on her heels. The Hollywood boys watched her leave, then after a moment, began to laugh. When they looked back, he waved them in and followed his partner's lead by pulling on nitrile gloves.

"What was that all about?" Sato said. "You into her or something?"

"I don't know what you're talking about."

"Right. Either the man's lying up there in a pool of blood, or he's not here. What he was like as a person doesn't really come into it."

"Unless he's dead."

His partner said nothing.

He interlaced his fingers to improve the fit of the nitrile gloves.

"I guess she had nice eyes," he said, casually.

Sato smirked.

"I noticed her *eyes* myself."

The two uniforms stood next to them now. A rookie in his early twenties with pale mottled skin, and an older man in his thirties with short sleeves and two chevrons.

"All right fellas, let's do a walk-through. It's your turf, but it might be related to our case. I assume everything's been explained?"

The older man nodded.

"If there's a body here the lieutenant says you can have it with her blessing. One less in our column at the end of the month."

The four of them set off through the front hall to a set of stairs. The entrance was cold as the back of it was cut into the ground and it was next to two double garages. As they climbed the stairs, he felt an immediate rise in temperature from the large windows on the floor above. He glanced back at the uniforms.

"You get much trouble out here?"

"Not really. Sometimes we get a DUI. The roads are narrow and twist about, if you've had a few drinks, it's easy to get caught out. Mostly it's noise complaints. Loud music, parties, barking dogs, like that."

Coombes nodded. Neighbors were terrible wherever you lived.

"The previous owner here had a pet tiger. It went wherever it pleased. No cage, no chain. I only know about it because a guy broke in to rob the place...and it ate him."

"Jesus Christ."

"We were chasing that thing around the yard with the guy's arm hanging out its mouth. It was my second week on the job. Craziest thing I ever saw."

They came out on the second floor, or maybe it was the first, since the previous floor was cut into the hillside. He looked around, didn't see anything obvious. He took a deep breath through his nose, filling his chest. The quickest way to find a corpse was with your nose, but he detected nothing but the hint of citrus and coffee.

They moved methodically through the building, starting from where they stepped out from the stairs.

He opened a door. A bedroom.

Unoccupied, tidy.

He moved on.

A place like this, he figured, it was going to have the best air conditioning money could buy. State of the art. Maybe it could clean the air of bad odors, as well as incoming pollution. It smelled better inside the house than it did outside. Normally, that wasn't so hard, but not if there was a body.

Another door, another bedroom.

Unoccupied, tidy.

The room was identical to the last. He wasn't the most imaginative man himself, but that seemed lazy. It was almost Spartan. No frills, just a simple bed frame, nightstand, lamp. These would be the guest rooms. If they were too nice, maybe people stayed too long. It could happen, he supposed, the rest of the house was amazing.

Coombes counted nine guest bedrooms, one master bedroom, a gym, a steam room, five bathrooms, a kitchen diner you could turn a Buick in, and a walk-in refrigerated storage room. It was a bust. They'd seen every room, every closet, and Schofield wasn't here.

Not dead, not alive.

No sign of a struggle, or of someone leaving quickly to catch an unexpected flight. The house was hollow, like a museum about to close up for the day. Something felt wrong, and he couldn't identify what it was. He turned to the two uniforms and shrugged his shoulders.

"I guess we're not going to need you guys after all."

"That's all right," the older one said. "A day without a body is a good day."

He didn't like being observed, it inhibited him.

"You mind if my partner and I stay a while longer, bounce ideas around?"

"Not at all. We'll just take off and get some lunch."

There was a large clock on the wall behind the man's head. 11:15. He remembered his time in uniform, you took breaks when you could. Nobody knew what was around the next corner.

When they were gone, he turned to Grace and saw she was sitting on a bar stool at the breakfast bar. She was rotating around and around like a schoolgirl.

"I don't think this guy is linked to our kidnapping."

Grace put her hand out and caught the edge of the bar, stopping her spin.

"Me neither. It doesn't fit."

It was four months and change since Maria López last heard from Schofield, but the drone video proved that he hadn't been missing all that time. All it meant was that he hadn't needed her services. There were any number of reasons for this, fewer trips for business, perhaps the breakdown in a relationship for another.

Yet the place was tidy like it was staged for sale. To his mind, that meant there'd been no relationship breakup because newly single men always returned to the feral creatures they were at heart.

He thought again about his wife and the lawyer. Is that what he was now? Newly single? Julie had cheated on him, but what right had he to get upset about it? He'd been having an affair himself, with Sato.

Whatever was going on here didn't smell right. The easiest explanation was that the two events were linked, even if that link was currently hidden.

"Maybe Schofield was in the wrong place at the wrong time and saw something he wasn't meant to see. An innocent bystander that became a loose end for somebody. It happens."

"You know, Johnny, you never asked how long this guy's been missing. It's fourteen days. This guy's been missing longer than Amy Tremaine. That timeline doesn't track for anything worth a damn."

Coombes sighed. She was right.

"Then why are we here?"

"You got me. According to Gantz, the request came from someone high up to find this Schofield character, whether it's part of this investigation or not. Seems like an odd choice to me to throw another case at us while we're looking for Walton's killer and Tremaine's kid."

Coombes walked to the window and stared out across L.A.

It was all there, spread out before him. Griffith Park on the extreme left, central Los Angeles and the towering downtown district, and Santa Monica on the right. It was nearly midday, yet the air quality was good and clear. Sharp. No heat shimmer, no smog. A reflection moved across the glass and he turned to face his partner as she moved through the room toward him.

"No sign of a struggle," she said.

He nodded.

"No sign of anything. Look at this place, it's immaculate. Straight out of a magazine. There's something about this place that's a bit off, don't you think?"

"What's off about it," she said. "Is that *we* don't live here, some bloody Nazi does. How much does a house like this cost? Millions. It's perfect. You know, it's too bad he's not lying back there covered in blowfly larvae, because it sounds like he deserved to be."

There was a darkness to Sato that he found seriously attractive. If her brain could somehow have been put into his wife's head, everything would've worked out between them, he was sure of it.

"What did Tremaine want?"

"To tell me that some psycho has been stalking him for years."

"Huh. I guess he forgot to mention that before."

"I guess so."

They walked through the house and down the stairs in silence. Whatever had happened to Schofield, it hadn't happened here. Most likely, he wouldn't be back.

On balance, he thought, Schofield was dead.

After sixteen years as an investigator, you got a feel for these things.

14

COOMBES WAS GLAD THAT he and Sato had travelled separately to Anton Schofield's home, as it gave him the whole drive back to the PAB to process the scene he'd witnessed beforehand between his wife and the lawyer. He'd seen so little of Julie recently that he was almost starting to forget what she looked like. Now, all he could think of was her on the bed with the gag in her mouth with the other man bucking away behind her. There was a good chance this was how he'd remember her for the rest of his life.

And I deserve nothing better, he thought.

What kind of hypocrite was he anyway?

At some point, he was going to have to tell Sato. It wasn't going to take much detection on her part to figure out that his marriage was over. He wondered how she'd greet that news. The fact that he'd been married had always limited their time together and added a *forbidden fruit* aspect. With that gone it was possible she'd tire of him very quickly.

He moved to the turn lane and pulled up behind a black GMC Yukon. A moment later, a faded blue Taurus pulled up to his bumper. Coombes frowned and glanced to the open lane to his left in time to see another black SUV slide into place next to him and stop.

A Chevrolet Suburban.

The Suburban's dark tinted window fizzed open and he saw the two FBI agents from the Walton crime scene that he'd been thinking of as Poured Concrete and Eyebrows because they'd never been introduced. He opened his own window and stared up, into the higher vehicle's cabin. Concrete's gray, lifeless face glared back.

"You were warned, Coombes. Pull that shit again and you'll see the inside of a federal prison. You feel me?"

"I don't even know what you're talking about."

"Stay on your side of the street. This is your last warning."

"Is this about me finding the tank in the kidnapping video?"

The glare seemed to increase.

"This is about you pulling Harlan Tremaine out of federal protective custody against the will of the US Attorney and the Department of Justice. But why don't you go ahead and tell us about the tank?"

The feds had heard nothing about it. Interesting.

"As soon as your boss starts sharing information with us, we'll start sharing it with you. Until then, adios. Now move your vehicles, some of us have work to do."

"You've got some nerve talking to us like that, Coombes."

"Just one of many fine traits, I can assure you."

Coombes gave him a humorless smile, then turned and faced front as he closed the window. Seconds later, horns began to honk around them as other drivers tried to pass the blockade. Poured Concrete had chosen a poor spot to box him in, both in terms of traffic density, and his close proximity to the PAB and all the backup Coombes would ever need.

He continued to feel the other man's fury through the glass. He'd said all he was going to say to the special agent. The Suburban pulled angrily away and a moment later, the Yukon followed suit.

He was back underway.

The feds had got the drop on him because he'd been distracted with thoughts of his wife, but it wouldn't happen again.

Next time, he'd be ready.

He got to the PAB without further incident and parked up.

Sato had beaten him back and had even picked up lunch for him along the way in the form of a foot-long sub filled with chicken, bacon, mayo, and lettuce. His stomach growled just looking at it. She winked at him and began to drink soda from a can with a straw.

He leaned in close. "I think I love you."

She laughed and some of her drink came out her nose and landed on the carpeting between her feet. This caused her to laugh some more, then get the hiccups.

"Now I *know* I do," he said at a normal volume, taking off his jacket.

He sat, unwrapped his huge sandwich and took a bite. His jaws mashed it up as he opened his soda. He was onto mouthful three before Sato got her hiccups under control.

"You can't say things like that to a girl, Coombes."

"Why's that?"

"Because she might believe you."

He wiped mayo from the corners of his mouth. His natural reaction was to tell her that she *should* believe it, but he'd learned long ago that smart women enjoy being teased, and that information related to the heart should be drip-fed.

"I had a run-in with our federal friends out on the street."

"What did *they* want?"

He took another mouthful and thought about how best to answer.

"It seems that John Coombes is an acquired taste."

She smiled and nodded like she agreed, then turned away from him to put the last of her sandwich in her mouth. She didn't like to be watched as she ate so he logged in to his computer and opened his email. One email subject caught his eye.

Member list for The Black Feather (eyes only).

He opened the email and went directly to the attachment, ignoring the body text from the detective that sent it. A long list of names appeared, almost a hundred in all. They were listed alphabetically by surname. His eyes went to the first name on the list: Ballard, Charles.

He'd struck out on James Anderson immediately.

Coombes continued to scan the list as he ate and soon came to understand why the email had been marked *eyes only*. He saw names he recognized. Judges, high ranking members of the LAPD, not to mention many from the world of entertainment and sport.

To his annoyance, Joachim Nelson wasn't on the list either. Seeing his name would have helped confirm his theory of an overlap between members of *The Black Feather* and *The Hard Limit*.

It made little sense to him that the elite represented by some of the names would choose to mix socially or sexually with someone like Nelson, but for all he knew that might be the appeal of the club.

No other names were jumping out at him so he forwarded it to Becker to check for links to Harlan or Amy Tremaine, or to Elizabeth Walton. There were a number of emails from Becker waiting for him, one of which he found interesting.

Becker had taken the abduction video to Rollins, their video expert, who had run it through analysis software that used the focal length of the lens, combined with the height of the camera from the ground and the likely distance to the subjects to calculate the height of their kidnapper. The analysis came back at 5' 10" - 6' 2".

Becker then got Rollins' software to estimate Amy Tremaine's height.

This came back as 5'8" - 5'11". Since they already knew Amy was 5' 10" and she was an identical distance from the point of capture, it could be assumed that the height of the kidnapper was closer to six feet.

It was a solid-gold lead from Becker. He wrote it in his notebook and then on a separate legal pad on his desk containing an overview of victims and suspects' details. He finished the last of his lunch then looked over at Sato and saw she was watching him closely.

"Everything okay, Johnny?"

She was on to him already.

"Freakin' fantastic. What are you working on?"

"Looking through Schofield's socials. He's on Facebook and Twitter. You should take a look. His profile picture *is* a profile picture, he's facing sideways like he's on a coin. I can't decide if that's evidence of a sense of humor, or not. I'm thinking not, based on his brow ridge and broken nose. Anyway, he's got six followers on Facebook and 856 on Twitter."

Coombes had seen this kind of disparity before. The larger number of followers represented fake friends, people who followed hoping to be followed back to boost their own numbers. The number of friends he knew that would be real, was six.

"I don't suppose any of his friends happen to be James Anderson?"

"No, although I do have something interesting. We think he's dead, right?"

Coombes perked up. "Why? Is he still posting?"

"Kind of. He's checking in. Restaurants, Starbucks, you name it."

"Has he posted anything since he was reported missing?"

"He wasn't posting that regularly in the first place. Let's see." Sato looked at her screen, checking both websites. "All right, no. Not a peep for nearly a month. Last thing he posted was a link to a YouTube video with machine guns and watermelons."

"So either he's dead and someone else is using his phone, or he's still alive and has forgotten the check-ins show up on his page."

"I don't think you'd forget that," she said. "We've seen before criminals co-opting platform features intended for one purpose to serve another. He's giving his location on purpose. I think he's meeting people at these places. Other criminals."

Sato was pleased with herself and it was a look that suited her. He'd never used the check-in feature himself and didn't much see the point of it.

"All right, what about these six friends of his?"

"Three of them went to the same school as him, the other three charmers are Russians."

"Russian-Americans, or the other kind?"

"The other kind."

"Uh-huh. We'll look into that later. For now, we need to get into James Anderson's life. Tremaine says Anderson runs a website about him that sells merch with pictures of his face on it. I want you to check it out, see what kind of a nutcase he is."

"I can tell you that without looking."

Coombes nodded. "I'll bet. I'm going to use Mark's computer to look up the databases. Just in case you-know-who is watching us."

He finished his soda and tossed it in the trash can under his desk.

15

COOMBES STARTED WHERE HE usually did, with a search of the NCIC criminal database. He got eighteen hits for different James Andersons that had each been charged with crimes and booked into the system. Without bothering to narrow the search result by age, height, or hair coloring, he flicked through the mugshots. None of them were the Anderson he was looking for.

Next, he tried the Department of Motor Vehicles.

The DMV was a huge resource in policing, providing verified photographic ID, age, height, weight, and street addresses for nearly every adult in the population. There was one hundred sixty-four *James Andersons* listed for the state of California, with twenty-eight of them located in L.A. County.

He scrolled through the digital copy of the licenses for the twenty-eight Angelenos. He found matches for the previously-identified Andersons from the criminal database, but saw nobody matching the man in the video.

The chance of Anderson not having a driver's license was zero. Given the amount of time he had been stalking Tremaine, it didn't seem likely that he was dealing with someone with an out-of-state license.

He sat back, his eyes moving over Becker's desk.

It was a mess of candy wrappers, empty coffee cups, and sticky notes. There were three pictures of Becker's wife at different ages, and she was smiling in all of them. Coombes had no photographs of Julie at his workstation, smiling or otherwise. He didn't even know if he had a printed-out photograph of her, everything was digital now.

Thinking of Julie and the divorce that would be to come made him wonder if James Anderson had had any other interactions with the legal system. Sometimes, it didn't matter how careful you were, some other fool could bring the trouble to you.

Coombes opened LexisNexis; a legal service used primarily by lawyers. It simplified the task of finding publicly-available court documents and made them searchable. He found his suspect in less than a minute. To his surprise, it was not as a defendant, but as a witness for the state. Unfortunately for the District Attorney, James Anderson could not be located to testify.

After giving his initial statement, Anderson had vanished into thin air. The prosecutor had been forced to get her investigator to read the witness statement into the official record, where Coombes was able to read it from the court transcript.

Anderson stated that on the evening of May 10th 2019, he had gone for a run along Venice Boulevard. As he came to the Angelus Rosedale Cemetery, he witnessed a dog being clipped by a passing motorcyclist.

Anderson carried the injured animal to a nearby veterinary clinic in Pico-Union.

When he arrived, he was presented with three men in ski masks armed with sawed-off shotguns in the process of robbing the place. Anderson took out all three using a fire extinguisher as a club, then waited with the terrified staff until patrol units arrived to secure the scene.

The dog, a German Spaniel, required only sedatives and rest and was later reunited with its owner.

There were two parts to this that told him this was his guy. First of all, was his easy use of violence to subdue the armed robbers. It spoke to him of a military-trained individual calm in the face of danger. Taking charge after it was over also inclined him to think of the man as an officer. It was what he would have done.

The other part he liked, was that the situation involved a dog and possibly linked to the kidnapping scheme identified by the Bureau. It was no stretch of the imagination to suppose that Anderson was in the process of abducting the dog when it got free and strayed onto the road and into the path of the motorcycle.

Becker appeared next to him, having returned from lunch.

"How you getting on?"

"I have a promising lead, but no photo ID or street address."

"Any idea how Tremaine filed a restraining order without an address?"

"That's easy. Anderson was standing outside Tremaine's residence at the time taking pictures. He was served right there on the street by the same twenty-three-year-old he'd been creeping on minutes earlier with his long lens. No address necessary."

"Damn."

Coombes stared off into space.

"What are you thinking, John?"

"This merchandise Anderson sells...it's got to be chickenfeed that brings in, right? On the other hand, we've got his kidnapping caper. First dogs, now people. That's making a *lot* of money. He's wanting five mill just for Amy. Why bother with the website?"

"I guess he's using it to wash some of the illegal money to give him an official means of support. Cash is great, but the real world operates on credit ratings, mortgages, and rent."

Coombes nodded and stood so that Becker could sit.

"You're probably right."

He returned to his desk and found Sato scrolling through a long grid of images. As he got closer, he saw that it was a shopping page and that all the images were of T-shirts. The format of all of them were the same; a photograph of the former governor with one of his famous quotes underneath. The quotes were either funny or inspiring.

"Bought anything?"

"Not yet. There's still a couple of months until your birthday."

"Anything interesting?"

"I asked myself who the hell would be buying this stuff and my answer, I thought, was nobody. Then I noticed something."

She selected one of the squares.

"What am I looking at, Grace?"

"Wait for it."

Just then a box slid up from the bottom of the screen.

Item bought by K. Reese of Stockton, California.

Ten or so seconds passed and another message was displayed. Another sale.

"Is this for real? People are really buying this shit?"

"Apparently. Interest in Tremaine has probably skyrocketed as a result of the kidnapping. If you look here," Sato's voice flickered as another sale was announced. "There's a counter that shows how many people are viewing this page. I checked one of the more obscure products by going on my cell phone at the same time. The count rose by one. It's real."

There were 63 other people browsing the page. Compared with the video of Amy in the tank of water it was nothing, but that didn't stop him being impressed.

"I've got a juicy lead on Anderson I want to check, you coming?"

"That's for sure."

Sato logged out her computer and they made their way across the detective bureau toward the elevator, pulling on their suit jackets at the same time. It felt good to be moving again.

"So what's the lead?"

"It seems that before Anderson was a bad guy, he was a good guy."

Sato smiled. "I love those."

As they drove into the parking lot for the animal hospital, he saw a surveillance camera aimed straight at their car. He saw three more cameras as he parked, on poles in glass domes that made it impossible to tell which way the lens was pointing. The lot was relatively small and he guessed that half the vehicles belonged to staff. He parked away from the entrance to leave room for any emergency arrivals and killed the engine.

"Did you ever have a pet, Johnny?"

"Yeah. I had a golden retriever before I joined the Army. How about you?"

"No. I wanted a dog, but I was never allowed one growing up. Later, when I had my own place, I was out all day. That's not fair to a dog."

"You're right about that."

They got out the Charger and walked toward the entrance.

He could feel his lunch sitting awkwardly in his stomach as if he hadn't chewed it at all and it was still a foot-long inside him. Maybe, he reflected, it was a heart attack. This could be the end coming and here he was mistaking it for indigestion.

The doors opened automatically. An empty waiting room. A receptionist looked up at the pair of them, eyebrows raised. She was a pretty brunette in her mid-twenties with long hair tied back behind her head in a ponytail. A name badge on the right collarbone of her pink scrubs said Ava.

He noticed a camera above her head looking straight at him, another over to the side toward a hallway leading to the rest of the facility, and as he turned back toward the door, two more covering the exit. The cameras were wall-to-wall and they looked expensive.

Coombes made a quick introduction, his face on a friendly setting.

"What can I do for you, Detectives?"

"It's about last year. May 10th."

Ava's face changed to one of pure horror before returning to normal.

"The worst day of my life," she said. "I thought they were going to kill me, those men. Actually, I thought they were going to do some other things first, *then* kill me."

Coombes nodded, his right palm raised a little to show that he took her meaning and she didn't have to traumatize herself any more by expanding on the thought.

"What can you tell us about the man that stopped them."

Her eyes lit up.

"James Anderson. I think about him every day. He saved me, he saved all of us. We wanted to thank him later but we had no address. Instead, we put up that."

Ava pointed behind him at a brass plate that was screwed to the wall.

For James Anderson
Not all heroes wear capes

He decided that the receptionist was better off not knowing about Anderson's fall from hero to villain. She was drawing strength from the idea of who he was, and it seemed to be offsetting some of the fear that the men with shotguns had brought into her life.

"He never gave you his number?"

"No, why would he?"

Because you're attractive?

Coombes smiled and tilted his head over a little. Maybe she was trying to get him to say the words. For sure, he'd never met a beautiful woman who didn't know it.

"I tried to find him online but it's a very common name and I got nowhere."

Coombes could believe it.

"When was it you looked? Recently, or back when it happened?"

"Both, actually. He didn't seem to have a social media account which I thought was weird, who doesn't have one of those? I checked again last week to see if that had changed."

Coombes made a note of this.

It meant that Anderson hadn't deleted himself prior to his big score with Amy Tremaine's kidnapping.

He pointed at the white rectangle in the ceiling.

"These cameras...they were added after the attack?"

"Yes. We also have a monitored alarm that summons an armed response."

"That must be reassuring," Sato said.

"I'd give it up in a heartbeat to have James sitting next to me."

"Was he married?"

The receptionist's face colored. "I don't know what you mean."

"Sure you do," Sato said. "I saw you check my partner's hand when we arrived. You were burned before, right? Now you do it without thinking. So, was he married?"

"He had no band on his finger, that's all I know."

Coombes cut back in.

"What kind of security system did you have before?"

"The kind that didn't work. The cameras were effectively dummies. There's no recording of those men, or of James Anderson, if that's what you're asking."

They were getting closer to Anderson, but the only chance of there still being any link between a year-old incident and the current case was if a relationship had formed between him and one of the people he saved. That person was not Ava and if it had been someone else here then her attitude toward him would be markedly different.

"I think we're done here."

"Wait a minute. What's all this about?"

"We can't comment on active investigations."

The fear returned to Ava's face.

"Those men aren't getting out of prison, are they?"

"No. Look, I wouldn't worry about them. The way I understand it, James took them out of commission. One can't lift his arms above his chest, another lost vision in one eye and needs a cane to walk, the last is stuck in a wheelchair drinking smoothies through a tube."

Ava went still as she thought about that.

After a beat, her chin popped out a little, defiant.

"It's their own fault, isn't it?"

"Yes, it is. If they hadn't killed someone here that day then I'm sure they would've somewhere else down the line, I have no doubt."

Ava liked that; the light was back in her eyes.

"Exactly!"

"Thank you for your time, ma'am."

"James has done it again, hasn't he? Saved someone. Why else would you be asking about him. Tell him he can come back here any time, we'd love to see him."

Coombes nodded like that was it, a forced smile on his face.

16

SINCE THEY WERE PASSING Elizabeth Walton's secret apartment on South Hill Street anyway, it made sense to take a look at it. The building was a modern high-rise made out of glass and steel and was new enough that Coombes could remember it being constructed. As was often the case, he could not remember what building had stood there before.

A roller shutter blocked the entrance and exit to the parking structure. The shutter would be fully automated, triggered by something in the owner's car.

The black box attached to Walton's sun visor.

Coombes fizzed down the window of his Charger and looked at a metal box that was mounted to a post. He located a button and held it in for a ten-count.

Longer than a mail man, he figured, to get some attention. An angry voice thundered out a speaker.

"What the hell do you want?"

"LAPD. Open the barrier."

The voice didn't come back, but the shutter began to roll up and he drove inside. He took off his sunglasses and tossed them onto the dashboard.

"You know, Johnny, we need to talk about your communication skills."

"I deal with the world the way I find it."

"I noticed that."

His eyes watched the numbers over the parking spots as they scrolled past. It appeared that each apartment was allocated two spaces, each wide enough to park a tank. Considering the SUVs some of the owners drove, this was probably a basic requirement. He saw Walton's number and parked in one of her spaces.

Now that they had stopped moving, frustration began to build like a static charge. There would be nothing useful in the apartment, but they had nothing else. About the best he could hope for was that something would trigger a new thought process and take him in a new, more fruitful, direction.

A concrete stairwell led from the parking garage into a beautifully-appointed lobby area. There was a ten-foot-long desk marked CONCIERGE in polished silver letters. A young man with a pinched, rat-like face, sat behind the desk giving him the evil eye.

Clearly the man he'd spoken with moments before via the box.

As they approached the desk, a second man in his late-fifties appeared from a doorway. He had bloodshot eyes and his hair was swept back into a ponytail behind his head like a coffee store barista.

"I suppose you're here about Elizabeth Walton."

He nodded.

"Detectives Coombes and Sato."

"Adam Finley."

"You're the building manager here?"

"That's right."

"We need to see her apartment, Mr. Finley."

"I thought that was it. Come on, I already have the spare keys."

Coombes had Walton's keys in his pocket but said nothing. They got onto the elevator and Finley selected the top floor on the panel. The doors closed.

"I couldn't believe it when I heard, I thought it must be a mistake."

He heard that a lot in Homicide.

"Did you know her well, Mr. Finley?"

"Just to say hello to. She was nice, why would anyone want to hurt her?"

He glanced at the other man, assessing him.

There was a quiver in his voice. Finley was upset about Walton, he realized, his red eyes were from crying. There were people Coombes saw for hours every day that he wouldn't shed a tear over, but that was just him. The elevator stopped and they followed Finley along the corridor.

Elizabeth Walton's unit was right at the end, away from the others. He figured this was the best setup, nobody walking past to get to their apartment, nobody even close to her door unless they had reason to be there. It's what he would choose, given the choice.

They pulled on nitrile gloves as the manager unlocked the door and pushed it open. Two locks, no alarm. Finley glanced at their gloved hands, his eyes wide.

"You don't think it happened here, do you?"

Sato answered, her voice soft.

"It's just procedure, Mr. Finley. Prevents any risk of contamination. It's also why you'll have to wait out here. We'll have some questions for you when we come back out."

The man's chest puffed up like he was about to complain, but then he just nodded his head. Sato had a soft touch, Coombes thought, that he doubtless lacked.

A short entrance hallway opened out into a shared space, with living, dining and kitchen areas. There was a glass wall to the north and west, filling the room with light. Through the window to the north was a narrow balcony.

An empty cereal bowl sat on the kitchen island with a spoon sticking out. Eaten at speed and abandoned to deal with later. Over by the sofa, sat a pair of high heels, one sitting on its side. A candle that looked artificial sat on a coffee table next to a glasses case and a hardcover crime novel.

Signs of a life lived, interrupted.

Coombes had visited hundreds of locations during his career and could always sense when he was somewhere that something bad had happened. He got nothing like that here.

It was calm, peaceful.

A murder victim had lived here, but she hadn't died here. The last breath she'd taken in the apartment had been happy, oblivious to any coming danger.

Sato gazed around, a dreamy look on her face.

He walked around the island unit into the living area. A flat-screen television was mounted on the wall to the south next to a partly open door. He pushed the door wider and stuck his head inside. A small bedroom, used only to store clothes and shoes.

Coombes stepped back into the living area.

Unlike in his own home, seating was arranged at right angles to the television which showed nothing but glare from the two windows on either side.

A telescope was set up on a tripod by the north window. It was aimed downward, into the city.

He put his eye to the eyepiece and an apartment two blocks over filled his vision. It appeared to be unoccupied and contained nothing of interest, but at night that might change. He saw a bedroom, a shower stall, and part of a living room. As with the apartment he stood in, there were no drapes, no privacy glass.

He'd misjudged Walton based on the formal business clothing she wore while working for Tremaine. The former governor probably liked the image she'd presented to him, but this telescope was who she really was.

Curious, maybe a little kinky.

The kitchen was small but functional.

Counters were clean and empty, except for a 6-bottle wine rack. One bottle missing. He looked at the drainer and the sink. Empty. It had, he supposed, been a number of days since she'd last been here. The hob looked new and unused.

He opened a cupboard next to the oven expecting to see pots and pans and instead found ten bottles of champagne. His nose wrinkled, remembering the scene at his own home, his wife with her lawyer friend.

The next cupboard he searched was full to overflowing with salted snacks. Chips, nuts, pretzels, puffed corn. Walton was a woman after his own heart. He found four more bottles of champagne in the refrigerator, along with two cases of beer, and some dips.

They were wasting their time; there was nothing here to move the investigation on. Grace stood watching him. It looked like she'd reached the same conclusion.

He pointed to the door of the freezer.

"Fifty bucks says the only thing in the freezer is ice cubes and vodka."

"I'll take that action," she said.

He opened the door. Three clear plastic drawers lay inside, all heavily frosted from lack of use. The top drawer was the coldest and looked the most used. He pulled it out and smiled.

"One bottle of Grey Goose, one tray of ice cubes."

"Shit."

The next drawer was empty and slid awkwardly on its runners. It looked like an inch of snow had fallen inside. A small smile curled on his lip, but he said nothing. He tried the last drawer and his smile vanished.

Three cartons of ice-cream.

"You almost had me there, Johnny."

He took out his wallet and pulled out a fifty.

"Keep it," she said. "Take me for dinner when we close this."

"I figure I'd be doing that anyway."

"You should be careful what you say next, Coombes."

There was a fire in her eyes that he'd seen before, although never during work hours. He nodded and put his money away. The fire was what he loved about her most of all.

"Tell me what you see," he said.

"She didn't cook here, that much is obvious. There's a lot of alcohol, snacks, and ice-cream. I don't know about you, Johnny, but I've never once drunk champagne on my own. I figure she used this place solely to entertain. It's her love nest."

A twitch started on his face, and he glanced away.

"What?"

"Nothing. Anything else?"

"Well, I hadn't figured Elizabeth Walton for a beer drinker."

"Me neither," Coombes said.

"So she kept her work and personal lives separate. She was dating someone."

"Looks like it," he said. "Let's check the master bedroom."

Bedrooms always revealed the most about a person. A public space like a living room or a kitchen the guard was always up. Anyone could walk in there. Family, friends, even a plumber. But the only people that got to visit the bedroom were people you wanted there, people that were going to see everything about you.

Elizabeth Walton had been 61 years old, but the first thing he saw in her bedroom was a teddy bear. Light brown, with short furry hair and a pink heart on each paw. The bear sat on a console desk under another television. The bear faced the bed, yet its small black eyes seemed to look right at him as he stood in the doorway.

Fairy lights had been draped over the top of the bed's headboard, leftovers perhaps, from a Christmas gone by.

Like the main space, the north side of the master bedroom was a glass wall. To his surprise, it led out onto a patio area with loungers. Unlike the balcony next to the living room, this outdoor space was at least as large as the bedroom it joined.

He could see City Hall pushing into the skyline.

Coombes saw City Hall about ten times a day and had never once thought of people looking at it from their bedroom window. He shook his head to clear the mental jam this caused him and tried to focus on the case.

Opposite the window, was a walk-in closet.

On quick inspection, it appeared that two women were living in the apartment. A woman that wore business clothing, and one that wore sexy, revealing clothes. He saw dresses that would've been risqué on a twenty-five-year-old. Sato nodded her head appreciatively.

Beyond the closet was the ensuite.

The layout meant anyone standing outside the front door would hear the shower running through the wall.

Coombes frowned as he walked back through the closet into the bedroom.

Something didn't fit right, but he couldn't place it.

Like a five-star hotel, everything was clean and tidy, with nothing left lying out, except for the teddy bear. It was a different type of living, minimalist. The apartment had almost no storage space or surface areas for anything you didn't need.

He pulled open the nightstand drawer and whistled.

Handcuffs, leather straps, a vibrator, and something that looked like a table tennis bat, but with spikes all over it. One thing was for sure, there was a side to Walton that she couldn't explore while at her residence within the former governor's home.

"I told you, Johnny," Sato said, suddenly next to him. "This is her love nest. She used it to get laid and whatever else using that shit."

She poked the spiked bat with a gloved finger like it was about to explode.

The spikes would leave a mark, he thought, but there'd been nothing like that on Walton's body. Which meant she wielded it, she wasn't the recipient. He wondered what someone got from being struck by the paddle, what need did that fulfill?

They returned to the living room and looked silently out the floor-to-ceiling windows at downtown Los Angeles spread out below. The view was amazing and it would be better still at night. The apartment would cost a fortune, he reflected, far more than Elizabeth Walton earned working for Tremaine. She had to have some other source of income.

It wasn't hard to work out what that was.

Barnes told him the dog kidnappers always knew who to hit, that they seemed to have inside information. Walton had that information. Her work supporting Tremaine's foundation gave her access to lists of donors, past and present. Names, addresses, size of donation. Coombes didn't like it, but everything was beginning to fit together.

Perhaps even the reason she was killed.

Taking her employer's daughter crossed a line and he couldn't see her willingly being a part of that. He recalled the photograph of Elizabeth Walton and Amy Tremaine that sat on her office desk. Shoulder to shoulder, a big smile on their faces. There was a bond in that picture that looked a lot like family.

No matter how bad things got for her, Coombes believed Walton would've come forward to help Amy. Identified her conspirators.

He noticed a Wi-Fi router underneath the TV with two steady green lights.

"No laptop or tablet," he said, almost to himself.

"I don't think she came here to work, Johnny."

He turned to look at Sato.

"No doubt, but I was thinking back to Schofield's place. Assuming he had a computer, and I do, then either he took it with him as he fled, or it was taken by whoever killed him."

"You think he's involved in any of this?"

Coombes thought for a moment. "No."

"A coincidental overlap then?"

He left that alone. Coincidence stuck in his throat.

"Let's see what ponytail has to say."

Adam Finley was still in the corridor outside the apartment where they'd left him. His head down, fingers typing into his cell phone. It looked like he had Facebook open, updating a world that didn't care about his treatment at the hands of the LAPD.

Finley's face flushed as he saw them and he put his cell quickly away. Coombes cut right to it.

"Does this building have security cameras?"

"Electric locks on public doors; deadbolt and mortice on private doors. Nobody likes being watched."

Coombes nodded. It was what he expected; he'd seen no cameras and he'd been looking for them. He took out his notebook and turned to a new page.

As he'd noticed many times before, the appearance of his notebook changed the dynamic of a conversation. Finley's eyes flickered nervously back and forth between his eyes and the pen in Coombes' gloved hand.

"How often did you see Elizabeth Walton?"

"Once or twice a week."

"And when would that be?"

"Weekends. Friday afternoon to Sunday night."

"You ever see a man with her?"

"There was *always* a man with her. Sometimes they didn't last a whole weekend. She'd be here on Friday with one, and I'd see her on Sunday with another lover."

"Friends, maybe? Business associates?"

"I know what I saw."

Finley was leaving something out. He was judging her about her dating frequency for sure, but there was something else. A negative energy that felt like fury. Coombes wondered if he was racist and thought for a second as he considered the best approach.

"Did she have a particular *type* of man that you noticed?"

"That's for sure. She liked them young."

Coombes felt a tingle move up his spine.

"How recently did you see her with a date?"

"Saturday."

"Early forties, short black hair, about six feet?"

Finley's eyebrows knitted together.

"That sounds about right."

Coombes took out his cell phone and pulled up a screen grab from the drone footage of his suspect walking behind Amy Tremaine in his smart clothes. The reconnaissance run. He sized the picture to clip off the victim and turned the phone toward Finley.

"This him?"

"Yes...I think so."

"Which? Yes, it's him, or you think it's him?"

"It looks like him, I can't swear to it. Look, I didn't care much for the way she lived her life, but Lizzie was nice to me. She would ask me how I was, if I was having a good day. Nobody else in here treats me like that. When she walked past, it was *her* I looked at, not some guy she was with. It hardly seemed worthwhile looking at someone I knew wouldn't be around for long."

Coombes understood.

"You wished the two of you had a relationship."

"It took me a long time to realize that she was nice to everyone. I thought she *liked* me; I thought I was *special*. Seeing her bring those men here was hard, a stab in the back. The age of those men, I knew she didn't see me at all. Not like that."

"But you kept putting yourself in places where you would cross paths?"

Finley nodded, his gaze down at his feet.

"She was beautiful. I would've done anything to be with her."

"All right," Coombes said. "Back to the man in the picture. Did you notice anything about him? Accent, tattoos, anything?"

"I never heard him speak. None of those guys spoke much."

"Just take a minute," Sato said. "Where were you when you saw them?"

"The parking garage. One of the tubes needed to be replaced."

"How close were you when you saw them?"

"Fifteen feet? I saw her Lexus drive in so I came down the ladder so I could see her properly. Her smile was always the highlight of my day."

Grace nodded, her face full of compassion.

"Picture him in your mind, try not to think about her. They walk up, you say a couple of words, then they walk over to the stairwell exit, yes?"

Finley's eyes lit up and he turned to Coombes.

"There was one thing. He walked like you do."

"Really. And how's that?"

"Like you're in charge, like you own the place."

Sato smiled as if Finley had told a joke, but Coombes wasn't smiling. Anderson was ex-military; he had no doubts left. An officer, like he'd been.

Amy's kidnapper had been here four days ago, right where they were standing.

Adam Finley's face changed as he thought about Walton's date. About her killer. Coombes took a business card out and began to write on it.

"This man," Finley said, "you think he murdered her, don't you?"

"He's a person of interest in a related investigation. If you see him again, I want you to call me, day or night. Here's my card, I've written my cell number on it."

Coombes had a new thought and swore.

"Wait here, Finley. Sato, you're with me."

He walked back into the apartment, putting his notebook away as he went. The kitchen again. He hadn't been thinking clearly the first time. Hadn't known what to look for. The clue was right there with the empty surfaces, the empty sink and drainer.

He found the dishwasher and opened the door. A stale smell rose to meet him; it hadn't been turned on. Not even a third full, not worth running it. He pulled out the top tray and took several photographs with his cell phone.

"What you got, Johnny?"

"The Holy Grail," he said.

There were four wine glasses inside the dishwasher. Two regular-shaped glasses, and two champagne flutes. The larger glasses had a red wine stain at the bottom. He lifted one out and held it by the stem up to the light. There was a soft pink bruise at the rim. Lipstick. He returned it to the dishwasher and took the other glass. No bruise.

The surface was covered with fingerprints.

Best fingerprints he'd ever seen.

He turned to Sato and saw she had an evidence bag ready. Grace held the top open as he lowered the glass carefully inside, then she sealed the bag shut. He decided to leave the killer's champagne flute where it was for now. The best chance at complete prints was on the wider glass, but if there was a problem with the legality of the first glass, the flute might give them a second chance at the same information.

Sato's cheeks were flushed as she looked up at him.

"Nice work, Johnny."

17

THE THREE OF THEM were silent on the elevator going down. Coombes gazed up at the ceiling and resisted the urge to smile. The kidnapper's fingerprints. He could hardly believe their luck. He'd expected nothing coming here, but this wasn't nothing. The doors opened in the lobby and they got out.

Adam Finley nodded his head wordlessly, then turned away.

Learning that he'd likely seen the killer hadn't improved Finley's day one iota. Coombes and Sato walked across the polished marble and through the door to the stairs down to the parking garage. It was poorly lit and there were no cameras.

This was where they should've found Walton's body.

The stairs were narrow. Falling into step behind his victim would not have aroused suspicion. From behind, it would've been easy for Anderson to snap her neck by rotating her head sharply to the side, or by slitting her throat and allowing her to bleed out on the stairs in front of her.

As he reached to open the fire door, Sato touched his arm to stop him. When he turned to her she kissed him on the mouth. Coombes felt himself blush in the half-dark. Her eyes were alive with mischief and something else.

"What was that for?"

She shrugged, casually. "Just checking something."

"Oh yeah? Like what?"

"To see if it's still there."

"It'll be there until I'm dead, Grace."

"You always know what to say to me, Johnny."

Coombes smiled and opened the door. He couldn't afford to let himself get distracted by Sato. Amy Tremaine was still out there somewhere, needing him. He decided to believe she was still alive, there was no upside to thinking she was dead.

They got back to the Charger and he drove around to the exit. This time the roller door opened on its own and he nosed out into the bright February sunshine. After almost a minute, a space appeared in the inside lane and they were out onto South Hill Street.

He thought about the spiked paddle in Elizabeth Walton's nightstand. She liked to be in control in the bedroom, perhaps she'd been in charge of the whole operation. He dialed a number he'd not long added to his cell phone and put it on speaker so that Sato could hear.

"Barnes. Who's this?"

"You don't write, you don't call…"

"Now's not a good time, Detective Coombes."

"Then I'll be quick. Did the dog kidnappings start about a year and a half ago?"

"Near enough, why?"

The same length of time Walton had lived in the apartment.

"Just chasing down a lead on *my side of the street*."

"That bullshit ambush was not my call. You were right before, we need to work together. I don't think Henderson cares how we get to the end now, as long as we get a good result. What do you think? Shall I sound him out, see what he says?"

"I'll have to get back to you on that."

"All right. Hey, how did you get my number anyway?"

"A magician never reveals his secrets."

Coombes disconnected.

He had what he needed, everything else was noise.

"Their investigation is stalled," Sato said.

"No kidding."

Above, a traffic light changed on them and their slow crawl came to a halt.

It was beginning to look like Walton set up the kidnapping scheme using men she picked up on dates to fund a lavish lifestyle and a view over Los Angeles that was second-to-none. There were a couple of problems with this theory that needed to be sorted out.

To begin with, Elizabeth Walton's murder in the former governor's house.

Her killer appeared to have bypassed a $28,000 alarm system and removed all trace of himself from security cameras. This seemed like a lot of extra work if he was a guest at her apartment just days beforehand with plenty of opportunity to kill her there.

The most logical explanation, was that the killer changed his timescale after his chance meeting with Adam Finley in the parking garage. Being the last person seen with a victim was a fast track to a prison cell.

By killing her later, Finley's role changed from being an eyewitness to a dark alibi. When questioned, the killer would admit to visiting Walton's apartment but would point to the fact that she'd been alive after he left.

Having an opportunity to kill her *and not taking it* was his alibi.

It was hardly airtight, but the defense would doubtless be able get Finley to repeat his claims about Walton's love life and the frequency of male guests at her apartment. Each one, a possible killer. The sexual appetites of those close to the top of society was pure catnip for juries and was a lot more interesting than the science of fingerprints.

He noticed Grace was smiling, the evidence bag held carefully in her hands.

"You know if he admits being in her apartment, that glass proves nothing."

"I don't believe that and neither do you. This gets us to the next screen."

"The next screen?"

"Don't be a fossil, Coombes. Like a computer game."

He nodded. *A fossil*. There was plenty there to dig into, but instead he chose to see her point.

The fingerprint evidence would confirm the identity of their killer one way or another and be enough for a warrant to search his address. If Amy Tremaine was locked in his basement, it wouldn't matter if he had left Walton alive in her apartment.

His train of thought returned to its previous track. Taking Amy by necessity meant killing Elizabeth Walton, which in turn meant the end of the lucrative dog kidnapping business.

This, he understood.

Even in L.A., the pool of potential targets was going to become exhausted pretty quickly.

If the dog caper had come to its natural end, then some form of diversification was going to be necessary. A crew like the one he'd witnessed on the drone camera would always migrate from easy low-value targets, to difficult high-value ones.

Unless they were stopped, Amy Tremaine would not be the last victim. His cell phone rang.

"Coombes."

"John, it's Mark. Are you on your way in?"

"No. We're fairly certain we've got the son of a bitch's fingerprints on a wine glass so we're running it directly to the lab ourselves."

"That's good news, brother. Well done."

"Yeah. You got something?"

"I've got Anderson's address if you're interested."

Coombes smiled so hard he felt his cheeks become tight.

"Today's getting better and better. How did you manage that?"

"I got it through his website."

Coombes felt himself deflate.

No kidnapper worth their salt was going to put their name on a website where it could be found by law enforcement. It went against logic, never mind his working theory as to why he could find no photographs of Anderson online. That he was smart and methodical.

"He has his postal address on his website?"

"Not exactly. I got it from his domain name. Actually, truth be told, Gonzalez did. She was always the technically-minded one. You remember my old partner, right?"

"Sure."

"Well, when Anderson registered his website domain, he didn't check a privacy option so all his contact details are right there. It also listed a company which I assume he owns, although I've not done anything with that yet."

Traffic was moving well and he'd coasted through a couple of yellow lights. They were already on Los Angeles Street, approaching 3rd.

"They just list all that online? You don't need a warrant?"

"Oh yeah. It's called a *whois lookup*. The internet used to be a free and open system remember, now people want their privacy on account of all the crazies."

"No kidding," Coombes said. "What's the name of his company?"

"Sequoia & Main. Weird name if you ask me."

Coombes smirked.

"Do you know what a Sequoia is?"

"Yeah, it's a huge tree. Oh. Tremaine, I hadn't got that."

"Send me the address and we'll head there next."

"You got it, John."

18

JAMES ANDERSON LIVED IN a run-down apartment building off Beverly Boulevard between a 24-hour launderette and a pawn shop. The structure had the charm of a state penitentiary but what Coombes found most interesting was that this squalid box lay less than a mile from Amy Tremaine's apartment overlooking MacArthur Park.

Coombes parked on the opposite side of the street where they could see the entrance and killed the engine.

He opened the door and waited for Sato to walk around the front of the Dodge so that they could cross over together. It was just after 3 p.m. and traffic on the street was in a lull period.

They got across quickly and were inside Anderson's apartment building less than thirty seconds later. The apartment was on the third floor, and although it was pretty much a toss-up time-wise, they took the elevator as it was the most likely way for a resident to travel. He didn't want to miss Anderson by taking the stairs.

The hallway on three was poorly lit and dirty.

It felt like something bad had happened there, or was about to. Coombes felt a steady increase in his heart rate as they moved towards Anderson's apartment. There were dark marks on the wall and floor that looked a lot like cast-off blood. He silently pointed to them with his left hand and Sato nodded grim-faced.

He drew his Glock as he closed the last few feet.

What they were doing here was the exact opposite of what he'd told Tremaine was the best course of action about trailing a suspect back to where Amy was secured. Instinct told him they were against the clock and that she didn't have much time left.

They were at Anderson's door now.

Sato moved past, so that she was on the far side of the door, the hinge side. When the door opened, she'd be hidden for longest.

Coombes put his head against the surface of the wood and covered his outer ear. Silence. No TV, no radio, no music. Not even an air conditioner.

He gave the door a cop knock with the base of his fist, pounding hard enough to flex the wood.

"LAPD! Open the door!"

His heartbeat was around one forty and the hairs on his arms were standing on end. In his head, Coombes imagined kicking the door down and shooting the creep until he dropped.

He was ready for it, he had to be.

Forward-thinking reduced reaction time. Decisions had already been made, all that was left was aiming. He pounded on the door harder than ever and shouted loud enough to fill the building.

"Last chance, Anderson! Open the door!"

He placed his head against the door again, hoping Anderson didn't have a shotgun ready on the other side. No muffled calls for help, no distressed thumps, no tinkle of breaking glass. Nothing. After the noise he'd made, the silence came back louder than ever.

He looked at Sato. "What do you think?"

"I don't think he's in."

He let a couple of seconds drift by. "Me neither."

Coombes re-holstered his weapon and Sato did the same. His body was jacked up on adrenalin and it felt good. His vision was turned up to 11, everything was enhanced. The grain of the wood on Anderson's door, the specks of dust hanging in the gloomy air of the hallway, the slight gap between Sato's lips.

"Let's check if his vehicle is outside."

"Something wrong with my mouth, Johnny?"

"Not a damn thing."

Grace smiled as they walked back down the hallway. The elevator hadn't moved and the doors opened when he pressed the button. They got on and rode it to the first floor in silence.

There was plenty of street parking, which was just as well as the apartment building had no dedicated lot. According to Becker's latest information, Anderson owned a pale blue VW Beetle that had entered the world six years before Coombes had been born.

The distinctive profile of the old bug made it an easy vehicle to spot even with the number of bulky SUVs that were now in use. Anderson's Beetle wasn't there. He should've checked when they arrived.

Coombes looked at his watch. 3:20 p.m.

If Anderson had gone out for lunch, he should be back by now. He was self-employed so they had no other location to check. A possibility, was that he was wherever he had Amy Tremaine secured. It stood to reason that he wasn't holding her in his apartment and walking her up and down public hallways and elevators. He'd have her in a disused warehouse, or a storm drain. Somewhere close enough to be handy, but not personally linked to him if she was discovered.

"What do you think, Johnny? Come back later, or sit and wait?"

"Let's wait for a bit."

They got back into the Dodge and an awkward silence fell on them.

Stakeouts were boring and it always seemed to him like time moved slower on a stakeout when he had company. On his own he could let his mind drift but the presence of another person meant he had to split his attention between them and whatever he was watching.

He considered telling her about catching his wife with the lawyer, then wondered why he hadn't told her already. It wasn't a conversation he knew how to start.

Coombes checked his watch again. 3:32.

They couldn't sit and wait all day like a private investigator, yet he could think of no shortcut. There was insufficient probable cause to enter Anderson's apartment, or ping his cell phone location. That's where the wineglass fingerprints would come in.

Going away and coming back later stood no more chance of finding Anderson since he could return and leave again within the unobserved window. They had, in any case, no other leads. Anything they needed to run down at the PAB they could get Becker to do for them remotely.

Waiting for anything could be a trap. You became reluctant to give up on something on account of all the time you had already invested in it. If you gave up, that time was all wasted. On the other hand, the amount of time you'd spent there surely took you closer to your goal. Whatever it was Anderson was doing, he had to be closer to being finished.

Coombes again imagined Anderson checking up on Amy Tremaine. Perhaps taking her some lunch and some bottled water. There were worse things he could be doing to Amy; she was a beautiful woman. Coombes blocked those thoughts out.

He turned to Sato and saw she was looking at him with a foxy expression.

"You want to make out to help pass the time?"

She smiled sweetly, like butter wouldn't melt.

"Grace, you're a class act."

"I'll take that as a maybe."

He nodded and turned to face the street again. One thing was for sure, Sato was a lot easier to resist when he wasn't looking at her.

It was possible that Anderson no longer lived here and that there was nothing at the end of the wait, no matter how long it was. A change of address might be a smart move before kidnapping Tremaine's daughter.

Coombes decided they'd wait until 4. No later. An absolute deadline. If Anderson wasn't back by then, he'd try something else. There was a contact form on his website, perhaps they could lure him out with the promise of an interview with Harlan Tremaine.

The street was getting busier now and more of the parking spots were filling up. The nearest space to the apartment was now a block away.

At 4:05 they were still there and, two minutes later, the pale blue Beetle drove past. It sounded like a Zeppelin and it was trailing a cloud of smoke. Anderson drove slowly down the line of parked cars. A gray Toyota pulled out and Anderson was able to get a space only thirty feet from the apartment entrance. Sato reached for the door release.

"Wait! Not yet."

Anderson came around to the side of his car and opened the passenger door. He pulled out a backpack which he put over both shoulders, then picked up three bags of groceries and closed the door with his ass. He locked it awkwardly with a key, then started along the sidewalk with his hands full of purchases. Anderson's head was darting around nervously.

"What are we waiting for, Johnny?"

"For him to be separated from his vehicle. I don't want this to become a car chase."

Anderson was almost at the front entrance to his apartment building now.

"Let's do this," Coombes said.

They opened the doors of the Dodge at the same time. Diagonally across the street, Anderson caught the movement and his head snapped around, locking on to them. There was a crash and Anderson turned and ran back down the sidewalk.

"Shit. He's rabbiting."

Traffic moved between them, preventing him from crossing. Coombes pulled his gun out and two cars came to an abrupt halt, allowing them to cross. They ran across the road, between parked vehicles to where Anderson's groceries lay spread out on the sidewalk.

Anderson was almost back to the Beetle.

Coombes sprinted after him, adrenalin flooding back into his system. With his long legs, he quickly left Sato behind, chewing up the distance to Anderson.

The other man had his car keys out and was trying to get them into the lock. No central unlocking on the old bug. Anderson glanced at him and then at the slow line of cars coming down the street.

If he got in the car, he'd be trapped there.

Anderson ran on down the sidewalk.

He had an odd faltering run. He bobbed up, and to the side, up and to the side. Coombes quickly closed on him. 30 feet. 20. He could almost smell him moving in front of him. The backpack had a handle on top, between Anderson's shoulder blades.

Coombes focused on the handle. That was the best way to grab Anderson, no doubt at all.

A large man appeared out of a doorway directly between them and Coombes was unable to avoid hitting him, falling onto the concrete. His gun spun out his hand against a car tire. The large man remained standing, his eyes fixed on the Glock.

"Sorry," Coombes said to the other man.

He picked up his gun and took off again.

Anderson had opened up a huge lead and had reached the end of the block. He took the cross street toward 6th Street. He focused on the spot where Anderson had turned out of sight and lost himself to the pursuit.

Ignoring the traffic to the right, analyzing the sidewalk for future obstacles, the regular thump of his shoes on the concrete.

By the time he got to the cross street, he'd halved the distance between them. Anderson kept glancing back, that was his mistake. It didn't matter what he did, Coombes knew the result would be the same.

He was a faster runner, with longer legs. A head start had only hidden what should have been obvious to Anderson from the very beginning.

They were two parked cars apart now.

Anderson's left leg was hurting, it had to be the way he was running.

They were picking up speed as Grand View dipped down onto 6th Street. MacArthur Park sat directly across from them. Traffic was well-spaced giving them clear sight of the sidewalk on the far side.

An invitation Anderson was intent on accepting.

Coombes grabbed the handle of Anderson's backpack just as he stepped out on the road and yanked him backward. A bus steamed past in the space where Anderson would've been, sucking the air away from both of them. He got Anderson on the ground and roughly cuffed him behind his back, his face pressed into the sidewalk.

James Anderson was panting, his face sweating.

"I know what this is, but you've got the wrong guy."

"You sure got a funny way of showing that, Anderson."

Coombes looked up and saw Sato running toward them. Her cheeks were flushed, her hips were twisting from side to side, and her suit jacket was fanned open to show her tight-fitting white shirt and her gun holster.

It was the hands-down best thing he'd seen all week.

He grabbed the other man by the left arm and pulled him to his feet. Anderson's teeth were all going in different directions, like tombstones in an old graveyard.

Close up, he did not look like the man in the security video. Probably, he didn't look like him from any distance, but he'd been too busy trying to catch him to notice. He glanced at Anderson's wrist and saw an old metal Casio.

No field watch, no NATO strap.

"I didn't kidnap that woman. That's why you're here, right? Because of Amy?"

"That's right. If it wasn't you then why did you run?"

"Because you're cops, man!"

It wasn't the stupidest thing he'd ever heard. In fact, he'd heard it before.

"We need to talk, Anderson. If I uncuff you, are you going to run away again?"

"I won't, I promise."

"I'm not running after you again. I'm wearing my best suit. I'm just going to shoot you next time. Okay?"

"All right!"

Coombes unlocked the cuffs and grabbed the handle on the top of the man's backpack with his left hand in case he took off again.

He didn't, he was through running.

"Let's go back to your apartment and have a conversation like regular people."

19

James Anderson's apartment smelled like the inside of a sneaker after a long run. Hygiene didn't appear to be a top priority and it was a solid bet that Sato was the first woman in the apartment since he'd moved in. Coombes resisted an offer to sit on a dirty chair opposite a laptop where Anderson presumably alternated his time between stalking Tremaine and watching pornography with his pants at his ankles.

Anderson was as far from being a buttoned-down officer as it was possible to get, and the only real reason he had remained a person of interest for so long was his personal paranoia and suspicious behavior. A single social media portrait photograph would have been enough, particularly if his teeth were visible.

This Anderson, he realized, *had* been on the DMV database.

"I knew you'd come for me," Anderson was saying, staring at his hands. "The outsider always gets blamed. Like Lee Oswald."

A large gray bird sat in a cage in the corner of the room and he went over to take a look. Coombes didn't like birds being kept as pets. The practice of keeping something that could fly in a small prison was plainly wrong, even a child could see that. The bottom of the cage was full of excrement and the bird looked embarrassed about it.

He turned back to Anderson.

"You remember what you were doing May 10th of last year?"

"How am I supposed to remember that? I don't remember last week."

Coombes let it go. It was obvious that the man in front of him was not the same person who had taken out three armed men with a fire extinguisher. He saw it now, that person had given a fake name and melted away into the L.A. landscape.

It didn't matter. The man he wanted was on the other end of a fingerprint on the wine glass he'd just dropped off at the lab.

This guy, was a clown.

"Explain to me your interest in Tremaine."

The other man came alive at the mention of his hero.

"He speaks to me. Everything he does or says, I relate to or agree with. I feel like I'm not alone anymore, that here's someone out there just like me. If he can be successful, can become the Governor of California, then I could too. You see?"

"Not really."

"I know how people look at me. How *you* look at me. Like I'm something they need to scrape off their shoe. I go outside and I feel two inches tall. *Look at that loser*, that's what people think. It's depressing. Then Harlan has a new podcast or a video, and I feel myself being lifted up. All my problems disappear, I can do anything, achieve anything. I listen to some of his speeches on my cell phone when I'm at the store. I feel 10 feet tall and strong, like I could flip my car over if I wanted."

"How long have you lived in this apartment?"

The question seemed to startle Anderson out of his daydream.

"About five years."

"Do you know where Amy Tremaine lives?"

"Why would I?"

"Give me a break, you sell T-shirts and tote bags with her dad's face printed on them. Why would you do *that?*"

Anderson frowned, like he didn't understand the concept of comparison.

"Because Harlan is amazing."

"So it would surprise you to learn that she has an apartment a couple of minutes' drive from this location and that she's been living there for roughly five years?"

Anderson's eyes opened wide in panic.

"You can't still think I had anything to do with her...situation?"

Sato was holding a laugh inside, her hand up over her mouth.

"Come off it, Anderson. What would *you* assume in my position?"

"I don't know! I didn't do anything to her."

"Yesterday morning, where were you?"

"Here. I was working on the website until after 2 a.m. so I slept late. By the time I woke up her abduction was all over the news."

Coombes wrote this in his notebook and glanced back up.

"Would I be correct in assuming that you were on your own?"

Anderson looked back down at his hands.

"Just me and Jennifer."

"Jennifer. Who's that?"

"She's behind you."

Coombes glanced back and saw the cage.

"You named the *bird* Jennifer?"

"I named her after a girl in my school I used to like."

"Uh-huh. What do you think, Grace?"

"Jennifer's probably under the floor, it would explain the smell in here."

Coombes nodded gravely, like he was considering it. Sato was getting good at this, she was spending way too much time with him. Anderson gripped his head in both hands and rocked back and forth for a moment.

"Look. I didn't do anything to Amy *or* Elizabeth. Jennifer lives in Phoenix and is married to a dentist that looks like a walrus - I looked her up on Facebook once. If you waste time on me, you'll be letting the real people get away with the killing and the kidnapping."

"All right. Let's say none of this has anything to do with you."

"Yes."

Eager, desperate.

"I'm just wondering if there is a single person in the world that knows Tremaine as well as you do. You're his biggest fan, right?"

"Definitely."

"And you know, a guy like Tremaine is going to be really pleased with you if you help us get his daughter back. He might take you out on his yacht, or on his private jet. Maybe have you around to his mansion. The two of you could be grilling meat on his back deck with some beers, smoking big cigars together."

"You really think so?"

"He'd totally do that," Grace said.

"You would probably get on the news, maybe even some chat shows. The man that saved Amy. This could be it for you, James, your chance at the big time. They'd make movies about it, you could write Tremaine's biography. You'd be all set."

Anderson's eyes were bright.

"What do I have to do?"

"We've seen your website. You've taken a lot of photographs. Tremaine doing this, Tremaine doing that. I bet you've got a bunch of photographs that you *haven't* uploaded. Hundreds, maybe thousands of images. I'm thinking maybe you got a picture of our suspect on one you didn't use. Someone that's been hanging around recently, acting suspiciously."

A sour look came over Anderson.

"Three weeks ago, I was in Brentwood taking pictures of Harlan welcoming guests for a charity lunch. This guy appears out of nowhere and stabs me in the leg with a long, thin blade. It was agony. I fell on the ground and my best lens broke. It was worth five and a half thousand dollars. He told me to leave Tremaine alone. Said if I didn't, he'd kill me."

"Can you describe him?"

"I can do better than that. His name is Nathan Marks, he was Harlan's head of security when he was governor. He's a total psycho. The next day, I was served paperwork that said I couldn't go within 200 feet of Harlan. I assumed the two events were connected, that Marks was back inside the tent. That he was feeding Harlan a line of shit about me. It's what he did last time."

"Last time?"

"Last time he worked for Harlan."

Coombes thought about it.

Tremaine claimed he carried a weapon in case Anderson came at him. He claimed he'd felt safer before, when he had his own security guy, presumably Marks. If he'd re-hired Marks it didn't seem likely that he would have made either statement.

He took out his cell phone and brought up the picture he'd shown Finley, the man trailing Amy Tremaine.

"Is this Nathan Marks?"

"That's him."

No hesitation, no doubt.

Coombes had been doing this a long time. The picture was terrible, Anderson should've taken a longer look. He'd glanced at it, then looked straight back into his eyes. It felt off. Like he said it was Marks because he *wanted* it to be.

Because he didn't like Marks.

"Show me where you got stabbed."

"I'd have to take my jeans down."

"James, we're trying to save a woman's life, you want my partner to avert her eyes? She's seen a man's leg before."

Anderson sighed then unbuckled his belt and lowered his jeans. A fabric dressing was wrapped around his left thigh. The dressing looked dirty from years of use and there were multiple blood stains on it from where the wound had leaked through and been re-applied.

"Take off the fabric."

Reluctantly, he did so. The wound was real and badly discolored. Anderson wasn't lying about being stabbed.

Coombes moved closer and angled his head for a better look. His nostrils filled with the smell of dried blood and with the sweet-sour smell of decay.

It wasn't poor hygiene he and Sato were detecting in the room, it was rotting flesh.

"Before I joined the LAPD, I was in the Army. I say that to give you some context. To let you know I have experience and that I'm not bullshitting with what I say next. Your wound is infected, James, and you need immediate medical treatment from a professional."

"It'll be fine."

"No, it won't. Either you lose the leg, or you'll get sepsis and die."

Anderson looked at him like he was expecting a joke and when one wasn't coming, he swore.

"That son of a bitch."

Behind him the bird kicked off.

"Son of a bitch! Son of a bitch!"

A talking bird. Maybe he should interview *Jennifer*.

"Get some stuff together, we're taking you to the closest emergency room."

Anderson seemed to deflate; his fight gone. He nodded meekly, then re-wrapped his dirty bandage and pulled up his jeans.

Coombes had come here ready to kill James Anderson and instead he was probably going to save his life. While they were waiting for Anderson to pack some clothes, Sato poured birdseed through the bars of the cage until it was piled up. As she did this, the bird pooped copiously into the tray below.

Homicide, it was a laugh a minute.

20

THEY TOOK ANDERSON TO the Good Samaritan hospital on Wilshire Boulevard and walked him inside. Coombes believed James Anderson would likely take off without being seen by a doctor, so they sat with him until he was, a process that removed 40 minutes from their day. When he came out with Sato the sky was half-dark and the sun was sitting low on the horizon, behind any building it could find.

He crossed the 110 on 4th Street, then turned on Main toward the PAB.

The miss-step with Anderson had cost them a lot of time, time Amy Tremaine could ill afford. Coombes thought about her again in that tank of water, doubtless believing her captors were trying to kill her. She'd pushed through her fear and shown strength and determination, something he couldn't stop admiring.

"Why do you suppose Nathan Marks let Anderson live? He had to know that he would be recognized and could place him near Tremaine before the kidnapping."

Coombes was quiet for a beat, the car moving slowly along.

"I think we can assume Marks is the man who did the hero act at the animal hospital. He takes those guys out then calmly waits for police to arrive. The two facts together - the being a hero and the waiting - means no one looked too hard at his story. He's out for a run, so he's not carrying ID. So he says his name is James Anderson because the guy's been annoying him for years. He doesn't know Anderson's address so he makes something up."

"Which is why the D.A. couldn't find him, but that doesn't-"

"Well, I was getting to that. I think Marks plans to frame him, knowing that Tremaine will instantly believe it. Anderson's practically been setting himself up as a patsy the whole time he's been stalking the former governor. As we know, he made a perfect suspect."

"But for that to work..." her voice trailed off; the thought left unfinished.

It didn't matter, he knew how it went.

For that to work, Amy Tremaine had to die. If she was alive, she would clear Anderson and identify Marks. It didn't mean she was dead already, it just meant that the kidnappers would have no use for her after they got their money.

As he entered the parking garage, Sato turned to him.

"I'm beat, Johnny. You mind if I take off?"

"Not at all."

She pointed to a vehicle coming up on their left.

"This is me here."

Coombes came to a halt. The question was on her face before she asked it.

"Are you okay? You've been distant all day."

"I don't want to talk about it."

His voice came out hard and angry. Sato's eyebrows lifted.

"This about us?"

"No, we're good."

She nodded, then got out the car and walked around the front without glancing back. Grace Sato wore flat shoes and had a muscular walk like she was ready to kick a man in the nuts. He smiled at the idea, then put the Dodge in gear and pulled slowly away.

When he got to his desk there was no email or telephone message identifying the wineglass fingerprint from Walton's secret apartment. This came as a disappointment rather than a surprise, as the lab had only received it about four hours earlier.

There were a number of emails from Mark Becker detailing his probe of Tremaine's charity foundation. Becker didn't mess about, his investigation was root and branch. Starting from the foundation's website he had built outward, analyzing first beneficiaries, then frequent donors.

Of particular note, was a crossover with the last case they'd worked together, a serial killer known as the Ferryman. An auction of rare goods and memorabilia for a children's charity where a pair of shoes worn by the killer had been bought. There was no link to the current case, but it had got Becker thinking about criminal connections and he had begun feeding names of donors through the NCIC database.

On the face of it, a fishing expedition carried out by a bored detective on desk duty with nothing else to do. So far, Becker was about halfway through the list of names and had already landed fourteen hits. The fish seemed small so far, but it was promising enough to let Becker continue, see what else turned up.

Coombes closed his email and sat for a moment looking at a stack of envelopes sitting on his desk. He'd been out all day and had missed the mail. He saw a thick envelope on top of the pile made from an expensive-looking light green board. It would be paperwork from the District Attorney related to an upcoming trial that was due to begin in just over a fortnight.

He decided that could wait another couple of days and took out his notebook and re-read his notes from the Anderson interview. He'd written *delusional?* on the top right-hand corner of the page and circled it.

The doctor at Good Samaritan had told him he'd probably saved Anderson's life, but that wouldn't mean much if he went after Tremaine later.

Saving Anderson made him responsible.

That brought him to Nathan Marks.

The positive ID was tainted by the source due to his personal dealings with Marks, but even a stopped clock is right twice a day.

He opened his browser and ran a search on Google.

There were hundreds of thousands of results. It always amazed him how many hits Google reported, but he knew there would be a lot of false matches or irrelevant part-matches that were worthless. He saw that Nathan had his own website and clicked on it.

The home page had a photograph of Marks standing next to Tremaine outside a building he didn't recognize, doubtless in Sacramento. The photograph was taken from across a street and showed both men full-length with a couple of feet of sidewalk below and three feet of building above.

Coombes moved his face up to the screen to zoom in.

Marks was looking toward the camera as if he'd spotted a potential threat, while the governor had his right arm up, holding a cell phone to his ear. It looked like a photograph taken by a newspaper photographer, except the quality wasn't quite good enough. A friend had taken it, he thought. Or maybe James Anderson, the memory card confiscated by Marks seconds after it was shot.

The face-on shot of Marks was perfect for facial recognition, but it was hard to compare it to the side-on kidnapping footage. That said, Marks was at least a 70% match for Coombes and he could see why Anderson would so quickly identify him.

He sat back and took in both men again.

Harlan Tremaine was six foot two inches tall, an inch and half shorter than himself. In the picture, Tremaine and Marks were the same height. This made him at the top end of Becker's height estimation for the kidnapper, but still within the ballpark.

This was his guy, he was sure of it.

The picture was eight years old, the 30% difference was easily explained by the time elapsed and by the angle of the drone camera. Coombes began clicking through the website, looking for a more up-to-date picture of Marks, but there were none.

Text on the website was small and filled with corporate security waffle that was of no interest to Coombes and he quickly began to skim, then abandon. It was clear that there had been no updates to the site in years. This in itself meant nothing. Everyone thought they needed their own website, but few realized what a cross they were making for themselves just in terms of security updates, even before you consider new content.

Anderson's website had consumed his whole life.

He flipped over to Facebook.

Social media required no maintenance from the user and new content was simple to upload. There was no bar you had to reach, you could upload a picture of your dinner or a cat, no-one would consider that unprofessional or irrelevant.

Nathan Marks had posted nothing in four years.

He still listed his employment as Head of Security, Governor of California. After leaving Tremaine's side, Marks had posted nothing anywhere online. It was as if he was unable to cope with losing a once in a lifetime job and gone into hiding.

The view from the top is amazing, but the fall is terrifying.

Aside from Facebook, the only other social media presence Marks had was on LinkedIn. His profile there was the oldest of all and the content pre-dated his work for Tremaine. It was possible that Marks had sanitized his social media, deleting anything that could be used to track him and he'd either forgotten about LinkedIn, or had lost the login.

Coombes decided to call it a day and get back to it when he was fresh.

21

THE FOLLOWING DAY IT took Coombes only eight minutes to drive to the PAB, a fraction of his usual daily commute. This was because he was now a guest at the Biltmore, his wife and her lover having spread the equivalent of nuclear waste around his home with their heaving buttocks and ball gag. He couldn't go back there, not even to pick up his stuff.

Everything was contaminated with fallout.

The detective bureau was deserted when he arrived and he got himself plugged in to his computer to resume his investigation of Nathan Marks from the night before. It took an hour to form a picture of the other man's life.

After leaving school, Marks had worked one dead end job after another. Gas stations, convenience stores, and fast-food outlets. The jobs were minimum wage, almost exclusively at night. This brought him into contact with members of a local street gang, who quickly pulled him in. He was arrested seventeen times in relation to fist fights, gun charges, and drug possession. Then the arrests stopped and something unexpected happened.

Marks enlisted in the US Marine Corps.

He served two tours, getting no closer to the action than Marine Security Guard at the American Embassy in Berlin, before being Honorably Discharged as a Lance Corporal. Not an officer, not even close.

Coombes hadn't been a Marine, but he knew how to read between the lines. Marks was a poor fit for the armed forces, having both a problem with authority and a low threshold for boredom. It made him wonder how Marks came to join in the first place.

The most likely reason, he thought, was that Marks had been offered service instead of prison time and he had taken it. There was no trace of any such deal in the system, nor would he expect to find any. Records would be expunged as part of the deal and to prevent blowback in the event that Marks died on active duty.

After leaving the Corps, Marks had done better for himself, leveraging his clean service record and good looks to gain employment as a high-end bodyguard. First to a series of A-list Hollywood actors, before landing the ultimate prize working for governor-elect Tremaine.

This was where the wheels came off.

After working for Tremaine, Marks disappeared.

In the last four years, Nathan Marks had not renewed his Driver's License, registered a vehicle, or updated his passport when the last one expired. He had additionally not filed any IRS returns, or paid for any utilities or telecoms. Coombes had yet to establish if Marks held active credit cards or bank accounts, but that information was beyond the scope of his access to law enforcement databases and public services.

Coombes ran his hands through his hair.

Ordinarily, he'd assume Marks was dead.

He reopened the photograph from Marks' website. The more Coombes looked at it, the more convinced he became that Anderson was right. As Tremaine's biggest fan, he ought to know what the former head of security looked like. The two of them had tangoed often enough. Being an expert with Tremaine by extension meant he was an expert with Marks.

"Hey, Johnny."

He turned and saw Sato standing behind him. When he turned her eyes dipped first to his shirt, then to his pants.

"Morning, Grace."

She seemed unusually interested in his clothes. Her mouth formed an O, her eyes zipping up to his. Her cheeks turning pink.

"She threw you out?"

"*What?*"

"C'mon. You think I don't know what you keep in your go-bag? That's the stuff you wear on out-of-town trips. I can even see the fold marks."

Coombes clenched his teeth.

"I don't want to talk about this."

"Why? Now we can move on with our lives."

He shot a look around to see if anyone had heard her, but the bureau remained quiet. Grace couldn't stop smiling and her happiness was getting on his nerves. He supposed he'd known this would be her reaction and that it was the reason he hadn't told her.

"I just pulled a knife out my back, okay? I'm not ready to party."

"I have no idea what that means, Johnny. At least tell me this isn't temporary, that you're going to divorce her."

He turned back to his computer.

"That's a safe bet."

On his screen he saw a reflection of her face. She was still smiling. The news had made her day. Her *year*.

Coombes took a slow breath, in, then out. He couldn't explain his rising anger, nor the overpowering sense of loss when he thought about Julie. They hadn't been in love for a long time, he'd even known she had been seeing someone else. Somehow, none of that mattered.

His mouth tasted of ashes.

After twenty seconds, Sato sat at her desk next to him and made a call on her cell phone. She spoke in a rush, excited. He didn't speak Japanese. No one else in the building spoke Japanese, it was basically encrypted.

She was telling someone about the tragic end of his marriage, he was certain of it. The excitement gave her away. The laughter.

His train of thought on Marks was totally derailed.

Coombes sighed and stared at his folded-over notebook in front of him.

Adam Finley had identified the man following Amy Tremaine as Elizabeth Walton's lover. The missing link between the two crimes. Assuming the man was Marks, that tied him not just to Amy and Elizabeth, but Harlan as well. Who better than Marks would know how to disable the alarm and wipe recordings? The extra connection reinforced the identification.

There was little doubt in his mind that he was waiting on fingerprint evidence he already knew the answer to. The results could come today, or in a fortnight, long after Amy was found dead. But there was a short cut to ID Marks that might also give Coombes his location.

He stood and pulled his suit jacket off the back of his chair. Sato was too busy with her call to notice him leave.

———

It took Coombes an hour and ten minutes to drive to Corona, a city in Riverside County to the south east of Los Angeles. The sun blazed the whole way, directly into his retinas. When he arrived he waited until after he rang the doorbell before he removed his sunglasses.

The door opened a couple of inches and stopped on a metal chain.

In the gap stood Abigail Marks, Nathan's mother. If Elizabeth Walton looked twenty-five years younger than she was, then it looked like she'd stolen the years from Abigail. Coombes assumed a casual stance.

"Abigail Marks?"

"Yes?"

"Ma'am, my name is John Coombes. I'm a detective with the Los Angeles Police Department. Can I come inside and talk?"

Her body slumped and her eyes filled with tears.

"Oh, god. He's dead, isn't he? You've found my boy."

Her reaction surprised him. He held up his hand in a calming gesture.

"That's not why I'm here, Mrs. Marks. I'm investigating the death of an employee of Governor Tremaine and the kidnapping of his daughter that you might have seen in the news. I was hoping to track down your son as he may have vital information, most likely without realizing it."

This was a script he'd worked up in his head on the drive over. He'd also decide to refer to Tremaine as if he was still Governor of California to make their son seem important by association. Abigail's eyebrows pitched downward in confusion.

"My son's been missing for years. I don't know where he is, I wish I did."

So much for that plan.

"Can we talk privately? No point letting your neighbors hear everything."

The woman's face hardened and she nodded. Among wide sections of the population, sharing your dirty laundry with the police within earshot of neighbors was a form of torture. Leaning into that was always a good way of getting into a property. The chain came off the door and he was waved inside.

Abigail had a walking frame held to one side and he had to wait for her to turn and move off down the hallway before he could follow and shut the door. He heard a television blasting from a room on the right.

She entered the room with the television and as she moved aside to pick up the remote control, he saw that Nathan's father lay asleep on an armchair with a clear plastic mask over his mouth and a pipe going back to a gas cylinder. She turned off the television and the sudden quiet seemed to rouse the old man.

"What! What's happening?"

"Bobby, this man is from the police. He's asking about Nate."

Robert Marks rotated his small, juicy eyes to look over his wife's shoulder at Coombes who towered over both of them. A skeletal hand reached up and pulled the mask down.

"You've come to the wrong place. My boy's not been here in almost a decade. Not since he worked for that fathead in Sacramento." Marks paused to get his breath back. "Thinks he's better than us now, doesn't he?"

It was worse than Coombes thought. His drive had been for nothing. He decided to press on, get some background information at the least. Get something from the trip.

"I'm sorry to hear that, Mr. Marks. Would you mind if I ask you and your wife some questions? Won't take too long."

Marks gave a small nod. Coombes glanced around for a place to sit and saw two other chairs, one obviously Abigail's, the other had an old poodle curled up on it. The dog eyed him warily as he approached. He knew from experience that it was better to pretend not to have seen the dog and to begin to sit anyway, it was the quickest way of getting a dog to move. The poodle shot off the chair with a second to spare.

Coombes took out his notebook then turned to Abigail who appeared to be the most capable of answering questions.

"How long is it since you last heard from your son?"

She paused for the briefest moment before answering.

"Four years, six months and twenty-two days."

"Did you see him at that time?"

"No. It's nearly six years since we last saw him."

"That would be just after he left Sacramento, yes?"

"Bobby, Alex, and I drove up to Los Angeles to see him."

She pronounced the city *angle-ease*.

"Alex?"

"Alex Holland, a childhood friend. He used to live across the street from our first home in La Habra. They served together in the Marines."

He nodded casually, like their son's tour of duty wasn't part of the reason he was sitting in their living room.

"How was your son that day?"

"Happy. He told us he was in love. Nate had never said anything like that before, he was very private about that side of his life. We were pleased for him." Her face hardened as she thought about the woman her son had fallen for. "What she said about him later was a lie. My boy would never do that. He wanted to marry her, spend the rest of his life with her. But she was rich, nobody wanted to listen to his side of the story."

This was why Marks had stopped working for Tremaine.

Not because he'd left office and didn't need him, but because of a scandal. An allegation strong enough to kill his career would prevent him from gaining further employment. In personal protection, word-of-mouth was everything. A bodyguard lived almost in your pocket. They went everywhere with you, saw everything, heard everything.

Nobody wanted someone they couldn't trust.

Coombes decided to move the conversation on before the allegation consumed the narrative. Whatever they might tell him would be nowhere close to the truth anyway, they were his parents.

"So, between the time you saw him in L.A. and the time he disappeared, you were only in telephone contact?"

"That's right."

"What about Alex, do you know if he saw Nathan again?"

"I'm sure he did, the two of them were close. They shared an apartment in Highland Park before he worked for the governor. Far as I know, Alex still lives there."

"Might Nate have gone back there after he lost his job?"

Abigail Marks shook her head.

"We hired a private investigator to look for our son. It cost a lot of money, money we didn't have. Alex helped pay for it. Thousands of dollars he's never asked us to pay back. I'm sure he would've mentioned if Nate was living in his spare room. Would have saved himself a lot of money."

The old man took off his mask so that it hung down by his neck.

"Cut the shit, son. You think he did something, why else would you be here?"

It was clear to Coombes that the father thought his son was still alive, while his mother thought he was dead. There was nothing to read into this, it was a fact that men were always the last to accept an awful truth.

He closed his notebook and stood.

"I have a picture. I want you to tell me if it might be your son."

"I knew it," Marks said. "Cops are all the same."

"Show me the picture."

Abigail's eyes were burning bright. She was desperate to see her son alive, no matter what that might mean he'd done. Coombes opened his iPad and brought up the screen grab of the man behind Amy Tremaine. He turned the screen toward her.

"That's not my Nate."

It was there in her face; he didn't think she could've lied to him.

"Then I guess I should get going. Thank you for your time."

Abagail Marks shuffled after him down the hall and through the door.

"Detective Coombes, just a moment. I want to give you something."

"What's that?"

"It's in the garage. Would you be able to open the door for me?"

He took a key from her and opened the up-and-over garage door. A cloud of dust rolled out toward him like he'd opened a pharaoh's tomb.

The inside was full of junk.

"The two cardboard boxes there."

He realized what they were.

"These are from the private investigator?"

"He couldn't find my boy, but maybe you will."

Like the three cases he was working weren't enough.

"I'll take a look, but no promises, okay?"

She sighed. "That's exactly what the investigator said."

22

As SOON AS HE stepped onto the floor of the detective bureau, it was clear to Coombes that everyone knew about his marriage. It was in the air, like a bad smell. A couple of detectives popped their heads up and glanced at him. He made his way toward his desk carrying the two box files on top of the other, his tablet balanced on top. Grace approached from the opposite direction, a nervous look on her face.

If she was coming to warn him, she was wasting her time.

Thomas Wallfisch stepped in front of him, a smile already on his face. The detective was one of his least-favorite humans and it burned him to see that he knew about Julie. Don McCreary and Ryan Cahill, two other detectives, formed up on either side, blocking his way.

"How's it going, Coombes? All right?"

The smile widened, Wallfisch could barely keep it under control.

"Bite me."

"Hey, that's no way to talk to a friend. I heard a rumor is all. Wanted to make sure you were okay. Not having any problems at home."

"Get out my way, lard ass."

The insult bounced off the man, like everything else.

"We always figured, you know-"

Wallfisch stopped, like he should know what came next.

"No, I don't know."

"Well, we figured you for a ladies' man. Like a dog chasing cars. No one here is surprised this has happened, it's your reputation. Everyone thinks you got what you deserved. You have this way with women, Coombes. You give them the bedroom eyes during an interview, then ask for their number. That how it works?"

His face colored, thinking about Schofield's property manager.

You into her or something?

"Step back, Wallfisch."

He wasn't going to back off, that much was obvious. The man was an imbecile. Coombes twisted to the side and put the PI's files on the floor then straightened up to full height.

"Want to know the secret to talking to women? It's simple. You give them your full attention and respect. You look into their eyes and listen to what they're saying. Try it sometime instead of staring at their cleavage, you'd be surprised what a difference it makes."

"You got all the answers, eh, Coombes?" Wallfisch smirked again. "For a second there, I almost forgot whose wife was banging someone else."

Coombes lunged at him, teeth clenched, fist already swinging. McCreary and Cahill sprang forward on either side to hold him back. It was a coordinated move, like they knew it was going to happen. Given his personal history with Wallfisch, it wasn't such a reach. Wallfisch laughed and walked away, shaking his head.

"Forget about him," Grace said. "He's an asshole."

He pulled himself free of the two detectives and made a show of brushing down his suit to get any wrinkles out. Around them, colleagues were looking over their desk dividers. Taking in the show.

Some days, the detective bureau was like high school.

He turned to his partner, if that's what she still was, and made no attempt to cover his hostility.

"You're wrong about that. Everyone needs an asshole."

Her eyes moved over his face.

"You think *I* told him?"

It was the only logical explanation, Wallfisch hadn't learned Japanese. Coombes looked away from her.

He didn't want to see her lie to him, to see how good she was at it. If he couldn't tell when she was lying, what then? Perhaps it didn't matter, she'd told Wallfisch, hadn't she? The closest thing he had to an enemy. She'd told *him*.

Sato tried to push her face into his line of sight like a guilty dog. He ignored it and picked up the box files.

"Let's just leave it, Grace. Damage is done."

"You honestly think I'd tell that piece of shit anything?"

She spoke loud enough that he heard Wallfisch say *Hey!* from across the room. Their eyes connected. She looked hurt. If it wasn't real, she should get an Oscar.

"My trust is at an all-time low right now, okay?"

"You suck at apologies, Coombes."

Sato turned and walked away, crackling with bad energy, her feet stomping on the floor. At least she hadn't kicked him in the balls.

When he got to his desk, she had her headphones on.

He set the files at his feet and opened the top box. A musty, mold smell rose to meet him.

Inside were a line of thick brown expandable folders close to an inch thick. They appeared to be in no order and he pulled one out at random and looked inside. It was packed with sheets of double-spaced typescript which appeared to be typed up from notes the investigator had made into his notebook.

Dates, times, descriptions.

His thought processes.

Coombes recognized the type of notes, he made plenty like it himself. Ideas that might pan out, some that go nowhere. If you thought of something and didn't write it down, chances were you'd forget it a moment later.

To Marks' parents, it probably looked like gibberish.

The back half of the folder contained photographs printed to 8 x 10 on high-quality paper. On top of the stack, a digital contact sheet showing 40 thumbnail-sized images, about twice as many as had been printed to full size. The PI had been following a young woman in a baseball hat. Where she lived, where she got coffee, who she met for lunch.

The woman was Cora Roche.

It appeared the PI was trying to locate Nathan Marks by looking at people close to Tremaine's inner circle. Potential love-interests. It wasn't a bad idea, but Roche didn't fit the pattern. For one thing, she wasn't on the scene when Marks worked there, and for another, he was fairly sure she was gay.

Coombes realized that everything in the folder related to a single day.

He glanced at the line of folders and noticed that he'd pulled the thinnest file. Going through it all would take a long time and there was the knowledge in the background that the PI's investigation had failed.

He set the first box to the side and opened the second.

This one was full of computer print-outs; Google searches, Facebook pages, maps. It seemed like the PI had printed out everything related to his investigation, no doubt to justify his costs and lack of results. He found an opaque plastic wallet with a zipper. It contained receipts for all the PI's expenses, and a thick envelope containing a settlement of account invoice for almost $10k.

The headed invoice showed the PI, whose name was Lester Crumb, had worked for just two weeks. The man sure generated a lot of paper.

Coombes sat back and stroked his chin.

What the hell kind of name was Lester Crumb?

He packed the boxes back together and carried them over to Mark Becker's desk on the other side of the detective bureau. A couple of heads followed him, but it seemed that his standoff with Wallfisch was already half-forgotten. Becker glanced up as he approached and did a double-take when he saw the box files in Coombes' hands.

"Oh shit. Are those for me?"

"Yeah, sorry. I'm looking into Tremaine's former head of security, Nathan Marks. He's a good fit for our suspect, but he turned himself into a ghost about four years ago. These files are from a PI the parents employed to find him. I'm hoping he missed something."

Becker glanced again at the boxes, at the way the sides bulged from all the paperwork inside. At the stains and torn spiderwebs spread across the cardboard.

His eyes came back up.

"This is going to cost you, Coombes. Four Roses Single Barrel."

"A bottle of whiskey."

"Two boxes, two bottles."

Becker shrugged his shoulders apologetically, like he could do nothing about it. As if to say *rules is rules, sir*. He'd seen the same thing many times over the years, usually when someone told him he'd need a warrant.

"All right. This is probably a long shot so finish what you're doing first."

As he walked to his desk Coombes took out his cell phone and dialed Tremaine's number. It went straight to an anonymous answering message and a beep.

"This is Detective Coombes. We need to talk."

23

He met Harlan Tremaine in the middle of the Temple Street footbridge, where Tremaine had positioned himself so that City Hall rose powerfully over his right shoulder. It didn't seem to Coombes that he had positioned himself where he had by accident, but career politicians can't turn off the need to be seen a certain way. The location was a single block down Main from the PAB and Coombes had walked to save himself the aggravation of parking.

Tremaine looked surprised.

"I expected your partner to be here after what you said last time."

"Yeah, well. Let's just say I'm over that. Why are we meeting here like a couple of spies in a Ludlum novel? Are the FBI still following you?"

"I've been busy running around trying to pull the ransom money together. Cashing in that much money at once isn't like going to an ATM and filling a sack."

"You're paying it then?"

"What choice do I have? Do you have good news for me?"

Coombes shook his head.

"We checked out James Anderson. The man's got a wallet full of three-dollar bills, but he's harmless. For what it's worth, pushing him away is the wrong move in my opinion. Give him a job in the charity; take him to a Lakers game; I don't know. Find a way to accommodate him and you'll defuse any tension. He needs a purpose. Aside from a talking bird with a potty mouth and a run-down apartment, you're all he has."

A pained look passed over Tremaine's face, either from being the unwilling recipient of advice, or from the prospect of spending time willingly with Anderson.

"He's definitely not involved?"

"No."

"Are you working any other leads?"

"Anderson had an interesting encounter with Nathan Marks."

Tremaine laughed.

"You think *Nate* is behind this? I've not seen him for four years."

"Marks stabbed Anderson in the leg and told him to get lost, to leave you alone. Three weeks ago, not four years. I assume he wasn't working for you, in which case, it looks like he was getting rid of a potential witness."

Tremaine opened his mouth but nothing came out and he closed it again. The laughter and smiles were gone. Coombes moved closer and dropped his voice to a whisper.

"If you told him to run off Anderson, tell me now. We can say the knife was Marks' idea and I won't charge you with half a dozen crimes. There's no time to waste if he's just going to be another dead end. You understand? I'm here for Elizabeth and for Amy. Not Anderson. His leg's a mess, by the way, but I'm not here about that."

Tremaine swallowed.

"I haven't been in touch with him, I swear."

"If you're lying to me, it could cost Amy her life."

"Jesus, Coombes. I understand. I've had no contact with Nate."

"Since you fired him, right?"

Tremaine sighed, then nodded.

"After you fired him, he disappeared. His parents haven't seen him since. All records of him vanish like he was abducted by aliens. Perhaps you should tell me what happened because the version I got from his mother has him wearing angel wings."

Tremaine glanced toward a bunch of tourists with big cameras around their necks that were coming up onto the bridge. They probably wanted the spot where the former governor was standing so they could take pictures of City Hall framed between the other buildings. Coombes and Tremaine left them to it, walking past them off the bridge.

All of the tourists were wearing face masks.

Coronavirus. People were starting to worry.

Off the bridge, they stopped on the other side next to some self-declared art. Coombes wasn't feeling it. They stood for a moment while Tremaine found the right words.

"Nate became infatuated with the granddaughter of Olaf Dekker, one of my big donors back then. Every chance he got, he'd be all over Kirsten. Asking her on dates, giving her jewelry, whatever. She wasn't interested in him, I could see it from across a room. Olaf asked me to make him stop. I told Nate it was over, but a part of me knew he hadn't heard me. The truth can be hard to hear sometimes. He thought she was the woman for him, I understood that."

"All right. So what happened next?"

"Months go by, Nate hasn't seen Kirsten. It seems like he's over her, problem solved. Out of sight, out of mind. The next time they met was charity dinner, a big one, 80 tables. About half-way through I noticed the chair next to Olaf was empty. His granddaughter's gone. I saw Nate was gone too, and I knew in my gut something bad was happening. Next thing she runs in screaming, clothes ripped, hair all over the place. She said he assaulted her, tried to rape her."

Coombes closed his eyes for a moment. It was worse than he thought.

"I'm guessing his story is different."

"A couple of minutes later, Nate walks in calm as you like with a smirk and her lipstick on his lips. I'd never seen him so happy and at peace. Everyone in the room stared at him like they wanted him dead. Olaf Dekker almost had a heart attack; it was a bad scene."

"What did he claim happened?"

"He said she flirted with him from the start of the evening. When she left to use the restroom, he followed her and they made out for about twenty minutes in a side room. He said she told him she was in love with him and always had been, but that her father had threatened to disinherit her so she had to pretended not to like him in public. Of course, at this point he thinks she set him up, that she ripped her own clothes to teach him a lesson."

"What do you think?"

"Nate and I spent a lot of time together campaigning, the whole time I was governor, the charity stuff. He was a good kid, there's no way he did what she said. I certainly don't believe he would calmly walk in if he'd torn her clothes off. I think he was telling the truth."

"But none of that matters."

"No, it doesn't. It became about survival. Not believing a potential victim of a sexual assault in this climate would finish me, finish the foundation. I fired him on the spot. Dekker said he'd keep the police out of it if he lost his job. I hated it, Nate was family by then."

"Then the last time you saw or spoke to Marks was on that night?"

"Yes."

"How did things end between you?"

"Not well. Nate said firing him validated her claims of assault. He said if I didn't believe him, no one else would. That his life was over."

"Why didn't you mention this to me already?"

"It was a long time ago, Detective. I assumed he'd moved on."

"Well, Anderson can place Marks outside your property three weeks ago carrying a knife with a five-inch blade. Maybe he hasn't *moved on* as much as you hoped."

"Anderson is a pathological liar with a grudge. Do you think it's a coincidence he supposedly has this meeting with Nate around the same time I file a restraining order on him? The man is a weasel and the idea that Nate would harm Lizzie or Amy is absurd."

Four years later, Harlan Tremaine was still defending the man he'd betrayed. But then, he hadn't seen the stab wound on Anderson's leg.

"To hell with it. I have a picture of our suspect who I believe is Nathan Marks."

Tremaine glowered and his voice became deeper, almost a growl.

"*Show me.*"

Coombes brought up the drone picture on his cell phone and again cropped Amy out of shot before flipping it around. The former governor stared at it for a long time.

"That ain't him."

"It's been years, Harlan. Is it *close* to being him?"

"All right, it's close but I'd recognize that kid anywhere. There's something else. Nate has a tattoo of an eagle on his right arm, you can't miss it. The man in the video has no tattoo."

Coombes returned his cell phone to his pocket.

Tremaine didn't want Marks to be the kidnapper, because if he was then it meant he was directly responsible for everything that had happened to Amy and to Elizabeth. Just the same, the tattoo was a problem.

Including Nathan's parents, that now made three people with a direct connection to Marks that had failed to ID him from the picture. That left James Anderson as the only positive ID so far. The case against Marks was fading fast. Maybe it was some kind of doppelgänger who by some twist of fate had chosen Amy as a target.

Of course, that was bullshit.

It was Marks, it had to be Marks.

"All right, Mr. Tremaine. I'll be in touch."

24

He picked up two coffees on the way back and put one next to Sato's mouse as he walked past her desk. She made a surprised face, but said nothing. It still seemed to him like she had to have told Wallfisch about his marriage, or at least told someone else who told Wallfisch, but he was trying to get past it. There was, he reflected, always a chance she was telling the truth and he didn't want to lose her because he was an asshole.

Coombes hung his suit jacket over the back of his chair and sat down. The new angle about Marks having a tattoo on his arm made him want to check the proof of life video again.

It surprised him that Tremaine was able to recall that the arm in the video had no tattoos. The temptation when watching the clip was to hold your own breath and watch what was happening to Amy. The disembodied arm coming down from above was of interest only to what was happening below.

He rewatched it all the way to the end first, watching for times when the arm was most visible and better lit. The optimal point was when the arm pushed Amy down for the second time, the hand gripping her hair. He paused the clip. At this point, almost the entire arm was in shot from midway between elbow and shoulder, right down to the man's fist.

Tremaine was correct, no tattoo.

There was also no sign that a tattoo had once been there and been removed, or been concealed by some kind of makeup. Coombes sat back and began to drink his coffee. He'd been hoping to see some differences in skin tone or tanning consistent with laser removal.

His phone rang and he lifted the handset with his mouth still full of coffee. Street traffic poured into his ear, distant voices. He swallowed his coffee.

"Coombes."

"You spoke to the owner at *The Hard Limit*. I saw where he put your card."

A woman's voice. Young, nervous.

"What can I do for you?"

"I'm a bartender there. Jax doesn't know, but I got evicted from my apartment and I've been sleeping at the club. I was there when that video was shot. I saw everything."

Coombes sat up in his chair and clicked his fingers to get Sato's attention. He angled the telephone headset away from his head so that she could hear.

"And what was that? What did you see?"

The woman was breathing fast into the microphone. There was a shake to it, like she'd just crossed a finish line after a marathon and was doubled over.

"Look, I'm scared. As soon as they find out about me, I'm dead."

"We'll make sure that doesn't happen, but the best way we can do that is by catching them, yes? Now, what did you see?"

"A man and two women. One of the women was the one who got put in the water. They had a hood over her head to begin with, she didn't know where she was. I thought they were going to kill her. Look, I'll tell you everything, but I need you to bring me in. I think I'm being followed."

"Where are you right now? Are you at the club?"

"No. I was heading to the station, but I realized I had no money for a ticket. There's a lot of tents on the sidewalk, people living on the street."

"Can you see a street sign?"

"No. I'll go up to the intersection."

He opened his desk drawer and took out a map of Los Angeles.

"What station were you going to? Union?"

"Yes."

He folded over his map so that it was showing the Fashion District and Skid Row. The caller was close, a half dozen blocks away.

"San Pedro, the intersection with 6th Street."

Coombes moved his finger to the spot and tapped it.

"I'll send a unit to pick you up, you're going to be perfectly safe."

"No, no, no! You send one of those cars, I won't be here. It has to be you. I saw you at the club, I trust you. I thought you had kind eyes. Come alone."

"What's your name, ma'am?"

The call disconnected.

Sato was sitting on his desk leaning over.

"She thinks I have kind eyes."

"I heard."

Her face showed nothing. No trace of amusement. Any other day she'd get a whole routine out of that but not today. He stood and pulled on his jacket. Sato walked with him to the elevator.

He glanced at her but said nothing.

The doors opened and they both got in.

She drew her weapon, ejected the magazine checked it was loaded, then pushed it back in. Coombes turned to watch. Sato drew the slide back a fraction to check the chamber was clear, then re-holstered her weapon.

"What are you doing, Grace?"

"Coming with you."

"She said I was to come alone."

"I heard that too."

They were in the parking structure now, moving quickly along a line of vehicles. He didn't believe that the caller was in any danger, at least not from the kidnappers. If she'd been discovered in the club then she'd be dead no question, but not a day later.

Just the same, he wanted to get there as soon as possible before the woman had second thoughts and disappeared. She was a vital witness and there was no telling what she might have seen. He blipped the remote and the Dodge's rear lights flashed.

"You're not getting in, Grace."

He opened his door, she opened hers.

Coombes glared at her over the roof.

"Grace, what the hell?"

"You're going to have to drive over my body to leave here without me."

He sighed. "Fine, but duck down when I say so."

She pouted, then got in.

Traffic was light and the drive took about five minutes. As he crossed over 4th Street, Sato pushed herself down in the seat, below the level of the dashboard.

He saw the tents the witness had mentioned.

His eyes swept along the sidewalk, looking for a young woman that looked like she might be a bartender at a night club. He imagined someone like Cora Roche, wearing a lot of tight black clothing. All he saw were people lying broken on the concrete.

The homeless, the addicts, the forgotten.

He knew many were veterans, sent to the same war he'd fought in Afghanistan. It could've been him lying there instead of them, all it took was an injury and the opioid addiction that often followed.

Coombes pulled over to the curb and killed the engine. Eyes turned toward them. Only a cop would park a car this new so near an encampment.

He drew his weapon, chambered a round, then returned it to his holster. Coombes wasn't a hundred percent, but it looked like the bartender had taken off.

He spoke to Sato without looking at her, just in case he was being watched.

"She's not here. I'm going to walk around, let her see me. Stay in the car."

"*Johnny.*"

"I'll leave the keys in the ignition in case you need to move."

Coombes stepped out and shut the door.

It was windy on the street and he squinted his eyes to keep the dust out. If she was on foot, the bartender couldn't have gone far, a couple of blocks max. He stared north toward Little Tokyo, then south toward the Fashion District.

No one was walking on the sidewalk, though plenty seemed to be slowly dying on it. He started off toward 6th Street. Maybe she'd given up waiting and started to walk back downtown.

If she melted away, finding her again might not be easy. She claimed to have been evicted, so any address the club had for her would be useless. If she thought she was in danger, there was a chance she'd disappear until she thought it was safe to resurface.

Coombes reached the intersection with 6th Street.

The sidewalk was clear all the way to Los Angeles Street, where city life seemed to normalize. He turned and began to walk back to his car. Sato was sitting in the driver's seat watching. Not even pretending to hide. Maybe bringing Sato spooked the witness. He sighed. The whole thing was a wild goose chase, the woman was wasting his time.

He caught a flash of movement to his right.

A young white woman with blonde hair stood in the doorway. Her skin was pure white with no trace of a tan. *Like someone that worked nights and slept all day*, he thought. When she saw him, she stepped back inside, into the darkness.

Not an invitation, she was trying to conceal herself.

It was a wide industrial unit, an abandoned toy factory. The front door had been forced, but not recently. He followed her into the building. It was dark inside, lit only by shafts of light from rusted-through bolt holes in the iron roof. He lost sight of her as his eyes adjusted from the blinding sunlight on the street.

Coombes drew his weapon and a flashlight and moved forward.

The light from the flashlight was dim, the batteries needed to be replaced. There were people nearby, shapes in the darkness. Squatters. Maybe she had changed her mind about telling him what she'd seen, but he couldn't leave her in here, it wasn't safe.

He heard a glass bottle fall over way at the back, then a man's voice thick with drink or drugs, calling out something angry. Coombes moved the beam of his flashlight toward it and there was a flurry of movement. He saw the bartender running through the darkness and he ran after her.

People were lying on the floor asleep or dead, he had to keep flipping the flashlight down to avoid standing on them or tripping over them.

The woman crashed up a set of metal steps, going up into an office above the main floor. He lost sight of her again as she entered the office. He took the steps three at a time, closing the distance with the blonde.

Coombes was pissed off. Much more of this, and he'd leave her to her fate with the derelicts.

The office door was closed. He tried the handle and found it locked. A frosted glass panel was in the middle of the door with the word MANAGER written on it. Hiding behind a wood and glass door.

It was stupid, the way a child might hide.

He kicked the door hard, his shoe landing right next to the handle. The latch tore through the wooden frame and the door slammed open, causing the glass panel to break and fell on the floor. In front of him, the woman was pressed against the far wall.

"I changed my mind! I don't want to get involved."

He holstered his weapon and walked into the room.

"Did you hear what I said?! I saw nothing. Those people are crazy."

Despite the low light from his flashlight, he could see her clearly.

She was not familiar to him.

He frowned. If she'd been at the nightclub when he visited, she'd stayed back out of sight. On the mezzanine level above maybe. But if that was so, she could never have seen his eyes.

His vision went black for a second, except for a bright purple and white crease that ripped through his vision like lightning.

Coombes dropped to his knees.

Pain soared from the back of his head, unrelenting and without end. He slumped forward and put his hand down on the floor in front of him to steady himself.

The woman seemed to change and become ugly. Her face became a snarl and she was looking over his head.

"Finish him! Kill the bastard!"

He turned to the space next to the door he'd just walked through.

A figure stood there.

He reached for his Glock but before he could get his hand on it, pain exploded across the top of his forehead. Blackness washed over him, but not for long, soon he was back only to find that he was flat out on the floor and the woman was kicking him repeatedly in the side of his chest.

There was no strength left in him, he doubted he could even stand. His hand fell back and touched against his side, his holster.

The figure walked toward him. It was too dark to see if it was Marks, all he could say for sure was that it was a man and that he was well-built. The man put his feet on either side of Coombes' knees and looked down at him. He was holding something in his hand.

A baseball bat.

He was going to be beaten to death in this shitty toy factory.

Coombes eased his Glock slowly out of his holster.

He didn't have the strength to raise it, never mind aim it. He rested the butt of the pistol on the floor and angled it up, toward the ceiling and fired.

His Glock held 17 rounds and he fired all of them about a second and half apart. The room filled with sound of gunfire, the smell of cordite, and the gentle *ding* of the ejected brass cartridges falling on the floor.

A moment passed and then he heard laughter.

"Hey, cop! *You missed*. You missed *seventeen* times!"

"Yeah, but my partner won't and now she knows where we are."

The bat hit him again and this time the blackness swallowed him.

25

WHEN COOMBES CAME AROUND, he was in utter darkness. He tried to sit up but it felt like a freight train ran over his head and he let himself lie still. The tips of his fingers felt the same dirty floor he'd been on before. He reached out his right fingers and found his Glock lay where he'd dropped it.

Before he'd been able to see enough to see the figure by the door. He'd seen the woman's face twist up with hatred. There'd been *some* light in the room, now it was black. The only thing that made sense was that he'd been unconscious all afternoon and that it was now night.

It had been just after 12:30 when they'd left the PAB. He didn't know when it got full dark, but it had to be at least 8 p.m.

There was no way he'd lost seven and a half hours. For one thing, he'd be starving and he was, at best, hungry. Going by his stomach-clock, he doubted he'd been out more than a couple of minutes.

His head pounded in time with his heart.

He heard movement next to him, shoes scraping on the floor.

He wasn't alone.

The woman who'd lured him here had to be one of the kidnappers and that the man and woman she described being with Amy in *The Hard Limit*, was herself and the man who'd hit him with the bat. Presumably, Marks.

It meant that they were tracking the investigation, and that they didn't like what they saw, so they decided to take him out.

He wished he knew which part they didn't like, because it didn't feel like he was making much progress.

If the person next to him was one of the kidnappers, then it followed that they were leaving him alone because they thought he was dead or unconscious. Changing them of that view would be a bad move.

He heard a sigh. It was a sound he'd heard before.

"Grace."

"John?" She never called him that, things must be bad. He felt a small hand on the center of his chest, then it held his hand. "You were out a long time, I got scared."

"I can't see anything, I'm blind."

"What about now?"

He saw something, a glow.

"Wait, I see that. What is it?"

"My flashlight, straight into your face. You have blood in your eyes. Don't worry, help's on its way."

"Did you see the two pricks that did this to me?"

"I saw."

"And?"

"I'm sorry, Johnny. They got away."

They said nothing for a moment. He felt ridiculous lying on the floor.

"Help me up, will you?"

He rolled onto his side, then part-way onto his front, the knee of his outer leg drawing up to brace himself like a sniper. He pushed down on the floor with his hands, then on his knee. He was half-way. The freight train returned, its steel wheels rolling fast over his head.

He put his arm around Sato's shoulders and paused for a moment, waiting for the pain to subside. His heart thumped fast in his chest and the room began to spin. He straightened his knees and back and took a couple of unsteady steps.

"Thank you, Grace. I'd kiss you, but I'm probably hideous now."

"Oh, you have no idea."

They were laughing as they left the office and came down the metal staircase together. He had his left hand on a rail, his right on her hip. They reached the bottom of the steps and moved across the factory floor. There were no shapes of sleeping squatters in old blankets, they had all cleared out for now.

They got out onto the street.

He'd never been so happy to feel the heat of the sun against his face.

He saw the edges of buildings against the bright blue sky. It was coming back. A siren approached, then a boxy shape pulled alongside and he heard doors slamming and hands were guiding him toward the vehicle where he sat on the back step.

"My name's Michael, I'm a medic with the Fire Department. What's your name?"

"John."

"All right, John. Let's take a look." Hands carefully moved his head and parted his hair to inspect impact sites. "You have sustained a blow to the left side of your forehead, the crown, and to the right rear of your head. Do you have any other injuries?"

"I decided that was enough."

"I'll bet. Let's clean up your face. Lean forward."

He felt a liquid lightly hitting his forehead, then his eyes. It took nearly a minute of rinsing but finally the world came back into focus. A young man was crouched in front of him with latex gloves and a bottle with a spray head. When he finished, he used cotton pads to clean the area then applied sutures to the open cut on his forehead.

There was a puddle between his feet that was pink with blood.

A second medic applied ice packs to his head and held them lightly in place while the first took a pen light from his pocket. Coombes knew what questions would be coming next.

"Grace, I left my flashlight and sidearm back there, could you get them?"

She was staring at his head with her eyebrows pitched up at an angle and her mouth drawn tight. It looked like she was about to cry.

"Grace! My gun?"

"Sorry." She left them and went back inside the building.

The medic shone the light into one eye, then the other. Back and forth.

"What day is it today, John?"

"Thursday."

"What year?"

"2020."

"Who is currently President?"

"Donald Trump."

"What's my name?"

"Michael."

"All right. Did you lose consciousness at any time?"

"No."

"No?!" There was disbelief in the man's voice. "How about a nap? Did you have one of those?"

"No."

Michael sighed.

"Very well. Using first your left eye, follow my finger." The medic moved his finger from side to side, then up and down. "And now with the right."

Coombes did as he was told.

"Your tracking is fine, but your iris response times are sluggish at best and your left pupil is visibly larger than your right. I recommend an MRI."

"I'm in the middle of a case and a woman's life is in danger."

"Isn't it always? Look, do me a favor. Let your partner drive for the rest of the week, leave your gun in its holster, and avoid any further impacts to your head. If your pupils don't match tomorrow morning *or* if you pass out again, go to the nearest ER immediately."

"Fine. Do you have anything for the pain?"

"We're the Fire Department, not a pharmacy."

Lying about blacking out had pissed off the medic. Coombes got down from the rear steps of their vehicle and stood carefully on the sidewalk. The dizziness had passed. Sato returned with his Glock and flashlight.

The medic turned to her.

"Your partner has a hard head, Detective."

"It's not hard," she said. "It's solid bone."

Coombes smiled, then thanked the medics for their help and walked back to the Dodge. His left hand held the ice packs in place. They seemed to be holding off the freight train. He got into the passenger side of the car and slid the seat back into place.

He felt stupid for being ambushed. Sato had saved his life, he had no doubts about it. Coombes glanced at her and was surprised to see that she was watching him.

"I don't think I said before. Thank you."

"You *did* say before, but it's not necessary. We're partners."

"Nevertheless, I owe you one. Not to mention another apology for being a dick."

"I'm not going to sugar-coat it, Johnny. It took a lot of work to break you in and I don't want to have to start over with someone else. I got a lot invested here."

"I feel the same way, Grace."

Sato started the engine and pulled smoothly away. The Charger's seat held his body perfectly. He was so tired he could barely keep his eyes open. If it wasn't for the pain in his head, he'd fall asleep.

"I suppose we're going to pretend that you didn't pass out back there?"

Coombes said nothing.

26

THEY STOPPED FOR LUNCH in Little Tokyo at a ramen place on Central Avenue that Sato liked. He figured he might draw a few looks, so they decided to get takeout and eat in the car. While Grace picked up their food, he tilted the seat back to something close to fifty degrees and lay there with the ice pack against the bump on his forehead. He closed his eyes and tried to picture in his mind the woman who'd set him up.

Shoulder-length blonde hair. Five-six to five-eight. Average build. Skin as white as a corpse. She'd been wearing boots, he thought. The chunky kind, with at least an inch heel, something to factor into her height.

He tried to think of anything else, but couldn't.

The figure with the bat he hadn't seen clearly at all. A man in his early forties, doubtless Nathan Marks. Luring him there like that, hitting him from behind.

What a chickenshit move. What a *coward*.

Rage surged around his system unchecked.

He recalled that Marks' service in the Marines was in protection which had set him up nicely for his future with Tremaine. He had no experience on the battlefield, or of going house to house, clearing villagers from combatants.

All defense, no offense.

Based on this experience, he wondered how things had really gone down at the animal hospital. Logically, more of the same. Using a fire extinguisher instead of a baseball bat, hitting the armed men from behind. The extra heft of the metal cylinder causing near-fatal injuries to the men with shotguns.

Where the comparison fell apart, was that Marks had no forewarning of what he was walking into at the animal hospital and had reacted with whatever was to hand. At the toy factory, he knew exactly what was coming. Coombes figured Marks was armed now, so the decision to use the bat was out of a desire not to kill him, only to set back the investigation.

The driver door opened and Sato got in.

"You better not be dead, Coombes. I just dropped twenty-five bucks on your lunch and it wasn't even my turn to buy."

He smiled and tilted his chair back up.

Why did he fight his attraction to her? Why did he seem to be trying to sabotage their relationship?

They ate in silence, the inside of the car filling with the smell of spices and garlic. He was hungry and ate quickly, a slight shake in his right hand fading away as the hot food went down. Ramen steaming in a broth with chunks of pork and handfuls of chilies, gyoza pan-fired dumplings, beansprouts with a lot of garlic, and a side of chili-salted edamame.

"What Wallfisch said about your wife. Was that true?"

He stopped eating and glanced at Sato.

"You mean, that she's seeing someone? Yes."

She dried the corners of her mouth with a napkin but said nothing.

"Yesterday, after my meeting with Tremaine, I went home for lunch. I was three or four blocks away, so I figure why not? I find wine glasses and an empty bottle of Champagne on the coffee table. We used to drink Prosecco a lot, Julie called it pre-sex-o. I should've just left but I had to see it to the end. I walked in on them going at it like he's pounding steak with a hammer. The man didn't stop to draw breath, he just kept going. Told me to get lost."

"Jesus."

He looked at the windshield, which was steaming up on the inside.

"I thought about shooting him. For nearly ten seconds I was good with being a murderer. I'd kill him, then I'd kill her. You know how that goes; I wouldn't have been able to stop."

"Is this because of us?"

Coombes shook his head and quickly regretted it. His brain seemed to swirl inside his skull, the pain coming thundering back.

"Me and Julie have been living separate lives. She's been seeing someone for a while now, I've known since before Christmas. Before us. You could call me a hypocrite and you'd be right, but it turns out there's a difference between knowing it and seeing it."

They finished eating in silence. The last third of his ramen had cooled but he finished it anyway and moved on to the edamame. Sato turned to him.

"What now?"

"Now we speak to Alex Holland about his old buddy Nathan Marks."

"I meant between us, idiot."

"Well, Grace. It looks like a couple more spots have opened up on my dance card if you're still interested. Unfortunately, I'm ugly now."

She touched his face, her fingers stopping short of the bump on his forehead.

"I've kissed worse."

———

THE ADDRESS HE HAD for Alex Holland in Highland Park had a new black Ford F-150 Raptor parked out front. If he still lived there, he was in. This suited Coombes just fine, he hated having to run down witnesses and suspects; whichever category Holland fell into. Sato pulled the Charger up behind the truck and killed the engine.

He'd spent most of the ride over catching her up on his investigation of Nathan Marks and what had happened to him that caused him to leave Tremaine's employment.

Holland opened his front door wearing a zip-up track top, camouflage shorts down to his knees, and a pair of open toe sandals. A cloud of marijuana smoke hung around him like a fog bank. He looked at the two of them standing there without surprise.

"Oh shit, 5-0! 5-0!" Holland grinned like he'd made a joke, then stared at Coombes' forehead like a rare butterfly had landed on it. "Hey man, what happened to your *face?*"

"Baseball practice. Open the door or it might be contagious."

Holland stepped aside to let them in and took a draw from a large joint in his hand. He smirked as Coombes passed him. They were the same height and build, but there was no focus in the other man's eyes. He'd smoked it all away.

"I know what this is about, Abigail called me this morning. Said some cop was sniffing around, asking questions about Nate. I'm guessing that's you?"

"Detective Coombes and Sato."

"Whatever."

Holland walked to the back of the property, toward the kitchen. He still walked like a Marine, shoulders swinging. It was amazing how much swagger could build up protecting diplomats in one of the safest places in the world.

Holland took a beer out his fridge, twisted the cap off and drank from the bottle as his eyes moved slowly over Sato's body. What a creep. Coombes cleared his throat and the sound brought the Marine back into the moment.

"If you're here looking for Nate, you're wasting your time. He's not here. I haven't seen him for four years. If you think he's hiding under the bed you're welcome to take a look."

"Is there somewhere we can sit?"

Holland sighed and walked them back through into his main living space and plopped himself down on a sofa where he stretched himself out horizontally.

Coombes sat opposite and took out his notebook. Sato remained standing.

"You think he's dead?"

"Do I think *who's* dead?"

"Nate. He disappeared. Even you, his best buddy, hasn't seen him."

"I never thought about it."

"Is that because the two of you had a fight and you killed him? If we come back with cadaver dogs are we going to find anything buried in your yard?"

"You can't be serious."

"Marks' parents say you helped pay for the private investigator to look for their son. That sounds like guilt to me, what does it sound like to you, Grace?"

"An alibi," she said.

Coombes nodded.

"*Right*. So how about it, Holland? Shall we get the dogs and a backhoe and pull up your yard?"

"You're crazy."

"Look at my *face*. I'm just getting started."

Holland took another mouthful of beer. Coombes understood now why he'd pulled it from the fridge, the beer gave him longer to think about awkward questions without it appearing like he was thinking for too long.

"I never thought of Nate as *disappearing*, I just stopped hearing from him. How many people have you ever met that just cut you off without warning? One minute they're there, you're having beers with them every Friday night, the next? Nothing. It happens."

"And yet you gave his parents what they needed to pay that PI."

"Nate dropping *me* is one thing. Dropping your family, that's not right."

"Still. Pretty generous, giving them that money."

Holland shrugged.

"I can afford it. You got to understand, Abigail and Robert are like second parents. Me and Nate were in and out of each other's houses growing up, eating meals, or candy, or soda. I was just paying back what I probably owed them anyway. They're good people."

Coombes glanced up at Sato and angled his head to the side. She uncrossed her arms and moved off, into the back of the property. Holland sat up and put his feet on the floor. His eyes flicking nervously between Coombes and Sato's retreating back.

"Where's she going?"

Coombes ignored him.

"What is it you do for a living, Mr. Holland?"

"I'm an ironworker. I put the beams in high-rises."

"No kidding. And you smoke that shit?"

"Not when I'm working."

"Are you currently out of work?"

"We're building a tower downtown but the site's closed. We get our steel from China and it's all dried up because of COVID. I get paid either way so I'm not bothered."

"The last time you spoke with Nathan, was that before or after he was fired?"

Holland took a draw on his joint.

It was almost finished and he had to hold it carefully with his fingernails which were heavily discolored. He blew out a cloud of thick smoke.

"After. He was framed by that woman and if you want my opinion, that rich old asshole was in on it."

"Olaf Dekker?"

"*Tremaine.*"

Coombes stared at Holland for a moment, letting the penny drop.

"You think Nate's involved in the kidnapping."

"That's right."

"There's no way, man! He's a boy scout."

"Not anymore. We have him on video grabbing Amy Tremaine and throwing her into the back of a van."

Holland stubbed out what remained of his joint into an ashtray. His joking face had hardened into a mask.

"Uh-uh. You got the wrong guy."

"Well, if it *isn't* him then the quicker we locate him, the sooner we can clear him and find the real kidnapper, right? He's got nothing to worry about."

"Like I said, I don't know where he is."

"Let's leave that for now. Tell me, you ever see Marks with a date?"

"Plenty of times. Women sure like that man's face."

"What age were they, these women?"

"Our age," Holland said, then smirked. "Older sometimes."

"How much older?"

"Twenty years? He said he didn't care what age they were as long as there was a connection. I'd joke about it sometimes, that he always seemed happiest when he was with one of his cougars."

He made a note in his notebook. *Cougars.* The term seemed offensive to him, but he understood many women applied it playfully to themselves.

Despite the failed IDs he'd had with Marks, this aligned perfectly with Adam Finley's account of the men Elizabeth Walton brought back to her apartment.

It seemed possible that after leaving Tremaine's service Marks and Walton had crossed paths again on the dating circuit and a new type of relationship had formed.

Sato returned and shook her head.

Hell, it wasn't like he'd expected Marks to be hiding in a closet.

"One last question. You said you thought Tremaine had been in on the frame-up with the Dekker woman. Is that what Nate thought too?"

"Of course!" Holland said, then froze, realizing he'd implicated his friend. "But that was a long time ago, you can't think this is revenge after all this time, that's insane."

Coombes put his notebook away and stood.

"Thanks for your time, Mr. Holland. We'll be seeing you again soon."

He walked to the front door with Sato alongside.

"What the hell does *that* mean?" Holland shouted.

When they got outside, he made for the driver's side of the Dodge before he remembered Sato was driving. The friction with Holland had made him forget about his injuries.

Once they were seated, they sat for a moment watching the house. After about twenty seconds the curtains moved and Holland looked out at where they were parked.

"He's lying about something," Sato said.

"That's for sure. Any sign of Marks in the house?"

"No. There's a spare room, but it's full of gear for Holland's job. Boots, harnesses, all that stuff. It didn't look like the room's been used as a sleeping space for a long time and I don't figure Holland and Marks are the type for sharing a bed."

"His reaction to the kidnapping seemed real."

"Nobody knows anybody," Sato said, starting the engine.

Holland was still watching them as they pulled away.

27

WHEN HE GOT BACK to the PAB, he walked straight across the detective bureau to catch up with Becker. Some of the other detectives made remarks about his appearance. Becker just whistled and allowed his eyes to move with frank interest over the damage to his face.

"What happened to you, Coombes?"

"I was ambushed by Nathan Marks and his psycho girlfriend."

"No kidding. Did he say what he wanted?"

"To play baseball, apparently. But we were all out of baseballs."

Becker laughed.

"I have news from TID about Tremaine's security system."

"Let me guess, they got zip."

"Correct. No recordings on the local drive *or* on the cloud backup."

"Whoever did this not only knew how to disable the alarm and wipe the recordings but knew about the cloud backups as well. Like someone that used to work there."

"Not exactly. The tech said that when a file is deleted it remains on the drive until it is over-written. Until then, all that happens is a pointer to the file is erased and the operating system sees it as available space. For a window of time the file can be found again, its pointer restored, and the file brought back. However, there *was* no deleted file to bring back."

Coombes nodded.

He knew about deleted files but let Becker finish. If you give a member of your team a moment to shine, it'll be something they'll want to do again.

"All right. Then our killer must've used a shredder program to permanently delete it so that there's nothing to bring back."

"Wait, John, it gets better. Our guy decided to look at previous recordings. He wanted to know what file format he was looking for, likely size, anything to help him find the missing data. What he found was that the last recorded file was over two months old. The system was off. It wasn't deactivated by some master crook, it just wasn't on."

"Goddammit."

Coombes found that he wasn't surprised.

He recalled a *Times* story about thieves whose m.o. involved putting cats over walls of target properties. The cat walked about, triggering false alarms. After being woken at 3 a.m. several nights in a row, the victims stopped setting their alarms. As soon as the thieves put a cat in and got no alarm, they knew it was safe to enter.

"Did TID have *any* good news?"

"If they did, they didn't mention it to me."

Coombes sighed.

"How are you getting on with the PI files?"

"More than half-way. I've looked at the timeline on this and I'm not hopeful. By the time he was hired, eighteen months had passed and all trace of Nathan Marks had vanished. The PI has nothing to work with and cast a pretty wide net hoping to get lucky."

"That may be, but the timeline's even worse now."

"For sure. I checked out this Lester Crumb character by the way. He used to be on the job, worked in the Real Estate Fraud Unit for three years. He solved no cases in that time. Not one. Looking at his notes here, I think I know why. He's a clown of the first order."

"Keep at it. Could be he had the answer and didn't know it."

"That I can believe."

Across the room, Sato was back to digging through the socials on Elizabeth Walton and Amy Tremaine.

They were at the end of day three and they were still looking for angles on social media. That told him all he needed to know about how well things were going with the investigation.

"Anything?"

"The only interesting thing is that Amy and her father don't follow each other on any platform. They both follow Elizabeth Walton and Tremaine's foundation, but there's no direct contact between father and daughter."

"You think there was a rift between them?"

"Maybe, or they just respected boundaries."

That didn't sound like the Tremaine he knew, but he'd been in Afghanistan for most of the former governor's time in office. Maybe he missed a memo.

"Any other links between Amy and Elizabeth?"

"Just one. Cora Roche."

"Hmm," he said.

It didn't surprise him that Cora added Amy as a friend, oftentimes people make friends through other friends and online was no different. The part that surprised him, was that she'd been so bitter about Amy's abduction getting media attention when it turned out they were friends.

"What kind of things did Cora post on Amy's page?"

"Funny stuff. Animal videos. Pandas farting and scaring themselves, you know the kind of thing. No politics, nothing about men. Early posts are signed Cora with a single x after it."

"And later posts?"

Sato smiled. "No x."

He nodded but said nothing. Cora wore her heart on her sleeve, she didn't hide it away. She had been attracted to Elizabeth Walton, then to Amy. They were completely different people, but they were both out there getting things done, which was attractive.

It didn't fit anywhere into their case, so he discarded the information. Sato spoke again.

"Assuming we're right and Nathan Marks is behind all this. That would mean Amy would recognize him, right? I mean, he must've been hanging around her dad through most of her teenage years and it's only been four years since he was fired."

His brain jumped to the proof of life clip.

"Oh, man!"

"What?"

"Amy *did* recognize him, don't you see? She's been telling us the whole time."

Sato frowned. "How?"

"The video in the water tank, she told us who it was."

Sato had only seen the video once and had been blocking it out ever since.

"All I remember is she punched the glass."

"Then what did she do?"

"Uh. She pointed at the camera."

He shook his head.

"I thought the same thing, but it's the water. *Refraction*. It distorted what she was really pointing at, which was the glass and what she'd done to it."

"To the cracks?"

"To the *marks*."

Sato's face twisted.

"That's a little cute, isn't it?"

"If she was only pointing at the person working the camera she would've pointed once or kept pointing. Same if she was pointing through the lens at her dad. *You did this to me.* Or whatever. But she didn't, she pointed, then pointed again. Two distinct motions."

"I don't know how to feel about this, Johnny. If you're right, we wasted all that time finding the tank, then James Anderson, all because we missed a clue right in front of us."

"Anderson wasn't a waste of time, he got us to Marks."

"What about the tattoo?"

"I figure Marks flipped the video left-to-right. I bet there's a pale band of skin on his wrist. He knew Tremaine would recognize his watch, so he took it off."

"This is bad, Johnny."

"It is what it is."

His cell phone vibrated. A text from Gantz.

My office, now.

Word of his injuries had obviously filtered through the office network.

He found Gantz sitting on the edge of her desk, head tilted forward like she was looking at her shoes. The glass window that separated her from the detective bureau had a venetian blind on it. The blind was closed. It was never closed.

Gantz closed the door then came up in front of him.

"Lift your arms up."

He frowned but did so anyway.

She stepped closer, put her head sideways against his chest and her arms around his back, under his jacket. She hugged him tight, her arms squeezing where he'd been kicked repeatedly by the blonde woman. Maybe twenty seconds passed, then she released him and stepped back.

She avoided looking him in the eye.

"Don't say anything crass, okay? In fact, say nothing."

He said nothing.

"You didn't black out, right?"

"Right."

Gantz turned away from him to go around the other side of her desk. She sat and began to fuss with items on her desk, still not making eye contact. He figured she knew the truth by looking at him. Maybe the medic had ratted him out.

"If you blacked out, I have to take you off rotation until you're cleared."

"Ellen, come on. It looks worse than it is."

She glanced at his forehead and flinched. He understood, he'd seen himself in the mirror. He had a lump on his forehead the size of a hard-boiled egg cut down the middle. As bad as it was, it wasn't nearly as bad as it had been.

"This thing with Becker trying to eat his gun and now this. It's brought things into focus. I don't want to lose any of you assholes, you're important to me."

Coombes smiled. "Thanks, L-T, that means a lot."

She waved that away, then cleared her throat.

"Tremaine's paying the ransom at Echo Park Lake tomorrow at 10 a.m. The feds will have half their field office down there, but I want you and Sato there to witness it all go wrong on behalf of the department."

"Once they get paid, Amy's done. You know that, right?"

Her face showed nothing. She thought Amy was dead already.

"Where are you with Schofield?"

"Nowhere, the man's missing. Not really my department. If someone finds his body parts I'll get right on it, otherwise he's on the back burner."

"You said he was on the abduction footage."

"No, I said he was on the *recon* footage. He was already missing by the time of the abduction. If he was involved in this at all it was in the early stages only."

"Regardless, someone with a lot of pull wants Schofield located and you were the only detective acceptable to this person. Clearly, you made an impression on him last time you met. He doesn't trust anyone else with this."

"You know who this person is then?"

"Obviously. I'm just not allowed to tell you, nothing personal."

"That's great. What about Tremaine and Walton?"

"Your friend knows they are the priority."

My friend.

"Then I work Schofield on my own time?"

"I knew you'd understand, John. Open the blind on your way out."

Gantz, she was all heart.

As he walked back to his desk, he couldn't help but feel that his lieutenant had given him something he wasn't meant to have. She'd told him this mystery shot caller was a man and that it was someone he'd met before. Using the word *friend* without irony told him this person wasn't a fed. If Block wanted something done, he'd use Wallfisch, not him.

Coombes thought about who had the juice to pull it off and realized the list was longer than he might've liked. He encountered many powerful people in RHD, any one of which might have seen him as a known quantity. If one of them was in trouble they might prefer the devil they knew over one they didn't.

It didn't matter who this person was for him to do his job, but by concealing the man's identity, his mind was working on *that* mystery and the reason for the concealment, rather than where this douchebag with a shaved head and neck tattoos might be found.

Anton Schofield.

Coombes sighed just thinking about him.

He didn't care anything at all about Schofield. Whatever happened to him, he had no doubt that the man had brought it on himself. The same could not be said for Walton, who was an innocent. In broad terms, he was part of the problem and she was part of the solution.

Yet for some reason, someone on high thought Schofield worthy of his time.

He returned to his desk and, thinking of no new direction to move in with Amy Tremaine, turned back to Elizabeth Walton. Her murder book was thin to say the least, he'd allowed himself to be consumed by the hunt for Amy, just as Cora Roche had predicted.

The official crime scene photographs were now available so he spent the best part of an hour going through them, looking for something, anything.

Seeing her again upset him, because he knew he wasn't giving her investigation any justice. He'd come to the conclusion almost immediately that her case was tied to Amy Tremaine's kidnapping and had promptly dropped all other work on it, trusting that solving one case would solve the other.

Objectively, there was no link between the two crimes except for the personal relationship between them, and the timing of the crimes.

He looked again at the positioning of Walton's nightdress. The medical examiner had confirmed that she had not been sexually assaulted, but there was something about the image that didn't seem right.

To feel a little better about her case he did some paperwork, appending the autopsy and the toxicology report to the murder book. Keeping the book up-to-date had to be done, but he couldn't help but feel like Lester Crumb, padding out his no-show work with lots of filler.

He shook his head, disgusted with himself.

It occurred to him that he'd never seen Schofield's file and brought it up on the computer. Everything he knew about the man had come from Sato's telephone summary and from a terrified property manager who assumed he was a Nazi.

The file came up and he clicked through to the missing person's report. A woman called Jolene Kendal had reported Schofield missing.

A girlfriend, he supposed.

He imagined a young woman with sun-bleached blonde hair carrying a surfboard along a beach to her VW bus. A free spirit that had somehow fallen for this monster from Germany. As hard as he tried, the image didn't hold.

Coombes switched to the DMV database and typed in *Jolene Kendal*.

Five entries, none current.

Two were dead, three had changed name as a result of marriage. The last name on the list was now known as Jolene Jackson, the Chief of Police's wife.

Shit.

The only thing that made sense to him, was if Jackson and Schofield were linked somehow. Business, or personal. Neither option made any sense to him, the chief was one of the more squared-away type of individuals he'd met on the force.

"Time to go, Johnny."

He glanced up and saw she had her suit jacket on.

"See you tomorrow, Grace. I'm going to work a little longer."

"No, you're not. I'm driving you to the hotel, then, tomorrow morning, I'm driving you back here. I'm your chauffeur, Coombes. If you give me any noise about it I'll tell Gantz I found you passed out on the floor and that you were out cold for at least five minutes."

"You wouldn't."

"Try me."

Sato put on her hard, frosty look.

It wasn't like he was making any progress anyway. He sighed quietly and logged out of his computer. As his wife's control over him waned, it was being replaced by increasing control from Sato.

"I take it you're at the Hilton?"

"No, the Biltmore."

"Really. Why?"

"It's next to the abduction point."

"You hoping it's going to tell you something while you sleep?"

"Something like that."

They stood and walked over to wait for the elevator next to four other detectives. None of them spoke to each other, all keen to get home.

Between dating and marriage, he'd loved his wife for half his adult life. But no longer. It was like a light that had been turned off. One minute it was there, undeniable, the next it was gone like it never existed.

All she had become to him, was a memory that was ten seconds long. It was seared into his brain like security footage, cued up, ready for playback at any moment.

The memory was destroying him, but he couldn't feel anger toward her, because the love that was needed to fuel it was gone. The same could not be said for the lawyer. A rage like something he'd never known burned inside his chest. *Beat it, man.* What kind of person could do that to another and feel no embarrassment, no empathy.

A lawyer, obviously.

Coombes realized he knew nothing at all about him, not even his name.

The elevator doors opened and they all squeezed on, Sato casually pressing herself against him barely five feet from Block, their captain.

Block's shoulders were covered in dandruff, like a light snow had fallen during the day. All their captain had to do was turn his head to the side and look down and they were both done.

Of course, that was never going to happen.

They were invisible to Block, who thought only of how to work his way up the slippery pole to the Chief of Detectives post he coveted.

The elevator opened again and they all emptied out. A short time later, he was lowering himself into Sato's personal vehicle and leaning his head back into the headrest.

In his mind he pictured the lawyer tied to a chair, helpless. He imagined a long knife in his hand, like the one Marks had used on James Anderson. Then he imagined himself pushing the blade slowly into the other man's chest. Right through the heart.

Coombes shivered; his eyes blinking closed with the strength of it.

"You okay?"

He turned to Sato. "Not even close."

She frowned, then drove her car around to the exit and out into the night air. After a couple of minutes, rain began to fall in big splashes on the windshield.

It was the first rain in almost two months and he wondered if that would be a problem for Amy Tremaine. If Marks had her stashed somewhere that might not be waterproof; that might not have much air. A hole in the ground or a storm drain, filling with water. Her mouth bound tight to prevent screaming, yet screaming all the same.

Then there was the ransom drop.

One way or another, Amy didn't have much time left.

28

THEY RODE IN SILENCE for the entirety of the short drive between the PAB and the Biltmore, each of them lost in their own thoughts. The daylight hadn't started to go yet and the traffic was moving well. When they got to Grand Avenue, Sato stopped in a yellow zone in front of the hotel and turned to him, the engine still running.

"I guess I'll pick you up here tomorrow morning."

It sounded like a question, but his mind was elsewhere.

"Grace, when we searched Schofield's home we found no laptop, no tablet, no phone. That means either he took them with him when he left, or they were taken by whoever killed him. It's not like a guy like that didn't have at least a cell phone, right?"

Sato nodded.

"Right. And there's nothing but tumbleweed on his socials, so he's probably dead. I thought you didn't care about Schofield?"

"Oh, I don't. My interest is whether any of his missing devices are still operational."

She frowned. "Why does that matter?"

Coombes said nothing for a moment and instead opened his tablet. He opened Facebook and slid the iPad toward Sato.

"Bring up Schofield's profile."

She took out her notebook and flipped through some pages to where she'd written down Schofield's Facebook ID. She typed it in then passed the tablet back and leaned across the gap between them.

"See? Tumbleweed. No new posts. *Machine gun vs Watermelon*."

Coombes clicked on the button to send the other man a message.

"What are you doing, Johnny?"

"Chumming the water."

He typed into the message box.

I got your money, tell me where to meet.

He pressed send and glanced at Sato. Her mouth had fallen open.

"Now we wait," he said.

"*What* money?"

Coombes shrugged.

"A guy like this? There's always money."

"He'll be able to look at your profile."

"Have you *seen* my profile? It's so empty that even tumbleweeds can't get a foothold."

A three dot animation showed someone was writing back.

Who's this? I don't know you.

Coombes smiled and began typing.

A friend of a mutual acquaintance. I fix his problems. He's passed the settling of your so-called debt on to me.

Your friend's name?

Not on here.

We're done asshole.

I'll tell him I gave you the $50k either way.

The three dots appeared again, then stopped. Coombes began to count in his head. If there was no response by the time he reached twenty he would write another message. At eighteen, the dots started again.

First letter of your friend's last name.

Smart. He couldn't duck it a second time and there was no reason not to supply the information as it gave nothing away. Coombes exhaled slowly. If his hunch was wrong, at least he'd get confirmation that the chief was not involved.

"You had a good run there, Johnny, but he's got you."

Coombes typed a single letter.

J.

The response this time seemed faster.

Your friend is light. He owes me a lot more than that.

So much for the chief.

"Who the hell is J? What aren't you telling me?"

Coombes typed again.

This is all he gave me. You want what I have now, or wait for the whole amount later?

As before, he counted in his head while the other man considered the offer. This time, he decided to wait, however long it took. Appearing to be desperate would give the game away. Coombes got to thirty before the next response.

I'll get back to you.

There was no more text, no more animated dots. The other person was simply gone. Coombes swore under his breath. He closed his tablet and sat back, the palm of his hand resting on the black pseudo-leather case while he thought about what happened next.

"Are you going to tell me who this J character is or what?"

He stared through the windshield.

"I can't," he said. "Not yet."

She said nothing, but he felt her gaze shift from warm and pleasant to the heat of the sun through a magnifying glass.

"Don't make *the face* at me, Grace. I can't get this one wrong. We're talking career-ending implications and I can't put that on you."

"For the record, Coombes, there was no *face*."

He nodded as if chastised, as if what she said was true.

Coombes knew every line and curve of her face and the micro-expressions she made that she didn't even know about. Not because he was the world's greatest detective, or because they'd been partners for two years. It was because he loved her.

"Who do you think was on the other end? Schofield, or his killer?"

It was a fair question and one he hadn't considered. The answer came easily.

"Schofield."

"Me too. He's been in hiding then."

"Looks that way."

He saw the way she was looking at him.

"You want to come in and have dinner?"

"And then what?"

He recalled her comment about picking him up in the morning and understood. She wanted to stay the night. Perhaps imagining he had a fancy room, worthy of such a grand hotel. One with a four-poster bed and a bath with carved lion's paws for feet.

"Nothing, Grace. I plan on lying in bed with the light out with a bag of ice on my head. I don't want *that* to be our first hotel experience, do you?"

She nodded.

"Then I'll skip dinner as well if you don't mind."

"No problem."

29

On a map, Echo Park Lake looked like a toddler reaching up with one arm to give a high-five. At the point where the toddler's shoulder would be, a fountain shot into the sky giving romantically-inclined couples something to look at while they paddled small boats around underneath.

Coombes was not romantically-inclined, but had visited the lake with three different women on dates over the years, not to mention his soon-to-be ex-wife. Now he was here again with Grace Sato and twenty-two members of the FBI.

Fridays were the third-busiest time to visit the lake, which was probably why the kidnappers had selected it as the time for the ransom drop. Not so full that it made escape difficult, but full enough that there were plenty of potential human shields to hide behind should things go sideways. It was a situation that went both ways, however, as it allowed the FBI to place agents in the field posing as couples and tourists with cameras.

A command post had been set up in a truck-sized RV with blacked-out windows on Park Avenue which sat on the north side of the lake near the entrance to a parking lot. It practically screamed *FBI surveillance truck* and he wondered why the feds thought it blended in so well. Henderson was glaring at him.

"What did I just say, Coombes?"

"We're here as a courtesy, blah, blah, blah. I kind of drifted in and out to be honest, but I got the gist of it. This is your operation and you're the big dog."

The SAC's face turned red.

"Watch the tone. I need you here like I need piles."

Coombes smiled and said nothing.

Like his captain, Henderson thought being a leader meant cracking a whip and diminishing those underneath to appear in command. He saw no respect in the agents around Henderson, only fear or disgust.

They were hooked into security cameras around the lake which were piped into a bank of screens along one wall. He stood and watched the screens and the people on them that knew nothing of their image being captured.

The images were suspiciously sharp, which made him think he was looking at high-res Bureau cameras. On screen, squares appeared over faces.

Facial recognition.

Live tracking and identification of private citizens outside of an airport setting was the thin end of the wedge to Coombes. It was an abuse of power, and a gross invasion of privacy. This was not why he became a cop, and he could see that soon it would become the default in all surveillance systems.

Barnes approached and glanced at his forehead.

"You been making friends again, Coombes?"

He ignored the jibe and the boyish smirk that followed it.

"What's the plan here, Barnes?"

"Tremaine brings the ransom, hands it over, that's it."

"And Amy?"

"Released later, after they've got away. She's their insurance."

"You know she's dead, right?"

Barnes flinched. "We don't say that."

"What's to stop them asking for more money?"

"Our plan is to track the kidnappers back to their nest and scoop them up before they can even count the money. Playing their game pulls them out of the shadows and makes them vulnerable. We've got jack so far."

It was a fair point, and it didn't seem like they had any other moves left to play. But assuming your opponent was going to make a mistake was a recipe for disaster. Coombes was about to say so when his thoughts were interrupted by the deep throated rumble of a vehicle passing them on the street. The floor was vibrating through his shoes and he glanced up to the monitor covering the car park next door.

"Look alive people," Henderson said. "He's here."

A silver-gray Rezvani Tank rolled through the lot like a huge child's toy. The vehicle was a military-spec SUV with enormous tires and a boxy design that was supposedly bulletproof. Despite his natural cynicism, Coombes had to fight the urge to exit the command post and take a closer look.

Harlan Tremaine stepped out, followed seconds later by a tall muscular man wearing black combat trousers, black T-shirt, body armor, sidearm, and sunglasses.

Sato leaned in close. "Check out the beefcake!"

A red box appeared around his head. *ID: Classified.*

Henderson swore, but Barnes laughed.

"I'm guessing he's not one of yours," Coombes said.

"Oh my god, that's Chris Thorne," Barnes said. "He was involved in my last case before I joined the Bureau."

"What about him?"

"He's like all four horsemen of the apocalypse."

"Why's he listed as classified?"

"I have no idea."

Thorne scanned the lot with a slow movement of his head then reached into the footwell of the SUV and pulled out a large gym bag. The armored vehicle, the military bodyguard; Tremaine had taken steps to ensure that nobody was going to by-pass the exchange by intercepting the money before it reached the park.

A woman with tousled TV-anchor hair and an Italian suit stood in front of Tremaine and talked to him as she appeared to adjust the lapels on his jacket. When she was done, she glanced at the camera and nodded.

Tremaine's voice boomed out a speaker in the truck.

"One, two, one two. That loud enough?"

"Just speak normally, Mr. Tremaine."

"How about now?"

Even at a low volume his voice was unmistakable, as if it too lifted weights.

"That's perfect. Good luck."

Harlan Tremaine entered the park at exactly 10 a.m. and made his way toward a statue known colloquially as *The Lady of the Lake*, where the money was to be handed over.

The former governor was an unusual sight in sneakers, jeans, and a corduroy jacket with elbow patches. He looked like a history professor, except for his highly worked-out body that was visible through his clothes. Then there was the canvas gym bag in his right hand.

It looked heavy.

People turned to watch as he walked past.

"You know, Henderson, this case *has* been in the news."

"What's your point, Coombes?"

"Everyone in L.A. knows Tremaine; knows his daughter's been kidnapped. And here he is in a public space carrying a bag that could only be filled with millions of dollars. You're not worried he's going to get robbed by one of these people?"

Henderson's face twitched.

"The venue was not our choice, nor was the decision to pay."

Coombes knew what the twitch meant; it meant the FBI had been so focused on the kidnappers that they hadn't thought about third parties being interested in the money. In this part of town, it probably wouldn't matter. Not too many gang members taking a walk in the park. He turned to Barnes.

"What's the play here?"

"The bag's got a tracker sown into it that they'll not find in a million years. If they ditch the bag, we have another tracker in the middle of one of the stacks of bills. We also put a really obvious tracker in the outside pocket. They'll know we'll track the money, so we give them one to find. People tend to stop looking once they find what they're looking for."

Coombes nodded, his eyes drifting across to Sato.

"That's certainly my experience," he said.

Sato flashed a huge smile, her cheeks turning pink.

Tremaine was almost at the statue when a woman in tight navy leggings and gray hooded top ran toward him. Her face was down, looking at a cell phone. She was moving fast, her Nikes tearing up the distance.

Tremaine moved to the side to get out her way, but they seemed to collide anyway. It was a hard impact, and she ricocheted off his huge frame onto the other side of the footpath and onto her back. Her hood fell back and Coombes saw blonde hair swept back into a ponytail before she got it back into place.

It was the woman from the toy factory.

"Henderson, that's the bitch who set me up, we have to arrest her!"

"Not a chance, Coombes. We stay with the money."

The blonde got to her feet and shouted obscenities at the former governor before running on. Tremaine, though shaken by the incident, continued on to the drop point. After a dozen steps, he pulled a cell phone out of his pocket and held it to his ear.

Nothing was coming out of the speakers.

Henderson turned to a tech.

"What happened to the audio?"

"His mic must've been knocked off by the impact."

"All right, but why aren't we hearing this through the wiretap?"

The man flipped screens, then looked up.

"His cell's not in use. That's not his phone."

Tremaine turned away from the statue, headed south, toward a place renting swan boats to the romantics. Coombes immediately saw the problem. Half the agents were at the top of the park, with the other half split in two by the thin strips of land on either side of the lake.

Soon, 3/4s of Henderson's agents would be neutralized. Marks was good.

"The blonde put the cell in his pocket when they collided," he said.

"Thank you, Coombes. Even *I* worked that out."

He checked the screens, to see if he could find her again, but she was gone. Not grabbing her was a basic mistake. She could have told them where Amy was, which was probably the same location where Marks would return to when he got the ransom.

Looking at the camera angles, the logical escape vector for the blonde was to walk around the edge of the parking lot and past the truck they were standing in. The FBI had no cameras pointed at the command post, it being the last place they expected to find the kidnappers.

Onscreen, Tremaine was approaching Bellevue Avenue at the southern end of the park. Which meant he was about to leave the area covered by the facial recognition cameras and the undercover agents pretending to take pictures of downtown.

The operation was going about as well as Coombes thought it would and he was glad the Bureau would get the blame. Although somehow, he thought, they'd find a way to blame the LAPD. They always did.

"Where the hell's he going?"

Coombes turned to the SAC.

"Don't you get it? The exchange isn't in the park. They're going to bounce him around the city to shake off his tail and then take the bag. Don't you watch movies?"

Henderson's face and neck were scarlet, like he was about to explode. Somehow, he managed not to take it out on Coombes and instead turned to his own people.

"Give me something!"

"Tracker one, two, and three are active, as is Tremaine's cell."

"Pérez, Hill, and Caruso are converging on his position."

"U/C vehicles holding at outer marker."

Through the soles of his feet, Coombes felt Tremaine's SUV roar to life and tear out of the parking lot. Thorne was changing position. It was a good plan; the former governor was moving off the grid. Henderson grabbed a radio handset off the table.

"Airship 1, this is Henderson. Principal is leaving on foot toward the southern corner of Echo Park and Bellevue. Move into position. Over."

There was a pause before a reply came back.

"Copy. Moving into position."

They were down to one camera, which had been panned around to face Bellevue from the corner of Glendale Boulevard. They saw Tremaine at Echo Park Avenue turn and make his way toward the camera. At the bottom of the picture, the Rezvani Tank appeared driving half on the footpath, half on a grass verge. It was heading straight at Tremaine.

Henderson swore and gripped the top of his head with his right hand.

"This is Airship 1. We have acquired the principal. Incoming vehicle closing fast on the footpath. Advise."

Henderson picked up the radio. "Ignore vehicle."

"Say again. Over."

"Incoming vehicle works for principal, not target."

"Copy."

They watched Tremaine walk along Bellevue, toward the approaching SUV, his hand holding the cell up to his ear. Still getting instructions. It would be difficult for him to reject the idea that Marks was the kidnapper after hearing his voice again. Just then, Tremaine came to an abrupt halt and turned to face a car that was parked in a tow-away lane.

The rear window of the car was wide open.

It was clear the driver wanted him to put the bag into the back. Tremaine stood there, the bag still in his hand. Reluctant to give up the money, the leverage.

The passenger window opened.

"This is Airship 1. We see a gun barrel."

"Acknowledged."

Tremaine threw the bag into the rear seat of the car and backed away, hands in the air. He moved across the grass strip and the concrete footpath behind it until his back was against a chain-link fence that bordered the park. The space between the car and the former governor filled immediately with the Tank, which seemed to get covered in sparks.

Multiple agents called out.

"Shots fired, shots fired."

Marks pulled out of the tow lane and raced toward Glendale Boulevard. He turned south, opposite the camera position, the back end of his car swinging wide. As the lens turned to follow, Coombes saw Tremaine in the background climbing into the passenger side of the Tank which U-turned onto Bellevue to give chase.

"This is Airship 1. Target vehicle has stopped under the Hollywood Freeway. We have no visual. I repeat, no visual."

Inside the command post, one of the technicians called out.

"Tracker one, two, and three are down."

"What do you mean they're *down?*" Henderson bellowed.

"They all died at once, sir."

"And how would they do *that,* Phil? Did they take out a satellite?"

"A Faraday cage," Coombes said.

The truck fell silent. Eight faces turned toward him.

"Get a beach bag and cover the inside with aluminum foil. That's your cage. Now, all you have to do is put Tremaine's bag inside and close it up," Coombes turned his hands palm-up as if to reveal his hands were empty. "*Adiós, muchachos.*"

Henderson turned to glare at the technician. At Phil.

"Uh. He's right. That would work."

"You're saying our best trackers can be defeated with turkey foil?"

"Unfortunately, yes."

"Jesus Christ."

Henderson's cell phone rang and when he answered the van's speakers activated, filling the interior with echo-filled traffic noise. The call was from Tremaine.

"I'm under the freeway. The car's here, no sign of the driver or the money. My associate found a tarp on the ground and some tire tracks. Looks like the bastard had a motorcycle hidden here. He could be anywhere by now."

Tremaine cut the call before Henderson could say anything.

Coombes shook his head. The dirtbags had been given five million dollars cash and the best possible chance to escape. Amy's only hope now, as far as he could tell, was if the kidnappers were greedy and asked for more money. The fact that Nathan Marks had tried to kill Tremaine after the hand-off did not bode well.

Marks was smart. He'd know it was time to tidy up loose ends and relocate.

Amy Tremaine *was* the loose end.

He threw the truck door open and walked down steps to the ground, Sato following after him. The former governor was going to be headed back this way in a foul mood and as the representative of the LAPD's best interests, he wanted none of the blowback.

"Where are you going, Coombes?"

The SAC was standing in the doorway like a big, sweaty meatball.

"Like you said before. This is your operation. We'll leave you to it."

Coombes put on his sunglasses.

"If it helps, Henderson, I do have one piece of good news for you."

"Yeah? What's that?"

"He'll have to open the bag to get at the money. Soon as he does, all those trackers come back to life."

30

WITH NATHAN MARKS IN the wind, there was little else to do but return to the PAB and search for a new angle to take the investigation and update Gantz on the ransom drop. It occurred to him as they arrived at headquarters that he'd never looked into Olaf and Kirsten Dekker who, from Marks point of view, had cost him everything. If what was now happening to Tremaine now was payback for his betrayal, had he sought to extract revenge from Dekker?

As Coombes stepped onto the elevator, he imagined a second scenario, one where Kirsten Dekker had blonde hair and corpse-white skin. He pictured Marks' accomplice the way he'd seen her an hour earlier in the park.

The hooded top, the hair tied back.

Tremaine's description of Kirsten's takedown of Marks held the possibility of the whole thing being fiction. If it was, and he was far from convinced, then they were dealing with a pathological mind. Deeply twisted and disconnected from the result of her actions.

Either Marks was drawn to erratic females, or they were the same person. The elevator doors opened and they got off, headed for their desks.

Would Marks take Kirsten back after she'd destroyed his life? It seemed unlikely, but when it came to matters of the heart, you never knew. The whole thing could've been a smoke screen designed to throw her grandfather off the trail and allow them to be together.

Coombes sat at his computer and logged in without stopping to take off his suit jacket. He'd talked himself into something and he had to find out the answer before he could do anything else.

He Googled Olaf Dekker first, cheating himself out of an immediate answer. The page refreshed, and a long list of clickbait headlines appeared, linking to newspapers struggling to stay alive in the digital age. Everything was more lurid now, it had to be.

Olaf Dekker, philanthropist, shot dead at 89.

Murder in Bel Air, prominent industrialist assassinated.

Arms manufacturer samples own product.

Coombes sat forward, his focus sharpening.

He clicked on one of the news stories and saw it was four years old.

A man dressed as a landscaper had waited outside the Dekker residence in Bel Air for almost two hours, trimming the hedge. As Dekker's gates opened and he began to pull his Rolls-Royce out onto the road, the unknown 'maintenance worker' had moved in close and emptied a seventeen-round magazine through the side window into Dekker's head and chest at a range of less than five feet. When his weapon was empty, the killer dropped it through the destroyed window into Dekker's lap and walked calmly away.

Everything had been captured on security cameras.

Coombes pulled up the criminal database and ran a search for the status of the case and found it was listed as open-unsolved.

Interesting.

He returned to the news article and found links to two newer related stories. One was a somber obituary, the other a hatchet job on a man too dead to complain about it. Coombes clicked on the second of the two.

According to the journalist, Dekker was a vile man that had driven his wife to suicide and his daughter to an early death at the hands of a drug addiction. His entire wealth went to his granddaughter Kirsten.

This time the related story was about Kirsten. He clicked it.

"Shit," he said.

Kirsten Dekker had long black hair and golden skin.

He pushed his keyboard angrily away and sat back in his seat. Another dead end. He'd known it was weak all along and had deliberately avoided going straight to the answer to avoid the inevitable.

Coombes tilted his head down from the ceiling tiles and caught Sato looking at him. At his forehead. Maybe she was realizing that he wasn't what she wanted anymore. Sometimes all it took was a small change to make you re-evaluate the whole thing, like a fly sitting on a slice of pie. Her eyes dipped down to his and she smiled awkwardly.

"*Grace,*" he said, reproachfully.

"Don't hate me, Johnny, but I was thinking I could help out."

"Help out. What does that mean?"

"Put concealer on your bump. No one would know it was there."

"No one, or you?"

"I don't understand."

"I disgust you now. I could put a paper bag on my head if you like."

Her face hardened.

"Keep going, Coombes, and it'll be a *plastic* bag."

He smiled. Sato was adorable when she was frosty.

"This conversation right here...this is why we work."

"We're on the same page," she said.

"Right."

He stood and took off towards Gantz' office. He wanted to tell her how it went down before Henderson got in there first and gave some version where he was somehow to blame. No, he thought. The SAC would bypass her and go straight to Block. His captain would then come in hot like a missile and he needed his L-T ready with the facts.

WHEN HE CAME OUT of Gantz' office, he found Sato standing next to her desk like she was waiting for him. Something had happened, her eyes were bright and alive with something that could only have been a break in the case.

"What is it?"

"Fingerprint ID confirms Marks at Walton's apartment."

He nodded. The fingerprints being Nathan's seemed like a formality at this point and he wasn't sure why Sato looked so excited about it.

"Okay, and?"

"Becker has a line on the accomplice, the blonde."

He smiled. "*Excellent.*"

They walked across the detective bureau together.

"What you got for us, Mark?"

"Grace was telling me about the woman that was at the ransom drop and the warehouse where you were attacked. White, thirties, medium-build, blonde hair. It got me thinking about something Lester Crumb turned up while he was looking for Marks."

"You realize that description probably matches about a hundred thousand people in the city alone?"

"Oh, no doubt. Anyway, do you want to hear about it or not? Isn't this why you had me go through those boxes?"

"Do you have a picture for me?"

After the Kirsten Dekker run-around he wanted to cut to the chase. Becker looked put out, like his big reveal had been spoiled. He opened the file folder and laid three 8 x 10 photographs down on his desk in a pyramid shape.

It was her.

Coombes leaned over to cut the reflections of the strip lights on the high gloss prints. The blonde coming out a store, hair billowing out behind her; the blonde sitting in the driver's seat of a red convertible, head turned toward the camera, sunglasses half-way down her nose; finally, the blonde putting gas into the car with her feet set wide apart like she was playing baseball, her short skirt stretched tight.

He looked up, at Becker.

"You may tell the interesting story."

"All right. When Marks left Tremaine's employment, he setup a mail forward. Anything sent to him at Tremaine's mansion was re-directed to a post box in Reseda. Crumb asks the manager there about the owner of the box. The guy gives him a mouthful about privacy, which goes away real fast after fifty bucks go in his pocket.

"At first Marks was getting almost no mail but after two months this changed. Now he's getting a steady stream of envelopes and the manager has to move Marks to a bigger box. These new envelopes are sent direct to the box, they're not redirects from Tremaine's place."

Coombes nodded.

"Okay, then these other envelopes are something new. He has a scam going. These aren't offers of a credit card or whatever. People are sending him money."

"That's a fair assessment, particularly since the new envelopes have a different recipient listed. These are addressed to Nolan Sawyer, same box number."

Coombes smiled. An alias.

"So Crumb put it together. Why didn't he solve it?"

"The manager tells him that Marks collects his mail like clockwork every Thursday afternoon so Crumb sets up on the place, only Marks is a no-show. He's spent four and a half hours in his car pissing in his bottle and it's for nothing. Then the blonde shows up and picks up mail. On the off-chance that Marks sent this woman to collect for him, he followed her home. He gets a dark picture of a man through a window and that's it."

"What do you mean *that's it?*"

"The man he sees her with is not Marks, there's no question."

Coombes took a deep breath, his eyes closed.

"Here's what I think. She saw him following her and went to the gas station in an attempt to confirm his tail, or lose him. He stops across the street and takes pictures of her gassing up, not realizing he's been made. When she's back underway, she goes to meet with her brother or a friend, knowing that Marks is the real target."

"That sounds right."

"So did Crumb try and re-acquire Marks at the post drop?"

"No. He gave up. It seems that our friend Lester believed the manager was leading him on, hoping for more cash. He thought that the reason for the name change on the envelopes was that the box had a new owner and that he'd seen that owner with the blonde."

"You're joking."

"I am not. However, he did do one more thing before he signed off. He ID'd the blonde from the license plate of her car. Her name is Cassidy Stone."

Coombes blew out his cheeks.

He couldn't believe any ex-cop would fall for such a simple deception, but there was a reason why Crumb solved no cases. He was an idiot.

Becker still had something; it was there on his face.

"You ran her through the system, right? She's got a record."

"She served one third of a twelve-year sentence for abduction, child endangerment, false imprisonment, and assaulting a police officer."

Coombes recalled the ugly way the blonde's face had twisted in the toy factory. Telling Marks to finish him.

"She was going to ransom a child?"

"Uh, no. Apparently, she saw the child in a store and decided on the spot she wanted to be its mother. The father was looking the other way and didn't notice that the stroller he continued to push around was now empty. At least, not until he got to the checkout when all hell broke loose."

"No kidding," Sato said. "Did you locate her parole officer?"

Becker looked pained and shook his head.

"Sorry guys, I'm losing my touch. Give me a second."

Almost a minute passed before Becker had the information. Coombes read the parole officer's name off the screen. Dale Pellegrino. Of course it was.

"You want me to send his details to your cell?"

"Nah. I've dealt with this asshat before. I know where his office is."

"Do you need anything else? I'm done with the PI files."

Coombes thought about it.

"Take a look at this Nolan Sawyer ID. Maybe he managed to get a real driver's license with his false paperwork and it's got an address on it. Then see if you can find out what he drives. This prick might be keeping his head down, but for sure he has a vehicle."

"You got it."

31

DALE PELLEGRINO'S OFFICE WAS located in an unmarked building on Highland Avenue in Hollywood opposite Yum Yum Doughnuts and a French restaurant. It had taken them forty-eight minutes to get there for what should've been possible by telephone. Coombes wasn't too worried about the loss of time, as he knew that Cassidy Stone's home address would be located relatively close to her parole officer and they'd have to drive there anyway.

Sato parked next to the French restaurant and killed the engine.

"You called him an asshat before, how is it that you know him?"

"We kind of go back, him and me. First time I met him, I was still in uniform. We were called to a party some yahoos were holding. They'd gone onto the roof of their apartment and were getting a bit rowdy. Loud music, drinking, shouting at neighbors, that kind of thing. By the time me and my partner roll up, people were jumping from the roof into the swimming pool below. As we get out, I see Dale Pellegrino throw an eighteen-year-old girl off the roof screaming. Fortunately, she landed in the water, but it could easily have gone another way."

"Was this a Spring Break type of thing?"

"Hardly, Pellegrino's has ten years on me."

Coombes saw himself reflected on Sato's mirrored sunglasses. He looked rough and only some of that was down to what Nathan Marks had done to him with the baseball bat.

"You said the first time you met. I take it there were others?"

"They say lightning doesn't strike twice in the same spot, but it's bullshit. Some people live close to the flame. Probably what got him into this line of work in the first place, being close to those on the other side of the line. He's no fan of us lot that's for sure."

They got out the car and walked across the lot to the building opposite. Coombes thought again of his appearance in Sato's sunglasses.

He wasn't sleeping too well at the moment. Thinking about Amy Tremaine in some hellhole. Bound, gagged, and thinking she was about to die at any moment.

Marks and Stone had their money now, maybe she was dead.

If she'd been kept alive as an insurance policy to get paid, then what use was she now? None. She had changed from being an asset, into a liability. The smart move for Marks was to get out of town and start over somewhere new with another alias.

Without a prisoner and without Cassidy Stone.

They got off the elevator and walked to Pellegrino's office. Thoughts of his wife with the lawyer weren't helping him sleep much either.

Pellegrino's door was locked, the light inside off.

No note, no *Back in Five Minutes*. No pretense at fitting in. Wasn't fitting into society the man's job? Coombes looked at his watch. A quarter after twelve. For some, close enough to lunch time, particularly when you knocked off work at four-thirty as he suspected Pellegrino did.

"What do you think, Johnny? Out for lunch?"

He thought of the doughnut store. That was Pellegrino's speed. The world would come to an end before he could imagine the other man going into a French restaurant.

"I think you're right, let's take a look."

They got into the elevator and went back down again. This part of the job they always cut out of TV shows, he reflected. Nothing but shoot-outs and chases. He sure wished *he* could cut it out, but the world didn't work that way.

Sato was looking at him again, at his face.

"Eighteen days," he said.

"Until what?"

"Until the bruises fade."

The doors opened and he walked out, leaving Sato behind, pouting. He was getting fed up with the way she was looking at him, like she expected him to keel over at any moment. All the same, he was sure glad that Marks hadn't hit *her* with a baseball bat.

Yum Yum Doughnuts was busy, but Pellegrino wasn't in there.

He replayed in his head the last couple of blocks of their drive and nodded.

"I know where he is."

Coombes walked out onto Highland and less than a block down reached a British-style *pub*. Dale Pellegrino sat alone at the end of the bar, half a glass of beer in front of him watching a muted TV above the bar. A news channel. He sat on the stool next to Pellegrino and waited for the other man to notice.

"Detective Coombes. What an unpleasant surprise."

"I didn't think it was possible, Pellegrino, but you've put on weight."

"You're not looking too great yourself. Did you forget to pull the parachute cord?"

"Something like that."

"What do you want?"

"An address for Cassidy Stone."

"Yeah? What'd she do now?"

Coombes didn't want to get into details, so instead pointed at his own face. Pellegrino laughed and some of the tension seemed to ease between them.

"You know what? I believe it. Raised by wolves that one. She's not in our half-way house so I'll have to get her address from my files."

Pellegrino returned his gaze to the TV, their conversation apparently at an end.

"Thing is, we're kind of in a hurry here."

"Relax. Have a drink, looks like you need one."

"I tell you what. If we go back to your office right now and get her address, I'll contribute twenty bucks to your beer fund for the inconvenience. How's that?"

What he'd just said was technically a felony.

California Penal Code 67, *Bribery of an Executive Officer*. It would be hard to argue that trying to get a man to do his job to save a life had a corrupt intent, but a conviction could result in up to four years in prison. Coincidentally, the same length of time served by Cassidy Stone for abducting a child.

Pellegrino turned to him, unfazed.

"Make it fifty and you got yourself a deal."

Grace Sato touched his arm.

"Johnny, look."

On TV, the news had cut to helicopter footage of a bus being pulled over on a desert road by six black SUVs with pulsing strobe lights. Suburbans. The doors of the SUVs opened and close to thirty figures in FBI vests poured out and surrounded the bus, guns raised.

Three boarded the bus, while the rest stood ready. After a minute, the three figures came back out, guns holstered. One of them held a familiar gym bag. Even from the high angle, he could tell that it was empty, the sides concave.

The figure holding the bag appeared to notice the helicopter for the first time and looked up, his gray poured-concrete face showing nothing.

Combes turned to Pellegrino.

"Let's go."

32

THE CALL CAME THROUGH from Gantz while they were inside Dale Pellegrino's office picking up Stone's address. She confirmed that the FBI had regained the tracker signal and swooped in, capturing only the empty ransom bag with three GPS trackers still inside.

Because of the live broadcast of the failed arrest, not only did the FBI have serious egg on their faces, but Marks and Stone would know their handling of the trackers had been successful and they were in the clear.

"You know what this means, right John?"

Coombes turned away from Pellegrino.

"It means she's probably dead."

"No," Gantz said. "It means we probably only have the rest of the day before we can assume the kidnappers have left town and are permanently in the wind. Whatever you're working on, do it fast. Harlan Tremaine is calling me every half hour for updates."

In Marks' place, he'd already be gone.

"We're running down a lead right now. I'll get back to you when we have something."

Coombes disconnected and turned to see the parole officer with a thin smile and his hand out. Now he was the one looking down the barrel at four years in prison. Instead of cuffing him, he gave him $50 and got Stone's address in return.

"Since you and me are old pals, I'll give you something for free."

"What's that?"

"Stone's been coming here since she got out. Most of that time she's driven a 1978 Jeep CJ-5 Renegade, but sometimes she's taken to driving a 1969 Pontiac GTO. I figure the GTO belongs to whoever she's with now, because she seems more like a Jeep-girl."

"Thanks. Do you know what color the vehicles are?"

Pellegrino shook his head.

"I only know this much because when she comes in here she has keys and a cell phone in her hand. Her pants don't leave enough room for imagination, never mind a set of keys. We don't have much to talk about, her and me, so when I saw the old keys I asked her about them. Same when I saw she had a different bunch."

Coombes read the address he'd been given. Cole Avenue, a block past Wilcox. It was about half a mile from where they stood. He'd worked Hollywood before moving to RHD and he knew the area well.

"Do other ex-cons live at this address?"

Pellegrino glanced at his watch, reminding him they were using up his beer time.

"Sure. There's two other women there, but they won't give you any problems. I'm not stupid, I only put one lion in each enclosure."

"One last question. Is she employed?"

"She works at the storm drain place across the street from her apartment. It's a weird shift pattern, try the apartment first. Now, if you don't mind, I'm getting thirsty from all this talking. If you have any other questions, ask me them in the bar."

Sato parked on the street outside Cassidy Stone's address and cut the engine. She took off her sunglasses and tilted her head to look up through the windshield at the apartment building. Like Elizabeth Walton's apartment, residents' cars were parked in a secure garage beneath the building, which meant it was impossible to tell if either Marks or Stone were home.

"Johnny, how is it that this child-stealer lives in a better place than we do?"

"I guess because she doesn't have to pay for it, and because this place is still cheaper than holding three cons in cells at Chowchilla."

"That's not right."

He fed a stick of chewing gum into his mouth as they moved along the sidewalk.

Access to the apartment building was controlled by an intercom system which released the door when the resident pressed a button. Like most systems, there was a button marked SERVICES for deliveries and suchlike. He pushed it and the door opened immediately.

"Imagine if criminals knew about that button," Sato joked.

The interior was cool so they took the stairs. He thought through what he was likely to find in the apartment. The answer was nothing. This place was all wrong as a hideout for two kidnappers. A single vehicle parked across the exit and Marks and Stone would be trapped and forced to flee on foot. They wouldn't get two blocks.

Coombes got to the door and drew his weapon. He took the chewing gum out his mouth and stuck it over the peephole then knocked with his knuckles. A firm, but polite knock. After a moment a woman answered through the wood.

"Who is it?"

"Delivery for Stone," he said, then winked at Sato.

"Can you step back? I can't see anything."

"Ma'am? I *need* your signature."

He heard a sigh then the door opened on a chain. Through the gap he saw a young woman's face and a bare, pretzel-thick arm. Her face registered that he wasn't a delivery man and the door began to close again. He had his foot ready and it stopped the door from closing.

"Open up. LAPD. Detectives Coombes and Sato."

"Cassidy's not here."

"She's not here when I see she's not."

"Have you got a warrant?"

"You're parolees, I don't need a warrant. It's like searching your cell."

The woman's nose wrinkled. Either from remembering her incarceration, or from the effort of thinking. She unhooked the door chain and stood aside to let them in. Coombes saw that she was only wearing a T-shirt and underwear. The T-shirt didn't cover the underwear, or her last rib.

"Is there anyone else in the apartment, ma'am?"

"Just me. Cassidy and Rosalie are out."

He walked past her down the hall, sidearm aimed low in front of him, braced for Stone or Marks to come charging out one of the doorways.

He wasn't going to be blindsided twice.

"Hey," Sato said casually. "I have those exact same briefs."

"*Really?*"

"No."

He smiled. Sato was on a roll.

The apartment had two bedrooms. The living room had been converted into a third, which was now the largest bedroom. It was obvious to him that this room belonged to Stone.

She wasn't there.

He checked each of the other rooms, the bathroom, closets, anywhere big enough for Stone to hide in, then holstered his weapon. He went over to the woman who had answered the door, noting that she still hadn't bothered to put any more clothes on.

"I told you, she's not here."

"Yes, you did. Where is she? At work?"

"How would I know?"

"What's your name?"

"Riley Atkins."

"Do you like her?"

"No, she's a bitch."

"And crazy," Coombes offered.

"She humps her boyfriend with the door open." Atkins imitated the throes of passion, her hands moving dramatically through her hair. "Oh! Oh! Oh! Who *does* that? What a *skank*."

"If you help us, Riley, we help you. Stone goes away."

"She's not at work. When Cassidy works her shift, she stays here. She can walk across the street and she's there. When she's off-shift she stays with that asshole at his place."

"Which is where?"

Atkins shrugged. "It's up by Dodger Stadium, that's all I remember."

"Victor Heights?"

"No, but it's like that."

"Angelino Heights?"

"That's it."

"Street address?"

"Hey, I'm just glad when the bitch is gone."

Some of the houses up there were old and had basements. A good place to put Amy Tremaine. Echo Park Lake was virtually on the doorstep, which meant Marks was probably home ten minutes after the money exchange.

"What color is her Jeep?" Sato said.

"Red, like a tomato."

"And the boyfriend's car?"

"Black. I don't know what kind it is, it's old."

He nodded at Grace and they made their way back to the front door.

"There is one thing," Atkins said.

Coombes turned back. "Oh yeah? What's that?"

"They called it the orange tree house. It sounded like an upscale coffee store but it was obvious from the context they were talking about his place. It was so I wouldn't know where he lived, like I care where that witch parks her broomstick."

33

Sato pulled away fast, forcing their Dodge into a gap in traffic that didn't exist a moment before. They were closer to Marks and Stone than at any other time and he felt good. He called Gantz and summarized their last two hours. Beginning with the ID for the blonde; her address and vehicles from the parole officer; and an approximate address for Marks from her housemate. He thought it was solid detective work, but a long pause from her said otherwise.

"So. Angelino Heights, that's all you've got? Are you kidding me?"

Maybe he summarized too much.

"Angelino Heights *and* two museum-grade vehicles."

"That's thin and you know it. A defense attorney would eat us alive. It's certainly not enough probable cause for a search warrant. We can't arrest someone for having a classic car, even knocking on their door is pushing it."

"It's not a big area, Ellen. I'm asking for you to get someone to drive over and look for either of these vehicles. We're forty minutes out. By the time we get there a single person could have covered every street."

She seemed to think about it, like she needed one more push.

"A tomato-red Jeep. You could probably drive past the *end* of a street and see it. This would take ten minutes, max. How we proceed from there legally we work out later, but if we miss them, they're gone forever."

"I'm sorry, John. That's just not enough."

It wasn't what he'd expected her to say and rage overflowed inside him.

"Enjoy your next call with Tremaine, Lieutenant."

Coombes cut the call and tossed his phone into a cup holder.

"I can't believe she didn't go for that," Sato said.

"You and me both."

Their front passenger tire hit a pothole and the purple crease flashed through his vision again. His head tipped over to the side and his right arm fell off the door armrest. It was all he could do not to scream at the sudden pain in his head. His injury wasn't through with him, not by a long shot.

"Shit," Sato said. "These roads get worse every day."

Coombes tilted his head back on the headrest and spent the next couple of minutes controlling his breathing, his eyes closed behind his sunglasses.

He couldn't *wait* to get reacquainted with Nathan Marks.

They were on the 101 about half-way to Angelino Heights when his cell rang. Sato answered it using the in-car hookup before he saw the caller ID. He figured Gantz had either changed her mind, or was calling back to chew him out for the way he'd spoken to her before.

"Lieutenant?"

"No, it's Becker."

Coombes realized they hadn't kept him in the loop and felt bad.

"What's new, Mark?"

"*What's new* is that we just had a visit from a dozen FBI goons who ransacked your desk pretty good before Block got there and shut them down."

"Did they get into my computer?"

"They tried, but they got nowhere. I guess they expected to find your login in your desk drawer somewhere like on a TV show."

The only part of this he couldn't believe was Block coming to the rescue.

"Block really kicked them out?"

"Some SWAT guys happened to be in the building. They bounced those feds pretty hard; they won't be coming back any time soon."

"Did they take anything?"

"Far as I could see they left empty-handed but there were a lot of bodies. They might've taken photographs of whatever they wanted. It's messed up pretty good, John. All your Post-Its, your papers, your mail. It's like a tornado passed through."

He thought of Grace's carefully drawn Kenji letters.

"What about *my* desk?" Sato said.

"Yours is okay. They went straight to John's, knew right where it was, then got tossed out on their ass before they could get any further."

Coombes wondered how the feds would know where he sat.

"This is a desperate move. They put everything into those GPS trackers solving the case and have nothing left now it's gone to shit."

"No doubt," Becker said. "Question is, did you leave anything on your desk that would help them?"

He thought about it. The computer was protected by a password; his cell phone, tablet and notebook were all with him, which only left his legal pad.

"Yeah, my overview of the main players. They now have Marks. I didn't have time to add Stone's name or the Nolan Sawyer alias before I left. But that's all."

"I think we can assume that won't hold water, John. When the feds look at Marks on the database, their system will tell them who ran the last search. They'll figure the hand-off play and will look at who else I've been investigating. That'll give them the whole nut."

"Damn, you're right."

"Anyway, that's only part of the reason I called. You were right about Marks getting a real driving license from the DMV to back his fake ID."

His breath caught in his throat.

"You have his address."

"It's in Hollywood. Apartment 23, 731 Cole Avenue."

He felt himself deflate.

"That's *Stone's* address, we were just there. Her roommate says he's in Angelino Heights somewhere. We're headed there now."

Becker sighed.

"I've seen nothing linking them to property there."

That didn't surprise him, there was no point hiding out where you could be found.

"All right. Take a look at rental properties in the area, maybe he's in an Airbnb. Stay off any federal databases, assume you're burned. In fact, use your tablet. They'll be scraping your web traffic from your terminal's IP address."

"Leave it with me."

They disconnected. Although Becker had given him nothing, the call had given him an idea on how they could find Marks before they got there and had to drive up and down looking for his car. Sato glanced over at him as he worked on his iPad.

"You got something?"

"Maybe. We can't use Street View to look for their cars, but if there's an orange tree out front, I might be able to see it. I figure they weren't calling it *the orange tree house* because it had a jacaranda."

"Nice!"

On screen, he drove the camera car along the streets of Angelino Heights, turning the camera to look at the passing buildings. If the process helped them save five minutes, it might be the difference between catching Marks before he took off, or the difference between saving Amy Tremaine and finding her dead body.

It took him ten minutes to check every street and he had returned one definite and two possibles. Possibles, because he wasn't certain he was actually looking at oranges or if they were peaches or even some kind of flower. This being the case, he decided they should go to the definite first, despite the fact that it was the farthest away. Which also made it the closest to Dodger Stadium, which Riley Atkins had mentioned.

He returned his focus to the road in front of them.

They were approaching their exit and he realized their route would cover the same ground as during the ransom exchange, only in reverse. Glendale Boulevard, Bellevue Avenue past the bottom of Echo Park Lake, then on into the heart of Angelino Heights.

Coombes took out his Glock, ejected the magazine and saw the ammunition inside. He put it back into his gun and re-holstered it. Next, he checked each of his two extra magazines that he kept on his belt. Fully loaded. He expected nothing else. They'd been with him the whole time, there was no possibility that he'd been sabotaged somehow.

It was routine, and routine always calmed him prior to conflict.

"So, you putting this guy in the ground or what?"

"It might not be my decision, Grace. You know that."

They took the exit ramp off the freeway.

"I mean, it's not like you don't need a new car, right?"

She remembered Tremaine's offer. He turned to her and said nothing.

"If you were *that guy*, Johnny, I wouldn't be with you."

"I'm not going to face Marks with a fruit basket or a bunch of flowers. I'm lucky to still be alive after our last meeting. You know what he did to those guys in the veterinary hospital. You want me to be like the guy eating nothing but smoothies through a straw?"

"Of course not."

"Then I don't know what you want from me."

"Yes, you do."

They moved along Bellevue Avenue in silence.

"By the way, I saw what happened back there when we hit the pothole. You almost passed out. You should be in hospital, John. Is it Amy that you're doing this for, or is it pride?"

When Sato called him *John*, he was in the dog house.

"I don't know how to stop," he said, almost to himself.

"What you said about the FBI putting everything into the GPS trackers?"

"Yeah?"

"What if we've done the same? What if Amy Tremaine's kidnap has nothing to do with Elizabeth Walton's murder?"

"Trust me, I know."

They were quiet for a moment before Sato spoke again.

"You want to tell me where we're going?"

"Turn left at Douglas Street then right at the intersection with Allison Avenue, heading toward the stadium. It's a couple of houses in."

34

Coombes' mouth was dry, his vision sharp. His heart rate was spiking as the adrenaline flooded his blood stream. Marks had got the better of him the last time they met and he was determined it wouldn't happen again. He spoke to Sato, his gaze fixed on the road.

"Regardless of what we see parked outside, I want you to keep going then make a U-turn at the end of the street and double back so we can watch the house from the hidden side."

"And then?"

Coombes shrugged.

"Simple. Confirm they're in, call for backup."

She shot him a look of disbelief. He supposed that was fair, he wasn't exactly a calling-for-backup kind of guy. There was no satisfaction catching bad guys if someone else did the heavy lifting for you. He lived for the *click-click-click* of handcuffs tightening around some dirtbag's wrists, their face pressed into asphalt. Sato reached the intersection and turned.

Time seemed to slow down.

The first thing they saw was the tomato-red Jeep.

The second was a man getting out of a black car.

It was Nathan Marks.

Marks slammed the door, locked it, and turned toward the house. His body moved easily in the manner of someone with nothing to worry about, someone with their own theme tune in their head. At the last second, he glanced across and saw their Dodge rolling slowly down the street toward him. His eyes locked on first the car, then on Sato behind the wheel, before finally landing on Coombes.

Time returned to normal speed.

Marks' body tightened up, and instead of running back to the GTO as Coombes expected, he made a break for the house and went inside.

"Shit!"

"We are *so* made," Sato said.

"Park in front of his car, box him in."

"On it!"

She swung across the road, blocking the Pontiac from moving forward and hit the strobes on the light bar that sat next to the rearview mirror.

They emptied out, leaving both doors open, and drew their weapons. He was on the sidewalk side of the car, which offered poor angles in the event of a firefight, so he moved around the hood to join Sato on the driver's side.

They moved along the side of their car, then along the side of the GTO. Marks' muscle car forced him to bend low to use it as a blind. When they got to the hood, Coombes had to get down on his hands and knees and work his way along to look around the fender.

The kidnappers' house, an American Craftsman, was set back from the sidewalk and raised up on a bank of earth to combat the steep angle of the street as it dipped down onto Sunset. A long flight of concrete steps led up to the front door, with the orange tree to the left.

He heard no movement from the house and the street was quiet. Coombes drew back from the fender and sat with his back against the rear wheel. He took out his cell phone and texted Becker.

Marks @ 1390 Allison Ave. Run background.

He put his cell into silent mode then put it back in his pocket. If the FBI were intercepting his text messages, so be it. By the time they scrambled HRT and got to his location, it would all be over anyway.

Sato leaned in close and spoke softly.

"You think he'll try to slip out the back?"

"It's possible," he said. "We're close to the corner, so there's probably a way out over a fence onto Douglas, or down, through a lot of back yards, onto Sunset."

Sato watched him closely, her face close enough to his that her breath was landing on his cheek. The adrenaline in her body had caused a rose tint to spread across her perfect doll-like face and her pupils to expand in her dark brown eyes. He'd seen a similar look on her before under very different circumstances and he glanced away to keep his mind in the moment.

They needed to draw Marks out quickly, he thought. Not give him time to think about escape, or about digging in like a tick for a prolonged stand-off. They needed this over, fast. The longer it went on, the more danger Amy's life would be in.

"All right," he said. "I've got an idea but it's a bit of a Hail Mary. I want you to cover me and be ready to shoot him if it goes sideways."

Sato said nothing.

She didn't want to shoot anyone.

"Grace, I need to hear you say it."

"I'll murder anyone to protect you."

Not quite what he was going for, but it would do. He stood and walked out, away from cover, along the middle of the street. When he was standing opposite the kidnappers' house, he turned square-on and put his Glock back in his holster.

Putting his gun away was a demonstration of power. He didn't need the gun, because it was already over.

The other man stood watching at a large window.

"Hey, Marks!" Coombes shouted. "You're *done*. We have the whole area locked down. Come on out with your hands up."

Marks stared at him through the glass.

The ex-Marine was projecting power in a different manner, with a thick silver pistol that extended down his leg past his knee. Even at this range, Coombes could identify it. A Desert Eagle .50. He'd heard the weapon could shoot through an engine block so he doubted his standard-issue LAPD bulletproof vest, currently in the trunk of the Dodge, would provide much protection.

Marks turned his head to the side.

He was talking to someone with him in the room.

Cassidy Stone, he presumed. Time to up the ante.

"End this like a man, Marks! Not like a mouse hiding in a hole!"

Marks twisted sharply away from the window and a second later the front door opened and in a flurry of movement he saw Marks appear at the top of the steps, his arm locked around Amy Tremaine's neck, moving her in front of him like she was weightless. Her long brown hair hung across her face and down the front of her cobalt-blue shirt, her head tipped forward by the pressure of the Desert Eagle against the side of her head.

"Get back, or the bitch dies!"

Through the tangle of hair, Amy was sobbing. He couldn't make out words, just high-pitched squeals of terror. Coombes held his hands up, emphasizing the fact that he was unarmed. Marks came down the steps toward him, throwing glances at Sato, but apparently not taking her as a real threat.

"You can't still believe there's a happy ending here, Marks. Let Amy go before something happens that can't be undone. I *know* you aren't going to hurt her; you've known her since she was twelve. You're practically her uncle."

Marks laughed and pressed the gun harder than ever against Amy's head.

"Yet she said nothing to defend me when that woman was spreading her lies about me. Just like her dad. These people threw me under the first bus that came along, they owe me. I owe them nothing. You know I'll do it,

Coombes, I'll do it even if your partner shoots me. A gun like this, it makes a real mess. Now back off."

Marks was at the bottom of the steps now, directly across from him.

Coombes backed away, using the movement to distract from the fact that he was lowering his hands to his sides. He stepped up onto the sidewalk opposite Marks. Backing off also increased the angle between himself and Sato. If Marks turned to aim at her, Coombes was confident he could shoot him before the other man could pull the trigger.

"Your mother thinks you're dead, Nathan."

"Nathan *is* dead. I'm Nolan now."

The mention of his mother had hit home.

"She's heartbroken. All she lives for is to see you again."

"Whatever, man."

Marks dragged Amy up the street to the Jeep, which was pointed toward the intersection. He matched pace on his side of the street and drew his weapon again. Sato moved around the back of the Pontiac to the same side as Marks, covering the opposite side.

It was no longer possible for Marks to use Amy Tremaine as a shield, if he turned his hostage toward Sato, Coombes could turn his head into a pink mist.

Once again, Marks chose him as the threat and held Amy between them.

"We're leaving, Coombes. I suggest for her sake that you stay here."

"She's only good to you alive. Your insurance disappears the second that changes."

Marks pushed Amy roughly across the driver's seat into the passenger seat, his arm extending so the end of the gun barrel remained within inches of her cowering head.

"Then I guess we have a stalemate, Detective. But we *are* leaving."

The framework of the Jeep now blocked Coombes from taking Marks out with a headshot and anything else probably guaranteed Amy would die as the last act of a bitter man. He glanced at Sato to see if she had a shot, but he could tell that she had no intention of shooting.

He glanced back at the house, expecting Cassidy Stone to come out, but saw no sign of her. The Jeep roared to life, then left six feet of rubber on the asphalt as it took off toward the intersection. Coombes ran into the middle of the street and raised his Glock, but the Jeep turned sharply right, putting Amy between them as Marks turned onto Douglas.

Coombes wanted to scream, but there was no time.

They ran back to the Dodge.

Sato spun the car around and took them back to the intersection. The Jeep was out of sight, but it wasn't hard to work out where it was going. Marks was making for Sunset on the other side of the triangle.

The intersection with Sunset Boulevard was clear, but they could see the Jeep continue straight on the other side of the crossing. Coombes frowned. For sure Sunset was less than ideal as an escape route, but Marks was headed toward dead ends.

"Where the hell is he going?"

Sato still had the strobes on and she used them with the siren to push her way across the busy road. When it came to heavy traffic and slower speeds, she had him beat. Her driving was downright muscular, if not insane.

They were on the other side now, on the section of Douglas Street that headed towards Elysian Park. They'd lost sight of the Jeep as they'd crossed Sunset.

"I'm sorry, Johnny, I had the shot. I couldn't do it."

"You did the right thing, Grace. It was a tough shot and it needed to be perfect."

"But you could've made it."

He turned and was surprised to see that she was upset.

"I was in the Army, Grace. My head is in a different place and always will be. Anyway, there's a reason why you're driving right now. I might have missed him and hit her."

The road twisted to the right but he remained looking at her. Beyond her face he saw a plume of dust rising and in the middle of it, the rear of the Jeep.

"There! He's cutting across the park!"

She hit the brakes and backed up fast one-handed, her head twisted around to look between the seats. In front of them was a utility entrance to Elysian Park. It was protected by a heavy steel bar that was chained in place. On each side sat a barrier like at the sides of a highway. On the left-hand side, the highway barrier ended next to a plant bed which Marks had driven over with the large wheels and ground clearance of the Jeep.

Sato took a moment to line up the Charger to the same damaged area and floored the throttle. There was a bang and the front of the car was kicked up in the air, followed by a dull scraping noise that moved from the front to the back as they passed over the flower bed before landing on the far side. The wheels caught on the paved road beyond and they shot forward into the park.

The road was little more than a wide footpath that wound through Elysian Park like a twisting snake and Marks had again vanished from sight.

This was his plan all along, Coombes thought.

Marks had explored the area, looking for ways he could escape if he was ever found. It might even have been one of the reasons that he'd chosen the house. The curving road came to an end at another steel bar, only this one lay open. An intersection. Scott Avenue. Left to Echo Park, Right to Stadium Way and on to the I-5.

"What do you think, Johnny?"

"He's trying to lose us, right? He figures his best chance of doing that is to be where we aren't looking. Go straight, stay in the park."

She looked across at the trail that continued opposite.

"You sure about this?"

"It's what I'd do."

They crossed Scott Avenue. On the far side, confirming his theory, tire tracks went around another steel bar. Sato followed them and within twenty seconds the Jeep appeared in front of them. It looked like Marks had eased off the gas to prevent his dust plume giving away his position because he suddenly accelerated again, the pursuit back on for real.

In these conditions, the Jeep had a clear edge. Four-wheel drive, high ground clearance, large all terrain tires, and a suspension setup perfect for off-road driving. Marks began to pull out a bigger and bigger lead.

"He's getting away," she said. "We need to call it in."

He remembered his earlier statement about calling in backup like it was a fragment of a long-forgotten dream.

"We don't need to catch him, Grace. Think about it, we just need to maintain line of sight. As soon as he makes his move back onto normal streets, we'll eat him alive."

The next crossing was Academy Road.

Marks did the same thing as before and drove straight across. Only this time, he drove the Jeep onto the foot trail next to the the road they'd been using. It was steep and narrow and intended for walkers. A sign prohibited cycling.

Sato braked, bringing them to a stop.

"Johnny, it's too steep, we can't follow."

He swore and punched the dashboard. The Jeep was already gone.

"All right, take the park road we were on before. Line of sight, remember? We can follow them from the side, maybe they won't see us."

Sato put the Charger in gear and resumed their pursuit.

"We've lost too much time, they'll be long gone."

"I don't think so. We'll be able to go a lot faster."

There were trees between the trail and the paved road and he saw no sign of the Jeep. It was possible, he thought, that the former Marine might anticipate this move and double-back to Academy Road. They could've lost them already.

Suddenly the trees fell away and a large empty area of dusty earth opened up. In the middle of it, was the Jeep sparkling in the sunlight like a jewel. The trail and the road were farther apart than he'd hoped and it seemed like Marks was making good on his escape.

The Jeep was tilted dramatically toward them as it traversed the slope, barely clinging to the side of the hill. Sato slowed to a stop so they could watch the other vehicle. It was rolling along at a walking pace. The downhill side was the passenger side and he saw Amy Tremaine's blue shirt as she gripped the windshield pillar to prevent herself from falling out.

She glanced at them, then sharply back toward Marks. A second later, the Jeep turned up the slope toward Park Drive. The windows of the Dodge were rolled up, but the sound of the Jeep's engine could clearly be heard, straining to push itself up the hill.

Dust and stones flew out the back as the big tires tore up the earth, but it was struggling to stay in place.

Realizing his mistake, Marks leveled out the Jeep again. Then he did something Coombes wasn't expecting.

He stepped out onto the side of the hill.

Without a driver nailing the throttle, the Jeep slid rapidly sideways, then began to roll dramatically down the slope toward them, a thick cloud of dust filling the air behind it. The Jeep had almost stopped rolling when he saw Amy Tremaine's body shoot into the air and land like a bag of rocks on the side of the hill.

When his eyes returned to the top of the slope, Marks was gone.

For a second, neither of them said anything.

"Call it in," he said. "I'm going up there."

He saw Amy on the ground. It didn't look good.

If she was alive, there wasn't much time.

Coombes picked his way up the slope, his shoes slipping on small stones and the dry, dusty earth. His eyes moved between where he was placing his feet to where Amy Tremaine's body lay the whole way. He slipped twice and had to catch himself with his hands both times to avoid hitting the ground. He kept going, his only focus being Amy.

He willed her to move. To roll over, to twitch a finger, anything.

Her face was turned away from him, back up the slope, as if she had turned to watch Nathan Marks run off. A man she'd known since she was twelve. A man who had sacrificed her to escape like she was no more to him than a bug stuck to his windshield.

Her blue shirt was dirty and torn from being thrown out of the rolling Jeep. A patch of dark blood had spread across one side, over her kidney. His eyes fixed on Amy's back as he closed the remaining distance.

The shirt wasn't moving as she breathed, it was still.

He knew she was gone before he got there.

For four days Coombes believed he could save her. Instead, he'd been the reason for her death. They'd given chase, forcing Marks to drive the way he had. Faster and faster, over terrain that didn't support high speed chases. This was on him.

He paused for a second, putting off the moment.

Finally, he reached down and rolled her over.

35

COOMBES LOOKED AT THE dead face in front of him. Not quite cold yet, but very far from alive. When she hit the ground, her right cheekbone had collapsed and her jaw had been broken and pushed to the side. The damage to her face, coupled with the missing spark that came from being alive, meant that it took him a second to understand what he was seeing.

Behind him, Sato shouted up.

"Is she dead?"

He stood and turned toward his partner.

"It's not Tremaine! It's Stone!"

"Huh?"

"It's Stone! She dyed her hair."

Sato said something he didn't catch; it might've been Japanese.

He swept his head across the top of the hill, looking again for Nathan Marks. The park was peaceful, but not silent. He could hear traffic on the I-5 and, closer in, the *tick, tick, tick* cooling sound coming from the destroyed Jeep engine.

Coombes walked around the SUV's debris field.

Broken glass, plastic, and twisted metal.

There was no sign of a bag capable of holding five million dollars. For sure neither of them had been carrying a bag when they came out the house and he hadn't seen one flying out of the Jeep as it rolled over.

Simple logic dictated that Marks didn't have the money with him because it hadn't been at the house. If the money had been at the house, it would be here. Why would he have the money somewhere else if they were preparing to leave?

He looked back down at Cassidy Stone's face.

She looked radically different as a brunette. Coombes realized that she'd also dyed her eyebrows, before they barely seemed to exist. The dark eyebrows made her face seem more three-dimensional yet also less real against her pale skin. He remembered the way Stone's face twisted while she was trying to bait Marks into killing him.

He nodded his head, understanding.

The money isn't here because Marks didn't trust her.

Either he thought she'd kill him for it, or that she'd steal it the second he fell asleep. So he hadn't brought it back to the house after the pick-up, he'd stashed it somewhere safe.

Somewhere she didn't know about, or have access to.

They didn't know where that was, they were going to have to track him down all over again and he didn't see how they were going to do it. He thought about cell phones, the gold standard in tracking someone down.

Stone wasn't carrying a cell; he didn't even have to pat her down. As her parole officer had said, there was no room for anything in her pockets. The material of her pants was so thin and tight he could see the shape of her underwear through it. There'd been no phone in her hand when Marks had brought her out in his fake-hostage play, which meant he'd carried it for her. It wasn't going to be anywhere around the crash site, it was with Marks.

He was done here.

With his back toward Sato, he took a photograph of Stone's face, careful to crop out the blue shirt. He checked it, then sent it to Tremaine. A message came straight back.

Who's that?

Coombes typed: *The getaway driver.*

What about Amy?

242

Still working on it. Hang tight.

Coombes stowed his phone and made his way back down the hill to where Sato stood. If Marks had brought a rifle, he could've shot them both where they stood, but they were well outside the effective range of any pistol.

"What do you think, Johnny?"

"Honest opinion? He's gone."

"In his place, where would you go?"

"I've seen no sign of the ransom money. I figure his only goal is to get the money and leave town. Nobody walks away from five million."

Sato looked at him, her hand shielding her eyes from the sun.

"Maybe he left it at the house? He came into the park hoping to lose us and planned to double-back to pick up the money when it was safe to move it."

It wasn't how he'd imagined it, but it made sense.

"Which explains why he took the Jeep, not the GTO."

Coombes nodded. It still didn't feel right, but he had nothing better.

"All right," he said. "Let's check your theory. If we find the five mill, nobody needs to know about it. We'll settle down on an island somewhere and grind out seven beautiful babies."

Sato pretended not to hear and pointed up the slope.

"What about her? I already called it in."

He thought again about Cassidy Stone. She hadn't just been pretending to look like Amy, she was wearing her shirt. The one she had been wearing when she was abducted, and the one she'd worn in the water tank.

Did that mean Amy was dead?

"We'll check the house, then come back. Amy's the priority. Stone isn't going anywhere."

36

THEY PARKED ON KENSINGTON Road, a street over from Allison Avenue. If Marks returned to the orange tree house for the ransom money, Coombes didn't want him to know they were there until it was too late. He paused as Sato stepped out the Dodge and knocked back more Advil while her view of him was obscured. It was the move of a junkie, he thought.

Allison Avenue was quiet, with only a delivery truck moving along it.

"What's your plan here, Johnny?"

"For what?"

"Getting in. This isn't Stone's residence; we can't use the parolee work-around to search it and we don't have a search warrant."

Coombes grunted. He hadn't been thinking about the legal aspect of entry, he'd been thinking about five million other things, all tied up in neat bands in groups of one hundred. The joke he'd made about finding the money and keeping it was not such a joke, he reflected.

They were at the address now. He opened the gate and walked up the path to the front door. The entryway of the house concealed their position from the rest of the street, giving him time to think in case Nathan Marks approached.

He took out his cell and put Becker on speaker.

"What's happening, Coombes?"

"Marks made a break for it through Elysian Park and rolled the Jeep he was driving down a hill. Stone's dead, he's in the wind."

"Is he injured?"

"No. He stepped out the Jeep and left her to her fate."

"What a piece of shit."

"Yeah. Look, we're back at the house on Allison. Did you find out if it's rented to Marks or to his alias?"

"I checked that. It's owned by a Mavis Kent, formerly of Providence, Rhode Island. She's in her late eighties and the chance of her renting her home is close to zero. I also checked for a familial link between her and either suspect and found nothing."

"Thanks, Mark."

He disconnected and looked at Sato.

"We might have to cut Becker in on the five mill."

"I can't even tell when you're joking anymore."

Coombes nodded. Sometimes he said the truth as if it were a joke, while other times he said a joke as if it were the truth. The gap between each seemed to be narrowing. It was getting hard to take reality seriously.

"I think we need to perform a wellness check on Mavis Kent."

"Agreed."

He pulled open a screen door and Sato held it while he tried the door handle. He always tried the handle and it never worked. This time, the door opened. He glanced at Sato, then drew his weapon.

Could Marks have beaten them back here?

He stepped into the house, moving his feet carefully to minimize sound. Sato followed, her own sidearm drawn. She closed the screen door gently against the frame and then the front door.

It was silent, the air hot and musty.

Just inside the door was a dent in the wall and a dark speck that might've been blood. Underneath, the bare wooden floorboards looked like they had been cleaned for several feet in every direction.

He pointed at the area to Sato and she nodded. Maybe the old lady had dropped a glass of grape juice.

Maybe someone had dropped the old lady.

Despite it being official policy for wellness checks, he didn't announce their presence.

Opposite them, was the kitchen at the back of the property. To the left, stairs up to the second floor, and on either side, half-closed doors to what he assumed would be a bedroom and a living room.

There were no sounds of Marks moving about or of Amy Tremaine trying to signal for help. It was so quiet that he could hear his own heartbeat.

They worked slowly, clearing each room, providing cover for each other as they moved. The house was a mess. It looked like Mavis Kent had owned the property for a long time and done no maintenance on it the entire time she'd been here. The house was about ready to be torn down. The stairs creaked dramatically as they moved to the second floor.

If Marks was in the house, he'd hear it.

At this point, the ex-Marine would still believe he could pull it off, that he could get to the money and disappear. Marks would kill both of them to get to that point, two last obstacles before freedom. Coombes moved his Glock to cover the second-floor landing in case Marks tried to ambush them. They reached the top of the stairs. Nothing.

The air was still and hot with dust hanging in it.

There was no air conditioning in the house and he guessed that Mavis Kent would look like a sun-dried raisin whether she was dead or alive.

The first door they came to was a bathroom. It was empty, with no sign of the ransom or foul play.

They moved on.

There was only one other door, the master bedroom. The door was wide open and he was able to clear half the room just walking along the hall.

Nathan Marks wasn't there, but he had been. His clothes lay on the floor where he'd pulled them off and in bags he'd been using to store them. Nothing had been taken out and hung on hangers in a closet. Marks had only been here for six months, he'd get to it eventually. Stone was no better; he could see her undergarments tossed aside like a tree dropping leaves.

Coombes holstered his weapon.

"Based on the smell in here, Marks and Stone were on intimate terms."

Grace nodded. "That's one way of putting it."

"All right, let's go. We need to get back to the crash site and give our statements."

They went back down the stairs.

It had taken too long to clear the property. It was obvious why, it was because of his relationship with Sato. His emotions were affecting his efficiency, he couldn't risk letting anything happen to her.

"Johnny, check it out."

The floorboards next to the stairs had a scrape about two inches long next to the wall. The scrape had a slight curve. He studied the wall and saw a keyhole. No handle, just a keyhole. He worked his way along the wall and found two recessed hinges. He made his way back to the keyhole and found a hidden lip he could put his fingertips into and pulled.

"It's locked. Stand back."

Coombes slammed the heal of his shoe against the keyhole. The wood was old and gave way on the first kick. He pulled the door open and looked inside. It wasn't a closet as he'd assumed, there were stairs down to a basement.

"Stay here," he said.

"What are you talking about?"

"Grace, if Marks comes back, I don't want us both down there. I need you to cover my back. If you prefer, *you* can go down and *I'll* stay here."

Sato didn't like that much either. She shook her head.

"This better not be a cock-block, Coombes."

"Wouldn't dream of it," he said.

A domed metal light switch sat just inside the doorway. He flicked it on and a dim light came on below. There were no shouts of fear or relief from

Amy Tremaine. He moved down the stairs. The ceiling was low and he had to lean forward to fit. Whoever built the house couldn't have been much over five-six tall.

There were no foul odors, just dust and cobwebs.

He reached the floor and stepped onto unfinished concrete. Part of him had expected to find a dirty mattress on the floor and a chain attached to the wall. Instead, he saw about eighty empty Mason jars lined up on a table. This hadn't been a prison, just some old lady's storage area. People from Rhode Island like to preserve food, he thought.

An old furnace sat against the wall on one side of the table and a chest freezer sat on the other. There was a suitcase on top of the chest freezer. His eyes fixed on it. The suitcase was easily big enough to hold five million dollars.

A smile formed on Coombes' face.

He walked over to the suitcase, his head dipped to avoid the ceiling. The case was old like everything else. It had been down here already; it hadn't belonged to Nathan Marks. He flipped open the catches and looked inside.

His smile disappeared.

It was full of identical hardcover books, packed in tight. He recalled a large empty space in the living room bookcase.

He lifted one out, then another.

They were encyclopedias, different letters of the alphabet. Heavy. Nobody used books like this anymore, they'd been replaced by the internet. As soon as something was published, it became out of date.

Coombes looked at the freezer underneath and his heart sank.

The bag was a weight.

He pushed the suitcase to the side and let it crash to the floor, books spilling out. It wasn't going to be five million dollars inside the freezer, he knew that much. He lifted the lid and a light came on brighter than the bulb in the basement ceiling. Coombes stood looking in for a moment, wishing he'd left well enough alone.

Sato spoke from the bottom of the stairs behind him.

"Is it Amy?"

"Mavis Kent."

"You think she was alive when they put her in there?"

The tips of the old woman's fingers and thumbs had been torn away from frantic scraping against the lid.

"Looks like it."

"That's horrible."

He closed the lid again to protect any evidence.

There was nothing here for Marks to return for, it was like he'd originally thought. Marks had kept the money away from Stone and wherever that was, was probably also where he'd been keeping Amy Tremaine. When he made it back there to pick up the money, when he was certain he had no more use for Amy, he'd kill her and disappear.

Coombes had no idea where Marks was, or where he was going next.

37

THE PICKUP TRUCK WAS still parked outside Alex Holland's address in Highland Park and his windows were lit up from within. There were no drapes pulled and Coombes could look right through the living room window at the other man stretched out on his sofa in front of a television that filled the wall. Holland was playing a computer game. The rear view of a life-sized figure was running down a street with a machine-gun. The volume was cranked up and he could hear sirens, gunshots, and music. Holland did not appear to have any company.

Coombes moved to the door and pounded on it with the base of the fist. He stepped to the side, his body overlapping Sato's. Shielding her. Holland didn't have a permit for firearms, but he'd never rely on a database when it came to guns.

Inside the property the television fell silent.

"Who the fuck is this?" Holland said through the wood.

There was no strength in the words, no bite.

A man with a shotgun had a strength you could hear.

"LAPD. Open up, Holland."

The door started to open and Coombes rushed forward, pushing his way inside and knocking Holland backward onto his ass.

"Hey, what the hell?! I was opening the door."

"You lied to me, asshole."

The edge of the opening door had split Holland's lip. He touched it with his fingertips and looked at the blood, then looked up with a frown.

"What did I lie about?"

"Seeing Marks. You lied to my face. Well, guess what jackass, you're going to be spending some time in prison."

Holland got to his feet and staggered slightly to one side. It looked like he'd been drinking all afternoon, getting the weekend started early. An inch-high slab of cell phone stuck out of Holland's pocket.

"*Prison!* For what?"

"Aiding and abetting, accessory after the fact. Listen, you better hope Amy Tremaine is still alive, because if she's not, you're going down for that too, conspiracy homicide. That's a full life term for you buddy."

"I didn't do shit."

He grabbed Holland's cell phone, pointed the display side at the other man's face and the screen unlocked. Coombes turned away, still holding the iPhone and opened the call log.

"Hey, you can't do that! You don't have my permission!"

He turned to Grace.

"Detective Sato, how would you assess Mr. Holland's current state?"

"Aggressive. Threatening."

"I agree. Draw your weapon. If he makes any moves toward us assume a hostile intent and put him in the ground."

Sato drew her Glock and aimed it at Holland's feet.

"Woah. Take it easy. All I did was call him. You can't shoot me for that."

Coombes nodded and scrolled through the call log.

Holland used his cell phone a lot.

Looking at the names he figured they were mostly women he was trying to romance. Booty calls. There were, however, sixteen calls to an un-named number that he took to be a burner cell belonging to Nathan Marks. He based this assumption on the fact that Holland had dialed this number within minutes of Coombes leaving the day before.

"Looks like you guys have been in touch pretty heavily. The two of you must be about ready to choose a ring." He glanced up from the screen. "I'm guessing it'll be *your* ring, not his." Coombes winked.

Sato laughed but the former Marine looked like he was about to choke. "*What!*"

"You know, Holland, that mustache of yours is going to be pretty popular in prison, those Aryan guys will eat you up like an all-you-can-eat buffet."

Sato glanced back at him.

"Actually, Johnny, it's the other way around. He'll be the one doing the eating."

He nodded. "I'll bet you're right about that."

"Oh, Jesus!" Holland said.

Coombes moved the text on screen again before the display timed-out and the phone would lock again. Alex Holland continued to deny it all but he tuned it all out and held up his free hand to silence him.

It took a long time to scroll back to the next part he was interested in, the part where the calls started. If Holland had dialed Marks' number from a saved entry, it would have his name on it, or a quick way to find him, there wouldn't be just numbers.

He reached a congested patch of calls around New Year's and gave up.

It wasn't there.

He realized he'd answered his own question. If it took this long to go back and find a new number that had called in, Holland would've added that number to the address book for quick access. The fact that he hadn't meant something pretty obvious.

"He was here, wasn't he? When?"

"I want a lawyer."

"Let me explain something. You're not under arrest, you've not been detained. You are helping us with our enquiries. I have not read you your rights, therefore anything you say to me can't be used against you. All I care about is saving that young woman's life. It's something you should want too, Holland. If she's dead, you're done."

The former Marine sighed, his chest deflating.

"All right. He stayed here one night about a month ago. I hadn't seen him for years like I said, then he showed up out of nowhere. He had some skanky chick with him called Cassidy. Man, she's damaged goods. If you ask me, she's been hitting the crack pipe. Anyway, we had a big fight the next morning and he storms out of here like his ass is on fire. I thought that was it for our friendship, but he came back on Monday and apologized for everything.

"Nate said he had a big score in the works. I didn't want to know what it was; I knew he was talking about something illegal. My gig pays well, I don't need to be messing around in anything heavy. He said people might come here asking about him and gave me a number to call if they did."

"You called him sixteen times. Some calls were before we showed up."

"If you say so."

"What did you talk about? From our perspective, it looks like you were involved."

Holland shook his head.

"You couldn't be further from the truth. I was trying to stop him from doing whatever he was was planning. I said I'd loan him money to get back on his feet if that's what he wanted. It wasn't. All he said was 'Someone's going to pay, but it's not going to be you.'."

"After we were here you called him, said we'd been."

"That's right."

"Did you ask him if he'd taken Amy?"

Holland seemed to lose track of the moment and his head moved around like he was looking at where he was for the first time.

"Yeah. I asked. He said I could choose to remain his friend and just hang up, or I could stay on the line and he'd tell me. I stayed on the line. He admitted that he took Amy and said that she was still alive, then he disconnected.

I have tried to call him back many times but it doesn't connect. He's tossed the cell."

"When was this?"

"Fourteen thirty...fifteen hundred?"

"All right, go back to when you said he came here the second time."

"Okay."

"Did anything about that visit seem strange to you?"

"Not really. We had a couple of beers, a couple of joints. Just kicked back, same as it used to be. The problem before was the woman, she's-"

"Damaged, I know. Go on."

"I don't know what you want."

"Here's the part I can't figure, Holland. Over the years I have apologized to a lot of women but I have never once apologized to a man. Not a friend, at least. I would avoid that situation the same as I'd avoid giving any of them mouth-to-mouth. But you're saying that Nathan Marks came here and said sorry for some drunken comment? The guy must be fixing to flee the country any minute, why bother come back here?"

"We grew up together-"

"No. That's bullshit. He hasn't talked to you for years. He came back here because he *wanted* something. What is it?"

"There's nothing, I swear."

"The night he stayed over, what did you talk about?"

"I don't remember. The past, mostly. I was hitting my stash pretty hard, makes it difficult for me to remember stuff later."

"Your work," Sato said. "You told my partner that you only smoke when you aren't working. Did you talk to Marks about the site being closed down?"

"Sure. He thought it was sweet that I was getting paid for doing nothing."

Coombes glanced at Sato and nodded.

"You have keys to get in and out?"

"Yeah, I'm the structural foreman. The site keys are on the board next to my truck keys and my ID. The keys have a big yellow plastic disk so you don't lose them."

"Show me."

They moved over to a set of wall hooks. There was no yellow disk. Coombes could tell it was gone before they got there, but Holland pantomimed searching through all the keys like it would suddenly appear.

"That motherfucker. I could lose my job over this."

"Give me the address."

Holland gave him a street number on Figueroa. As Coombes copied it into his notebook, he realized he knew the building, he'd seen it going up over the last eight months.

"How near is it to completion?"

"We're glazed and weathertight up to 30, the next 2 floors are open to the elements, after that you're talking steel beams and crane. Go above 30 without a harness and you're asking to be blown out onto the street. At that height, wind can appear out of nowhere."

Coombes moved toward the door.

The time for talk was over. He walked to the Charger with Sato, Holland trailing after them in bare feet. She started the engine. Alex Holland tapped on his window and he fizzed it down.

"Don't use the crane elevator, he'll hear you coming."

"Thanks."

"Do me a favor. Don't kill him, okay?"

"That's up to him."

Sato hit the gas and they were gone.

38

THE BUILDING ON FIGUEROA was being built on land that previously operated as a parking lot. About half the lot still remained and Sato was able to get a spot still warm from a silver Toyota. Coombes glanced at the clock on the dashboard as he stepped out the Dodge and saw it was just after six. Neither of them had eaten since half eleven.

He tilted his head up to the top of the building.

Coming here was a stroke of genius by Marks, he had to hand it to him. The building could be seen from all over L.A. but it would never have made anyone's list of potential locations. Only a small number of people knew the site was closed and fewer still had access.

He opened the back of the Charger and they changed into running shoes and put on their bulletproof vests. He didn't mention to Sato how little protection the vests offered against Marks' gun, there didn't seem to be much point.

The base of the tower was surrounded by eight feet high wooden boards with a single security gate that was padlocked shut. He brought the thick jaws of their department-issued bolt-cutters up and began to squeeze on the hardened steel of the padlock.

"We *are* calling for backup, right?"

"We don't know he's here yet, Grace."

"And if he is, when do we find out? When it's too late?"

The jaws of the bolt cutter chewed through the padlock hoop until it broke in half and fell on the ground.

He turned to face Sato.

"Look, I'm not waiting. It might already be too late but on the chance it's not I'm going in. If we call for backup, we have to wait for it to arrive before we do anything. Maybe word gets back to Block and he decides we need to get a judge involved. Get a search warrant, or an arrest warrant. We don't have enough evidence to connect Marks with this property, so then what? Judge says no, do we still go in?"

"Ask forgiveness, then?"

"You're goddam right. Tell me this isn't the very definition of *exigent circumstance*."

Coombes didn't wait for her to answer. He opened the security gate and walked toward the tower. She ran to catch him up.

"Johnny, I asked so we're on the same page. I don't disagree with you."

"All right then."

"It's just," Sato said, "I think we should have a fallback position."

"What did you have in mind?"

"I don't know. Like if we confirm he's there we call for some uniforms to lock down the base to prevent him from escaping."

Coombes said nothing for a moment, thinking how best to say it.

"Actually, I want to face him alone. I think he sees me as some kind of fellow traveler. We both served. In some ways we're different halves of the same whole."

"You're talking about a guy that tried to kill you."

Sato hadn't served, she didn't understand what it was like. On the other hand, it was a long road between Afghanistan and the Taliban to protecting diplomats in Berlin. Marks' tour of duty had been a walk in the park, there were no two ways about it.

Coombes saw a track going up the side of the building like a railway line. At the bottom sat a wire cage and a generator. He supposed this was the crane elevator Holland had mentioned. He turned back to Sato.

"If Marks wanted me dead, I would be dead. His goal was to put me out of commission and sink the investigation. At the very least, he didn't want a dead cop against his name. That's a one-way ticket and he knew it."

"You think you have a *connection?* C'mon, that only happens in movies."

"It might not be much, Grace, but it's a hell of a lot better than a SWAT team rushing him with face masks and riot shields. He sees me, sees my *face*, I'm a known quantity."

He walked to the doors to the building and saw a chain with a padlock on it. The chain hung down, wrapped around nothing. Either Marks had forgotten to lock it behind him, or he was inside. Unlike the gate, this could not be locked from the inside, the glass prevented it.

They went through the door into the building.

There were no lights on in the lobby and little of the early evening sun made it past the wooden perimeter and the dust-coated windows. Two elevators sat open and in darkness. No power. There were stairs at either end of the lobby. Coombes walked to the doors at the far side and fed the legs of the bolt cutters through the handle to prevent them from opening.

Only one way out.

He turned on his flashlight and walked to the other stairwell.

"Johnny, we don't know what floor he'll be on, or if he's even here."

"He's holding Amy Tremaine prisoner. His friend tells him the site's shut down so he knows he's got the pick of the building. Any floor he wants. I say he chooses one far enough from ground level that even if she were to start screaming it doesn't matter."

"That makes sense but I'm afraid where this is going."

"Yeah. My guess is he's on the highest finished floor, or one close to it. That way he probably figures he'll get plenty of warning when anyone is on their way up even if they don't take the elevator."

"I knew you were going to say that."

They began to climb.

Each floor was separated by two flights of steps connected by a half landing. Between the two was a gap wide enough to drop a former Marine Lance Corporal without too many regrets.

They reached the second floor.

Coombes aimed his flashlight at his feet. Ahead of him he saw recent footprints in the thick layer of concrete dust that covered the floor like snow. The prints went on up the stairs, not out through the door.

He turned to Sato. "You see that?"

"I see it."

Coombes put his shoe next to one of the prints. His shoe was a quarter inch longer which made it a good match with Marks who was three inches shorter than him. He walked across to the start of the next stairs and played the light across the steps. The concrete dust faded away the farther he moved from the exit to the second floor.

"I only see Marks' prints. No Tremaine, no Stone."

"Only a man's stupid enough to climb 30 floors when there's an elevator."

"An elevator that could run out of gas and trap you in a wire cage."

Sato said nothing and they began to climb again.

The dust was the same on the third-floor exit, the footprints not stopping, feeding around to the next steps and up.

Coombes had worried they could miss Marks on a lower floor without realizing it, but the dust would tell them exactly what floors he had been on.

He was getting into a rhythm with the climb, barely needing to check the floor for prints. When they reached the eighteenth floor the purple crease pulsed through his vision and his head pounded with pain almost as great as that first impact with the baseball bat.

His foot stumbled and he gripped the rail. Sato piled into his back.

"You can't be done, Coombes, we're barely half-way."

She cast her flashlight at his face, filling his vision with burning after-images. He turned away from the glare and raised is hand to shield his eyes.

"Do you mind?"

The pitch of her hushed voice changed.

"What's wrong? Is it your head again?"

He ignored her and started up the next set of stairs. Slower now. Better to keep moving. Having a rest was like giving his body permission to quit. Maintaining forward movement prevented his partner holding a flashlight on his face and seeing for herself his physical state.

When they reached the twenty-sixth floor, he felt a breeze coming down the stairs from somewhere above. They'd nearly run out of building. There was no layer of dust on the floor now, the breeze had been enough to push it down onto lower floors.

He paused and looked at the door out of the stairwell.

Logically, they had to check if Marks or Amy were there. He knew they could expect the dust to be the same on the next four floors. Clearing each of those floors would take too long, he knew it in his gut. He decided to continue, follow his hunch to the end.

On the landing for the 30th floor he paused and drew his weapon. According to Holland, this was the last floor that had been glazed. He eased the stair door open and looked around the gap. The space beyond was lit by the evening sun which shone through the windows.

He saw no sign of Nathan Marks or Amy Tremaine.

Coombes pocketed his flashlight and moved carefully through the doorway, his eyes scanning the space he found himself in. Thick plastic sheeting divided up the area, preventing him from quickly clearing the floor.

They moved forward, guns dipped but ready.

He used his left hand to move another plastic sheet aside. Right in front of him was a saw table with a large black backpack next to it. Coombes pulled back the zipper and found that it was packed with bundles of cash.

The ransom money.

Their climb hadn't been for nothing.

They came to an area that appeared to have been boxed in on three sides with stacked drywall and the fourth side left open to the wall of glass. A bed of sorts had been set up with layers of cardboard acting as a makeshift mattress and a blanket covered in dark stains. A steel cable snaked out from a bolt on the wall and disappeared under the blanket.

He bent down on one knee and touched the blanket. There was no warmth to it. When he turned his head to the side, he saw blood on the floor. It was fresh and bright. He realized he could smell it now too, his nose filed with the distinctive metallic tang.

Whatever happened to Amy had happened recently, and close by.

Sato spoke to him in a hushed voice.

"It's not hers, Johnny. It's yours."

Coombes reached up and wiped his face. His fingertips came back covered in blood. Thick and dark. The medic had warned him, now his body was warning him. The purple crease, now the blood. His body was ready to collapse, but he wasn't through yet.

He got to his feet and moved clear of the bed area before he contaminated the scene any further.

Marks had kept Amy here for four days, but she was gone now. The obvious conclusion was that she was dead and that the other man had disposed of her body somehow.

The saw table.

Coombes moved reluctantly over to it and studied the blade for signs of blood. Nothing.

Suddenly a voice filled the room.

"DO YOU EXPECT ME TO BELIEVE THAT? YOU COULD PAY TEN TIMES WHAT I WANT AND NOT EVEN NOTICE IT."

Marks. Coombes and Sato glanced at each other.

The other man sounded close, yet not on the same floor. If anything, it sounded like it came through the window from outside.

Sato tilted her head up to look at the ceiling.

Right. They moved quickly back to the stair door. Despite the long climb, he felt a sudden burst of energy flow through him. Marks was here, he was close, and it sounded like he was trying to ransom Amy Tremaine again, which likely meant that she was still alive.

On the 30th stairwell again, Coombes now saw lines on the wall where someone had reached out with their fingernails to try hold onto something. He'd been too busy looking at the floor, he'd missed it.

He followed them to where the stairs went up again. A sheet of plastic blocked the next set of stairs that rose up into the unfinished section of the building.

Down the middle of the plastic, was a four-foot cut.

The lines, the cut.

Nathan Marks had dragged Amy Tremaine across the landing and taken her up into the unfinished section of the building.

A large drop of blood dropped from his nose and landed on the webbing of his right hand between thumb and forefinger.

"YOU HAVE A YACHT, A PRIVATE PLANE, THREE HOMES, FIF-TEEN VEHICLES, AND A FIFTY PERCENT SHARE OF A RESTAU-RANT CHAIN. DON'T TELL ME YOU'RE RUNNING ON EMPTY."

Coombes stepped through the hole in the plastic into cool night air. The landing of 31 and 32 were the same as all the others, except that a metal device was fitted over the exit door handle to prevent the door being opened.

He began up the steps to 33.

The setting sun bathed everything in a golden light. As he looked up, he could see unfinished steel reaching up into the night sky like the rotting hull of a shipwreck.

With the fingers of his left hand, he pressed Sato back against the last remaining piece of concrete stairwell and held up his left hand, then pointed two fingers at his own eyes.

Wait. I'm going to have a look around.

He saw anger on her face.

She thought he was dick-blocking her again, and maybe he was, but he was the senior detective and he had that right. Coombes moved clear of the stair riser and out onto one of the steel beams. Wind pushed past his body fast enough to whip his trousers side to side.

He saw Amy Tremaine first.

She was bound with her hands behind her back and was hanging from one of the beams by a long orange rope. The wind was causing her to sway dramatically to the side, over the edge of the building. If the rope snapped, she'd be blown onto the streets below.

He swung his head around to place Marks.

The sharp movement caused the purple crease to move through his vision and pain tore through him like ripping paper. The pain was unbelievable and it caused him to double over.

Above him the air seemed to explode.

His feet skidded and he fell so that he was now hanging from the beam he'd been standing on, his right hand still gripping his Glock.

Never relinquish your weapon.

He heard Marks laughing.

"OH, MAN! I NEVER SAW ANYBODY DODGE A BULLET BE-FORE, THAT'S AMAZING."

Coombes was breathing fast, his lungs trying to catch up with his heart. Blood was running off his chin. He located Marks standing in the beams on the partial corner of what would eventually be the floor above. He had the huge Desert Eagle in one hand, and a cell phone in the other, his feet bracing him into the beams.

Coombes assessed his situation.

Pulling himself up without releasing his pistol would be difficult. He could wait and see if Marks came close enough to shoot, but why would he? Time was on his side. He could stay up there in the beams like some kind of rooster, waiting for him to either drop the gun or drop a whole floor onto the concrete below.

He glanced down.

It was about fifteen feet. Survivable no doubt, but it would take him out of the picture. He'd be no use to Grace, or to Amy, and a sitting duck to whatever Marks decided to send his way with his hand cannon.

Climbing back up surely committed him to losing his weapon and even if he got it back in his holster there would be a point between hanging over the side and regaining his footing where he was unarmed.

Marks held the cell phone to his ear again.

"NO, NO. SHE'S FINE. I JUST GOT A VISIT FROM THE LAPD."

Marks had to shout, because of the airflow up in the beams. Out the corner of his eye, he saw Sato at the side of the concrete stairwell. With the other man distracted by the call to Tremaine, this might be his only chance to get his footing back on the steel.

There were worse things than dying he figured, and seeing Grace die in front of him trying to save his life would be one of them. He'd rather be dead than see that. So he did something he'd never done before.

He let go of his gun.

39

Coombes watched his gun fall onto the concrete below, knowing that losing it might cost him his life. He pulled himself up onto the steel, then stood slowly up to full height. Hanging from his arms had taken a lot out of him, more than he'd expected.

Marks jumped down and landed on the same beam as him, his arms spreading wide to maintain balance. At almost the same moment, the wind that had been pushing past them eased and became still.

"You don't look too good, Coombes."

"Don't make me your problem, Marine. You served eight years as a door stop while I was fighting the Taliban. You really think a nose bleed gives you a chance against me?"

"Well, this *door stop* still has a gun and you seem to have lost yours."

Marks put on a big smile, like they were on a TV show and he was waiting for the canned laughter to stop.

"I'm here for the governor's kid, not you. The FBI want you to themselves and I've decided that I can live with that. Far as I'm concerned, you were already gone when I arrived. I found Amy where she is. What do you say?"

"That's very *generous* of you, Coombes, but I'm not finished with that brat."

"Then we have a problem."

Marks laughed.

"I'm not the one with the problem, Detective."

"It's going to take you an easy fifteen minutes to run down those stairs. That's if you leave right now. Five minutes after that, and you're going to be looking at close to thirty cops standing there waiting for you. But you'll have to allow some extra time to find that bag full of cash because it's not where you left it."

The smile fell away from Marks' face.

"Let me tell you how it is, *cop*. You're going to tell me where my money is or I'm going to shoot that brat right through her head. If that doesn't work, I'll blow one of your legs off. You'll tell me anything I want after that."

"All right, but she stays with me."

"I'm just not getting through to you, am I Coombes?"

"Your margin of escape is now about three minutes. How quickly can you carry a hostage down those stairs? Face it, Marks, you wouldn't make it ten floors."

"The bag!"

"I dropped it between the stairs. It's at the bottom waiting for you."

Marks lifted his gun and pointed it at Coombes.

"That saves me carrying it *and* the woman."

"You know, you were right before. I have lost my gun, but she hasn't."

Marks glanced over his shoulder at where Coombes was looking. As soon as he turned, Coombes rushed forward, halving the distance between them. Marks turned hurriedly back, away from Sato.

"Stay where you are!"

"This seems familiar, doesn't it? You can't cover both of us, Marks. You shoot me, she shoots you. We die together. You turn your gun toward her again, she shoots you, you die alone. Neither of those work for me, do they work for you?"

Marks was thinking about it, but he didn't want him to think too much, he wanted to keep things moving.

"I'm going to offer you the same deal I started with. Take the money and leave. Amy stays with us. You get what you want, we get what we want. No hard feelings. Just know there's no version of this where Amy Tremaine leaves here with you."

Between them, the gun dipped a couple of inches.

It was heavy.

"All right, but you're coming with me to the stairs. Call it insurance."

"Works for me."

They started back along the beam.

Now Marks had three things to look at; Coombes, Sato, and where he was putting his feet behind him. To keep things interesting, Coombes used the opportunity to close up on the other man again.

The automatic zipped up to his chest.

"Back off, Coombes!"

He fanned his hands as if in surrender, but he stayed where he was, just out of reach. As long as Marks was thinking about him, he wasn't thinking about Sato, and whether she could actually pull the trigger.

They were ten feet from the stair exit now.

He figured Marks planned to use him as a shield from Sato, then shoot him and disappear down the stairs. A gut shot, something she'd have to deal with instead of pursuing Marks.

Sato was watching him, looking for instruction.

The building was one long dead end, and as good a hiding place as it was, it offered no escape routes once discovered. Either Marks had thought the risk of being discovered was low and he could wait out the manhunt above the city, or he *wanted* to be caught and lacked the nerve to give himself up.

"You couldn't do it, could you?"

"What?"

"You came here to pick up the money and kill Amy. But you couldn't do it, so you called Tremaine, started that bullshit second ransom. It was a stall."

"You don't know what you're talking about."

He knew he was right, but it didn't help him.

Marks had been in a few tight spots recently and had managed to survive each time with a mixture of skill, ruthlessness, and luck. Why would he assume this time would turn out any different?

Coombes brought his left hand up to his face and wiped the blood away from his nose and chin, then swung his hand to the side to shake off the blood. Marks smiled, his head turning to follow the movement of his hand and the arc of blood droplets that flew out from his fingertips. It felt like two whole seconds passed before Marks turned back to look at him and saw that he'd moved forward again and a split second later when Coombes' right fist struck his face, twisting him around.

Marks had to windmill his arms to stay on the beam and as he did this, he fired a round from the Dessert Eagle into the sky. Before he could recover, Coombes popped him again, right between the eyes. It was a solid hit, forcing Marks to take several fast steps backward. He began to slip on the beam and pushed off sideways to the platform that surrounded the stairs.

He landed badly, his knees making a hard impact on the steel. Marks grunted in pain and pulled himself slowly to his feet, his jaws clenched tight. He began to lift his gun toward him when Sato called out.

"Hey! Wouldn't do that if I were you."

Marks backed away toward the stairs.

"We'll finish this dance another time, Coombes."

"I don't think so," said a deep voice. "That pressure you are now feeling against your spine is a Remington 870. Drop the piece and put your hands behind your back."

Marks glanced wide-eyed behind him.

"Drop it! I just climbed a million goddamn steps and my trigger finger is getting *real* twitchy, you know what I mean?"

Marks dropped the gun.

Sato moved across to cover Marks while he was being cuffed. Coombes saw him slump, relaxing into the arrest. The relief of submission, something he'd seen many times before.

Becker stood behind Marks holding nothing but a flashlight.

"Becker, *buddy*, am I glad to see you."

"I'm technically still a cop until midnight."

"You don't stop being a cop, you just stop getting paid for it."

"Ain't that the truth."

He turned back toward Amy Tremaine.

As far as he was concerned, she was the real reason he was here. With Marks and his huge gun dealt with, the roof of the building seemed to shrink. He moved quickly across the lattice of steel beams to where she was still hanging mid-air.

The rope was wrapped around and around her body, then it went up over a horizontal beam, then back to where it was tied off at the side against another beam. The rope was thin, it didn't look strong enough to take a person's weight and he didn't much care for the way the rope was bent over the sharp edge of the steel.

He pulled Amy Tremaine toward him with both hands. Her eyes were close to his, wide with terror and slick with tears.

"Amy, my name's John. I'm a detective with the LAPD and I've been working with your dad to get you home safe."

She had the tape over her mouth, but it looked like she understood.

He turned his head to the side and nodded to Sato. She unfastened the rope from around the steel support and let it slowly out as he carried Amy back toward the stairwell.

Adrenaline still flooded his system and she felt as light as a feather.

Coombes was about halfway across the roof when the wind returned, blowing fast through the structure. His arms instinctively tightened around Amy. He saw only her face; he couldn't see where his shoes were positioned on the steel. Her eyes locked on his, pleading with him to make it all stop. He returned her gaze and did a slow blink.

I'm a professional, ma'am, I got this.

They were being pushed backwards, along the beam toward the edge. He could feel the steel moving past through his sneakers.

Coombes crouched down to make their wind profile as small as possible. Their movement slowed but did not stop. He was running out of time, they couldn't be too far from the edge.

It was a rare opportunity for a homicide cop to save a life and he wasn't going to give it up lightly. He was going to take this all the way to the end.

There was no point looking at the approaching edge if he could do nothing about it. Instead, he looked into the eyes of the woman he was holding. She'd stopped crying now, and was looking peacefully back at him.

He felt his shoe catch on something, a bolt or a rivet, and their drift backward stopped. He turned to the side and saw Sato holding fast against the upright, her hair blowing across her face. You could hold yourself against an upright all day, all night.

Grace was safe, and it was all he needed to know.

The wind took close to five minutes to ease off and he spent all that time looking into Amy Tremaine's green eyes. They were giving each other strength, he realized. There was nothing sexual, or creepy about it. Just two humans bonding at the edge of a 500-foot drop.

When the wind dropped away, he wasted no time in carrying Amy back down the beam toward safety. The wind could return at any time and he'd had about enough of it.

In the safety of the concrete stairwell, he peeled the tape slowly away from Amy's mouth. Her lips flared up red and puffy as the adhesive pulled at them.

"Thank you! Thank you! Thank you!"

Coombes nodded and said nothing. He found gratitude difficult to deal with and always had. He removed the rope as Marks looked calmly on.

"That psychopath was going to kill me!"

Marks laughed at that, but said nothing.

He'd unwound the rope from her shoulders down past the bend of her elbow. She was wearing a light pink T-shirt with a cartoon character printed on it. He assumed it belonged to Cassidy Stone, swapped for the blue shirt the other woman had died in.

"You've had a tough week, Miss Tremaine."

"Looks like I'm not the only one."

Coombes smiled. "I'll live."

"And it's Amy, like you said before. Not Miss Tremaine."

Once he got the rope past her hips the rest fell away onto the floor.

He took out his cell and dialed Harlan Tremaine, then passed it to Amy. It rang six times before he heard the former governor answer with a fearful, *yes?*

"*Daddy?*"

It was the only thing he heard her say, because she started to sob and Coombes left her to it as he helped Becker wrestle a handcuffed Marks down the stairs.

40

THEY WERE SET UP for Nathan Marks in interview room 4. Coombes went out into the hallway to watch him arrive. He'd had Marks stewing for an hour in holding to soften him up. The former Marine was now wearing shackles on his wrists and ankles with chains up the front of his body connecting everything together. The setup required Marks to walk in a shuffling motion as he was led down the hall and into the room.

The chains were a message, in case his new surroundings didn't get the job done. His old life was over. The task for him now was to get used to it and not waste Coombes' time believing there was still a way out.

Once Marks was seated, the chains were drawn forward and connected to a post on the table, at which point the uniforms that had brought him from the cells backed out the room.

"Are the chains really necessary?"

"You've tried to kill me twice, Mr. Marks. There won't be a third time."

"I'm unarmed."

"As am I. Let's get to it, shall we? I'm told that you're waiving your constitutional right to have an attorney present today. Why's that?"

Marks shrugged. "Why pay someone $500 bucks an hour to tell me not to say anything?"

"You can't use lack of legal counsel as a defense."

"It's not going to matter."

Coombes opened a leather folio and took out a legal waiver and a duplicate then placed them on the table in front of Marks, followed by a pen. There was a line at the bottom with a cross next to it and the other man signed both documents without reading any of the text. It could've been a typed-up confession for all he knew.

He gathered up the signed papers and glanced down to check that Marks had used his real name and not Nolan Sawyer or some other name. If he signed using the name of a Dodgers second baseman the document would be worthless, along with the whole interview.

Satisfied, he returned everything to his folio.

"All right," he said. "Interview of Nathan Marks by Detectives John Coombes and Grace Sato. Today's date is Friday, February 28th 2020. Time 8:15 p.m."

Coombes sat opposite Marks, while Sato remained standing over to one side, arms folded. He took a moment to pull out his notebook and straighten his suit.

He'd been rotating the same two shirts for four days in a row, and while he'd been able to use the hotel laundry service, he was convinced that he must cut a disheveled appearance on camera.

"I've got to admit that I'm not sure where to start, Mr. Marks. How about we begin with the kidnapping of Amy Tremaine. How did that come about?"

He'd started with something Marks couldn't deny, having been found with both Amy Tremaine and the ransom money. Once a ball was rolling, it was easier to keep it rolling.

"It all started with that damn dog."

Marks fell silent for a long moment. Coombes did nothing to interrupt it.

"I was out for a run minding my own business when this dog shoots across the sidewalk in front of me and gets clipped by a motorcycle. The guy floors it, leaving the dog at the side of the road howling. I couldn't have that, so I carried it to a place a mile away."

Marks took them through the story of his unexpected hero act at the veterinary hospital, taking out the would-be thieves with a fire extinguisher, then leaving the name of another man to avoid legal problems.

The story was familiar to Coombes, but he made notes as the story unfolded to prevent Marks from knowing when he was getting new information.

"A couple of nights later, I'm out on another run. I see these fliers around the area it all happened. A picture of the dog with the word REWARD in big capitals across the top. It was the owner wanting to give the man that saved his dog a $1,000 reward. I realized I couldn't claim it, I gave a false name. Part of me suspected it was a police sting to capture me. I'd seen the news, those guys I hit were in a bad way. A month passes. I'm over it. I meet Cass at a bar-"

"Just a moment. This is Cassidy Stone?"

"Right. I tell her about that night, thinking it would impress her, that she'd go home with me. I was half in the bag and not thinking straight. I figured if I didn't make something happen soon, I was just going to call it quits and head home.

"But it *did* impress her. She became obsessed. With the story, with what I did, then with the injustice of not being able to collect the reward. Cass thinks maybe there's another approach.

"I already proved that there are some wealthy owners out there, it was just about finding the right ones. Next thing I know, we're kidnapping dogs and making thirty thousand a week."

Coombes made a note *find the right ones* and glanced back at Marks.

"What led you to start kidnapping people?"

"Money of course. It was almost the same amount of work but much more lucrative."

"How many were there before Amy?"

Marks looked up like he was counting in his head, but whatever number he reached, he didn't share. There was a flicker of what looked like pride in his eyes, before he remembered where he was and his face fell.

"It doesn't matter, none of this matters."

It was the second time Marks had said it didn't matter. Coombes sensed that the other man was taking more stock of his situation and was keen to keep things moving.

"Why did you kill Mavis Kent?"

"I don't even know who that is."

"The lady you stuffed into her own freezer."

Marks laughed. It sounded all wrong, fake.

"Shit, I forgot about that! We *really* liked her house, that's all."

Coombes sat back.

For the first time, he questioned whether Marks was working an angle. Perhaps going for a diminished responsibility defense by acting crazy in an interview. Even waiving his right to an attorney fitted that profile.

"When you were talking about the dogs' owners you said that you needed to find the right ones. I assume that was the case with the people too?"

He shrugged, wordlessly.

Once again Marks dodged the question about other kidnappings.

"Information you got from Elizabeth Walton."

Her name put energy into Marks.

"Not true. I knew all those donor people myself from my time working for Tremaine, she had nothing to do with it."

"Then why did you kill her?"

Marks clenched his teeth hard together, fury burning in his eyes.

"I *didn't*."

"Let me get this straight. You expect us to believe that you kidnapped Amy Tremaine, half-drowned her on camera; that you froze an old woman slowly to death; that you killed Cassidy Stone in front of us...but that you didn't kill Elizabeth Walton?"

"That's right."

"Why would we believe that?"

"Because she was important to me."

"And your girlfriend wasn't?"

"Oh, please. Cass was never my girlfriend."

"The two of you had a physical relationship, Marks. The air in the bedroom of that house was saturated with it. I could've cut it with a knife."

"Look, we had sex, so what? It didn't mean anything to me and it certainly didn't mean anything to her. It passed the time. She was pretty good at it, you know?"

"Was Elizabeth Walton good at it?"

Marks hung his head then simply nodded. This was his weak spot.

"Were you in love with her?"

Marks nodded again. Coombes saw tears roll down the other man's cheeks and drip onto the table. He didn't see a lot of criminals crying, but he saw plenty of victims' families crying and that's what Marks looked like.

"Is that why you beat her head off a floor and strangled her to death?"

"NO!"

"Sure, you did. She found out about the kidnapping plan and you had no choice."

"That's bullshit! I would never-"

"So, it was about the other men? You got jealous and lost it."

"*What* other men?" Marks turned to Sato. "Is this a good cop - stupid cop routine? Lizzie didn't have time to see anyone but me and she wouldn't have even if she had. She knew her way around the track, sure, but she was traditional. One man at a time."

Coombes moved his eyes slowly over Marks' face.

He saw no doubt, only anger.

"And *you* were that man?"

"Is this because she was older than me? Look, we had a connection, she made me laugh. She was smart. She read books. She didn't spend every waking moment with her face in her cell phone. Most people thought we were the same age anyway."

"You miss my point. On the one hand you say that you loved Elizabeth, on the other you're having sex with a crazy ex-con just to pass the time."

"I can't help you with your hang-ups, Detective."

The interview was getting away from him so he glanced at Sato to take over.

"All right," she said. "Let's take a step back. Help us understand. Imagine for the moment that Elizabeth is still alive and you've still got your millions of dollars. What was your plan? Was she part of your future?"

"What difference does that make now?"

"Indulge me."

"We were going to move to Vancouver. I told her I'd inherited money and I was just waiting on it coming through. I said it was a lot, that neither of us needed to work again. She was all-in. The charity stuff wasn't doing it for her any more. She said things were so bad now that nothing the foundation did made a difference. That they were trying to empty the Pacific with a shot glass."

"You must realize what you're saying, Nathan."

Her use of Marks' first name caused him to pause and glance at Coombes.

"That I would never do what he says to Lizzie? That someone else did that?"

Coombes shook his head.

"What she's saying, is that for your little retirement plan to work, Amy had to be dead. Otherwise, as soon as you release her she'd tell us who took her. Even if you skipped town, it would make the news wherever you went. Amy was like a daughter to Elizabeth. She'd turn you over to the police in a heartbeat."

"Oh."

His face fell. It looked real, like he'd never connected the dots.

"I just wondered again, *Nate*, if maybe Elizabeth got wind of your scheme and that you had no choice but to shut her up."

"Stop saying that!"

"What would *you* think in my position?"

Marks' face twisted awkwardly.

"The same as you. Why do you think we rushed the ransom demand?"

"Say I believe you, when did you first hear about her death?"

"It was just after we took Amy. Me and Cass were watching the news for developments we needed to know about. When I heard about Lizzie, I lost my lunch."

"You don't seem the type."

Marks ignored that and continued.

"I realized you people would connect Amy and Lizzie, that you'd think they were linked. I almost released Amy just to get you to focus on the Lizzie case. I couldn't be the reason that someone got away with murdering her, but I knew no one would believe me."

"I'm going to level with you, Marks. We hear the same song in here all the time. It wasn't me, it was someone else. Blah, blah, blah. The problem is that we've already got enough to put you in a cage for the rest of your life. Additionally, I should probably tell you that there's a detective down the hall waiting to speak to you concerning the murder of Olaf Dekker. I'm pretty sure you're good for that as well. Why not get it all off your chest? Tell us what happened to Elizabeth, her family and loved ones deserve to know. Lying about it is a further assault to them and to her memory."

Marks tried to put his head in his hands, but the chain that was looped around both of his wrists stopped his hands short. After a moment, a wordless animal whine came out of his mouth. The sound became louder and louder until Marks arched his head back and brought it down fast on the sharp edge of the interview table.

Blood shot out in all directions and his arms and legs began to convulse. Coombes jumped back, almost falling out his chair, and slammed his hand against the panic button on the wall. A siren filled the air and blue strobes pulsed on the ceiling.

Marks' body jerked against the chains and it took Coombes and Sato working together for close to a minute to unlock his handcuffs and get him to the floor and onto his side. The door flew open and Cahill and Gonzalez rushed in, weapons drawn. He looked up.

"Call a goddamn ambulance!"

Blood stopped pulsing out Marks' nose and his body went still.

Coombes touched the other man's neck. Nothing. He rolled him over on his back, tilted Marks' head to clear his airway, and began CPR. After what felt like an eternity, he glanced up and saw that the detectives were still standing in the doorway with glazed expressions.

"WHY ARE YOU STILL HERE? CALL AN AMBULANCE. GO, GO, GO!"

The two detectives scuttled away.

"You're not doing mouth-to-mouth on this clown, John."

"*Grace?*"

"I won't let you. He could have the virus."

She meant Coronavirus, he thought, not HIV.

From what he'd seen on the news, Coronavirus was airborne. If Marks had it then he'd been filling up the room with it since he arrived. It was doubtless blood and saliva-borne too, it was the new bogeyman.

Every generation got a plague, this was theirs.

Whether it had any merit, her warning was enough to hold him off. Just the same, Marks would be long dead by the time any medics arrived. CPR was a sticking plaster, not a solution. He glanced up at Sato and spoke between chest compressions.

"All right...get the defibrillator...break room."

Sato paused for a second.

"Promise me. No mouth-to-mouth."

"I promise."

She ran off, leaving him alone with Marks.

The positioning of the body beneath his hands made him think about how Marks must've crouched over Elizabeth Walton as he crushed her throat.

It would be easy for him to stop trying to save the other man. That's what Harlan Tremaine would want; for him to just lift off the throttle and let nature take its course. Revenge as a by-product.

He couldn't do it.

Coombes fought to keep him alive, not because Marks deserved to live, but because he had to pay for his crimes.

Sato reappeared with the defibrillator which she set up on the floor next to him. They lifted his T-shirt and applied the electrodes. Marks' chest was covered in a thick black hair and the pads barely stuck down.

When the defibrillator finished charging, he moved clear and Sato pushed the button. Marks' body lifted up off the floor and sank back down. The display showed no heartbeat and began to charge again automatically.

In the movies it always took three zaps to bring someone back, but Marks took only two, his heart returning at a leisurely 64 beats per minute, his breathing shallow.

Coombes sat back on his heels, his hands shaking.

"Help me roll him on his side, I'm beat."

They moved Nathan Marks into the recovery position and Coombes got unsteadily to his feet. He saw arcing trails of blood everywhere he looked and somehow none of it had got on his clothes.

It took medics another quarter hour to arrive.

In that time, Nathan Marks still hadn't regained consciousness.

41

Coombes picked up Korean take-out on the way back to his hotel and started to eat it before he was off the elevator. He'd hardly eaten anything all day and there was a tremor in his right hand. Not ideal for a right-handed shooter. He unlocked his door and let the automatic closer pull it shut behind him as he set his take-out and a six-pack of beer onto the room's only table. The food was going to make the room smell bad for days, to say nothing of the effect it would have on his body, but the heart wants what the heart wants.

He put on the television and changed it from a classic movie channel he was watching the previous night, to one of the local news networks to see if there was any breaking news on the Nathan Marks arrest and the safe return of Amy Tremaine.

Commercials.

He took off his suit jacket, sat on the edge of his bed, and began to shovel the food into his mouth using chopsticks from a previous take-out.

One thing was for sure, his diet had gone to shit. It always did when he was on rotation, but this time it was worse because he no longer had Julie to keep him grounded.

After a minute, the news was back.

Over in China, the authorities were spraying something on city streets to hold back the virus. Thousands were dead, perhaps tens of thousands, and the cities were being locked down.

He saw people wearing protective suits with masks that covered the whole of their head. It looked like a scene out of a movie. What amazing foresight, he thought, that they would happen to have vehicles capable of spraying who-knows-what on the local population.

Coombes opened a beer and took several long pulls.

He liked to think he had a high tolerance for spicy food, but Korean food always cut right through.

The news segment ran on and on.

A lot of people were getting pretty worried about the virus now that it had made landfall in the US. He had finished both his fire chicken and the beer before they cut back to the studio anchor and another mini-summary of the day's events.

Amy Tremaine's rescue was front and center, as was her father, the former governor. Now that her story had reached the end and it was good news, the broadcasters appeared to have lost interest in it. Bad news, that's where the ratings were. He saw a four-second shot of himself taken with a long lens and he raised a fresh beer in salute to the television.

His cell phone rang. Sato.

"Hey, Grace. What's happening?"

"Where are you, Johnny?"

He heard laughter and voices talking over each other. She was in a bar.

"I was about to hit the shower, why?"

"You've not forgotten, have you?"

Becker's retirement party.

"I'll be thirty minutes, tops."

"Skip the shower and make it fifteen. I'm surrounded by creepy cops and I'm worried that in my drunken state I might go home with one of them."

"All right, take it easy. I'm pulling on my jacket."

————

HIS UBER DRIVER MADE conversation like that was part of the job. In his opinion, Coronavirus was a cover story for a nuclear disaster. The Chinese were spraying the air and the streets to wash out radioactive particles. Telling everyone to stay indoors so they wouldn't be contaminated. Coombes agreed with the man just so he didn't have to think about it.

After they reached their destination the driver turned to him.

"Watch yourself in there."

"Why do you say that?"

"It's a cop bar."

Coombes nodded. "Thanks. I will."

There was no sign of Sato inside the bar but at a little over five feet tall, she was an easy person to lose. He'd lost her once behind an office chair. The first person to find him was Becker who came over, a big smile on his face.

"Thanks for coming, John. I know your hands are full right now."

"What you going to do? Wait for people to stop killing each other?"

"Ain't that the truth, brother."

To his surprise, Becker embraced him and slapped his back. Coombes slapped back, embarrassed. They had only worked one previous case together and had had minimal contact during their shared time together at Robbery-Homicide.

"L-T said you fought for me to be on the *Ferryman* case. You have no idea what that means to me. And now this, with Tremaine's kid. To help save her. *Thank you*. There will be a place at our table anytime."

"Forget it. I should be thanking you."

"Regardless. I appreciate it."

A silence fell between them, as silences often fall between men in bars. Becker did what he couldn't, he took a long drink from the glass in his hand. Coombes noticed a bruise on his index finger as he lifted the glass. It was from firing a handgun with it pointed backward at his own head. Recoil had twisted it sideways.

"What am I going to do now, John? I've been a cop my whole life."

"Did you see what Lester Crumb was charging?"

Becker's eyes lit up. "A PI. That's not a bad idea."

"You're going to need those sky-high PI fees to pay for your boat."

"I told you about my boat?"

Coombes smiled. "What kind of cop would you be if you didn't get a boat?"

"A cliché, huh? There's a lot of those going about."

His smile melted away. Even Becker had heard about his marriage.

"You heard about Julie?"

"Who's Julie? I was talking about Grace."

"Who told you?"

"Relax, John. Nobody told me. When she looks up at you it's like a flower gazing at the sun. Don't you know what that *look* means? I thought you were a man of the world."

Coombes knew exactly the look Becker was talking about. He'd seen it, liked it, and thought no more about it. She was his partner first, before anything else, she was coming at him from a blind spot.

"Shit. I need a drink."

He moved toward the bar but Becker put his hand on his chest.

"Do you know why I never made D-III?"

"I never thought about it. I suppose I assumed you'd been overlooked."

Becker shook his head.

"It's because I never wanted it. I made it clear that my wife was more important than the job and I never regretted it. After all these years, my wife still looks at me the way Grace looks at you. Do not choose the job over a life of happiness, that's my advice. *Now* you can get your drink, I'm supposed to be mingling here."

After Becker left, he scanned the room.

He'd visited the bar before he even served in the Army, it was part of him. But it wasn't like it used to be, there was no cigarette smoke anymore. You could see everything in disgusting clarity. Sato wasn't there. He wondered if she'd made good on her promise to go home with another cop.

If it was true, it would break him.

To his right, the crowd opened up and Wallfisch pushed his way through. Judging by his face, he was either furious or drunk. Maybe both. If they were ever going to have a fight, here would be the place to do it.

Cop bars were neutral territory in the blue religion and a fight would go on until someone stopped swinging, or furniture started breaking. He shifted his weight so that he was ready for anything that came his way.

"Look, Coombes, I got carried away talking shit about your wife. I'm sorry, that crossed the line. How about you and me bury the hatchet and start over?"

Coombes studied the other man, trying to gauge if he was earnest, or if this was a setup to further mockery. The fact was, he was bored with the hostilities and the energy required to maintain them. Wallfisch just wasn't worth the effort.

"All right."

"I'm hardly in a position to comment, I've been married five times. You know the divorce rate among cops is north of seventy percent? Being a cop's wife is no pleasure cruise."

"Back up. You've been married five times?"

Wallfisch shrugged helplessly.

"What can I say? I'm irresistible to ladies."

Despite himself, Coombes smiled.

"I'm sure."

"Just forgive yourself. Forgive *her*. When I married my first wife, I thought apple pie was the best kind of pie. Every chance I got, I'd choose apple, right? Why wouldn't I? It was my favorite. One day out of the blue, I decided to try cherry. Let me tell you, my mind exploded. I became a cherry man until again I tried something else. Pecan. I was ready this time, I embraced it. Then there was peach-"

"Are you seriously comparing your wives to pie?"

"All I'm saying, is that when you fall in love it's based on how you feel *up to that moment*, not how you feel later. It's like pain, it's on a scale and that scale changes depending on your situation. You get shot, you think that's the most pain you'll ever have, that's your 10. Then maybe you have an arm blown off, your 10 changes, see?"

"Women really find you irresistible?"

Wallfisch laughed.

Behind him, Coombes saw Sato emerge from the restroom and stop as she saw who he was talking to. She diverted to the bar, which was a pretty good instinct.

He decided to try and get Wallfisch back on track so he'd get lost.

"So peach is your new favorite pie?"

"Right, no. That's my point. I'm back on apple again. Sometimes all you really need is a break to make you realize how good something was."

"Then that means-"

Wallfisch nodded somberly.

"I remarried my first wife. Turns out she was the right one after all."

"Tell me something. How did you hear about my marriage anyway?"

"I was standing next to your desk when the kid came around with the mail. I saw you had a light green envelope. It looked familiar, so I turned it over and saw the name of a legal firm printed on the back. Two of my ex-wives used the same firm, so I joined the dots."

Coombes sighed and said nothing.

This was the closest Wallfisch had come to actual police work in the whole time he'd known him. The envelope was still on his desk, he'd never got around to opening it.

He supposed this meant that Julie had started the paperwork on their divorce long before he'd caught her in bed with the lawyer.

"I hope you didn't like your home, Coombes, because that's hers now."

"It kind of always was."

Wallfisch gave him a knowing nod, then moved off.

Sato had a Sapporo waiting for him at the bar. It wasn't his usual beer, but it was light and went down easily. He felt like he needed to put some drinks between himself and Wallfisch's pie analogy.

Coombes turned to catch the eye of the bartender and found she was already looking at him, a friendly look in her eye. He indicated two more beers.

Under the bar, Sato let her hand rest casually on his thigh as she pretended to look around the room. The heat from her small hand soaked through the thin material of his pants and spread out across his skin.

"Did you speak to Gantz?"

"No," he said. "Just Becker and Wallfisch. Why?"

"When they got Marks to the hospital a nurse checked his wallet to see if he had medical insurance, or a card listing any drugs he was on, or allergies they had to know about."

His focus sharpened. "*And?*"

"They found a *do not resuscitate* card. There was also a folded legal document signed yesterday morning allowing a lawyer to take criminal action against anyone breaking the DNR in the event that Marks was incapacitated and unable to do so himself."

"Grace."

"I'm sorry, Johnny. He coded minutes later. He's gone."

Coombes looked away from her so that she didn't see the anger in his eyes. This was why Marks kept saying nothing mattered, he had an exit plan. There would be no justice for Olaf Dekker, Mavis Kent, Elizabeth Walton, Cassidy Stone, or Amy Tremaine.

The single hour Nathan Marks spent in custody was all he'd ever serve. Coombes felt himself sinking into the dark space inside himself where he stored his demons.

A single hour, it was a joke.

"Hey," she said. "It wasn't for nothing. We saved Amy *and* fucked the FBI."

Sato was right, that was something worth celebrating.

"I meant to ask you, when did you ask Becker for backup? Was it on the way up the stairs, or at the top?"

"Are you kidding me? I sent him a text before we left Holland's place. I know what you're like asking for help."

"Well, it was a good call. He saved my stupid ass."

A silence fell between them for a moment before she spoke again.

"I know this isn't our arrangement, Johnny, but you're staying with me tonight."

He glanced at her, an eyebrow raised.

"Oh yeah?"

"It's been a long week and I need to forget about the world for a couple of hours. The way things are between you and your wife, I don't really see the point of maintaining all the cloak-and-dagger stuff."

"That was never about Julie, Grace. You're in my chain of command, they'd split us up if they knew. It's against policy."

"Pffft! Chain of command!"

Sato laughed, and he liked hearing it. Coombes sensed she was a few drinks ahead of him and decided to catch up. He finished his first beer and pulled over one of the new bottles.

"Go easy with that, Johnny, I'm going to want more than a hug."

He studied her face closely and, for the first time, wondered what it would be like to spend the rest of his life with Grace Sato.

Not awful, he concluded. Not awful at all.

42

COOMBES OPENED HIS EYES and saw Grace next to him, watching closely. Waking up in bed with his partner should've taken some time to adjust to, but he had found that it did not. It was as natural as breathing. Her eyes moved a fraction and she smiled. He realized she'd been using the time he was asleep to study the damage to his face.

"How is it?"

She rolled on top of him and kissed him until he forgot what it was he'd asked her. Afterward, he lay calmly looking at the ceiling fan that rotated slowly above the bed. He thought about the way Marks had described what he and Walton had between them.

The more he thought about it, the more he recognized his own relationship with Sato.

There wasn't a two-decade age gap between them, but the rest. Being smart, having a connection, making him laugh. Basic things maybe, but there was a truth in his words that couldn't be denied. Marks had been in love with Walton, he was certain of it.

She poked his face playfully.

"Why the big frown?"

"Marks could've done what he did in that holding cell."

"Probably would've been easier," she said. "A lot of hard surfaces. No chains."

"So why didn't he?"

"I guess he wanted us to see it. People are fucked up, Johnny. You know that."

Coombes shook his head.

"He admitted to everything except Walton's murder. He could've claimed Stone was responsible for everything, but he didn't."

"Why say he didn't do it, if he was going to kill himself anyway."

"Right."

"You believe him, then? That he didn't do it?"

"Yeah," he said. "Those tears looked pretty real."

"Some people can't accept what they've done, the guilt becomes too much to carry. Is it not possible that he killed himself out of remorse?"

It was true, loving someone was no barrier to murder.

"I don't think so, not in this case."

Sato sat up in bed and sat facing him, legs folded.

"All right, then Schofield killed her like we originally thought. Say Marks and Stone did the kidnappings while he sat back and ran the operation. Marks decides he's had enough, he's taking all the risks, why pay this other guy anything?

"So he decides to do one last job, keep all the money, then disappear off to Canada with Walton. Schofield gets wind of it and kills her to show Marks who's in charge."

He nodded.

Sato's analysis was a little movie-of-the-week, but it fit the facts available. It had also never been difficult for him to imagine Schofield as Walton's killer.

"That's not bad, Grace."

On the nightstand, his cell phone chirped. He picked it up and saw it was a Facebook message.

A smile spread across his face.

"Speak of the devil and he shall appear."

He clicked on the message as Sato watched over his shoulder.

I'm back in town, you got the money?

Yeah, I got it. All of it.

Good. Meet me in front of Sidecar Doughnuts on Fairfax at 10.

Coombes thought for a second, he had to play this right.

My friend wants this to be over.

He knows the score. He pays me, he gets his files.

Coombes knew better than to respond. The longer any conversation ran, the more chances he had of exposing his own ignorance of the situation. Schofield, if that's who he was communicating with, had the advantage.

"You ready to tell me what all this is about?"

Files. These days that meant digital, which also meant that they could be endlessly duplicated. A thumb drive of files didn't end a blackmail situation.

"Not just yet."

Sato shoved him hard in the shoulder and walked toward the shower.

"Jackass," she said.

She was almost right, he reflected.

COOMBES WAS CARRYING A padded envelope in his left hand with a copy of *The Devotion of Suspect X* inside. He'd taken the novel from Sato's towering bedside pile of books to give the envelope a believable heft. He had no idea how much money Schofield expected, but based on their previous chat, he was assuming around $100k.

The profile picture on his Facebook account was almost eight years old and was taken around the time he joined the LAPD. He didn't look too much different now, but the picture had been taken in a bar, making him appear more casual. Schofield had to have looked at his profile to check him out if only to know who to look for at the handoff.

He'd been on the news the day before, albeit for only four seconds. It was possible that Schofield could recognize him and place him as a cop. Coombes wondered about this, before deciding that it might actually be *better* if Schofield realized he was in a box.

A cornered animal fought to survive.

That's what he needed. He needed Schofield to be the criminal he was and react appropriately. Otherwise, what did he have? There was no case to make against him for Elizabeth Walton *or* the kidnapping of Amy Tremaine.

All he had on Schofield was a possible scheme to blackmail the Chief of Police and he was pretty sure that Jackson didn't want whatever it was coming out at trial.

His cell vibrated in his pocket, a text from Sato.

Parked in Du-Par's, opposite Trader Joe's. All clear.

Coombes turned onto Fairfax at 4ᵗʰ Street, two blocks down from the meeting point. He was on the shaded side of the street where he hoped his bulky department-issue polyester jacket wouldn't seem as out of place as it felt. If Schofield saw what he was wearing under it the whole gig would be up whether he wanted it or not. Another text came in.

He's here! It's Schofield. He's big, John, be careful.

To suddenly appear as he had told Coombes that Schofield had walked through the pedestrian footpath between Paper Source and Trader Joe's, which likely meant he had parked in the lot on West 3ʳᵈ Street.

As an exchange point, the location was terrible.

If Schofield had run the kidnapping operation, he hadn't been the brains. He was a gangster with no tactical training. Marks would never have chosen a place like this, so close to a busy road and so many pedestrians, any one of them potential undercover cops.

Coombes saw Schofield. He was about the same height as he was, but pumped out in every other direction. The man was a beast and obviously spent a lot time lifting weights and injecting himself with steroids.

Schofield was staring across the street at Sato.

He'd made her.

Coombes shot a quick glance at her and was in time to see her do a dramatic laugh, like she was handsfree on her cell phone with a friend.

When he returned his gaze to Schofield, he had moved on from Grace to a white Impala that was driving down the street toward him.

The man was on edge, nervous.

It was perfect. The way things looked, he'd only have to confirm Schofield's fears about being set up, to trigger him into doing something that he could actually arrest him for.

But what *would* he do?

The number of pedestrians weren't just a problem for Schofield, each of them was a potential victim. Coombes ducked into Blackburn Avenue, then along an alleyway behind the Writer's Guild of America, which dumped him out on West 3rd Street.

He took out his cell phone and sent Schofield another message.

Stuck in traffic on the 10, going to have to re-schedule.

The app showed him that Schofield had read the message, though there was no response. He imagined the other man was irritated, but not angry. Getting stuck in traffic was the most L.A. of traditions.

A text message arrived from Sato.

He's leaving! Where are you?

Coombes didn't have time to reply, because he saw Schofield walking down the footpath toward him. His eyes were downcast, his shoulders slumped. *Or maybe that's just his enormous trapezoids.*

Canceling the meeting seemed to legitimize it for Schofield, that it wasn't a setup. Cops don't cancel stings due to traffic delays.

Schofield wasn't looking around anymore; he was focused on finding his vehicle in the rows of cars and SUVs. A hard line formed across his forehead.

When he'd parked, he had anticipated walking back with a nice chunk of change in his pocket and it hadn't happened.

Coombes crouched behind a high-sided Mercedes SUV and watched Schofield move down the lot. He realized he was still holding the padded envelope with Sato's book inside and he put it down on the asphalt beside him. The play with the envelope was over.

He drew his pistol as Schofield pulled out his key fob and blipped the remote. Two spaces over, a black VW sedan unlocked, its turn indicators flashing.

Coombes popped up from behind the Mercedes, his gun pointed.

"LAPD! HANDS IN THE AIR, SCHOFIELD!"

Schofield turned his head sleepily toward him, like he was waiting to pull out at a bad junction. There was a beat as he recognized him from his old profile picture, and another before it dawned on him that he *was* in the middle of a police sting after all.

Instead of raising his hands, Schofield dropped down fast as if he'd tripped on something. Coombes had no sight of him and had to work his way around the side of the Mercedes.

He felt his pocket vibrate. Sato again, he assumed.

By now she'd probably worked out what happened and was telling him to wait for her. But he didn't want to wait for her, not with a piece of work like Schofield. He wanted to take care of things himself.

He moved his head around the front of the SUV and saw Schofield lying sideways on the ground with a compact machine pistol in his hand. The air filled with noise as the vehicle next to him was torn to shreds.

Nothing hit him, not even a ricochet.

He got his head back behind cover after a second and another second later the pistol ran dry. People were screaming and horns were blaring as they tried to get clear of the firefight.

Coombes fired a single shot at Schofield and saw him fold at the waist, an angry bellow of pain coming out his mouth. Schofield got a fresh magazine into his pistol and let loose another two second burst at the side of the Mercedes.

The other man's hands were shaking, the shots going everywhere. Even with a shoulder stock, firing a machine gun could make your hands shake as if in sympathy with the recoil of the weapon. Again, Schofield's pistol ran dry and he heard it clatter to the ground empty.

Coombes popped up in time to see him draw a Walther P99 diagonally across his body. *Another gun, great.* Unlike his previous weapon, Coombes knew the Walther was highly accurate and decided not to wait around to find out what Schofield could do with it.

He fired four more shots aiming to pin Schofield down; but ended up hitting him again with one of the rounds going through his left forearm.

Rage drove Schofield on, charging straight at him like a crazed bull.

Three shots from the Walther hit him in the chest, knocking him backward onto the asphalt and tilting him up to look at the blue sky. Coombes struggled to breathe and was only able to watch as Schofield blew past him with a stumbling gait toward West 3rd Street.

Coombes rolled over onto his front, then pushed himself to get up on his hands and knees. He coughed and felt the tightness ease across his chest and air begin to return to his lungs.

It was his first time being shot wearing a bulletproof vest and though he wasn't in a hurry to repeat the experiment, he wasn't going to let Schofield get away.

He got to his feet just as Schofield stepped up on the sidewalk.

"FREEZE ASSHOLE!"

Sato had been waiting for Schofield at the side of the parking lot. Squatting down, feet wide apart, holding her Glock in both hands.

She seemed to surprise Schofield as he approached the road, his eyes turning toward her. He was still looking at her as he stepped out onto the road and a half second after that when a one-ton Dodge RAM slammed into him at thirty miles per hour with a force strong enough to separate his head from his body.

Anton Schofield's head bounced off the truck's windshield and flew twenty feet up in the air before falling back under the wheels of a BMW that was driving behind the Dodge.

It wasn't exactly how he'd pictured his morning, but he wasn't overly sad about it either. He walked calmly over to Schofield's sedan before the doors re-locked.

He found a messenger bag in the trunk containing a high-end Apple laptop, an external hard drive, and a pouch filled with memory cards.

Schofield's entire blackmail setup.

Coombes took the bag, slipped the strap over his shoulder and closed the trunk. It felt like he'd broken a couple of ribs and it hurt if he drew too deep a breath.

On West 3rd Street, the driver of the Dodge RAM opened his door and stepped onto the road. He took a couple of shaky steps, then passed out in front of Schofield's headless corpse.

Coombes knelt next to the body.

He didn't have much time. Soon there would a crowd of witnesses. No matter how unsavory the view, a crowd always appeared to take it in and capture it on their cell phones. He located another memory card in Schofield's right pants pocket and palmed it as a Highway Patrol cop approached on a motorcycle.

You owe me one, chief.

He straightened up and let the cop see his badge.

43

COOMBES WAS ABOUT TO sit down at his desk when he caught sight of Block on the other side of the detective bureau. His face was scarlet and he was looking straight at him. *Great.* His captain tilted his head down at the person in front of him, who was apparently holding him back. It was Gantz. Henderson's words came back to him *I pity your lieutenant, Coombes, putting up with this all day.* He supposed it was true, he had come to rely on Gantz to have his back and it couldn't be a lot of fun dealing with Block.

After a moment, Block was past Gantz and was striding across the floor toward him. His face had lost a little of its color, whatever Gantz had said to him had taken the edge off.

"You're on a goddamn roll, Coombes! Three dead! You're going to put the courts out of business with all this *Dirty Harry* shit. The Police Commission and the ACLU are going to expect someone's ass for this and it isn't going to be mine, you feel me?"

Coombes said nothing for a moment. His captain was wearing sweatpants with a faded Pink Floyd T-shirt tucked into them and both were better than a size too small. Block had been in such a hurry to come into the office that he hadn't bothered to change clothes.

"Stone was killed by Marks, Marks killed himself, and Schofield was hit by a truck. Where do I fit into any of this?"

"Don't get smart with me you little shit. You're on notice. I'm referring you to IAD."

"For what?"

The color was back in Block's cheeks and there was a fire in his eyes.

"For whatever they can find."

The man was an idiot and his answer served only to relax Coombes. He had nothing to worry about, this was no more than an old beef resurfacing. His captain thought he saw an opportunity to get him out the department and he was going to take it.

"Then I guess you haven't heard, Block. The chief's pinning a medal on my chest in about an hour's time in front of the mayor, the former Governor of California, and whatever remains these days of the press corps."

Block's eyes bulged like an airbag had gone off in his head. He seemed to register for the first time that Coombes was wearing a brand-new Class A uniform and not his suit.

"*Which medal?*"

"Preservation of Life."

Block had no comeback. The medal was a big deal and was respected by cops everywhere, including Internal Affairs. Next to him, Sato took off her huge headphones and popped up, her face all smiles.

"Have you heard about our medals?"

"You're getting a medal too?"

"Yeah, same as John. Mark's getting a Meritorious Service Medal."

"Jesus Christ, *Becker?* The whole world's gone to hell!"

Block stomped off radiating anger like an exposed reactor core.

"You know, Johnny, I don't think he likes me."

Coombes sat in his chair and started his computer. He had yet to file his report on Schofield's death but it wasn't the accident he was thinking of, it was the kidnapping. He pulled up the surveillance videos taken from the electronics store.

The footage was the only link between the two men. He'd watched it so many times hoping to see something new. The clips were short. Each one was ten seconds long, the time it took Amy to cross the space in front of the store.

He'd had Becker create the clips from the originals so that they were easier to re-watch. When they got to the end they replayed from the beginning automatically. He watched both through several times then stopped them.

There was nothing new to see.

He found the original unedited clips and opened the one showing the abduction. They now knew that Cassidy Stone was the getaway driver and that Schofield wasn't behind the wheel. He watched the clip from ten minutes before until ten minutes after on double speed, waiting to see if Schofield appeared anywhere.

He did not.

Coombes switched to the second clip, the reconnaissance run. Chronologically, the first recording. He did the same thing, set it playing ten minutes before Amy appeared and began fast-forwarding it. After only two minutes, Schofield entered the shot. Coombes hit regular playback and watched as the dead man walked over to his spot at the edge of the sidewalk next to the road, facing the camera.

Schofield was a brutal-looking individual and it was no surprise to Coombes that Maria López had been scared of him.

Sato appeared next to him; her arms folded.

"Why are you looking at this again? We got him."

He glanced up at her.

"We got him all right, but for what?"

Sato frowned but said nothing, so he continued.

"What do we honestly have linking Schofield to the murder or the abduction?"

Sato pointed at the screen in front of him.

"He's right there! He watches Amy Tremaine with that other creep. Schofield was the ringleader, the man that controlled Marks and Stone."

"Or he's just a guy standing at the side of the road."

"You're saying we hunted this guy and he's got nothing to do with anything?"

"I think so, yes."

"That doesn't make sense, Johnny. Why did he shoot at us?"

"Because he's a bad guy and because we're cops."

"You can't be serious."

"What about James Anderson? We rolled up on him and he ran like his life depended on it. No doubt he's a weirdo, but that's not against the law."

On screen Schofield's head turned to follow another woman, then a short time later, another. The man was a hound dog. Next to him, Grace stiffened. She'd seen it too. The case against him was falling apart by the second. After almost another minute, Schofield glanced at his watch.

"He's waiting for someone," Coombes said.

"And it's not Amy Tremaine."

They watched it play in real time. He didn't want to fast-forward it and miss seeing who Schofield had been waiting for. Finally, a dark shadow passed in front of the lens as someone walked close to the front of the store. It was what Schofield was waiting for, and he walked toward them, then out of shot at the last second.

Coombes groaned.

"What is it? Where did he go?"

"Don't you see? He was waiting for the store to open, he's a customer."

Sato sat on the edge of his desk and grabbed his hand.

"That means we got an innocent man killed."

"Listen to me. That's not what happened. This asshole tried to blow us away, he had something going on, something we don't know about. Innocent people don't shoot at cops."

Tears rolled down her face.

"I hate this, I really hate this."

He stood and without checking to see if anyone was looking, put his arms around her and gave her a hug. Sato pressed her head into his shoulder and he felt her silently sob for the piece of shit that was now dead. Coombes felt no more regret over Schofield's death than he did for pizza that fell face-down on the floor.

Her sobbing began to wane and he released her.

She nodded at him, her mouth pulled down at the corners.

Coombes glanced up and saw Wallfisch standing behind them, sipping coffee out a large paper cup. He shook his big head in disapproval. Wallfisch was old school. The only time you could touch your partner was to press a wound shut, or to hold their hand as they died in front of you. Hugging was never okay.

"Let's take a walk," Coombes said.

They walked through the detective bureau, took the elevator to the first floor, then walked out into bright February sunshine. He screwed up his eyes at the onslaught. His sunglasses were in the Dodge. They crossed over 1st Street and into Circle Park in front of City Hall where the trees provided welcome shade.

Sato looked up at him, her face hard to read.

"Not that I don't enjoy spending time with you, Johnny, but why are we here?"

"We made two mistakes. First, we assumed that Walton's murder was incidental; that she either interrupted a robbery, or that her killer was there for Tremaine. Then we assumed she was caught up somehow in Amy's abduction and was killed by one of the kidnappers."

"What does that leave, except for two different cases?"

"Nothing. They were never connected."

"That's crazy."

"I know."

Sato was struggling with the idea. He'd struggled with it a bit himself but he was farther down the track than she was and some of the crazy had evaporated.

They stood and watched people around them in the park and on the sidewalk. At least half were wearing masks or had some kind of fabric over their mouths. The virus was here now, it wasn't an ocean away.

"This is going to be a problem for me, isn't it?"

He turned to Sato.

"How so?"

"People are calling it *the Chinese virus*. They're looking for a scapegoat."

He'd tell her not to worry, but he knew she was right. It would be a waste of time telling someone like that she was American, or Japanese-American.

The hatred would remain, because it had always been there.

"Wait, what did you just say?"

"I said they're looking for a scapegoat."

A scapegoat.

He recalled what Barnes had said at the ransom drop about the concealed trackers.

People tend to stop looking once they find what they're looking for.

He kissed Sato on the forehead.

"You're a genius, Grace!"

A goofy smile flashed across her face.

"Remind me why?"

"Let's say someone wanted to kill Walton. Someone close to her, close enough to be considered a suspect. It's enough to hold the would-be killer in check. Then he or she finds out about the plan to kidnap Amy. It's a window of opportunity. The killer would know Marks would become the focus of the investigation and would be blamed for the murder no matter what. It wouldn't matter if he was caught and denied it, no one would believe him anyway. It's a perfect frame."

Sato thought about it for a moment.

"The only person who knew about the kidnapping was Stone. The medical examiner said Walton's killer had to have big hands to crush her windpipe. Stone had small hands, like me."

"I agree, but logically someone else had to know about it."

"Someone that hated Marks almost as much as Walton."

He nodded.

"That follows, yes."

"Unless Walton's death was just a way to hurt Tremaine."

Reluctantly, he nodded again.

Finding someone that disliked both Marks and Tremaine might not be that hard, they'd worked together for a decade and it would only take someone that Marks had roughed up in that time to start something.

Someone like James Anderson.

Stabbed by Marks, then served with a restraining order by Tremaine, his hero. Had Anderson gone rogue? It was possible. For years, Anderson had stalked Tremaine. Lurking in doorways, staying hidden but close to his target. Close enough to take a photograph with a long lens, or overhear something private. Sato seemed to read his mind.

"Anderson," she said.

"Maybe."

"Why only maybe?"

"Walton's head was repeatedly bashed off the floor before she died. That's personal. We found no connection between Anderson and Walton."

Silence fell between them and when Sato spoke again, she changed the subject.

"You never said why we're standing in front of City Hall."

"Oh. We're not really. We're standing in front of *our* building; you can see it better from this side of the street."

She turned to face the PAB.

"So why are we standing across the street from headquarters?"

"Because the person that filed the missing person's report on Schofield used their maiden name. I guess because her married name would've raised too many questions."

"Why? Who is it?"

"The chief's wife."

"Oh, shit."

"The store with the drone sells surveillance equipment, hidden cameras, microphones. Schofield ran a blackmail operation and that was simply where he bought the equipment of his trade. He was targeting the chief among many others."

"What are we going to do about it?"

"Nothing. The world has other things to worry about than the death of a blackmailer."

"Can we do that?"

"He got creamed by a truck crossing the road. We were asked to find him. We found him. I imagine the chief's pretty pleased with the way things panned out. Dead men tell no tales."

"But his laptop-"

"There was no laptop, Grace. You're mistaken."

He smiled a little, then walked out from under the trees onto the sidewalk and continued back along 1st toward the crosswalk. Sato did a couple of quick steps to catch up.

"You think the chief put people onto him to hunt him down?"

"We *are* those people, Grace."

"You know what I mean. Like the big guy Tremaine had with him at the ransom drop. An ex-military whack job bristling with guns and attitude."

"Still kind of me."

Sato sighed, exasperated.

"He was on the run from somebody before we ever heard of him."

"The chief wouldn't send us after this clown if he'd sent an assassin after him first. Think about it. He'd want *no one* looking for this guy, never mind people tied directly to him. Schofield had Russian friends on Facebook; the tattoo on his neck, that's Russian. I should have thought of this before. That eagle with the two heads, it's on their damn flag. I'm thinking he was *Bratva* and simply fell out with his former associates."

"We're never going to know, are we?"

"All we need to know is that he wasn't involved in the kidnapping of Amy Tremaine, or the murder Elizabeth Walton. Which means her killer is still out there."

44

COOMBES HAD RECEIVED MEDALS before. Twelve in the Army, five in the LAPD. The Preservation of Life made his sixth serving Los Angeles. He'd become jaded with the whole thing, but this one was different. It was Grace Sato's first medal ceremony, and her face was beaming with pride. He saw her face and he felt his heart surge.

The former governor seemed to draw quite a crowd, none more so than when he arrived in his battle-scarred vehicle and parked half on the sidewalk. As he walked toward him, Coombes noted that Tremaine was wearing cowboy boots with a thick heel, at least two inches. It meant that when they stood side-by-side they were almost the same height. The line of Tremaine's suit jacket sat awkwardly, indicating a concealed weapon.

Beneath his wide, mall-opening smile, the other man was in crisis.

Chief Jackson launched into a big speech, overflowing with superlatives for the work of his three officers. His eyes reaching out first into the crowd, then landing solely on him. He gave an almost imperceptible nod, his only thanks for dealing with Schofield.

Becker got his medal first. He'd been a cop for a long time and he had received a lot of medals, too many to count. Then it was Sato, her face tight with emotion, her right hand doing little waves to her family at the back of the audience. Finally, it was his turn, the chief standing directly in front of him, eyeball to eyeball.

Jackson leaned in and spoke quietly.

"The other situation. It's dealt with?"

"Yes, sir."

"You saw it? The video?"

"No, sir, none of my business. There is one thing, though."

"What's that?"

"Next time, come to me direct. Don't keep me in the dark like a potato, it's not necessary."

Jackson nodded. "That's fair."

They were shaking each other's hand now, then everyone was shaking hands, he even ended up shaking hands with Becker and Sato. He wanted to embrace Sato, but there was a time and a place. The mayor shook his hand last, her grip tight, her eye contact total.

"Good work, Detective."

"Thank you, ma'am."

"The boys at the federal building might not be too pleased about the way this shook out. You get any problems from them I want you to let me know and I'll take it straight to the director. I'm sick of the unchecked testosterone."

Coombes thanked her again, but said nothing about her offer. He preferred to carry his own beer. He'd gone around the chain of command once before and paid a price.

The crowd was melting away. He wondered if any of the press coverage would be used or if it would be seen as a non-story and binned as he thought it would. It was three days since he'd been attacked and, some bruising aside, his face was almost back to normal. The bump on his forehead, the only one not hidden by his hair, was little more coin's depth deep. If they published a group shot, only the smudge of a bruise would be visible.

"Could I borrow you for a moment, John?"

It was Tremaine, he'd come around the back of Sato and had his arm out around his shoulders guiding him away from the group.

"I can't thank you enough for bringing my little girl home safe. She's my world. I don't think I realized that before this happened. You went above and beyond."

"You're embarrassing me."

"Good!"

The former governor flashed a big smile and slapped his back.

"Actually, I wanted to ask you something about that morning."

Tremaine flinched, his happy-go-lucky persona falling away.

"I still can't believe Lizzie's gone. She was part of my life for so long. I think of things I want to say to her all the time and then realize I can't. It's unbearable."

"I understand, sir."

"Call me Harry. My friends call me that, I never liked *Harlan*."

"Mine call me Johnny. John is my work name."

"What was your question, Johnny?"

Were they friends now, is that what just happened?

"It's a little delicate. You told me that you adjusted Elizabeth's nightdress. I wondered if there was anything else you changed before we arrived."

Tremaine took a deep breath, his huge chest swelling up, then relaxing.

"Yeah, but it was nothing. The bastard covered her face with one of her shirts."

"*Really.*"

"Does that mean something?"

It meant the killer felt guilty about what he'd done, which fit all too well with Marks as the perpetrator, despite his denials. He said none of this to Tremaine.

"It meant the killer went into her room to get the shirt. But we fingerprinted in there and got nothing so I guess he was wearing gloves."

"You said killer - wasn't it Marks?"

"We're running down some loose ends before we close the file."

Tremaine nodded, satisfied. *Procedure.* It was the cop's magician's flourish that could be used at any moment to disguise what was actually happening. The former governor glanced toward where his bullet-damaged vehicle was parked. Coombes saw that Amy was inside.

"My daughter wanted a word with you if that's okay."

"Sure, Harry."

WHEN HE GOT BACK to his desk, he found that Sato had already changed into her normal clothes, her uniform now gone. He felt the need to do the same. Sato looked up.

"How's Amy?"

"She's taking over from Walton running the foundation."

"I guess that makes sense."

Coombes took off his Class A jacket and hung it over the top of his suit jacket on the back of the chair and sat down. He had to think through what, if any, were the implications of the shirt that had been on Walton's face.

Sato stood and looked over their partition.

"You remember that guy down at the aquarium that fed us the story about the sex club and the water tank?"

"What about him?"

"Well, I got to thinking about how everything fitted together and how we got onto Marks. I kept coming back to this idiot with the mop who just *happened* to have the information we needed. In hindsight, it kind of stunk."

Coombes' back straightened.

"*Tell me.*"

"I called the aquarium. He doesn't work there. I gave his description in case he gave us a false name. Nobody knew who I was talking about. They told me they don't even use mops; they have a motorized thing you sit on."

He leaned back in his chair and stared at the ceiling.

When you got good intel, it was always easy to overlook the source and not question *why* you were receiving the information in the first place.

He returned his gaze to Sato.

"That's fantastic work, Grace."

"I wasn't sure you'd want to hear it."

"Never hold anything back, okay? I'd rather hear it from you than from a defense attorney in court."

"What do you think it means?"

It meant that someone had helped them and tried to hide it.

"Did you call the number he gave us?"

"Of course," she said. "It's the number for a carpet-cleaning company. It's fake."

"Did you run his name through the system?"

"I only just found out before you got here."

Coombes realized that he couldn't remember the mop-cleaner's name and flicked through his notebook to find it.

Joachim Nelson.

It was a stupid name, he thought. Now that he was thinking clearly, it seemed made up. Instead of going to the criminal database, he typed it into Google. To his surprise, he got a hit.

Nelson was listed in a production of *As You Like It*.

"He's an actor," Coombes said. "Community theatre. *Shakespeare*."

Sato groaned.

"I *hate* Shakespeare. The way everyone talks, I just want to punch them."

Coombes glanced at Sato. "No doubt."

He clicked back to his Google results and found an actors' directory entry for Nelson with a list of credits; his work addresses; and his real name, which was Andrew Jones. The work address was a carpet-cleaning company in the valley.

"He really does work at that cleaning firm."

"What are we saying here, Johnny? That *mop-guy* murdered Walton then pointed us toward Marks as a misdirect?"

"No. I figure her killer saw the video of Amy in the water and grew a conscience. The easiest way would be to call in a tip, but we would wonder where that came from down the line. So he has this actor provide us with the information we need in a way that seems organic. The quicker we get to Marks, the quicker he's in the clear for Walton."

Sato thought about it for a moment.

"Oh my god! Nelson didn't think we were real cops!"

"What are you talking about, Grace?"

"At the end of the interview he said something weird like *how did I do?* Then asked if we'd be in touch."

"Like an audition."

"Exactly. He thought it was a real-world casting."

Don't call us, we'll call you.

"Well, as fascinating as this is, it gets us nowhere. Dollars to doughnuts the killer used the form on his directory page to contact him, which will only have the website's email address on it, and any name given setting up the meeting will be fake."

"You're killing me here. It's not worth checking out?"

"I'm not spending an hour and a half driving to the valley, then an hour and a half driving back just to talk to that idiot."

"This really gets us nothing?"

Coombes thought about it for a moment, his fingers playing with an elastic band that had been on his desk. The revelation *wasn't* for nothing, he thought. He could see that a patron of a sex club might be reluctant to come forward with information about the water tank, but to go the extra step of using the actor meant only one thing.

The tipster had more to hide than embarrassment. To his mind, this confirmed that Marks wasn't Elizabeth Walton's killer and confirmed the framing of Marks that he'd suspected.

Her killer had followed the Marine long enough that it led him to the sex club. As he'd discovered, there were a lot of videos of the water tank online if you knew where to look, and knowing the name of the club would be enough to connect the pieces.

"Maybe we're thinking about this all wrong," he said. "What if the original target was Marks not Walton. Our killer follows him, waiting for the best moment to strike."

"Because Marks is bigger and stronger than him."

"Yes," he said. "Go on."

"Finally, the two fight. Caught by surprise, maybe even drunk, Marks still out-matches our killer. He takes the other man's knife off him and stabs him in the leg."

Silence fell between them for a beat, then he laughed.

"Come on, not *Anderson* again."

"Why not? We thought he was good for it before."

"Yeah," he said. "Before we actually met him." Coombes paused for a moment as he tried to pack away a vision of Anderson's rotting leg wound. "Tremaine told to me after the ceremony that the killer put a shirt over Walton's face. That's shame or remorse."

"Doesn't that bring us back to Marks? Someone that thought he loved her."

Coombes was about to shut her down when he stopped himself.

"What?" she said.

"Marks wasn't the only person in love with Walton."

"*Right*. Adam Finley and Cora Roche."

"Bring up Facebook on Roche, I'll do Finley. Go back to December."

Coombes pulled himself closer to his computer and opened Facebook. Finley's profile picture showed him looking younger, without the ponytail. Walton's building manager was in denial about his age, no doubt about it.

"What am I looking for, Johnny?"

"A visit to a theatre to see *As You Like It*."

"I don't see Roche liking Shakespeare any more than I do."

"Whoever hired that kid saw him act, they didn't find him on Google."

He scrolled and scrolled. Adam Finley posted a lot. Every day, ten to fifteen posts. Pictures of himself, pictures of his food, videos from YouTube. Christmas lights flicked past and he slowed his scroll.

"Nothing incriminating on Roche's feed."

"No," he said. "There won't be. It's Finley."

Sato scrambled around to see his screen. He brought up a picture of a theatre brochure with the title printed on it. Above, Finley had typed:

All the world's a stage...

Coombes pulled back the elastic band and fired it at the screen.

"Gotcha."

45

ADAM FINLEY LIVED ON Navy Street, just a block away from the end of the Santa Monica Airport runway. In front of his home stood a huge Indian Laurel Fig, the tree's thick silver roots piled up and crisscrossing over one another in the tight rectangular space between the footpath and the road. A faded blue minivan sat on the driveway.

He wasn't at work, but he wasn't in the wind either. Perhaps waiting for everything to blow over and the dust settle back into place.

News of Marks' suicide in police custody and had been seen by all as an admission of guilt over both Amy Tremaine's kidnapping and Elizabeth Walton's murder. The media hadn't been that invested in Walton's murder to begin with, so seemed perfectly happy to join her story onto the solved kidnap case to save time.

Sato parked across the drive, blocking the minivan's exit.

"What are we doing here, Johnny?"

"Arresting this bozo, what else?"

"All we've got on him is that he went to a play."

Coombes smiled.

"Then let's not mention that, shall we?"

"We're just going to bluff out a confession? That's the plan?"

"That's it."

She smiled uncertainly at him, doubtless thinking he was crazy. Twenty feet back, out of sight of the house, a Santa Monica PD cruiser pulled to a stop and cut their engine. Finley lived in their jurisdiction so they had been looped into the situation.

Coombes climbed out the Dodge and gave a small nod up the street at the two uniforms then walked across Finley's driveway to the front door of the house, rang the doorbell politely and took a step back so not to crowd the smaller man in the doorway.

The situation called for a bit of finesse.

A circle of light indicated that it was a video doorbell.

In his experience, few used the video function to screen callers. The camera instead being used as a failsafe for unreliable courier companies, or to deter burglars. Sure enough, Finley opened the door with no idea what he was about to see because his expression nosedived before he could get it back under control.

"Detectives! I wasn't expecting to see you here."

"No? Where were you expecting us?"

A plane whipped past overhead and Finley used the distraction to regroup.

"Why don't you come inside?"

Coombes nodded and said nothing, walking straight toward Finley so that he was forced to back away into his property. It was a power move, but also one that prevented the other man from slipping around behind them and escaping, or grabbing Sato as a human shield.

Only now that he was inside, did Coombes take off his sunglasses and hang them from one leg from the top of his shirt. He saw a big bookcase filled with old books, many with leather bindings.

No modern crime novels, as favored by Walton.

There was another unit with a turntable and a stack of records. He'd heard vinyl was making a resurgence, but everything looked old and well used. The other man was living in the past, pure and simple, this was no cultural front to impress the opposite sex.

He gestured Finley to sit on a sofa, where it appeared that he'd been sitting prior to their arrival. A French press coffee maker sat on a glass table next to a full mug and a television remote control. Coombes put his cell phone down on the table in front of Finley.

"I hope you don't mind, just procedure. 'Interview of Adam Finley by Detectives John Coombes and Grace Sato. Today's date is Saturday 29th February 2020. Time 5:25 p.m.'"

Finley was staring at the cell phone and the digits that were now counting up on the display as it recorded. Somehow, he wanted to get Finley to forget about the cell phone and the recording and what it might mean for him.

He looked around the other man's home as he spoke.

"You told us previously that there are no security cameras in the South Hill Street parking garage, but it turns out that's not true. Many of the vehicles have their own cameras, designed to record activity close to them. For thieves and suchlike. A bit like your doorbell there."

Coombes' gaze returned to Adam Finley's face. It looked worried.

"This is a really nice place you have here, Mr. Finley."

The complement threw the other man off balance.

"Thanks."

"How are you today? You look like you've seen a ghost."

"I'm fine," Finley said.

"That little rat-like fellow at the apartment building said you haven't been at work all week. In fact, he said you took off right after our visit."

Finley glanced quickly toward the door behind Coombes, then back. *Interesting.* Part of him hoped he would make a run for it.

"I've been unwell but I'm feeling better now. That's all I meant."

Coombes smiled, but put no light in his face.

"Really. Because you look like you're about to throw up on the floor. What do you think, Detective Sato?"

"He doesn't look good at all. Maybe he's got the virus."

"The virus. Of course. You think that's possible, Mr. Finley?"

"Look, what's all this about?"

"Our technical people traced a message from you to an actor in the valley who uses the stage name Joachim Nelson."

Finley's eyes widened, and again his gaze shifted briefly to the door beyond. *Please*, Coombes thought, *make a run for it, I'm needing a laugh.* The other man said nothing, but in the context, saying nothing was an admission. It was all he needed.

"No? Well, I'm sure you remember his performance in *As You Like It*, you described him as *stunning* on Facebook, an actor to watch out for. Five stars you said."

Coombes turned to Sato next to him, hoping the break in eye contact would be enough to make Finley run for the door.

"Five stars, that's good. Right?"

"The best," Sato said.

"All right, I sent him a message, so what? I was trying to help you."

"Help us?"

"Find the girl in the tank. It helped, didn't it? She's back safe."

"Why do you suppose we're confused by that, Mr. Finley?"

"I don't know."

"Well, it did help us. We found the tank and eventually found both Amy Tremaine and the man that took her. A man called Nathan Marks, who I'm sure you're heard about on TV."

Adam Finley smiled a little, sensing he was out of the woods.

"Here's the thing, Mr. Finley. You're not a member of the club you directed us to, we checked."

This was a pure guess by Coombes, the club kept no names.

"I saw it online, okay? On their website."

"You *happened* to visit a website for a sex club you weren't a member of that *thankfully* showed the very tank we were looking for? That's what you're saying?"

"You're twisting my words. I thought it was familiar so I passed it on."

They were going nowhere so he decided to move things along.

"The next day we came to your apartment building. You described a man you'd seen with Elizabeth Walton. This man later turned out to be Nathan Marks, Amy Tremaine's kidnapper. But you knew that already, didn't you, Mr. Finley?"

There were beads of sweat all over Finley's face.

"I don't know what you're getting at."

"Sure, you do. You followed him in your car to the sex club. That's how you knew about it. In fact, it's the *only* way you could've known about it."

"That's not-"

Coombes held up his right hand, fingers spread open.

"Before you say any more, you should be aware that there are close to a dozen security cameras outside the club and on the buildings around it."

A twitch started on the side of Finley's face.

"All right, fine! I followed him, big deal!"

"Because he was dating Elizabeth Walton."

"Yes."

"Because she'd been dating him for *eight months*, he wasn't some flash in the pan like you told us, she was serious about him."

Finley's head dipped. "Yes."

Sometimes, with an interview it was like backing the suspect closer to the edge of a cliff, leading them right up to the precipice and blocking off all escape routes. Getting the suspect to admit to small details that weren't damning on their own, but led to only one conclusion.

"You were in love with her."

"I'm *still* in love with her."

"Right. But this other guy, Marks, he didn't love her like that, did he?"

"No."

"In fact, he was a criminal."

"That's right! I overheard him on his cell phone in the parking garage talking about Amy Tremaine. It was obvious he was going to kidnap her."

"The whole time Marks was romancing her, it's for this, to take Amy. He wasn't in love with her, he was using her."

"Yes!"

Whenever he used language that was supportive, Finley came back quickly, with relief, not thinking through what he was saying. Above them another small jet flew past. He waited until the sound dissipated before he continued. Everything had to be recorded.

"You followed him again, this time back to his house in Angeleno Heights. How long did you sit there, Mr. Finley?"

"Three and a half hours."

Coombes nodded, like it tied in with something else he knew.

"That's a long stakeout. Long enough for you to figure out he was in for the night, that it was where he lived. He wasn't visiting a friend."

"But he was! He had another woman there; I saw them through the window."

Coombes knew the house on Allison Street was on a hill with steps down to the road, Finley hadn't seen Marks and Stone through the window from his car, he'd gone up the steps to look in.

"What age was this other woman?"

"Young. In her twenties. She looked like she was on drugs. She was dancing with him in her underwear and singing. I could hear music."

Finley seemed withdrawn, like he was describing the scene from his position outside the window. His voice was bitter.

"Seeing them together made you mad, didn't it? You'd do anything to be with Elizabeth Walton, yet the man she loved was cheating on her with someone less than half her age. He had no class, no culture. She deserved better."

This time Finley only nodded.

"When you got back to the South Hill building Elizabeth was gone, her Lexus missing from her spot in the parking garage. You knew she worked for the former governor during the week, the address was in your records."

"I had to warn her about him. He was going to kidnap the girl."

The heels of Finley's shoes were at the edge of the cliff now. He had to know where this was going but he seemed not to care. Some killers, in their hearts, want to be discovered.

"What time was it when you got to Tremaine's mansion?"

"Nearly four a.m."

"She'd be asleep, the governor too."

"It felt like the whole city was asleep."

Coombes nodded again.

"But you had to warn her about Marks, about Amy. It was your duty. So, you climbed over the fence and go in the back door."

"When she saw me, she screamed. It was so loud. I put my hand over her mouth to keep her quiet and tried to explain, but she kept on screaming into my hand. The next thing I know we're on the floor. I'm crouched over her, my hands around her neck. She's not moving. It felt like a second had passed, but she was already cold."

It was what he'd waited for, the drop over the cliff.

"Adam Finley, I am arresting you for the murder of Elizabeth Walton. You have the right to remain silent. Anything you say can and will be used against you in a court of law. You have the right to have an attorney present during questioning. If you cannot afford an attorney, one will be provided for you. Do you understand?"

The building manager nodded, his face frozen and distant.

"Mr. Finley, I need you to confirm that you understand your rights."

"I understand."

The tension on Finley's face was ebbing away. It was over. There was peace there, and Coombes hated him for it. He'd brutally murdered Walton, he deserved no peace.

"I'm curious why you didn't tell us about the kidnapping plot before Amy was taken. Let the LAPD take care of everything."

"Because she had to know it was me, that *I* was the one that saved the day."

"How does murdering Walton save the day?"

Finley screwed up his face.

"I didn't mean to; she just wouldn't stop screaming."

He'd got Finley to admit to killing Walton post-Miranda warning on a recording, but he didn't want the DA to go for an easy involuntary manslaughter charge, when it was obvious to him that it was a premeditated killing with malice aforethought. A first-degree murder. The former carried a sentence of four years, the latter, twenty-five to life.

"You had her cell phone number in your records too, but you didn't call her to pass on what you'd heard in the parking garage. You drove across town three times. First to Marks' address, then back to Hill Street, then out to Brentwood where you broke into Tremaine's home. How do you explain that?"

"It was late, I wasn't thinking clearly."

"I don't think so. When you saw Marks dancing with his younger girlfriend you got angry. You got angry at them, then angry with Walton. She just kept walking past you. You were right in front of her for years and you were *nothing* to her. Pocket lint. A servant. But when you saw her boyfriend with this other woman you realized what it all meant."

Finley looked up at him, a sick smile forming.

"And what was that, Detective?"

"That you could kill her and not one person in the world would ever think it was you, not after Amy was taken. You knew that nothing would change with her if you *saved the day*, you said it yourself, Elizabeth didn't see you that way. She liked younger men."

"It worked, didn't it? I heard that poor sap killed himself. He died thinking he would be blamed for her death. I got my revenge. I took everything from him, with *your* help. I should've just left that Tremaine bitch to her fate."

Now he showed them his true form.

"All right, Finley, on your feet. Hands behind your back."

"There's nothing you can do to me, Detective. Don't you see? I'm already paying the price. I wish I could take it back, every second of every day. She was beautiful and she's gone because of me. I'm in hell."

Coombes pulled out his handcuffs and physically turned Finley to face the other direction, pulling his arms back and cinching the cuffs tight. A lot of cops liked to do an extra couple of clicks on the handcuffs to cause the wearer pain, but he wasn't one of them. Besides, his cell phone was still recording audio and he didn't want any yelps of pain to get Finley's confession kicked on grounds of torture or coercion.

He directed Finley out the door toward the awaiting patrol car.

46

It was after 7:30 p.m. when they finished with Adam Finley. They had re-interviewed Finley two more times, once in a Santa Monica PD interview room, then again at an LAPD interview room in Pacific Division, which happened to be the closest. Each time, Finley told as good as the same story he'd told them in his home. His responses becoming increasingly robotic as his initial relief at confessing gave way to fatigue.

After formally charging Finley, they returned to headquarters to finish up their paperwork. He had no intention of coming in the following day, so it was worth the extra effort. As they approached the Dodge to leave, Coombes paused.

"You know what? It's my turn to drive."

Sato frowned, thinking about it.

"Okay."

"I thought that was going to be more difficult."

"What you did with that guy today blew my mind. It was like you were dancing. Whenever I thought you were going too heavy, you pulled it back at the last second and seemed to be holding out your hand to help him. There's nothing wrong with your brain, Coombes, you're just a bit dog-eared."

"Dog-eared, huh?"

He adjusted the seat, then the mirrors.

It was good getting back behind the wheel. For all he hated driving in Los Angeles, he had missed the focus of being the driver. Choosing lanes, speed, the distance from the car in front. Sato drove about a foot from the car in front and it made him tense.

He drove the Charger around the parking structure toward the exit. They were just about to pull out onto the street when a figure stepped out in front of the car and stood with his feet planted wide apart. Coombes hit the brakes and skidded to a halt.

Henderson.

The man came around the side of the car and knocked on the glass. Coombes glanced in his mirrors to check that there wasn't a team of armed agents coming out the walls.

He fizzed down the window and looked up.

"You're not allowed in here, Henderson. This place is for real cops."

"I came to give you a message, Coombes. We work the same town, there's a good chance we're going to meet again. Next time, won't go like this time, you can bet on that."

"After the way you bungled your investigation, I'll be surprised if you're not transferred to a Nebraska field office within the week. You're an utter disgrace to the badge."

The other man's face turned crimson with rage, his eyes ready to pop right out of his face. *Nobody* talked to him like that, consequently, he had no way to handle it when they did. Coombes smiled at him, closed the window, and pulled away out the exit into the night.

"Why didn't you tell him what you *really* thought, Coombes?"

"I considered it."

Sato seemed to notice their direction for the first time and turned to look at him.

"We're not going to *Bestia*?"

"Just need to clear the Walton apartment first."

She groaned. "I thought we did that?"

"Couple more boxes to check off. I promised Gantz we'd get it done."

Sato shrugged her shoulders, apparently unfazed, but her face showed irritation.

The distance between the PAB and Walton's apartment building was only nine city blocks and the Saturday evening traffic moved without too much trouble until they were once again looking up through the windshield at the building ahead.

This time the barrier lifted automatically, triggered by the black box that was now clipped to his visor. He drove under the still moving shutter, into the parking structure. He parked in the same space as before and climbed out the vehicle.

The doors to and from the stairwell were both locked but Walton's security dongle still worked, just as he'd been told. He walked to the concierge desk, Sato trailing behind, her head somewhere else.

The concierge nodded his head as he saw who stood in front of him. He handed Coombes the replacement keys for apartment 1224. Two mortice, two deadbolt, two dongles for the parking structure. Elizabeth Walton was dead and cold, but the world kept on turning. A diamond-shaped plate was attached to the keyring with the number of the apartment on it, like a motel in years gone by.

"You want me to come up with you?"

"That's all right."

The man nodded and turned back to his computer and whatever thrills it offered. Doom-scrolling news about the virus probably. It was wall-to-wall now, like a good carpet.

Sato looked bored as they walked to the elevator. She was hungry, and he'd pulled this on her at the last moment. Coombes regarded the building's lobby area. It was clean and expensive-looking.

It should be, he thought.

He pressed the call button and the elevator opened without delay. They got in and he selected the top floor. His partner's shoulders slumped and she stared vacantly at the changing floor numbers. She was pissed off.

Never get between a woman and food.

His father had said that once, but what did he know?

He'd been married to the same woman for the last fifty-six years.

The elevator opened, and they walked along the corridor until they came to the apartment. New brass locks shone in the deep gray metal. Coombes took out a knife and cut through the police tape sealing the apartment and unlocked the door. He gave the door a push and indicated for Sato to walk on ahead of him.

The place had been cleaned and freshened up. No personal effects of Walton's remained, although the apartment was fully furnished. Sato did quick 360, taking it all in. There was nothing for them to do here, no official boxes for them to check off.

Resealing the door had been the concierge's idea.

"It's been totally cleaned," she said.

He waited for her gaze to return to him.

"That's right."

He smiled a little and tilted his head.

"What's going on, Johnny? You've been acting weird all day."

"When we were here before it seemed like you liked it. Maybe not as much as Schofield's, but well enough. You seemed happy and at peace."

She got it then, her mouth dropping open a fraction.

"You're crazy, you can't afford a place like this."

"It belongs to Amy Tremaine. Her father got it for nothing for greasing the wheels that helped get this place built. The former mayor has an apartment on the other side. Anyway, her father gave it to her when she turned twenty-one, but she never liked it. She thought it was corrupt, so she let Walton stay here in exchange for paying the mortgage of Amy's apartment in MacArthur Park. She's offered me the same deal. Seems she's gone off high-rise buildings."

"How much does the mortgage come to?"

"About four times as much as my bungalow."

"Jesus!"

Coombes nodded. "It's going to be tight, but we'll be fine."

Her cheeks turned pink.

"You're asking me to move in with you?"

"To start with."

Grace looked at him with an expression he couldn't read, her eyes moving slowly over his face. At his mouth, the stubble on his chin, then his eyes. It looked like anger, he thought, maybe disbelief. It was a fine line to walk, getting a romantic gesture right. At a certain point, you were overstepping, making decisions without the other person's consent.

The doubt in her face vanished and she screamed.

She ran the short distance between them and jumped onto him. He caught her as their bodies slammed together, her arms and legs wrapping tightly around him, her mouth pressed against his. Grace was small but highly muscled and he had to take a step back to balance himself. Her arms tightened around him as he moved.

God, she was strong.

She was crushing him, taking the air out his lungs.

Coombes reached his hand back until it connected with the edge of the door and swung it shut behind them. He carried her through the living room to the bedroom. The teddy bear, the fairy lights, it was all gone. At his insistence, even the bed and nightstands had been changed. He wanted nothing in the apartment that emotionally connected to a dead woman.

He felt Grace's breath landing on his neck, fast and excited.

She'd called the apartment a love nest. It was true, Elizabeth Walton had never really lived here, it was only used to meet up with young men. You could take that information anywhere you liked, but Grace found love there, and maybe they could find more, together.

She looked him in the eyes.

"This better not be a rebound-thing."

"It's not," he said.

Coombes lowered her onto the bed and she clung on for dear life.

NEXT IN SERIES: Johnny Coombes will return.

Follow me on Amazon to receive updates.

About the Author

I live on the outskirts of Edinburgh with my fiancée and young son. I would like to thank my family for their support and encouragement, it means the world to me. I am the author of Night Passenger, The Dark Halo, and The Scapegoat.

If you enjoyed The Scapegoat, please consider writing a quick review, it would be greatly appreciated. To stay up-to-date on new releases, click Follow on my Amazon author page.

Printed in Great Britain
by Amazon

37576610R00189